# THE POPE'S HITMAN

AF865860

**ALSO AVAILABLE BY JM BERGER**

**Optimal: A Novel**

*Essential Knowledge: Extremism*

*ISIS: The State of Terror (with Jessica Stern)*

*Jihad Joe: Americans Who Go to War in the Name of Islam*

# THE POPE'S HITMAN

A NOVEL

J. M. BERGER

CROOKED LANE

NEW YORK

Books should be disposed of and recycled according to local requirements.
All paper materials used are FSC compliant.

This is a work of fiction. All of the names, characters, organizations, places, and events portrayed in this novel are either products of the author's imagination or are used fictitiously. Any resemblance to real or actual events, locales, or persons, living or dead, is entirely coincidental.

Copyright © 2026 by J.M. Berger

All rights reserved.

Without limiting the exclusive rights of any author, contributor or the publisher of this publication, any unauthorized use of this publication to train generative artificial intelligence (AI) technologies is expressly prohibited.

Published in the United States by Crooked Lane Books, an imprint of The Quick Brown Fox & Company LLC.

Crooked Lane Books and its logo are trademarks of The Quick Brown Fox & Company LLC.

Library of Congress Catalog-in-Publication data available upon request.

ISBN (hardcover): 979-8-89242-851-4
ISBN (paperback): 979-8-89242-852-1
ISBN (ebook): 979-8-89242-853-8

Cover design by Nebojsa Zoric

Printed in the United States.

www.crookedlanebooks.com

Crooked Lane Books
34 West 27th St., 10th Floor
New York, NY 10001

First Edition: October 2026

The authorized representative in the EU for product safety and compliance is eucomply OÜPärnu mnt 139b-14, 11317 Tallinn, Estonia, hello@eucompliancepartner.com, +33757690241

10 9 8 7 6 5 4 3 2 1

Nobody must say, "He can't forgive
me my sins."
"How can't he, being almighty?"
"But," you say, "I've sinned so much."
And I say, "But he's almighty."
And you: "I've committed such sins as I can't
possibly be cleansed and
delivered from."
I reply, "But he's almighty."

*The Sermons of Saint Augustine, No. 213*

CHAPTER

1

# Hellbound

IT HAD BEEN years now, but Father Francis Loyola had never grown accustomed to being seen. His finely honed reflexes rebelled at the feeling of eyes on him, activating a tactical bearing that he wore like a second skin. He gripped the edges of the pulpit like a steering wheel, out of a deeply learned instinct to assert physical control over his environment.

But when he spoke to conclude the reading, his graveled voice was steady and clear: "Through the words of the Holy Gospel, may our sins be wiped away."

Loyola swept his eyes over the congregation in front of him with practiced precision. The eleven AM Sunday Mass was typically well-attended, and today was no exception. Women in hats and brightly colored dresses, men arrayed in starched white shirts. Children fidgeted in semiformal straightjackets soon to be cast aside. It was an old-fashioned sort of scene, shaped in equal parts by the Boston neighborhood's diverse immigrant demographics and by the aura of respect and dignity that its pastor quietly engendered.

Maybe two hundred fifty people in attendance, filling pews that fanned out from the center in four sections separated by three aisles. The balcony, reserved for the choir on special occasions, was closed and dark. A man in the north wing discreetly slipped out the back, hand reaching inside his blue blazer in a manner that stirred the priest's old alarms. But Loyola recognized him—Ronny Gold, a heavy smoker, indulging his vice. On the west side, a young mother, Sarah Jelen, carried her fussing newborn out to the vestibule. Loyola had baptized the child, Christine, just last month.

The priest himself cut an imposing figure—six-foot-one, broad shoulders, unruly dark brown hair turning gunmetal gray at the temples, and a craggy, weathered face that was habitually stern but rarely judgmental. He was dressed in the purple vestments of Advent, and three of the four Advent candles were lit next to him, signifying the approach of Christmas. In honor of the pope's proclamation that 2025 would be a Jubilee year, he had prepared a sermon on the traditional Jubilee theme of the forgiveness of sin, a topic close to his heart.

Loyola's sermons followed his conversational habits, direct and concise. No one would ever call him voluble or even forthcoming, but people listened all the more when he spoke. It was not a conventional style of preaching, but it had its charms. He projected a rare authenticity that was seen perhaps too infrequently in the Catholic Church these days.

"Forgiveness is the hardest thing God asks of us," he began. "It's hard, isn't it? When someone has wronged you, it burns. You don't *want* to let it go, right? Maybe they don't deserve it. Maybe you resent even being asked. Doesn't matter if it's a stranger or someone you love. Sometimes it's *worse* when it's someone you love."

Some light murmurs and rustling, vaguely appreciative. A woman got up and headed for the lobby, not an unusual occurrence during a sermon. But she stopped short of leaving, putting her back to the rear wall. Loyola didn't recognize her. She wore a conservative indigo blazer and slacks. Her hair was silver-gray, possibly premature, although it was hard to be sure at this distance. She was tall, but that could be heels; he couldn't see her feet.

She watched him intently, leaning back in a posture that was almost but not quite casual. He frowned. Something was off, but he couldn't put his finger on it, so he continued.

"Imagine how God must feel," he said. "When we ask Him for forgiveness. When we have wronged Him. When we keep wronging Him and coming back for more and more forgiveness. We go to confession, every week, every month maybe, and ask for forgiveness, and He always comes through, no matter how many times we bring Him the same old sins. Without confession, every one of us would be hellbound. The confessor speaks the words of absolution and the gates of heaven are reopened."

He paused for emphasis.

"But it never ends, right?" he said. "We're always screwing up, always coming back to confession, always asking forgiveness. We always return to sin."

A second round of murmurs.

"Lucky for us, God is more patient than man. He never stops forgiving. Sometimes I wonder, though. How must He *feel* about it? We know He feels things. He's a God of infinite love, but we also know He can get angry. It's right there in the Bible. Is God always angry with us? When we walk into the confessional, asking for His forgiveness yet again, is He thinking: Why don't we just do better?"

Dead silence. Hopefully that meant they were thinking about it.

"Here's the thing," Loyola said.

Something moved on the balcony.

Loyola blinked, keeping his face pointed at the flock and letting his excellent peripheral vision do the work. Could a kid have snuck up there?

No. Something poked out from the railing. Black, cylindrical.

Gun. With suppressor.

A brilliant red dot suddenly appeared dead center on the stole draped over Loyola's chest. Instinctively, he dropped to one knee, taking cover behind the pulpit.

A loud thumping sound emanated from the balcony, and a corresponding hole cracked open in the brick wall at the back of the sanctuary.

The pulpit rocked in sync with a second thump from above. One night, about five years ago, Loyola had slipped into the sanctuary and affixed a thin Kevlar panel to the rear of the stand, covering it with a discreet veneer. The armor held, thanks in part to the pulpit's thick wood, which slowed the bullet. Loyola reached up from where he crouched and grabbed the microphone.

"GET DOWN!" he bellowed then bounded down the center aisle.

It would take Loyola about two seconds to clear the fifty feet between the sanctuary and the lobby doors, not accounting for the aerodynamic drag of his heavy vestments. Crowds were unpredictable. The muffling effect of the suppressor meant most people didn't yet understand what was happening. Quite a few had followed his shouted command, ducking their heads and taking cover in the pews, but they wouldn't stay put for long.

Father Francis Loyola was not a gambler by nature, but he had just placed two very large bets. First, that the sniper was expecting Loyola to stay behind cover or flee, rather than rushing toward danger. Second, that the sniper would not start firing into the congregation.

If he lost either bet, people would die.

Loyola was about a third of the way down the aisle when the suppressor thumped again. He heard the bullet kick up a divot on the floor of the aisle behind him, but he was moving faster than the sniper's aim could adjust. The robes made it awkward, but Loyola had practiced endlessly for just such an occasion. He balled his fists in the flapping vestments and thrust his arms forward, streamlining his profile for a tiny improvement in speed.

Loyola's heart pounded in his ears, and behind that he could hear screams. The shock was wearing off, and the congregation was starting to understand what was happening. People in the pews leaned away from the center aisle as he passed, as if he were cutting a wake through water.

The woman in the indigo blazer was calmly walking toward a side exit. No time to do anything about it, no time even to think about it. File it away for later.

Loyola smashed through the lobby doors, to the surprise of the ushers and the young mother sitting on a bench rocking her baby.

"Clear out!" the priest shouted. "There's a shooter!"

The ushers scrambled for the exits, the woman not far behind. They probably thought they were rushing, but they were painfully slow and uncertain from Loyola's adrenaline-soaked perspective.

The balcony had only two points of egress—a stairwell on the north side and another on the south, both of which emptied into the lobby. Behind him, the panicked voices of the congregation rose like the roar of an approaching tsunami. In moments, the foyer would be jammed with fleeing people, constricting his freedom of movement.

Another life-or-death decision, with only a split second to choose. If he picked the wrong stairwell, the shooter would escape, or worse.

He knew the building better than anyone. The exits on the west side of the lobby led to the front steps and a busy street. From the east, the sniper could access a corridor that led to a parking lot and a less-trafficked alley in the rear.

Had to be east.

Loyola hit the stairwell just as the wavefront of the crowd burst out of the nave and flooded the narthex. He sprinted up the stairs, his breathing heavy but steady. The shooter wasn't on the steps.

Loyola reached the top and dropped to his belly. There was no door to the balcony, just an archway. He shimmied forward carefully until he was next to the threshold. Reaching beneath his vestments, he found his phone. Switching on the camera, he angled the device so that he could see around the bend without sticking his head into the line of fire.

The balcony was dark, only dimly lit by the chandeliers in the nave. A couple of metal music stands stood toward the front of the balcony, untidily pushed to the side. He could see the sniper's tripod by the rail, but no sign of the rifle or its owner. The back of the balcony was shrouded in deep shadow.

Loyola knew the precise location of the balcony's three rows of pews. He pulled himself up into a crouch, one knee forward, muscles taut, and took a deep but silent breath. If the shooter had taken the west stairs, there was no danger in front of him, but also no way Loyola could catch up. If this was an ambush, nothing would happen until he moved.

He took a precious moment to collect himself.

When he was ready, he threw his phone forcefully over the threshold, flicking his wrist to send it on a high arc above the pews. It landed on the far side of the balcony with a loud clatter.

Nothing happened. No shot, no shout. But there was a movement, a rustle, so small only Loyola's practiced ears could have picked it out amid the growing din of the fleeing parishioners. The disciplined reaction confirmed Loyola's worst fear—the shooter was a professional, lurking in the shadows at the rear of the balcony.

One crucial question remained. Had the assassin drawn a bead on the spot where the phone landed? Or the spot where it originated?

Hesitation would not improve his odds.

Loyola uncoiled with explosive force, leaping through the doorway and onto the back of the nearest pew. His powerful legs propelled him over each pew and toward the sniper. When he hit the third row, he launched himself like a missile, arms extended to protect his head, vestments whipping like a sail in the wind.

His opponent had traded the rifle for a pistol but didn't have time to aim. Loyola crashed into the shooter with brutal velocity, his momentum absorbed by the stocky man's barrel chest. The priest heard a satisfying crack as the assassin crunched against the brick back wall.

Loyola disarmed the shooter easily and tried to trap him in a standing shoulder lock, but his opponent twisted free and put some distance between them.

The shooter wore black pants, a matching turtleneck, and gloves. A black N-95 obscured his identity without attracting much attention during flu season. The assassin produced a knife from somewhere, spinning it with his fingers in an unnecessary flourish before adopting a pragmatic hammer grip.

Loyola could hear the sound of distant sirens, getting rapidly closer.

"Who do you work for?" Loyola demanded, adopting a defensive stance.

The man lunged forward. He was good, but not good enough. Loyola executed a hip throw, turning his opponent's momentum against him. The shooter slammed to the floor and went limp.

Loyola quickly dragged the man to the front of the balcony and searched him in the dim light. No wallet, no phone, just a single car key. Loyola reached beneath the turtleneck and found a large, flat, stylized silver cross on a chain. The two-barred cross was etched with an intricate moiré pattern that seemed to throb. He recognized it as the totem of the Brotherhood of the Epoch of Martyrs.

Worst-case scenario.

Loyola yanked the chain from the man's neck and stashed the cross and key in his robes. The sirens were close. There would be questions. Too many questions. He made the sign of the cross over the assassin's head, and whispered, "Remember, man, that you are dust."

The priest retrieved his phone. The screen was smashed, but it was still operable, and he was able to take a photo of the assassin's face. That accomplished, Loyola hauled the shooter over to the front pew and, using the hard wooden armrest as a fulcrum, efficiently snapped the man's neck.

Crouching at the rail, he scanned the nave calmly and methodically, never rushing despite the blue and red flashing lights he could now see through the stained glass. The security cameras were forward facing, meant to cover the altar and the sacristy, where most of the valuables were concentrated. All of the people had cleared out. No one had eyes on the balcony.

Satisfied, Loyola heaved the assassin headfirst over the rail. Fresh screams from the direction of the lobby, followed by barking tones of the police.

If they had arrived a moment earlier . . .

But they hadn't.

* * *

"The rifle's an SR-25," said a uniformed cop named Duffy. "Could be thirty years old, but it's in pristine condition. Serial number has been filed off. Same deal on the pistol. No ID, no car keys. Flat hard-shell case for the rifle. No one saw the perp enter, at least not so far. We still have quite a few witnesses to work through."

"Got it," replied Martina Rocha, the homicide detective who had arrived to take charge of the scene. She wore a suit that would have been businesslike if it were less rumpled. She turned back to Loyola.

"I know you're probably already sick of telling it, Father, but I'm going to have to ask you to do it one more time, please," she said.

"I was giving my sermon when I saw the gun poking over the balcony railing," Loyola said. "I assume it was meant to be a mass shooting."

"Just another Sunday in America," Rocha said grimly. Loyola nodded.

"I tried to draw his fire," he said. "I ran up to where I'd last seen him, hoping to distract him while the parishioners got away. He had his head in his hands when I got here, agitated. I tried to counsel him, but he jumped."

"Real heroic," she said, in a pointedly neutral tone.

Loyola shrugged.

"Not a great height," Rocha said, looking over the railing. "But he managed to land on his head. What exactly did you say to him?"

"I told him God loves him," Loyola said. "I said no one had been hurt yet, and we could still turn this situation around."

"And he said?"

"'No one can help me' or something like that," Loyola said. "Something else that sounded like gibberish, and then he jumped."

"Gibberish like a foreign language gibberish?" she asked. "Or like speaking-in-tongues gibberish?"

One of Loyola's mentors had been a police detective. *Always send them home with something to gnaw on*, the man had said. *Give them a mystery that goes nowhere.*

"Maybe a language? It's all kind of a blur," Loyola said and shrugged again.

"There are security cameras?" Rocha asked.

"Covering the altar and the sacristy," he said. "The assistant pastor can show you where the hard drives are kept. I don't think we have coverage of this area, to my recollection."

"Any enemies?" Rocha asked. "Any reason that someone might have a grudge against you?"

"I can't imagine," Loyola said.

"A lot of people frustrated and angry with the Catholic Church these days," Rocha said. "Just in general, but also sometimes for very specific reasons."

"Sure," Loyola said.

"Is there anyone who might have a *very specific* reason to come after you?" Rocha said with a tone that was somehow even more pointedly neutral. "An angry parent, maybe?"

"No," Loyola said flatly. It was a reasonable question, all things considered, and he shouldn't have resented it, but he did.

Rocha nodded, as if satisfied.

"Right," she said, handing him a business card. "If something occurs to you, call me. In the meantime, we've got a lot of work to do on the scene here."

"If you need anything, please let me know," Loyola replied, pocketing the card.

"We sure will, Father," Rocha said. There was something about her tone that made Loyola uneasy, but he had done all he could to throw her off the scent.

Loyola went down the stairs into the lobby. A coffee station and doughnuts had been brought up from the activity room in the basement, and a couple dozen parishioners were milling about waiting to be interviewed by the police. Someone saw him and started clapping. Others joined in, crowding around him. Loyola wasn't very social by inclination, but this was the job that God had chosen for him. He doled out handshakes, brusque hugs, and terse reassurances.

A lieutenant warned Loyola that the TV people were on the front steps of the church, and his officers couldn't hold them off much longer.

"Hero priest," the cop said. "They're very hot to get you on camera."

Loyola thanked him and decided to make a quick exit, out the back doors, and a short walk down the alley to the rear entrance of the rectory. As he moved to leave, a wan young woman in a green dress and an old-fashioned pillbox hat placed a hand on Loyola's arm.

"I'm sorry we didn't get to hear the end of your homily, Father," she said. "What was the lesson going to be?"

Loyola sighed, suddenly exhausted.

"God forgives, but He doesn't forget."

She frowned, not sure what to make of it. Loyola felt like he should say more, but he could only muster a shrug. His world had turned upside down in an instant, and he feared he was the last person who should be giving anyone guidance.

Through the power of the confessional, God had forgiven him for the sins of his past life, but out in the material world, it seemed Loyola was not yet done paying the price.

CHAPTER

2

# The Dead Man's Vice

THE CATHEDRAL WAS empty, illuminated only by shafts of fading late afternoon sun passing through stained glass. Father Francis Loyola straightened his cassock and made his way to the confessionals, entering the furthermost booth. The man on the other side of the screen slid the shutter back with a scraping sound.

"Bless me, Eminence, for I have sinned," Loyola said. "It has been two weeks since my last confession. These are my sins."

He could hear the cardinal breathing, waiting.

"I killed a man," Loyola confessed. "I lied to the police about it. I removed evidence from the scene. I ran two red lights on the way here to be sure I wasn't being followed."

He paused.

"And I took the Lord's name in vain while making a comment about another driver, in connection with one of the aforementioned red lights."

"Who was the man you killed?" the cardinal asked, unperturbed.

"I don't know his name," Loyola said. "All I know is that he was with the Brotherhood of the Epoch of Martyrs, and he was trying to kill me."

"Epoch of Martyrs?"

"Military order, established about nine hundred years ago."

"Weren't they disbanded?"

"About two hundred years ago, officially," Loyola said. "Unofficially, they're still very much alive and kicking. But no longer under the auspices of the Holy Father."

"Did you kill this man in self-defense?" the cardinal asked.

"In cold blood," Loyola replied. "I disabled him, but I didn't want him alive to be questioned by the police."

"To protect yourself?" the cardinal asked.

"To protect the Church," Loyola said.

He could almost hear the frown through the confessional screen.

"It is a grave sin to lie during confession, my son," the cardinal said.

"It's the truth," Loyola shrugged. "What happens to me doesn't matter, but it would be disastrous for the Church if the history of the Epoch of Martyrs was exposed, or if other details of my past activities came to light."

"What will you do now?" the cardinal asked.

"The assassin was carrying a car key," Loyola said. "He was very professional, so my assessment is that the police are unlikely to find his vehicle any time soon. I'm going to try to track it down and hopefully find his token. Then I'll report back."

"Your penance is fifty Hail Marys and five Our Fathers," the cardinal said. "Now say your act of contrition."

"O my God, I am heartily sorry for having offended Thee," Loyola recited. "I detest all my sins because of Thy just punishments, but most of all because they offend Thee, my God, who art all good and deserving of all my love. I firmly resolve with the help of Thy grace to avoid sin and avoid the near occasion of sin. Amen."

"God, the Father of mercies, through the death and resurrection of His Son has reconciled the world to Himself and poured out the Holy Spirit for the forgiveness of sins," the cardinal said. "Through the ministry of the Church, may God grant you pardon and peace, and I absolve you from your sins in the name of the Father and the Son and the Holy Spirit."

The two men sat in silence for a moment.

"What is said during confession is a sacred trust that stays between us," the cardinal said. "But is there a message you want me to relay?"

"The Holy Father should be notified of the key facts, and I have no objection to you reporting them to him," Loyola said. "The only question is whether it would be better to wait until I have more information."

"It should not wait," the cardinal said. "I think you know that."

"I'm accustomed to working independently," Loyola said. "That's how I work best, and limited communications make for better security."

"You *were* accustomed to working independently," the cardinal replied, gently. "Those days are behind you. You retired. You came in from the cold."

"But the cold came back for me," Loyola said grimly. "The media is already having a field day with this. My picture is everywhere. It's not safe to stay put, but if I just disappear, it will raise a lot of questions."

"We can manage that," the cardinal said. "We'll tell them you had a nervous breakdown or some such. You've gone on retreat to meditate and pray on what happened. But that only works if you stay out of sight."

"I'll try," Loyola said.

"You are not tasked with doing anything beyond retrieving the token," the cardinal said. "Let me emphasize that. Investigate the car, then report back for further instructions. Do not take further action without a direct order."

"Acknowledged," Loyola said.

"Go in peace," the cardinal said.

"Seems unlikely," Loyola said.

He cracked open the confessional door and scoured the church for any signs of movement. Satisfied that no imminent danger lurked, he knelt in a pew, took out a rosary, and recited his penance.

* * *

Loyola slipped into the rectory quietly, seeking to avoid attracting the attention of the reporters stationed out front and the housekeeper inside, who would be cooking dinner at this time of evening.

He moved silently up the back stairs. In his bedroom, he went to his laptop and connected his smashed-up phone with a USB cable. He dragged his photo of the assassin onto the desktop, then deleted it from his phone.

Loyola went to the closet, removing a stack of identical cassocks and dumping them on the bed. A hidden switch opened a secret panel, revealing a pegboard with hooks that held an assortment of carrying cases—a duffel bag, two backpacks, and several hard cases of varying size. Stacked on the floor were boxes of ammunition in different calibers.

The duffel was a go-bag containing civilian clothes, three thick rolls of cash, several wallets, and four burner phones with chargers. Loyola took out one of the phones, one roll of cash, a credit card from one of the wallets, and a baseball cap, then changed into a navy blue crew-neck shirt and tactical pants with lots of pockets. Black socks and black running shoes. A short, charcoal gray coat, appropriate for the winter chill and bulky enough to cover the bulge of his gun. His ensemble was sufficiently dark for a night mission, but visually distinct from his typical garb. A charcoal-colored knit cap finished the ensemble.

Loyola opened one of the hard cases and retrieved a Glock 20 pistol, two ten-round magazines, and a silencer, which he pocketed, along with the ammunition and the cash. He donned a shoulder holster and put the gun in it. A larger case contained a fully automatic APC rifle and night-vision scope. Loyola left the weapon but took the scope. From yet another case, he retrieved two throwing knives with nylon sheaths that attached to his belt.

Suiting up quickly, he replaced the bag and cases in the secret compartment, closed the panel, and replaced the cassocks.

Back at the laptop, he called up recordings from the hidden cameras that he had not told the police about. Fast-forwarding through the footage, he found nothing suspicious around the rectory; the shooter had probably assumed, correctly, that Loyola's safeguards would be strongest there.

The cameras covering the church's parking lot and back entrance had caught the sniper entering from the alley around four AM while it was still dark outside. He was alone, carrying the wide, flat case that the police had recovered. Although the rifle had been broken down to keep a lower profile, the dimensions of the case were unusual enough to attract attention—if anyone had seen him, which seemed doubtful given the hour.

Loyola copied the photo of the sniper onto the clean phone. then used a file-shredding app to delete the image, the surveillance video footage, and the app that controlled the cameras from his laptop.

Opening a private browser window, he typed a series of numbers into the URL bar. A web page opened with an empty text box and a single button that said "send." Loyola typed into the box: "Wheels, 3 am" followed by a lengthy alphanumeric code. It was late for a drop-off, but he needed time to investigate the sniper's car. With any luck, that task could be finished early, and he could grab some shut-eye in his own bed, which he might not see again for some time.

He clicked submit, closed the window, then closed the laptop. In his en-suite bathroom, he dropped the smashed-up phone into the toilet tank, then added some bleach to the tank before replacing the lid. In the medicine cabinet, he found a box of COVID-era latex gloves. Donning them, he wiped down his knives, the new phone and the scope.

Twilight had fallen, but the exterior of the rectory was well-lit, and he could discern no lurkers when he checked the window. Loyola made a stealthy exit, creeping silently to the rear door, past the kitchen where the housekeeper was making stew with the TV on. The smell of food reminded him that he hadn't eaten since breakfast, and the sound of the TV reminded him that everyone in the vicinity would instantly recognize the face of the hero priest.

* * *

The shooter would have chosen a route that avoided surveillance—as much as that was possible in the twenty-first century. Any number of houses in the neighborhood had doorbell cameras, which the police would poll first, since most homeowners would give up the footage without a warrant.

Loyola knew the assassin had entered the church from the back alley. To find the man's car, he would have to follow the gaps in camera coverage.

The alley stretched for a few blocks in either direction, north or south. An auto shop's lot opened onto the alley just to the north, no doubt protected by a security system, so he headed south.

After six blocks, the alley terminated facing a middle school and another bank, both of which would have lots of cameras. If the car had been stowed nearby, it must be back the way Loyola had come. He turned and began to retrace his steps.

Many of the houses were brightly lit and filled with the sounds of families having dinner, easily excluded from his search. Some of the houses were dark, but only a few of those had vehicles parked in back. Loyola tested each one with the key, but none matched. One house had a garage in its backyard, which contained a lawnmower, a snowblower, and assorted junk, but no vehicle.

Soon, Loyola found himself back by the church. He leaned against a telephone pole in a dark spot and pondered his next move. He'd quit smoking many years before, but the craving occasionally kicked up. He tried to ignore it.

He looked back to the south. If the assassin had a partner—his memory flashed on the woman in indigo—that person could have moved the car. Loyola couldn't rule it out, but he had doubts. The sniper had the key on his person. If this were

Loyola's operation, he would have secured the car somewhere discreet, where it could sit for a while without attracting notice.

His eyes roamed to the north again, returning to the auto shop. The lot was not well-lit, and at this distance, he couldn't make out much detail. Loyola fished the rifle scope out of his pocket and switched on its night vision. He made out three cameras—one on each corner of the building's rear face, and one in the center. One high-mounted spotlight bathed the lot in a faint yellow glow. Perhaps enough shadow that a person could slip through, but too much light to park a car without being detected. And the police would have gone through the business records to make sure everything in the lot had been checked in for a repair.

Unless the car was being repaired. Knock out a taillight, drop the car off at closing time on Friday. Easy fix, no need to check the trunk. Only a few steps to travel exposed while carrying the rifle case. If the shooter had managed to escape unseen, he could have picked the car up Monday afternoon without attracting scrutiny.

The trick would be to search the lot without getting caught on camera. Loyola pulled out the scope again. The mounting on the center camera was slightly skewed to the left, creating a blind spot on the center right, which might be enough, combined with the low light.

Zipping up his jacket, Loyola dropped to a crouch and moved forward in a duckwalk. If he had calculated the angles correctly, he could navigate most of the lot without getting captured on video, so long as he stayed close to the cars and below their hood level. Crawling on his belly would have been more discreet, but it could fatally slow his response time if trouble broke out. He looked ridiculous, but from a duckwalk, he could instantly spring into at least three different melee attack positions, or he could drop one knee to the ground, draw, and shoot with a two-handed grip.

Ridiculous was better than dead.

Once behind cover, he shifted to the right and began working his way through the twenty or thirty vehicles packed into the large lot. He checked the driver's side door of each, one by one, even the ice cream truck, even the car with the pizza delivery topper. Some people had funny ideas about camouflage.

When he got to the thirteenth vehicle, a baby blue Honda Accord, the key clicked, and the door opened—loud in the silence, made worse by a creaky hinge. A skittering noise followed, probably a startled rat or a racoon. Loyola paused. The animal was gone, but something else—so faint it was almost subliminal—a crinkling, settling sound. The rustle of clothing? The faint squeak of a shoe carrying its load at the wrong angle, as if bearing the weight of someone in a deep crouch?

Loyola drew one of the throwing knives, quieted his breathing, and waited. He didn't want to expose himself to the cameras unless it was absolutely necessary. He spared a glance at the car. No time for a thorough search, but that wasn't needed. He reached in and grabbed what was to all appearances an ordinary phone charger plugged into the auxiliary power outlet—the socket once meant to hold a cigarette lighter. He slipped the device into the zippered jacket pocket that held his phone. A Faraday pocket liner would block any trackers or other wireless signals.

Loyola pulled out the scope and surveyed his immediate vicinity. Nothing. He duckwalked around the open door toward the front of the car, peeking around the bumper, first with his eyes, then with the scope, sweeping from left to right. Nothing. He turned toward the rear of the vehicle just in time to see a woman come around the bend, below the camera level, using an *aikido* knee-walking technique. When she saw him, she rocked back onto her heels.

Gray-silver hair, just a strand peeking out from under a knit cap. She was wearing jeans and an indigo T-shirt under a light but warm jacket that was unzipped despite the winter air. In her left hand, she held a semi-automatic pistol, equipped with a silencer. He recognized it as a Luger, which meant it must have a customized left-handed grip. Not a casual purchase.

The sound of the car door had given her a distinct advantage—she had known exactly where to find him. The open door was between them, giving Loyola some cover, but he was too close to it, without enough runway to lunge forward.

Their eyes met through the driver's side window. He caught her fleeting glance toward the nearest camera, figuring the angles. They were doing the same calculus. Exposure versus range of movement.

Her calculations were faster. From the kneeling position, she sprang straight forward, ramming into the car door with her full weight, bending back the hinge and smashing the window into Loyola's face. While resistance blunted the force of her charge, he had failed to anticipate the move and the price he paid for that lapse was his balance. He tumbled backward.

Loyola converted the momentum of his fall into a backward somersault, landing on his feet just clear of the car's front bumper. No chance of avoiding the cameras now, but at least that opened up some freedom to maneuver.

Indigo bounced back from the impact to land in a kneeling stance, two-handed grip, right elbow resting on her knee. Loyola dived for cover in front of the car then dropped flat to the ground, peering under the chassis. In the dim light, he could see her rear leg. He flicked the throwing knife, flat on its side, like a frisbee. Because of the angle, he couldn't put much force into it, but he heard her grunt as the razor-sharp blade sliced through her jeans and into her calf. Probably just a graze, not enough to disable, but hopefully it would sting and bleed, at least slowing her down.

Loyola tried to put some distance between them, keeping low. A Jeep offered improved cover. He put his back to it and drew his trusty Glock. No time for the silencer. He looked up. Loyola was a good shot, probably good enough to take the light out, but the darkness was not necessarily his friend. He couldn't aim his pistol while holding the scope in his other hand.

For a long, tense moment, everything was quiet. Then he heard the muffled retort of her silenced pistol. A car alarm erupted near him. A good strategy, intended to throw him off balance and perhaps cause him to expose his location, but Loyola maintained a glacial stillness forged by years of experience.

He considered returning the favor but decided against it. One car alarm was just the background noise of the city. Multiple alarms would be more likely to attract attention from the neighbors. He needed to end this swiftly and as silently as possible.

The ice cream truck was a couple vehicles to his left, and he decided to seize the high ground. Staying low, Loyola scuttled over to the truck, then hoisted himself up using the side mirror, ending flat on the roof. The blaring of the alarm covered the sound of his movements, or so he hoped.

From this vantage point, Loyola spied his adversary, who was closing in on his previous position, limping slightly thanks to the knife wound. He pulled the silencer out of his pocket and screwed it on.

He was still waiting for a clean shot when something intruded on his vigilant peripheral vision. Two men were approaching. For a moment he feared they were police, but they were equipped with black body armor, night-vision goggles, and suppressed automatic rifles.

If they were here to reinforce Indigo, Loyola's best option was to retreat. He drew a bead on the woman again. If he took her down, they might stop to assist her, giving him time to escape. The distraction would be more effective if she survived, so he zeroed in on her left shoulder, which would have the added benefit of taking her left-handed gun out of play.

But she had also clocked the men, and she didn't look thrilled to see them. Not one bit. Keeping as flat as possible, he watched to see what happened. Whatever this thing was, it seemed to include multiple factions, and he desperately needed intel. Loyola told himself he was being practical, but he had arguably fallen prey to curiosity—the dead man's vice.

Keeping her head below the car line, the woman quickly shifted from a stalking posture to an ambush stance. Her position suggested she was concerned about a sniper on the roof. Loyola looked up nervously. The truck was white, and he was prone on top of it, completely exposed.

But none of this felt particularly planned.

Indigo was undoubtedly after the same thing he was—the covert device that looked like a phone charger. That was a stealth mission, but the goons were not at all stealthy, and they were armed to the teeth. They were here for him, or they were here for her. No other reasonable explanation came to mind.

Loyola began calculating escape routes, estimating the strength of the car roofs that lay between him and the alley. He was four jumps from freedom.

Indigo had taken a page from Loyola's book, flattening to mount an attack by shooting beneath the cars. He couldn't see for certain, but she was undoubtedly targeting the back of their combat boots, the Achilles tendon, where the armor would be weaker and the result disabling. A muffled gunshot, and one man went down, cursing in some language that was not English. The woman was an excellent shot under very bad conditions. She quickly circled the car and put two bullets in the man's head.

The parking lot suddenly went dark.

Bad conditions indeed. The men down there were not alone.

Loyola fumbled for his night-vision scope. A sweep of the property revealed four more targets approaching from the alley, putting a crimp into his escape plan. Not only that, they were closing on his location. Which meant someone had spotted him, maybe from the roof or the second floor of the auto shop. Probably the same person who had cut the lights.

Time to go.

Loyola rolled off the roof of the truck and landed hard on the ground, only to find himself face to face with the woman. They each stepped back a pace and drew up, staring at each other over their gunsights.

At this range, he could see that she was fairly young, despite her silver-gray hair, probably early thirties. They locked eyes for a moment, as the armored men rushed up loudly—five now, minus the one she had killed. Four behind Loyola, one behind the woman. She took her aim off of him and shot one of the incoming men in the face. He reciprocated and took out the one behind her.

The three remaining interlopers took up positions behind nearby cars and began firing indiscriminately, as Loyola and

Indigo dove for cover—him behind a car on the left, and her on the right. Their eyes met once more.

"*Pax vobiscum,*" she said. "Until we meet again."

Moving as fast as she could in a medium crouch, she fired a couple of wild shots to discourage pursuit. She disappeared quickly into the inky darkness, despite her limp.

A hail of gunfire came from the armored goons, mostly aimed in her general direction. Loyola thought he could make out two firing positions in front of him from the sound and the occasional muzzle flash. More and more car alarms started blaring. Police involvement was now guaranteed, and the clock was counting down. He had to end this, fast.

The third man would be trying to flank him. He looked down the row of parked cars. It was too awkward to reach for the scope now. While the two shooters were focused on Indigo, Loyola dashed up the row, staying low. He paused behind each car and swept each aisle with his pistol. Just past the fourth car, he found a target and pulled the trigger.

The shot would have penetrated his opponent's heart if not for the armor. Even with the armor, the man was knocked back a step, thanks to the Glock's considerable stopping power. The man squeezed off a wild burst of gunfire as he stumbled. Loyola's second shot went into his head.

The other two abandoned pursuit of the woman and set into motion after Loyola. They advanced from aisle to aisle, shooting first and checking for a target second. The leading attacker was three rows of cars back from Loyola's position, and the second was four rows. The sloppy tactics strongly suggested these commandos were not even close to Loyola's league, but they had superior firepower, and at least one person in reserve, maybe more.

The noise was deafening now, a surround sound cacophony of car alarms on top of the volleys of gunfire. Loyola crouched behind a station wagon, holding himself steady as the lead attacker fired his weapon up the aisle to the left. When the lead attacker was shooting to his right, and the second attacker was shooting to his left, Loyola made his move.

He leapt on the hood of the car and ran up onto the roof. When his foot hit the trunk, he jumped onto the next car and repeated the maneuver. The lead attacker panicked, swinging his rifle in a wide arc while firing continuously. As Loyola landed on the third car, an old Buick, he fired down on the lead attacker, a clean head shot. The priest rolled off the hood of the car and hit the ground hard as the second gunman let off a volley that decimated the Buick. Loyola covered his face with his arms as shattered glass rained down around him.

The remaining attacker, realizing his compatriot was down, adopted a more cautious approach. Loyola pulled himself up into a kneeling stance and waited. As soon as the gunman came around the corner, Loyola fired two shots. He was aiming for the head, but hit center mass. The gunman staggered.

Loyola had a clean shot then, but the Glock's magazine was empty. He pulled his remaining throwing knife from its sheath and aimed for the man's neck. He hit the target, blood spurting everywhere. The bastard didn't go down, but he dropped his gun. Loyola rushed forward and tackled his enemy, knocking him onto his back. The priest sat on the man's chest, his knees pinning the man's arms.

Loyola swapped out his empty magazine for a full one while he waited for blood loss to do its work. It didn't take long.

He retrieved the knife from the man's throat. Loyola thought about going back for the one he had used against Indigo, but the enemy team had at least one more person on the premises. It nettled him to leave anything behind, but he was wearing gloves, and the knife was clean and untraceable.

Sirens were now drowning out the chorus of car alarms. He was out of time. Patting his jacket pocket, he confirmed that the phone charger had not slipped out during the melee. Loyola would win no points for stealth, but he had accomplished his most important objective.

"*Gratias agimus tibi,*" Loyola whispered. "I give thanks to Thee." He performed the Sign of the Cross, then let the Holy Spirit move him to an expeditious retreat.

CHAPTER

3

# Perps With Ambiguous Intentions

Pope Eugenius III was distressed to hear that Raymond II, Count of Tripoli, had been murdered. Not that Raymond was anything special—a mediocre crusader, an ineffective politician, and a brutish human being whose cruelty had reportedly driven his noble wife into the arms of another.

No, it was the manner of the murder. Count Raymond had died miserably, his throat slit, ambushed by the Muslim Assassin cult, his body left by the side of the road to be ravaged by rats and dogs. Lurid tales of the Assassins were well known throughout the land. Eugenius III had paid them no mind, because they had mainly killed other Muslims, an activity that suited the Church well enough.

But now! The murderous cult had dared to strike at Christendom, and the Holy Father could not let it stand. People were already saying he was dull and weak. His own advisors said it! To his face! Despite his anointment by God! His crusade had ended in humiliating defeat, and his own mentor had called him a peasant in front of the entire Curia. Enough was enough! This would be a turning point, he swore, the very last affront he would endure.

Eugenius III had no shortage of militaristic religious orders that could execute a routine retaliatory strike. Military orders were all the rage in those days, the Knights Templar, the Knights Hospitallers, the Brotherhood of the Epoch of Martyrs, the Knights of Saint Peter, and on and on, with new ones springing up constantly.

But the Holy Father wanted to fight fire with fire—a secret society, answerable only to God, and God's representative on Earth. What Eugenius III needed was a band of perfect killers, cut from the same cloth as the Assassins, but better. The Assassins had become enthralled with their own mystique, and the cult's love of its own reputation had led its fanatical adherents to become loud and unsubtle. The Holy Father needed a different sort of tool, quiet, invisible, unstoppable.

Let them think he was weak. They would never see his killers coming. History would not soon forget the name of Eugenius III.

Thus was the Order of Saint Uriel consecrated with a secret papal charter in June of the year of Our Lord 1153, taking as its patron the archangel chosen by God to strike down the firstborn of Egypt.

Eugenius III died of typhoid fever two weeks later and was forgotten by history in due course. But the Order lived on.

* * *

Loyola hadn't been expecting a firefight when he left the rectory, and now he couldn't go back. Even the laziest cop in Boston would instantly connect the shooting at the church to the massacre at the car lot, and he hadn't gotten the impression that Martina Rocha was lazy.

His nerves still jangling from combat, Loyola decided to walk. For seven blessed years, he had not raised a hand in violence, and his body had changed. Physical reactions coursed through him like the rumbling of tectonic plates, indistinguishable from emotion, equal parts excitement and dread. He did not love violence, but he had undeniably mastered it and using his well-honed skilled brought a certain satisfaction.

Unlike his pastoral ministry, Loyola had a natural talent for violence. But God didn't ask his children to do what was easy; he asked them to do what was hard. For Loyola, the path of peace was a daily challenge, but one he had accepted gladly and come to treasure. He worried that the day's events signaled the end of that pursuit.

For the first hour, he kept a brisk pace, burning off excess energy and putting miles between himself and the church. He often went running late at night, but this time he avoided his usual routes. Today's attacks were clearly professional in nature, and his enemies had undoubtedly studied his movements. Keeping a low profile now would be key to his survival. He walked the harbor waterfront for a time, keeping to side streets. After a while, he circled back through town, passing through quiet residential areas and moving deeper into the city.

Preoccupied with dark reflections, he was slower than he should have been to notice a shadowy figure pacing him. His old instincts roused at the intimation of danger. Another assassin? As he approached an intersection, the street signs suggested a simpler explanation—Massachusetts Avenue and Melnea Cass Boulevard, known to locals as "Mass and Cass" or the "Methadone Mile." The city had been working to make the area safer, but it was still dangerous, especially after dark. Loyola's ministry had brought him here many times, most recently to retrieve the son of a parishioner who had fallen prey to heroin.

After the incident at the car lot, he couldn't take any chances. Quickly scoping the location, he diverted to a side street. A county-run halfway house was about a block away, staffed by the sheriff's department, which meant there would be at least a handful of armed officers on site, whom he greatly preferred to avoid. He slipped into the parking lot of a Unitarian church instead, pressing himself against the graffiti-covered wall.

The sound of footsteps accelerated, and then a man careened around the corner and darted past him. Gaunt, pale, unshaven, and underdressed for the cold in a jeans-jacket with its sleeves ripped off, the man overlooked Loyola entirely, skidding to a halt in disappointed puzzlement. Loyola pushed away from the wall.

"What are you doing, son?" he asked.

The man wheeled about, extending a switchblade in a twitchy hand.

"Give me your wallet and your phone," the man demanded. "And your coat," he added after a moment's thought.

"I can't do that, son," Loyola said, deliberately slowing his breathing and tamping down his reaction. This man was not even remotely a danger to Loyola, but the reverse was not true. Loyola's body was tuned to other threats and eager to react. Had all his worst impulses come back to him so quickly?

"I'll cut you!" the man said. "Don't think I won't!"

"Tell you what," Loyola said. "I won't give you my wallet, but I'll give you a hundred bucks, and we'll go our separate ways. No harm, no foul. I won't call the cops. Nobody gets hurt."

"Do you think this is a game, old man?" the man hissed.

He lunged forward. Loyola turned his body to one side with a minimal movement and removed the knife from the man's hand, gently, as if correcting a child. Confused, the man moved to grab it back, clutching, but Loyola sidestepped again. The man swung a fist high and wide, and Loyola simply leaned back and let it whoosh past his face. The man swung again and again, without making contact. Finally, he seemed to realize that he might have made a serious mistake. He extended his palms and slowly backed away.

"Take the money," Loyola said, fishing in his pocket and producing a hundred dollar bill. The man took it from him gingerly, as if fearing a trap.

"Use it for food, not drugs," Loyola said. "There's a Catholic Charities shelter four blocks in that direction if you want to get clean or just need a safe place to sleep. Tell them Father Loyola sent you. They'll help."

Loyola held up the knife, retracted the blade and put it in his back pocket.

"But no more of this," he said. "If you give them any trouble, I *will* find you."

"*Father* Loyola?" the man asked incredulously. "You're a fucking *priest*?"

Loyola sighed heavily. His effort to keep a low profile was off to a bad start.

"Look, no one needs to hear about this," he said. "OK?"

He stepped forward, trying to project a friendlier vibe, but the man yelped, then turned and ran. Even on the best of days, Loyola cut an imposing figure. And this had not been the best of days. Not by a long shot.

He threw up his hands in exasperation and walked on into the night.

* * *

"What a mess!"

Rocha was exhausted. It had been a long day investigating the shooter at the church, which was more than bad enough. The perp was a cipher. No fingerprints or DNA in the database, no ID on his person, no vehicle to be found, no serial numbers on the guns, and according to the priest at least, he was spouting some unknown foreign language. His clothes didn't even have tags. Nothing about this was routine.

The whole thing smelled like a professional hit, but why? On a hunch, she had run the priest through the system and found no criminal record. Something was amiss, but she had figured that something could wait until Monday.

Maybe not.

A bustling team of officers and city workers had erected glaring spotlights over the auto shop's back lot, illuminating the spectacular scene—more than a dozen bullet-ridden cars and six dead bodies lying in pools of black blood. The dead men were dressed like commandos and equipped with slick, expensive gear. Three White, two Black, and one indeterminate, but maybe Arab or Desi. Not an ID on any of them, and she was sure her officers would find the guns were clean as well.

Rocha looked back over her shoulder. All of this had unfolded just steps away from the church. The massacre was obviously connected, but how? What was it about?

"Malone," she called out to one of the officers. "Send someone over to the rectory to check on the hero priest. Assuming he's alive, tell him to bring an overnight bag. In the unlikely event I'm done questioning him by tomorrow, he's going to be in protective custody until further notice."

Rocha returned her attention to the car lot. The damage was extensive, and a fire truck was stationed nearby because the shooting had punctured some of the vehicles' fuel tanks. It was clear a gunfight had taken place, but all the corpses were outfitted identically, suggesting they were all on the same team. Whoever killed them was still at large. That meant probably five or more armed and dangerous perps with ambiguous intentions.

She walked up and down the aisle, trying to reconstruct events from the spread of bullet damage. None of it added up. All of the damage was down range from the placement of the bodies, meaning the dead guys had done almost all the shooting. Ballistics would say for sure, but it looked like the team that killed the commandos had barely fired their guns. Had they been killed by a sniper? Snipers? Most of them had been taken out by head shots, like in the movies. One had his throat slit.

She sent two officers to check the roof.

Near the perimeter of the destruction zone, she came upon a blue Honda Accord. It too was damaged, but differently, its driver-side front door bent at the hinges as if from a blunt impact. Rocha squatted for a closer look. On the ground near the rear door, she found an exotic-looking throwing knife with blood on it.

"I need someone over here," she called out. "Run the plates and the VIN on this car, blue Accord, and get forensics over here ASAP. I want this thing under a microscope."

"Nothing on the roof, Detective," someone shouted from above.

As she straightened up, Rocha saw Malone sprinting back from the rectory, and she just knew it wasn't going to be good news.

“No sign of the priest,” Malone said. “But no sign of a struggle. The housekeeper hasn’t seen him since this afternoon. His bed hasn’t been slept in. The assistant pastor is calling the diocese now to see if they know where he is.”

Rocha checked her watch. 11:36 PM.

“What a fucking day,” she said.

Malone just nodded.

* * *

Loyola checked his watch for what seemed like the hundredth time. 2:55 AM.

“What a fucking day,” he muttered.

After the attempted mugging, he had pulled his hat brim down low and grabbed a spicy chicken sandwich at a fast-food joint. He hadn’t eaten at all since breakfast, and his body was aching for fuel. The caffeine in the watered-down Coke didn’t hurt either.

Then it was back to the streets, assessing the day’s performance as he killed time.

Loyola didn’t like what he saw. He was rusty and complacent, his instincts dulled after seven years of civilian life. To be sure, he still had his habits, his muscle memory. Otherwise he would have died at the church this morning, or in the parking lot. But at a deeper level, his head wasn’t in the game. He was engaged with paranoia as an professional exercise, but he had stopped *feeling* it. And it was the feeling that kept the knife’s edge sharp.

He should have stashed extra weapons and ammo somewhere outside the rectory before searching for the car. He should have anticipated more trouble.

But he hadn’t, and that was that.

He looked at his watch again. Almost time.

At three sharp, the car rolled up.

The BMW E32 was a 1980s muscle car dressed up like a dadmobile, its advanced age offsetting any glamor associated with the brand. Its sedate four-door form belied a V8 engine and gas tank big enough to offset the fuel efficiency. The paint job was a deliberate matte brown, well-maintained, but dingy-looking, with a few minor dents. You could find faster cars, and sexier cars, but the combination of power and discretion made the heavily customized E32 Loyola's favorite. A cop wouldn't look at it twice.

The driver stepped out and lit a cigarette. He was lean, dressed in a smart suit and wearing glasses, his hair in tight, neat cornrows. Stepping out of the shadows, Loyola allowed himself to vicariously enjoy the smell of smoke.

"Deacon," he said.

"Frank," the man replied with a warm smile. "I honestly thought I was never going to see you again. But don't worry, I've kept her in fighting form." Deacon patted the hood of the car affectionately.

"I never doubted it," Loyola said.

"I assume this is about what happened at the church this morning," Deacon said.

Loyola grimaced.

"I know better than to ask," Deacon laughed. "But this is not our usual situation. I've never known anything about your work, and I don't want to now. But, my friend, you are the lead story on every single television and radio station right now, local and national. Get used to questions."

"Shit," Loyola growled. He had been reticent to use the phone, but it would have been worth the risk to cultivate his situational awareness about the entirely foreseeable outcome of the firefight. Another rusty instinct.

"The world's changed," Deacon said. "It's a lot harder to keep secrets these days."

"Yeah," Loyola said.

"Fortunately for you, discretion is my business," Deacon said. "You can still count on that at least. I've updated the Beemer's systems, let me give you a rundown."

"Yes, but . . ."

"Make it quick," Deacon laughed. "Frank never changes."

Deacon gestured toward the small white box affixed to the front windshield.

"You have EZ Pass," he said. "But the transponder is special. Every time you go through a toll booth, it'll ping to a different account belonging to a real person who lives and actively drives in this part of the state. There are 50 IDs in rotation. As long as you don't rack up crazy big tolls, no one will notice."

He opened the door and gestured inside as he highlighted features.

"The glove compartment is now a Faraday cage, so you can always toss the transponder in there if you prefer not to leave an electronic trace, but the toll plazas all have cameras now, so you might just want to avoid them entirely."

Loyola grunted with approval.

"The radio works just like it used to, but now it's got Bluetooth for your tunes, and more importantly, an embedded Wi-Fi router that will automatically jump on any open or weak security networks nearby. While you're in the city, you should have a reliable and fairly untraceable signal."

"Got it," Loyola said.

"Outside the city, it switches to satellite," Deacon said. "Slightly less untraceable but still better than pinging cell towers. Turn off mobile data on your phone whenever possible and use the car's Wi-Fi instead."

"Got it," Loyola said.

"This next one is pretty cool," Deacon said. "Get out your phone, and try to take a picture of the license plate."

Loyola complied. When he pointed the phone at the plate, the camera went out of focus. He tried a couple of different angles, but none of them produced a clean image. Deacon grinned.

"The plates and the windows are treated with a digital camouflage coating," he said. "Invisible to the naked eye, but digital cameras won't get a clean image of your plates or your face through the windshield."

Loyola nodded approvingly.

"Everything else is pretty much as you left it," Deacon said, "except refreshed. Oh, and I replaced the old laptop with something newer and more secure." He handed Loyola a small slip of onion-skin paper marked with symbols vaguely reminiscent of the Zodiac Killer's code. "This is everything you need to log on, both the computer and the Wi-Fi."

Loyola nodded.

"You know where to reach me if you need anything else," Deacon said.

"Probably better have a backup vehicle on call just in case," Loyola said.

"No problem," Deacon said. "It might not be the same make and model, but I know what you like, and you'll have something suitable if and when you need it."

They shook hands, and Deacon handed Loyola the keys.

"Don't suppose you need a ride," Loyola said.

"Never," Deacon said, as he walked into the shadows. "Go with God."

"Always do," Loyola said.

* * *

After a series of elaborate maneuvers designed to throw off anyone trying to follow him, Loyola drove west in the dark for about an hour and a half, heading toward the Saint Meinrad Benedictine monastery in Plainfield, a sleepy rural community on the far side of the state. He played Johnny Cash on his new phone to stay alert.

*From his hands it came down*
*From his side it came down*
*From his feet it came down*
*And ran to the ground*

Loyola took comfort in the sacrifice of the Cross. He had seen and done terrible things, and he had to believe that violence and suffering could somehow be transubstantiated into meaning.

*And the blood gave life to the branches of the tree*
*And the blood was the price that set the captives free*
*And the numbers that came through the fire and the flood*
*Clung to the tree and were redeemed by the blood*

He pulled off the road about half an hour before he reached his destination. Twisting one of the BMW's custom knobs, he reduced the brightness of the headlights, then drove a short way up a service road into a wildlife management area, where he parked. In the trunk, he found clothing options suitable for different occasions. He donned a black clerical suit and white Roman collar.

Like Loyola, Abbot Konstantin Stefanidis was a veteran of the Order of Saint Uriel. They had worked together about fifteen years ago, on a mission that had left no witnesses, and they had encountered each other only briefly since. They were connected by a shared experience of violence, but Loyola didn't like the abbot and definitely didn't relish the prospect of asking him for help. Stefanidis was extraordinarily skilled, but he took pleasure in work that should have haunted him.

But Loyola had cut ties with the Order after "entering ordinary time," while Stefanidis maintained lines of communication.

After the parking lot firefight, Loyola couldn't go back to the cardinal. Deacon had not exaggerated; his face was leading every website, newspaper, and TV station, an intensely uncomfortable situation he'd never had to face before. Loyola was a creature of the shadows, instinctively averse to the glare of the spotlight. Fortunately, the abbey was focused on silent contemplation. The monks had foresworn TV, Internet, even newspapers. No one other than Stefanidis would be likely to recognize him.

Fog rolled in as he got back on the road, thick and gray in the tentative early morning light. Leaving the highway, he took a series of smaller roads and then turned onto a wide, unpaved logging trail that continued for more than a mile through the woods. When he reached the end, the first beams of sunlight sliced through tree branches to part the mist. The abbey emerged in spectacular silhouette, an ornate shadow amid fractalized shafts of smoky golden light.

The looming structure was an artifact dislodged from its rightful time and place, proudly incompatible with the modern world and American aesthetics. It had been painstakingly reconstructed from the ruins of a medieval British abbey.

About thirty monks lived in the architectural marvel, while an incongruously shabby collection of trailers set back from the road housed a dozen or so "guests." Some visitors were ordinary people or clergy who had come to seek solace in solitary prayer and meditation. Others were priests who had been sent here for a period of silent retreat after becoming "problems" in their home parishes—a practice that set Loyola's teeth on edge.

Some people were better suited to jail cells than monastic cells. If God saw fit to redeem them, He could find them just as easily in prison or the grave.

Loyola parked a short distance from the abbey, pointing the nose of the BMW toward the road in case a quick exit was needed. The sounds of Monday morning Mass, already underway, drifted from the compound. Loyola followed them to a chapel, opening the door as quietly as possible and slipping into a rear pew. A handful of congregants were priests, dressed as Loyola was, the rest were monks wearing simple brown habits.

Stefanidis was standing at the pulpit, preparing to give the gospel reading. He was only a few years older than Loyola, but his balding head and gray-streaked beard gave him the look of an elder statesman. The abbot's voice was deep and resonant, with hints of sly humor. His accent faintly evoked his native Greece, although a less practiced ear might miss it.

Despite Loyola's effort at discretion, Stefanidis immediately noted his presence, acknowledging with a nearly imperceptible nod. A gleam in his eye was replaced with a glint.

"And Jesus told his disciples another parable," Stefanidis read. "The kingdom of heaven may be compared to a farmer who sowed wheat in his field. While everyone slept, his enemy came and sowed weeds among the wheat. When the wheat grew up, the weeds did too. The farmer's servants came and said to him, 'Master, did you not sow good seed in your field? Where did these weeds come from?'"

Stefanidis paused and cast his eyes over the congregation, as if searching for the source of the weeds. His gaze passed over Loyola but did not linger. But some of the "visiting" priests squirmed in their seats.

"The master answered, 'An enemy has done this.' The servants said to him, 'Then do you want us to go and pull the weeds up?' He replied, 'No, for you will pull up the wheat as well, and it is not yet time. Let them grow together until the harvest, and then I will tell the reapers to gather first the weeds, binding them in bundles and setting them ablaze. Then gather up the wheat and place it in my barn.'"

Stefanidis closed the book with a clap.

"This is the Gospel of the Lord," he said.

"Praise to you, Lord Jesus Christ," the brothers replied.

"Through the words of the Holy Gospel may our sins be wiped away," Stefanidis recited. He looked down at the pulpit for a long moment. When he began the homily, his tone was casual, almost genial.

"The wheat and the weeds," he said. "Older editions of the Bible call them tares, referring to a specific kind of weed. Tares look just like wheat, so much so that they were sometimes called 'false wheat.' When the master tells his servants that they will bring up the wheat with the weeds, he wasn't simply telling them that the roots are intertwined, although they are. He is saying it is too soon to know."

Stefanidis paused, placing his hands on the book in front of him.

"When the harvest comes, the wheat ripens brown, but the tares turn black," he said. "That's why the reapers can sort them out so easily."

He looked up again, and out at the congregation.

"God intends that we live in the midst of evil," Stefanidis said. "That is our burden in this world. We take nutrients from the same soil as evil. We drink the same rain as evil. No matter where you dwell in this temporal world, evil is there. Next to you. It looks just like wheat until the harvest comes, when God reveals all. We cannot root out the weeds until the time is right. We must not. If we act too soon, we risk destroying the righteous alongside the wicked."

Stefanidis's roaming eyes suddenly landed on Loyola with an impact that was almost visceral. Loyola remained perfectly still, impassive as a fortress. Stefanidis was trying to bait him, but Loyola couldn't afford to revive old grudges.

"God counsels patience," Stefanidis said. "Evil will reveal itself in its appointed time. Now please stand and join me in the profession of faith."

When the Mass concluded, Stefanidis exited through the left transept, rather than using the main entrance. The monks did not seem to expect otherwise, shuffling out through the rear of the church to start their day. One of them, a massive man with a boxer's pug nose, looked at Loyola appraisingly.

Hopefully none of the brothers had a bootleg Internet connection.

Loyola remained, kneeling in prayer, until they were all gone. Crossing himself, he got up and made his way to the transept door. A short corridor led past a small library to an open-air cloister that surrounded a fading lawn. A majestic old maple tree sat in the center of the courtyard, its branches dusted with snow. Stefanidis stood next to the trunk, running his hand over the bark, as if studying its health. He seemed immune to the cold and did not turn his head as Loyola approached.

"Abbot," Loyola said.

"Francis," Stefanidis said.

"Can we speak privately?" Loyola asked.

With a flourish, Stefanidis led Loyola on a winding path through the rooms of the abbey, ending in a spacious suite. Taking a seat behind the large mahogany desk that dominated the sitting area, he gestured toward a low-set stuffed chair. Loyola remained standing.

"I'm pretty sure that wasn't supposed to be today's gospel reading," Loyola said.

Stefanidis smirked.

"God moved me to make an adjustment," he said.

"And you just happened to have the pages in front of you?" Loyola asked.

"I have a photographic memory," Stefanidis replied. "But enough. I don't need to ask why you're here. While the brothers do not partake of the outside world, I carry that burden for them. Meaning I've seen the news reports. Now tell me what really happened."

"The shooter at the church was a member of the Brotherhood of the Epoch of Martyrs," Loyola said. "Or at least he was carrying their insignia. I removed it from the body before the police came."

He drew it out of his pocket. Stefanidis examined it closely.

"Authentic," he said.

"I concur," Loyola said.

"The news said the shooter committed suicide," Stefanidis said. "A mortal sin."

"I did what had to be done," Loyola said.

"And the shootout in the car lot?" the abbot asked.

Loyola gave a concise account.

"You think the commandos were not the Epoch of Martyrs," Stefanidis said.

"Hired guns," Loyola said. "Good, not great."

"And the woman?"

Loyola shrugged.

"They have a women's order," Stefanidis said. "The Sisterhood of the Epoch of Martyrs."

Loyola hadn't known that.

"They work together?" he asked.

"Not necessarily," the abbot said. "You have the token?"

Loyola pulled the Faraday bag out of his pocket and placed it on the table. The abbot opened the bag and found the phone charger that Loyola had retrieved from the sniper's car. Stefanidis pulled a small electronic device from his desk and waved it over the dongle. A light blinked green, and he nodded with satisfaction.

"No tracker," he said.

Stefanidis unlocked the center drawer of the desk and pulled out a laptop, which he booted up. From another drawer, he obtained a bricklike power converter with a circular port. The abbot plugged the dongle into the socket, then connected it to the PC with a USB cable. A command-line window popped up on the laptop's screen and lines of code marched up the screen.

"Give it a minute," he said.

"Sure," Loyola said.

"You must have some theories," Stefanidis said. "What do you think this is about?"

Loyola frowned.

"I had a run-in with the Epoch of Martyrs some years ago," he said. "In Medjugorje, Bosnia. It was messy."

"Messy enough to make enemies?" Stefanidis asked.

Loyola shrugged.

"Loose ends?" Stefanidis asked.

Loyola kept his expression still, but his jaw tightened. The abbot nodded.

"What about the commandos?" Stefanidis asked.

"They could have been after the woman," Loyola said. "I'm reasonably sure I wasn't tailed to the car lot, but I can't rule out exotic surveillance, drones, satellites, that sort of thing."

Stefanidis snorted.

"Hardly exotic these days," he said. "You are behind the times."

The computer beeped. Stefanidis turned away from Loyola and typed a few commands on the keyboard. Another beep, and a screen full of data appeared.

"What have you got?" Loyola asked, leaning forward to see for himself.

"What you would expect," Stefanidis said. "Mission-critical documents. Your name. A recent photo of you. The address of your rectory, the habits of police patrols in your neighborhood. Contact info for a local gun dealer and a local fixer. Hotel reservations. No rental records for the car, it was probably stolen."

He opened another screen of data.

"Flight itinerary. There's a name, presumably fake. He entered the country from Europe, had a return flight reserved," Stefanidis said. "Sarajevo. What is that, two or three hours' drive from Medjugorje?"

Loyola nodded.

"Anything else?" he asked.

"Nothing," Stefanidis said. "You're going to go?"

"I can't exactly go home after all this," Loyola said.

"You remember the Order of Saint Uriel's first directive."

"Death before exposure," Loyola said.

"You have already made a big noise," Stefanidis said.

"Was I supposed to just take the bullet?" Loyola asked, genuinely wondering.

Stefanidis shrugged.

"Maybe," he said. "Maybe not. But perhaps something to think about going forward. Do you want me to hear your confession?"

"No," Loyola said.

Stefanidis turned back to the computer. He pressed a key, calling up another headshot of Loyola that looked to have been taken ten years ago or more.

"You kept your face when you entered ordinary time," Stefanidis said. "Why?"

Another small shrug.

"If I changed my face, I might forget," Loyola said. "I might start thinking that someone else did all those things. That it was someone else's burden to bear."

"You sound perhaps like a man who wants to die," Stefanidis said.

"I want to live," Loyola said. "But on my own terms."

"Now you sound like a man who is *definitely* going to die," Stefanidis said. "Are you sure you're up to this, Francis? You've been out of the game a long time."

"Don't have much choice," Loyola said.

"You do have a choice," Stefanidis said. "Stay here. I can guarantee your safety. Pray, meditate, walk in the woods. Let the Order handle it."

Loyola frowned.

"Asking me to sit back and trust the Order is asking a lot," he said.

"The trust or the sitting back?" Stefanidis asked.

Loyola shrugged again, and the abbot scowled.

"I could order you to stand down," Stefanidis said.

"I retired," Loyola said. "I'm not yours to command."

"You didn't retire from the Church," Stefanidis said. "I can speak for the Vatican in this matter."

Loyola arched an eyebrow.

"Is that so?" he asked.

Stefanidis smiled thinly and held up his hands, palms pointing toward heaven.

"I will not stand in your way, Francis," the abbot said. "But heed me. You need to keep a much lower profile. And don't leave any loose ends this time."

Loyola nodded.

"That's the plan," he said.

"Man plans," Stefanidis said. "God laughs."

"God laughs either way," Loyola said. "At least this way I have a plan."

CHAPTER

4

# That Can't Be Right

WHO THE FUCK was Father Francis Loyola?

Martina Rocha had gone to sleep asking herself that question, and it was still there when she woke up a few short hours later. She just knew it was going to swallow her entire day, so she got up ahead of the alarm, already tense in anticipation of the ten AM press conference.

When she got into the station, she saw her captain talking to two suits, undoubtedly ATF and FBI, the all-powerful federal government coming to the rescue of the outclassed local cops. She was going to need more coffee before facing that, and anyway, she had to make notes for the media scrum. Arming herself with a cup of the precinct's vile caffeine beverage (she refused to call it coffee), Rocha fussed with the chaotic stacks of paper on her desk before logging into the computer.

Francis Loyola, born in Cleveland nearly forty-eight years ago. Family and education details pending. Enlisted as an Army chaplain in Afghanistan after 9/11. She was still waiting for details of his deployment, but he had rotated out in 2004.

According to the assistant pastor, Loyola then worked as a missionary somewhere in Africa. She was annoyed that he couldn't name a specific country, but she had a query into the archdiocese for more details. At some point after that, Loyola had worked in the Vatican as a diplomatic liaison, whatever that meant. Rocha didn't know much about the hierarchy of the Catholic Church, but it seemed odd that he would go from Rome to a mundane parish in Boston. Seemed like a step down.

All of which added up to what? Why send a small army after this guy?

Maybe terrorists with some kind of grudge? Had he baptized the wrong kid in Afghanistan? Or was it an Army thing, some kind of bad business, or some deal with a military contractor, or the CIA? What about the Vatican? Had the chaplain stumbled onto some kind of dirty dealings? Wasn't there some kind of conspiracy theory that Pope John Paul I was murdered because he uncovered corruption? She was sure she had seen that somewhere. Rocha had been raised Catholic but left the church as a teenager, when a priest had informed her in a matter-of-fact tone that she was destined for hell for the sin of being gay. She had put all things religious out of her mind after that, and she resented this case for dredging it all up.

Rocha heard her name being called from across the room and looked up. The suits were looking at her, and the captain was waving her over. She checked her watch. Half an hour until the press conference. They would want to compare notes. They were, understandably, focused on the gunmen and their guns, and Rocha couldn't argue with that. But she kept coming back to the same question.

"Who the fuck is Father Francis Loyola?" she mused aloud.

"Isn't that the hero priest?" asked the desk sergeant sitting next to her.

"That's what they say," she muttered as she got up and crossed the room.

* * *

Loyola accepted Stefanidis's offer of a guest room. After propping a chair against the door, he sprawled onto the bed fully clothed and fell asleep instantly. He woke up as the sun was going down. Quiet murmurs and the clinks of glasses and plates indicated that the brothers had gathered in the dining hall.

He gave them a wide berth. Further conversation with Stefanidis would be pointless at best, and probably counterproductive. If push came to shove, the abbot would undoubtedly side with the Order of Saint Uriel over Loyola. Nothing yet suggested the Order was involved with yesterday's attacks, but its leadership might decide to shut down his investigation rather than risk any further exposure. Sharing information would create unnecessary risks without any obvious rewards. And Loyola was keeping one vital piece of information close to his vest.

In the fading light, Loyola popped the trunk of the BMW and took inventory. Deacon had provided multiple passports, but these wouldn't do him much good with his face plastered on every screen in New England, and disguise had never been his strong suit. After consulting the paper map he found in the glove compartment, he decided to make for Nova Scotia. Avoiding major highways as much as possible, the drive to Halifax would take about sixteen hours. It was far enough away that, with a little luck and another day's worth of stubble, he might be able to get through security without being noticed. From Halifax, a direct flight to Frankfurt, then by car to Sarajevo.

A short distance from the abbey, he pulled into a wooded copse to change his clothes, choosing a beige ballcap and a pair of glasses with antiglare lenses. He stopped for gas, careful of the camera angles, paying at the pump with a card provided by Deacon.

Eager to escape the bright lights, Loyola set off on the first of many backroads. The moon was new, and streetlights were few and far between. The trees lining the road were bare and desaturated in his headlights, flickering past him in monotonous patterns, broken up only by Christmas lights in the windows of the occasional houses he passed. Golden snapshots of ordinary family lives, a concept that Loyola had lived vicariously through his parishioners.

Loyola had never really known "ordinary" people, and the last seven years at Saint Bridget's had been a revelation. Before Boston, his world and his work had been consequential, shaping the fortunes of a two thousand-year-old institution and changing the course of human events. Civilians could never know the extremes he had experienced, the magnitude of his victories and the depths of his defeats, and above all the burden of blood that he carried wherever he went.

Many veterans of the Order of Saint Uriel took up lives of silent contemplation when they could no longer continue the Great Work. Others pursued atonement, ministering to the world's most desperate and impoverished communities. When Loyola prayed on it, his mind returned again and again to the nature of the institution he served. Everything he had done, he had done for the Catholic Church, but he had never really known the believers who made up its body.

Working with them, for them, these past seven years, he had come to understand the dignity of their lives, the true and vital worth of simply existing within a family and a community.

Nothing in his experience had prepared him for the intense grief of parents who had lost a young child, the patient kindness of a middle-aged woman toward a father who no longer remembered her face, the authentic forgiveness extended by a young man toward an abusive mother, the radiant faces of a couple newly wedded before God and their families.

In ministry, Loyola could finally put faces and voices to the abstract Church he had once served so furiously. This gentle work had given him rewards that the Great Work could not. Every life was a deep story. Loyola took great satisfaction in his newfound role cultivating such stories rather than unceremoniously ending them.

Well, those days were over.

Whatever happened next in Medjugorje, the Vatican could never allow him to return to his flock. At best, he might be permitted to live out his life in a solitary monastery in some remote location. At worst, he would find himself looking down the barrel of a gun into the eyes of a killer much like himself.

Call it poetic justice, or God's mercy.

* * *

Five hours in, Loyola crossed into Maine, a Red Bull in the cupholder and the stereo blasting Creed, both courtesy of Deacon's thorough provisioning. He would have preferred coffee, but he didn't want to risk stopping anywhere until he was close to or over the Canadian border. Snow had been falling for hours, and it was picking up.

Loyola finished the energy drink after passing Augusta, and he began looking for a sheltered spot to pull off and urinate, which would also allow the vehicle behind him to pass. The driver had been with him for maybe ten miles. It was probably happenstance. No one could have followed him from Boston, but Loyola saw no reason to take chances. Spotting a widened shoulder ahead, he put on his turn signal and began to pull off.

The other driver slowed. Loyola moved off the road and decelerated further, and the other driver matched his pace. Loyola abruptly switched gears and slammed on the gas pedal, prompting the BMW's powerful eight-cylinder engine to roar with delight. The other driver allowed a short distance to open up between them but kept the pace. Loyola increased his speed to sixty miles per hour, well beyond the posted limit, and the other driver matched him.

The road was a single lane in either direction, narrow and twisting, with lights few and far between, and a thin sheen of snow making it slippery. No one would take these curves at this velocity without reason. Happenstance was off the table.

Loyola came out of a curve and put the pedal down, but a pair of taillights abruptly pulled off the side of the road and into his path. The new car was a black Ford SUV, a model favored by police, and it was moving at half his speed. Loyola jerked the wheel to the left and entered the oncoming lane. As soon as he was past the SUV, he swerved back to the right, narrowly avoiding a head-on collision with a pickup truck that blared a horn at him in protest.

The SUV had accelerated and was now keeping pace, a second pursuer. All three cars blasted through a stop sign. On the next curve, Loyola felt his tires start to spin out, fortunately only for a moment. But it was obvious that the roads presented at least as much threat as his pursuers. On a clear day, they would have been going way too fast; on a snowy night, he could only call it madness. And the distraction of his full bladder wasn't helping either.

His rear window suddenly fractured, a spider's web of cracks emanating from a central impact. The glass was bulletproof, of course, but not indestructible. A couple more shots, and the windshield would give way. In the meantime, he could no longer see through the central rear view mirror.

Unsustainable.

Loyola had been driving roughly parallel to Interstate 95, the major route north through the state. His best bet now was to get on the highway, but he would have to drive through a town to get there. He spared a quick glance at the dash. 10:43 PM on a cold Monday night. In rural Maine, not many people would be out. It was worth the risk—as if he had a choice.

They ran two more stop signs, then a traffic light, where another car barely stopped in time to avoid a collision. Loyola's peripheral vision picked up the lights of other moving vehicles, civilians probably, on intersecting and surrounding roads. The ramp onto the interstate was still five miles away.

They burst into the main stretch of a town called Sidney, according to a sign that flashed past almost too quickly to see. Loyola was relieved to see there was no walkable downtown, but ahead he spotted the lights of a roadside bar that was still open. A red car was in the process of pulling out, and he swerved violently, barely missing, the sound of shouted vulgarities compressed and distorted as he left the scene behind. The SUV also avoided the red car, but the other pursuer clipped it. With only the side mirrors, Loyola couldn't tell how bad the damage was, or whether the impact had taken the driver out of the chase.

A bullet hit the back of his car, then another, but there was nothing he could do about it. The on-ramp was ahead of him, finally within sight—a tight one hundred eighty-degree loop, which he was approaching at eighty miles per hour. Loyola slammed on the brakes and jerked the wheel to the right. He was still doing sixty as he hit the ramp, and the car lurched, threatening to fishtail on the thickening snow, but he somehow kept control as the centrifugal force of the turn pressed him against the door. His relief was palpable as he snapped back into a straight trajectory, exiting the ramp onto the highway.

His pursuer, or pursuers, might be skilled drivers, but they were not as confident. By the time they hit the ramp, at a considerably safer speed, Loyola had managed to open up a lead, pushing the BMW's speedometer up to a hundred. The snow was falling heavily now, but the highway was in pretty good shape compared to the backroads he had left behind.

Loyola allowed himself a moment of relief, which quickly faded when he saw the flashing yellow lights ahead—a snowplow, going perhaps thirty miles an hour, kicking up a substantial amount of snow and ice in its wake.

He slowed down and looked off at the shoulder. The plow tracks made it hard to be certain, but it seemed at least four inches had fallen. From the way the BMW was handling, he was reasonably certain Deacon had outfitted him with snow tires, but the improved treads could only handle so much, and he had already come dangerously close to losing control.

Another bullet hit the back windshield, shattering it. A gust of freezing air spilled over his neck, but at least he could see. Two pursuers still, and closing fast. Loyola pressed the gas and the engine responded, oblivious to the weather. As he closed in on the plow, its driver laid on the horn hard.

Loyola ignored the noise, focusing intently on the plow's immediate wake, where the freshly turned snow would be looser and more dangerous as he tried to pass. His plan was to forge ahead at maximum speed, alternately tapping the brakes and the clutch as lightly as possible to mix up the wheel rotations and hopefully avoid a skid. It sounded like a terrible idea, and he would never advise anyone to try it.

Somehow it worked, and he lurched past the plow onto a field of pristine powder.

"I give thanks to you, oh Lord," he said, crossing himself. "As always."

The road was completely covered, so he situated himself parallel to the guardrails and hoped for the best. The flashing lights of the plow receded behind him, but another vehicle was closing in. From the height and shape of the headlights, he made it out to be a Jeep. On a clear road, the BMW could easily outrun it, but the weather put them on a roughly equal footing. Trying to go any faster would be suicide.

Someone was leaning out of the Jeep with an assault rifle. Loyola heard a burst of automatic weapons fire, but he didn't feel an impact on the car. Their velocity and the current visibility made it hard to shoot accurately, but his opponent would eventually get lucky.

Loyola considered getting off the highway again, but the roads would not be any better than this, and the risk of collateral damage would be higher in populated areas.

His bladder, which had quieted as he concentrated on passing the plow, suddenly reminded him that it required urgent relief. But his attention was immediately jolted back to the road as a massive shadow loomed in front of him. Considerably bigger than the BMW, its powerful antlers swiveled toward him and tossed back as if in challenge.

Loyola had never seen a moose before, and now he was speeding toward one, over snow, at ninety miles per hour. It stood in front of him like a brick wall, and Loyola was pretty sure that the impact would be similarly catastrophic. Without time to think, he just reacted, slamming on the brakes and twisting the wheel. The car hydroplaned over the snow, spinning completely out of his control. He downshifted and started pumping on the brakes for what seemed like forever, until his rear bumper hit the guardrail, stopping his rotation with a grating sound about twenty feet from the moose, which seemed to be glaring at him.

Loyola sat there for a moment, panting, trying to get his bearings. And then the Jeep came barreling out of the snow and struck the moose with an awful sound. The front end of the Jeep crumpled like a wad of paper, and the moose's torso toppled into the windshield, smashing it. The man who had been hanging out of the passenger window with a gun was pinioned as the frame bent back, one arm trapped in the vehicle and the other going limp and dropping the rifle.

Loyola paused to consider his next move. Between the snow and the shooting, he had no idea how much time had elapsed since they passed the snow plow, but he was pretty sure he had gone past at least one exit. He wanted to question any survivors of the crash, but he didn't want to be seen by the plow driver or any other civilian. And at least two more cars had been pursuing him.

He would have to be quick. Jumping out of the car and drawing his gun, he headed toward the Jeep, wading awkwardly through the deep snow.

The crash site was gruesome. The driver had been crushed, presumably to death, beneath the massive girth of the moose, which had somehow survived and was quietly whimpering. Loyola looked it over, trying to determine whether it might recover. When he got to the rear legs, he could see both were broken.

Loyola put a bullet in its head, regretfully. He had killed countless times before, but the moose was innocent in a way that men could never be. He made the Sign of the Cross over the animal's head and whispered a prayer, then turned his attention to the passenger, who was thoroughly trapped and moaning softly. He was wearing the same type of body armor used by the commandos in Boston.

The snow plow might catch up at any time, but one piece of business couldn't wait. Loyola relieved himself by the side of the road, cleaning his hands with a fistful of snow, then returned to the Jeep.

"Help me," the man moaned.

"Weren't you just trying to kill me?" Loyola asked.

The man paused, as he didn't really have a good answer for that.

"Have mercy," he wheezed, finally.

"Who do you work for?" Loyola asked.

"Bridgewater," the man said. It was a moderately well-known private security company, with the emphasis on "private" and a very broad definition of "security." Its name was shared with its owner, Lloyd Bridgewater, a former Special Forces operative turned cryptobro entrepreneur specializing in high-tech intelligence gathering. He was also, Loyola recalled, a particularly reactionary type of American Catholic convert, for whom the Latin Mass symbolized the good old days when the Church was less compassionate.

"Who's the client?" Loyola asked, already knowing the answer.

"They don't tell us shit," the man coughed.

"What *did* they tell you?" Loyola asked.

"Capture or kill," the man said.

"How did you find me?" he asked.

"We were given a general vicinity and a description of the car," he said.

"What else?"

"They said you were a priest," the man said, then paused. "That can't be right, though. Wouldn't you have to help me?"

Loyola looked back up the road. Through the snow, he saw the flashing yellow lights of the plow approaching slowly. He looked back at the man. Stefanidis had advised him to keep a lower profile, and he had already left a significant pile of dead Bridgewaters back in Boston.

"God would want you to help me, right?" the man said.

"I tell you what God wants," Loyola said. "You don't tell me."

The man moaned.

"The snow plow is coming," Loyola said. "As far as they know, you haven't committed any crimes. Tell them the truth: You were traveling too fast for conditions, and you hit a moose. And hope they don't ask about your gear."

Loyola plucked the man's assault rifle from the snow, walked back to the BMW, and drove off through the storm at a decidedly unsafe speed.

CHAPTER

5

# The God of It All

LOYOLA TRIED TO focus on the dark, snow-covered road, but his mind was racing.

How did they know where he was? The most obvious explanation was that he had been betrayed either by Stefanidis or by Deacon. The Deacon network, a secular organization employed by the Vatican, had an unimpeachable reputation for discretion and trustworthiness. Stefanidis was far more likely to play the role of Judas, which would mean that his enemies probably also knew that he was headed to Bosnia.

But what game could Stefanidis be playing? Was the Order of Saint Uriel involved? The commandos were off-the-shelf goons. If the Order wanted him dead, it had plenty of tools at its disposal that would be more subtle and far more likely to succeed at taking him out.

Had Bridgewater been surveilling Stefanidis? The abbot would surely detect any on-the-ground operation, but Bridgewater would have access to drones, maybe even satellites. Even the most proficient assassin could not be expected to detect a watcher at orbital heights.

Whatever the source of the problem, the car was compromised. If they were tracking him via satellite, they had probably lost contact during the snowstorm. That might be why their ground forces had moved on him aggressively, instead of waiting to see where he went. If Deacon's countermeasures worked as advertised, they might not have his license plate. But based on his trajectory, they had to know he was headed for the border.

He was going to have to ditch the car, the sooner the better. But driving something stolen through a border checkpoint presented an unacceptable level of risk, even at a remote crossing like the one he had been heading for. He was about an hour away from Bangor, or would be in normal weather. Bangor was big enough to find a decent car, but also big enough to have cameras everywhere.

Decisions, decisions.

Loyola decided to head for Bangor. It would be almost two AM by the time he got there. He could steal a car and hopefully make it to the border before anyone woke up in the morning and found it missing. He might even be able to hide the BMW from any eyes overhead before the snow stopped. Once he was on the other side of the border, he could steal a fresh car with much less risk.

It wasn't much of a plan, but it would do for now.

* * *

The streets of Bangor were silent, muffled by snow, with only the occasional rumbling and scraping sounds of plows at work. Loyola focused on avoiding them, cruising up and down the streets of residential neighborhoods, looking for a place that met his needs—far from any commercial facility with surveillance cameras, no lights to indicate anyone was awake in the house, and ideally a detached covered garage where he could work undetected and leave the BMW hidden from prying satellite eyes, at least until morning.

After a few passes, Loyola identified a likely candidate, an aging mansion behind a snow-caked wrought-iron gate, with a three-car garage that was accessible through an alley behind the property. He rolled into the alley with his lights off—tricky in the snow, but he managed. Retrieving a small kit from the trunk, he left the car sitting in the middle of the alley, some distance from the house, and proceeded on foot to investigate the garage. A locked window presented him with no challenge, and he saw no signs of a security system. He entered silently, closing the window behind him. Turning his flashlight on low, he surveyed the scene.

Jackpot. Two cars in the garage, along with a snowblower and other lawn equipment. An empty bay big enough for the BMW.

The first vehicle was an extremely rare 1970 Plymouth Fury GT in pristine condition, with a glossy red finish. He admired its lines, but it was hardly discreet, and its astronomical value would make it a high priority for the cops. The second vehicle was a dull gray 2010 Nissan Murano, oddly downscale in comparison but equipped with all-wheel drive and snow tires. It was an easy call.

Back out in the alley, Loyola put the BMW into neutral and rolled it toward the garage. It was a substantial car, and managing its heft was even harder in the snow, but he couldn't risk starting the engine. By the time he got it into the bay, another half hour had passed. He lowered the door silently and took a minute to rub his aching arms.

Deacon had packed the BMW's trunk with maximum efficiency, using a frame-and-divider system that could be lifted out as one unit. Loyola moved everything, covering it with a blanket he found in the hatchback.

Time to get back on the road.

* * *

The snow continued to fall—fat fluffy flakes that would have been pleasant if viewed through a window of a house with a fireplace, with a mug of hot chocolate in hand. On a dark Maine highway in the dead of night, it was far less charming.

Loyola was forced to proceed at a crawl, at times uncertain about his lane, or whether he was even on the road, although the GPS kept him vaguely on track (he hoped). On the bright side, no one seemed to be pursuing him.

The snowfall was so intense that he almost didn't see the blinking hazard lights, let alone the woman standing next to her car, waving her arms.

Braking gingerly, he felt the Nissan slide underneath him, but it slowed and eventually stopped. He cast a wary eye backward to be sure no one was following. Loyola was cautiously optimistic that he had thrown off his pursuers, but he was far from certain. The last thing he needed was entanglement with a civilian, or even worse, a first responder. But the Bible was quite clear about how God expected him to respond to a person in need.

Loyola turned on his own hazards then quickly inspected the interior of his vehicle. His pistol was holstered beneath his jacket. A spare magazine was stowed in the driver's side door pocket, not too visible. Anything else that would be difficult to explain was in the hatchback, under the blanket. Hopefully whatever this was would not require him to go into the trunk.

“Thank you, thank you, thank you!” the woman cried, obviously exhausted. Beneath her parka, he could see she was wearing pajama pants that disappeared into snow boots. Clearly, this wasn’t a planned excursion.

“What’s the problem?” Loyola called out, as he trudged through the snow to reach her. “I can guess some of it.” The falling snow cast an aggressive white-noise hush over everything, and he felt the need to raise his voice.

“My baby has a bad fever,” she said. “I wouldn’t come out in this otherwise.”

Loyola looked at the car, which had gone off the side of the road and was sitting an angle that suggested a ditch somewhere beneath the powder. Inside, a tiny baby fidgeted in a car seat, and a girl of about five or six was riding shotgun. Both were heavily bundled against the cold. The woman had wisely turned off the engine, since the snow was deep enough to cover her car’s tailpipe, but that meant no heat. Not good for a sick baby.

“Do you have roadside assistance?” Loyola asked.

“I don’t have any bars on my phone,” she said.

Loyola looked back up and down the road. The good news was that the road remained empty, and he saw no signs of enemy pursuit. The bad news was that he had no idea when any other help was likely to arrive. A snow plow would surely be along eventually, but the child’s fever was serious.

“I’m Evelyn,” the woman said, sticking out a mittened hand. “Billy was running a temperature of a hundred and two when we left the house. I can’t afford to wait for someone else to stop. I hate to ask in this weather, but could you please help us?”

“I’m Frank,” Loyola said, returning the handshake. “I don’t live around here. How close are we to a hospital?”

"Half an hour," she said. "Uh, normally."

That meant at least an hour in this weather, probably longer, and undoubtedly back in the direction he had come. There was no chance he could tow her car out of the ditch under these circumstances, and it would be a waste of valuable time to try.

"OK," Loyola said. "Everything is going to be all right."

"Bless you," Evelyn said with evident relief. "A Good Samaritan."

"Let's get you all into my car."

The girl climbed into the front passenger seat, while Evelyn got in back with the baby, a diaper bag, and several blankets from her vehicle. She fished a baggie out of the bag and filled it with snow, holding the ice pack to Billy's flushed forehead. Loyola had very little experience with babies beyond baptizing them, but even he could tell the child was suffering. He helped the little girl put on her seat belt, then started the car.

"I'm Frank," he said to her. "Your brother's going to be just fine."

"I'm Tina," the girl replied. "Are you mad?"

"What? No," Loyola said.

"Tina!" Evelyn said. "Be nice to Frank! He's helping us!"

"He looks mad," Tina said solemnly.

"I'm mad at the snow, not at you," Loyola said.

She thought about that for a minute.

"I'm mad at the snow too," she said.

"Good," Loyola said. "We have something in common."

He found the nearest hospital on his GPS, and inched back onto the road. At the first exit, he pulled off the highway so he could turn around. A gas station's lights flared up through the whiteout, and he was tempted to stop and see if someone else could help. But God had put this family on his path, and he didn't especially trust anyone else on these roads. He got back on the highway going south, as fast as he dared.

"What brings you out on such an awful night?" Evelyn asked. "I mean, I'm glad you are."

"I'm visiting my mother in Oromocto," he said. "New Brunswick." Fortunately, she didn't follow up with any informed questions about the town, which he had seen on the map while planning his route.

"Are you Canadian?" she asked.

"By birth," he said. "But I've been here a long time."

"Are you married?" asked Tina.

"Tina!" Evelyn said. "I'm so sorry! She can be very, uh, direct."

"Something else we have in common," Loyola said.

"So are you?" Tina asked.

"My wife died a few years ago," Loyola said. "Cancer," he added for Evelyn's benefit.

"What was her name?" Tina asked.

"Lois," he said, with a sinking feeling. Why hadn't he just said "no"?

"Do you have kids?"

"No," he said. He congratulated himself on getting it right this time.

"Let the nice man drive," Evelyn said. "He needs to focus."

"My mom isn't married anymore," Tina continued. "My dad went away."

"Tina!" Evelyn said, in a pleading tone.

"He looked mad all the time," Tina continued, relentless. "Like you."

"I don't look mad *all* the time," Loyola said, defensively.

"It's a sin to lie," Tina said solemnly.

"I'm well aware," Loyola said.

"Sir, I am so sorry," Evelyn said. "She's very curious, and it's so late."

"Why are *you* up so late?" Tina asked him.

"It's my mother's birthday," Loyola said. "I didn't want to miss it."

"Is she having a party?"

"Yes."

"Is there a cake?"

"Yes."

"What kind of cake?"

Loyola had endured less brutal interrogations in Kazakhstan.

"Lemon?" he said.

"I like chocolate," Tina said.

"When's *your* birthday?" Loyola asked, seeing an opening.

"How old is your mom?" Tina countered. "Is she pretty? Does she look mad all the time? Does she have a nice house? Does she have a dog? What's the dog's name?"

It was all Loyola could do not to groan audibly.

The questions continued for one of the longest hours of Loyola's life, until the lights of Bangor's hospital mercifully emerged from a wall of white. Loyola helped his charges out of the car and into the emergency room, where a nurse took Billy's temperature and told them a doctor would be right out.

"I have to go," Loyola said.

"Thank you so, so much, and I'm so, so sorry about Tina," Evelyn said. "Nobody expects the Spanish Inquisition, right?"

"You'd be surprised," Loyola said. "I'll pray for Billy, but I'm sure everything is going to be all right now."

"Thank you," she replied, her eyes shining.

"You still look mad," Tina said. "I don't think you're very nice."

"Tina, please!" Evelyn said. "He's done so much for us! He's very nice!"

Loyola sighed.

"I'm really not," he said. Then he turned to Tina and presented her with the most overwrought scowl he could muster. She shrieked and hid behind her mother's legs. Loyola winked at Evelyn, who burst out in relieved laughter as he made his retreat.

* * *

The snow was finally abating, and he opted to take the interstate. It was still dark and the roads were deserted, but the plows had finally gone by, so he could make decent time at close-to-normal highway speeds. After some hours, he came to a rest stop, where he changed into a warm, dry flannel shirt and a pair of tough jeans provided by Deacon. A pair of calf-height hunter's boots finished off the ensemble.

Maine's large forested border with Canada, running north to south, had minimal security other than the weather, which routinely claimed the lives of those who sought to cross undetected. Loyola could defend himself against threats that most people would never be able to imagine, but he was as vulnerable as anyone else to subzero temperatures.

By the time he approached the border, a faint glow on the horizon foreshadowed the arrival of daylight. The shortest possible route through the forest involved about two miles of hiking from the terminus of a dead-end road on the American side, where he would have to ditch the car. After crossing on foot, he would have to find a fresh car, but he would be back on the beaten path. A long walk didn't frighten him, but freezing to death in a snow drift did.

In the small town nearest the crossing, Loyola found a diner open for breakfast and decided to risk it. He hadn't eaten proper food in twenty-four hours and didn't know when he would next get the opportunity. Plus he was facing a strenuous day, even if no one was shooting at him. He took a booth and ordered a stack of pancakes, two eggs, a steak, bacon, home fries, toast, orange juice, and a coffee.

The size of his order didn't seem to faze the waitress, whose name was Louise and who called him "hon" three times in the course of four sentences. Two burly truckers at the counter had similar plates in front of them.

As he waited for his food, Loyola booted up his current burner phone. He'd lost his secure Wi-Fi along with the BMW, but he needed situational awareness. The good news was that a quick news search showed no reports about heavily armed commandos getting killed by a moose. Unfortunately, his face was still plastered over Boston-area media. He watched video of a press conference about the parking lot massacre. He could see Martina Rocha among the gathered cops.

He slipped on a pair of Bluetooth earbuds to listen. No one had any explanation for what had happened. The theories under investigation included terrorism and organized crime, possibly connected with Loyola's missionary work.

Rocha looked extremely uncomfortable, standing alongside agents from the FBI and the ATF, then stepping forward to give a short and technical description of the scene at the car lot and the Boston PD response. A spokesman from the archdiocese followed, explaining that the hero priest was on retreat in an undisclosed location for his own protection and to recover from his ordeal.

Rocha looked particularly unhappy during this part of the presentation, no doubt wishing to question Loyola further. The cover story of his personal history was probably robust enough to withstand a significant amount of scrutiny, but the body count in the car lot guaranteed an extraordinary amount of scrutiny. The Order of Saint Uriel was no doubt fully engaged with backstopping his legend. At least no one seemed to be actively searching for him at the moment.

He took out the earbuds and activated the phone's VPN, using the browser to visit a website identified only by a numerical IP address. A blank page appeared, containing only two empty fields and a button labeled "Next." He typed an unreadable series of letters and numbers into the first field, and a similarly composed password into the second, then clicked next. An unadorned text page appeared, reading "no messages."

Loyola frowned. The Order was aware of his situation, and although he was retired, he would have expected them to reach out with "guidance" about how to proceed—most likely that he should report to a safe house and take no independent action. He had been fully prepared to ignore any such guidance, but its absence worried him. He closed the browser window.

He was puzzled to hear Rocha's voice again; his phone was no longer playing video. When he looked around, he spied small TV mounted above the diner counter displayed the morning news, which was now showing his face. One of the truckers glanced at him, then elbowed his comrade. The waitress was also looking at him.

"You're that guy," the trucker said. "The hero priest!"

Loyola groaned inwardly but deflected outwardly.

"Nobody tell my old lady," Loyola said with as much humor as he could muster.

Louise laughed.

"Don't listen to these idiots, hon," she said with a wink, as she brought his food to the table. "You're better looking than that priest, any day of the week." The trucker gave Loyola a long searching look, before shrugging and returning to his meal.

Loyola applied hot sauce to his eggs and maple syrup to his pancakes then proceeded to devour them at an unsafe speed. He left cash on the table, with a generous tip, then visited the restroom. Thankfully, the truckers did not show any further interest in him or his famous face.

Hopefully Halifax was far enough away to put the publicity behind him. In an ideal world, he would lie low until the furor died down, but he couldn't afford any further delays. He could only hope he wasn't too late already.

* * *

Just off the end of a dead-end road, he said good-bye to the SUV. Popping the hatchback, he took stock of his inventory. Deacon's frame-and-divider system could be converted into a rucksack, and he had also included a large backpack. Loyola considered dragging everything over the snow, but the crossing would be miserable enough with just the necessities.

Inventory, then decisions.

Key supplies went into the pack: bottles of water, cash, a thermos, protein bars. Two of the four provided changes of clothing. One of the suits was the clerical garb he had worn at the abbey. His DNA was on it, so it went in the bag. The other was a thermal-lined sport ensemble. He donned a pair of waterproof hiking boots, and put the shoes he had been wearing into the pack, along with a battery-powered beard trimmer. In a small leather pouch, he found a rugged brass rosary, which he secreted in his inner coat pocket. An N-95 mask, which he would wear whenever possible to reduce the odds of anyone else recognizing him.

Identity: Four sets of passports, matching driver's licenses, and credit cards. He pocketed the set that showed him wearing a beard, and put the rest in the pack.

Gauze, tape, a small bottle of rubbing alcohol, a suture kit, and industrial-strength antibiotics all went into the pack, along with a Leatherman multitool, and a small butane torch. A handful of zip ties and a bungee cord. Loyola found an outdoors-oriented tool watch that included a compass, which he strapped on, stowing his personal watch in the pack.

On to the technology: A compact laptop, two more phones, and a bundle of power cords zip-tied together. A pocket-sized VPN-equipped hotspot.

Weapons: The Glock was still in its shoulder holster, and Deacon had packed a Colt 1911, with a fair amount of ammunition for both, which went into the pack. There was an ankle holster, but it wouldn't go over the boots, so he tucked the 1911 into the back of his belt. Among the several blades on tap, he pocketed a butterfly knife, and put the rest in the ruck.

Loyola had covered the essentials and couldn't fit much more into the backpack. Everything he hadn't picked went into the ruck. None of it was likely to lead back to him, but when it came to evidence, less was more. He couldn't take it the whole distance; he would need all of his stamina to brave the cold. But he would drag it as far as he could and scatter the individual pieces out in the woods. With some luck, they would remain buried under snow until the spring thaw. Finally, he wiped down the Nissan with a cloth and some of the alcohol, including every surface he had even considered touching and the entire seat.

Spinning to gather momentum, he tossed the ruck sack as far as he could into the woods, then walked up the road some distance and circled back through the forest to pick it up, careful not to leave footprints leading from the car to the border.

Tired, but not yet exhausted, Loyola began the long hike, quietly chanting one of his favorite Latin carols to honor Advent and pass the time.

*Veni veni, Emmanuel*
*captivum solve Israel . . .*

* * *

Rocha spent nearly an entire day at the church, interviewing witnesses. After a while, the stories began to blur together.

A young woman with a baby. "He doesn't say much. Or I guess, it's more like, he doesn't use a lot of words. He says a lot without saying a whole lot. And he listens. He listens more than he talks. Does that make any sense?"

A heavyset middle-aged man. "I lost my job, then I lost my house. I was sleeping in my car. Somehow, Father Loyola found out about it. He introduced me to other people at the church who helped me find work and a cheap room to rent. He always seems to know what's going on with the parishioners. I think he just pays attention. Most people don't."

A freckled woman with red hair. "When my son was being bullied, we went to Father Frank. He suggested Jamie take a judo class. Even showed him a couple of moves. I guess he took it in college or something. He said, 'You don't need to fight. You just need to know you can.' It made such a difference."

A married couple. "He organized a group of us to volunteer for Habitat for Humanity. While we were working on this one job, a scaffolding collapsed, and it was falling toward this young woman. Father Frank saw it and somehow grabbed her out of the way in the nick of time. Like Superman or something."

A young man. "I was going through a crisis of faith. The sex abuse stuff . . . Well, I don't want to talk about it that much, but I was so angry at the church. I confronted him about it, and he doesn't say a lot, but I think he was angry too. I asked how he could still believe in the church with all that. He said, 'People fail you. Institutions fail you. God won't fail you.'" The man paused for a moment, somber. "He said our faith was in trouble if good people like me stopped fighting for it, but he wouldn't blame me if I did. He said it was on them, not on me. I guess I'm sticking around. For now."

Another middle-aged man: "He runs in the Boston Marathon every year. I did it one year, and it nearly killed me. I tried to keep up with him for a while, but I couldn't for even an hour. I'm kinda surprised he didn't win. He hardly broke a sweat."

A woman in her forties. "He shows up for people. Anniversaries, birthdays, illnesses, wakes. He don't talk much, but he shows up. People respect that. You can do a lot just by being there. You don't need a lot of flowery words."

An older woman wearing white gloves and fingering a rosary. "Some priests, it's just a job. One that happens to involve God, but you get the impression they're here for the job, or for the people, or the community, and not so much for the God of it all. I go pray during the day sometimes when I need some peace. I see him there too, in the middle of the day, kneeling and praying. I don't think he notices I'm there. Father Loyola is great at the job, but I think he's mainly in it for God."

A stocky man in his forties. "To be honest, he's kind of a jerk. Never says much, just looks at you like he's always judging you. Holier than thou, that's what they call it. And he's not from around here. My wife will disagree, I'm sure, but I simply don't care for the man."

Rocha rubbed at her eyes and thanked God for the last guy. It was getting to be a bit much. She had been at it all day, without anything to show—at least nothing of investigative value. Loyola didn't talk about the past much, and when he did, he spoke only in vague generalities. But it seemed like (almost) everyone had a story about how he had helped them, often through deeds, sometimes with a few economically chosen words. She was almost convinced that he should be fitted for a halo, although the recent incident probably had people feeling generous.

None of it explained a dead sniper and six dead commandos.

The captain sauntered over to her desk, and she could tell by his demeanor that he was looking forward to dropping something on her.

"Where are you at with the car-lot shootout?" he asked.

"I've been interviewing the parishioners at Saint Bridget," she said. "Loyola is beloved, but kind of cipher."

"He's also not a suspect, so I'm not sure why you're wasting time on that," the captain said. "But at any rate, you can stop. The case is going upstairs."

"What's the deal?" she asked.

"The diocese sent over his history," the captain said. "He apparently got on the wrong side of the cartels while working in Mexico as a missionary. And the feds IDed one of the parking-lot shooters as cartel-connected, so this is officially an international investigation and henceforth the FBI's problem. Or DEA. Or ICE. 'Not us' is the important thing."

"No one I talked to said anything about him having any history in Mexico," Rocha said. "Where exactly is this coming from?"

The captain shrugged.

"Someone from the church sent over a pretty detailed dossier," he said. "Pictures and credit card receipts and passport stamps and everything."

"The diocese keeps receipts and passport records for their priests?" Rocha asked, not bothering to hide her incredulity.

"Or the Vatican," he said. "Who gives a fuck? It's not your case anymore. Go find me a suspect in that Dorchester home invasion I gave you last week."

Annoyed, Rocha went into the system and found the dossier, which had been emailed by one Monsignor Gasparo Biancardi. A Google search indicated he was an employee of the Vatican's Secretariat of State. Was that like the State Department? Maybe that explained the passport thing. She thumbed through the photos, which showed Loyola at an orphanage. The pictures looked perfect. Maybe a little too perfect. Whatever that meant.

The cartel might explain the sniper. Even the commandos in the car lot. But who had killed the commandos?

Rocha sighed. Was she losing it? Did it matter? The feds were taking over, right? Not her problem anymore.

She went back to the Google search. Gasparo Biancardi's name appeared on a number of press releases. One had to do with the killing of a priest by neo-Nazis in Ukraine in 2019. Another pertained to a priest found dead in Sudan in 2017. A political scandal involving a cardinal and a dead diocesan administrator in Malta in 2012. A financial scandal and suicide in Switzerland in 2011. An al Qaeda attack on a religious order in Medjugorje in Bosnia in 2015 that left twenty-three monks dead, and their abbot badly injured. The name of the town rang a vague bell, so she Googled it. The first hit was Wikipedia.

*Our Lady of Medjugorje (Croatian: Međugorska Gospa), also called Queen of Peace (Croatian: Kraljica mira) and Mother of the Redeemer (Croatian: MajkBa Otkupitelja), is the title given to the visions of Mary, the mother of Jesus, said to have begun in 1981 to six Herzegovinian Croat children in Medjugorje, Bosnia and Herzegovina (at the time in SFR Yugoslavia). The children (Ivan Dragičević, Ivanka Ivanković, Jakov Čolo, Marija Pavlović, Mirjana Dragičević and Vicka Ivanković) ranged from ten to sixteen years old at the time of the first claimed apparition.*

The fuck? She went back to the Biancardi search and found more cases where priests and other church people were adjacent to violence, crime, or scandal. His entire portfolio seemed to consist of "nothing to see here."

She looked over at the captain's office.

*It's not your case anymore.*

Like hell it wasn't.

CHAPTER

6

# The Medjugorje Affair

THE HIKE THROUGH the woods took hours longer than Loyola had hoped. Wading through snow up to his knees, he had too much time to think and found himself indulging in a measure of self-pity. It was barely two days since his life turned upside down, a life in which he had grown comfortable, perhaps even complacent. But it was a life of service, and he had served his flock well and wholeheartedly.

He had begun to believe that he had earned a measure of rest. He could almost convince himself that he didn't deserve to lose it. But he knew better.

Since the shooting in the church, he had been preoccupied with survival. But as he trudged through the ice and snow, stamping his damp feet against the cold, he finally had time to consider *why* this was happening. He didn't have the entire picture yet, but he knew where the story began.

**The Vatican, 2015**

Father Francis Loyola had walked into the Sistine Chapel many times, but the forty-foot tall fresco looming over the altar never failed to stir his heart.

Michelangelo's *The Last Judgment*, the culmination of the mission of the Church. Jesus Christ the Savior sending humanity to its final fate, rewarding the righteous and damning the evildoers. All of man's hopes and fears decided, with finality.

His well-worn path took him to the left of the altar. Directly over the door he sought, the fresco showed the dead rising from their graves. Loyola was haunted by the image of one soul seemingly caught between heaven and hell—an angel fighting to lift the man up while a strange ghoulish creature sought to drag him down. It was a small scene in a work overflowing with detail, but it stayed with him, sometimes showing up in his dreams.

Loyola didn't know what it meant. He could have asked, of course. He was surrounded by the Church's leading scholars. But he didn't want to. Explanations were only words. Art, like faith, was in the feeling.

Shaking off his reverie, Loyola left the opulent hall and entered the Room of Tears. The chamber was plain, its walls largely bare. In this place, newly elected popes donned their official robes for the first time.

In between papal elections, the room was used for meetings that required the greatest discretion. As such, it was protected by multiple countermeasures designed to foil electronic surveillance. To protect against unearthly intrusions, an order of nuns worked in shifts in the chapel's basement, praying novenas continuously. Or so Loyola had been told. It might have been a joke, but he had seen stranger things.

Cardinal Niccolò Macerata was seated at a spartan desk reading through a sheaf of papers in a brown folder. He stood, and Loyola kissed his ring. The cardinal acknowledged the gesture then indicated that Loyola should take a seat on a red couch against the wall. Macerata was somewhere in his sixties, with a face that was sharp like a blade, whetted by years of intrigue. It was rumored that he was a direct descendant of Niccolò Machiavelli, and Loyola had no reason to doubt it.

"The Lord be with you, Father Loyola," Macerata said.

"And also with you, Eminence," the priest replied.

"You are familiar with Our Lady of Medjugorje?" Macerata asked without preamble.

"I have heard the story, Eminence," Loyola said. "Miraculous appearances of the Blessed Virgin Mary to some children in Bosnia, yes? Back in the 1980s, if I recall, but I think they are still having visions?"

"The jury is out on miraculous," Macerata said. "The Holy Father believes the situation represents an opportunity to bring people to grace, but he has not taken a position on the authenticity of the visions. Especially the more recent ones."

Loyola nodded.

"The children communicated ten secrets to the Holy Father, the contents of which are irrelevant to this conversation," Macerata said. "Many pilgrims have visited the site and had their own experiences since the first apparitions in the 1980s, but none were so memorable."

Loyola nodded again.

"But one recent exception has come to our attention," Macerata continued. "A local boy, age fourteen, by the name of Mirsad Mujovic, started having visions earlier this year. His case has been investigated by the Dicastery for the Doctrine of the Faith, and it has stoked their interest. But . . ."

Macerata paused.

"There are some complications."

It sounded complicated enough already, as far as Loyola was concerned. He was innately suspicious of people who claimed to have visionary experiences, at least in the modern age. If God spoke to people directly, they would not have to do the work of faith, which mattered to Loyola for reasons he could not quite articulate.

But such theological questions were not for him to assess. His skills were firmly grounded in the secular realm. Macerata scrutinized Loyola, as if the priest's face had betrayed his thoughts.

"As you know, claims of miracles are always delicate matters," Macerata continued. "In this case, more so. The boy's visions come with seven secrets, disclosed only to the Holy Father. But they are attested by a different set of secrets, secular secrets, information about certain indiscretions related to the Curia, which are offered ostensibly as proof that the seven secrets are true."

Loyola arched an eyebrow.

"Surely this is a matter for the Dicastery for the Doctrine of the Faith, Eminence," he said. The institution formerly known as the Inquisition was responsible for verifying the authenticity of alleged supernatural events.

"The boy is under the control of a monastic order," Macerata continued. "A military order, the Brotherhood of the Epoch of Martyrs, is sheltering the boy in their abbey, just outside of Medjugorje. The secrets were transmitted by their abbot, Vaso Belosevic."

"Both sets of secrets," Loyola said. "You fear it's a blackmail scheme."

"The secular secrets could create significant political problems and even endanger the lives of some Church officials," Macerata said. "The Holy Father has informed me that the other contents of the visions are even more problematic, verging on the heretical. Dangerous to the very survival of the Church. The interests of the Church are best served by transferring the seer from the Epoch of the Martyrs into the custody of the Vatican.

"Thus we turn to the Order of Saint Uriel," the cardinal said. "Your mission is to investigate, to determine whether a blackmail plot is afoot, and if so, who is behind it. Should you confirm that our suspicions are correct, the Holy Father directs that you resolve the situation *in aeternum terminale*. Be warned that the Epoch is likely to be heavily armed."

*In aeternum terminale*, a permanent and complete solution, a form of consecration that Father Francis Loyola was uniquely authorized to dispense.

"If you are captured or killed, the Secretariat of State will disavow all knowledge of your actions," Macerata said. It was an unnecessary reminder. Loyola suspected the cardinal had seen it on television and just liked the sound of it.

The cardinal handed him the brown folder.

"*Hoc est mandatum Sancti Patris*," Macerata said. This is the command of the Holy Father.

"*Mandatum Sancti Patris accipio*," Loyola responded. I accept the command of the Holy Father.

"Go with God," Macerata said.

"Always do," Loyola said.

As he left the chapel, he genuflected before the altar, and his eye was drawn again to the dead spirit Michelangelo had painted over the door to the Room of Tears. A soul caught between heaven and hell; his better angel trying to lift him up while his personal demon sought to drag him into the abyss.

**Sarajevo, 2015**

Sarajevo's Old Town was a hopping neighborhood surrounding a crowded pedestrian bazaar—shops, restaurants and stores tightly stitched into a patchwork with a diverse collection of religious sites—Muslim, Catholic, Orthodox, and Jewish.

Loyola wandered the cobblestone streets for a while, watching the tourists pore over tchotchkes as he cased his meeting place—a steakhouse with a picnic-table patio, a picture menu, and the English words "STEAK HOUSE" in large letters over the door. Satisfied that the site was secure, he took a seat at one of the picnic tables and ordered a soft drink.

His dining partner had been lurking nearby for ten minutes, scoping the street for threats in a similar manner, while Loyola pretended not to notice.

Calvin Coll was a former Black Panther from Chicago who converted to Islam in the early 1980s and volunteered with the anti-Soviet mujahideen in Afghanistan. After the Russian withdrawal, he had come to Bosnia to fight the Serbs and stop the genocide. He stayed after falling in love with a Bosnian woman and, Loyola suspected, the less-than-strict version of Islam practiced by the locals.

After the war, Coll worked as a fixer for journalists and other parties. Loyola had met him on a previous mission in the former Yugoslavia, and they had bonded during a particularly hair-raising mission.

"My brother," Coll said, approaching the table. Loyola stood to shake his hand, but Coll pulled him into a bear hug instead.

"How is Zerina?" Loyola asked.

"Good, good," Coll said. "She wants to get on with starting a family. I keep telling her I'm way too old for that shit. But we're talking about it anyway."

Neither of them wanted to expose their backs to the street, so Coll came around, and they sat side by side. He was wearing a black T-shirt and ballcap, and he kept his sunglasses on despite the fading daylight. His energy was youthful, but the lines of experience on his face hinted at his age.

"Better view of the local ladies from this side. I know you know what I'm talking about," Coll said, elbowing Loyola, who smiled. Very few people in Loyola's professional circles knew he was a priest, but Coll was among them, and his ribbing was good-natured.

"Whole reason I came to Bosnia," Loyola said.

"Me too," Coll laughed. "Most beautiful women in the world."

They ordered steaks, and Coll got a Coke. They chatted for a few minutes, catching up on Coll's life while saying nothing about Loyola's. The food came out, and Coll ordered a second Coke.

"So what are you up to, Frank?" Coll asked. "I know you didn't come here for my tales of domestic bliss. I got a phone for that."

Loyola chuckled drily.

"I need a driver for a few days," he said. "Someone discreet and smart, who can take care of himself if things get rough. But I couldn't find that kind of guy, so I called you instead."

Coll laughed.

"What's the mission?" he asked.

"We're going to Medjugorje," Loyola said. "I'll supply the car."

"There's only one thing to do in Medjugorje, and that's pray."

"That's why I'm here, to pray," Loyola said.

"You traveling as a priest?" Coll asked. "Might as well. Plenty of Catholic types in Medjugorje, you won't stand out."

"Sure, why not," Loyola said. "But not under my own name." He slid his passport over to Coll, who looked it over and nodded.

"Any other special needs?" Coll asked. "Car? Guns? Equipment?"

"I got a guy," Loyola said.

* * *

The stiff brutalist lines of the neighborhood's apartment buildings had been rigidly crafted during the Communist years then fractured by the scars of war, their massive concrete expanses pockmarked by Serbian artillery decades earlier. The effect was an impression of chaos slowly overtaking order.

At three AM sharp, a BMW E92 M3 pulled up to a deserted street corner. Into the uncertain illumination of a buzzing streetlight, Loyola emerged from the shadows.

The driver opened the door and stepped out of the car. He was thin, with a pointed face, wire-rimmed glasses, and a jaundiced complexion. His expensive Italian suit reeked of cigarettes.

"Deacon," said Loyola.

"Father Francis," said Deacon, his English tinged with a Bosnian accent. "I apologize for not being able to meet your exact specifications on such short notice. I trust this vehicle will suffice."

Loyola looked it over and nodded. Plenty of power, excellent handling, a little less discreet than he would have preferred.

But the paint job was a drab brown and weathered. It would do. Deacon gestured toward the dashboard through the open door.

"Satellite phone link, encrypted GPS," he said. "The usual customizations with respect to the lights and air filtration."

Frank stuck his head in to take a look. The car also smelled like cigarettes, and he was starting to feel a serious craving.

Deacon walked around to the trunk and opened it to reveal a standard supply pack, including food, coffee, clothes and four secure burner phones. A Glock, as he had requested, and an AWM sniper rifle of antique vintage but in excellent condition, outfitted with a night-vision scope. Two bricks of C4 that he had not requested, with detonators. An adequate Kevlar vest. He had asked for throwing knives, and he had received shuriken.

Loyola turned to Deacon, who shrugged.

"Bosnia is awash with weapons, but the exact contents of the supply chain are unpredictable," Deacon said. "You may remember this from your last visit."

"No one in Bosnia has knives?" Loyola said crossly. "It's not like I asked for nerve gas." Shaking his head, he went to close the trunk and spotted several packs of Marlboro lights in one of the divided compartments. He frowned.

"Your brand, yes?" Deacon asked.

"I quit since I was here last," Loyola said.

"Congratulations," Deacon said. "Not to worry. I will dispose of them."

"That won't be necessary," Loyola said, closing the trunk.

* * *

The Military Brotherhood of the Epoch of Martyrs was founded in 1132 by Antipope Anacletus II, whose challenge to the legitimacy of Pope Innocent II drove the incumbent into exile in Pisa. Innocent II excommunicated Anacletus II and his followers, then dispatched the Order of Saint Uriel to undertake a covert effort to reclaim Rome from the heretics. The Epoch of Martyrs was commissioned to fight fire with fire and defend Anacletus from Innocent's assault.

The conflict continued until Anacletus died under mysterious circumstances in 1138, after which the schism was healed, and the Brotherhood of the Epoch of Martyrs was quietly brought back under the auspices of Innocent II's now-vindicated papacy. If the Epoch played a role in settling the schism, it was not recorded by history, not even in the most heavily restricted accounts preserved in the Vatican's Secret Archives.

Although it had been fully restored to orthodoxy, the Epoch remained in a state of limbo over the centuries that followed, due to lingering suspicions that the Brotherhood had become embroiled in a papal coup and ultimately betrayed its founder. Later popes would suspect the Epoch of taking sides in the Curia's constant infighting.

All of this history informed Cardinal Macerata's suspicions about the secrets of this so-called visionary. The apparitions of the Virgin in Medjugorje already sat toward the edges of orthodoxy, tolerated only grudgingly by the Church. The arrival of a new visionary with ties to the infamous Epoch was doubly suspect.

According to the briefing materials supplied by Macerata, the Epoch of Martyrs maintained an abbey in an elevated spot just outside of Medjugorje. While Coll drove from Sarajevo, Loyola pored over the layout of the compound. They checked in at a hotel and ate an early dinner, waiting for night to fall.

"Reconnaissance first," Loyola said.

"Got it," Coll said.

They set out after dinner. Coll parked about a mile from the abbey, just off the side of the only road that led to its elevated position atop a massive bluff. Popping the trunk, Loyola pulled on thin leather gloves, then armed himself with the Glock, a silencer, and two magazines. He attached four shuriken to his belt with a magnetic clip and pocketed a night-vision scope. The Kevlar vest was too bulky for a stealth mission. Loyola was very good at not being seen, but just in case, he donned a clerical collar and cassock. In the unlikely event someone spotted him, he could try to talk his way out of trouble.

"Wait here," Loyola said. "Normal readiness. I'm not expecting drama at this point, I just want to have a look around and see what we're dealing with."

"Easy money," Coll said, taking a pack of cigarettes from the trunk and lighting one. "Be careful."

"Never not," Loyola said.

He approached the abbey on foot, avoiding the driveway and sticking to the woods. The compound was relatively new, clearly postwar, and barely religious in appearance. The modern-looking church, sited at the highest point on the property, was surrounded by boxy dormitories and other outbuildings.

Pulling out his scope, Loyola counted four sentries in monastic robes, armed with assault rifles that looked like Kalashnikovs. Two were roving and two were standing outside what appeared to be a small bunkhouse—almost certainly the seer's quarters.

Loyola climbed a tree and pulled out a notepad, mapping the sentries' patrol patterns and marking the bunkhouse's location. After about half an hour, he had committed the sentries' timing to memory. Using the night-vision scope, he methodically scanned the scene for cameras or sensors. Finding none, he climbed down and cautiously proceeded onto the property.

He took a circuitous route to the church. From its front steps, he could see in the distance the illuminated cross atop Mount Krizevac, a local landmark popular with apparition-minded pilgrims. It was outlined with large white bulb lights, which Loyola found to be slightly gaudy, like a Las Vegas sign.

After checking the door for an alarm, he quietly let himself in to the chapel.

The interior seemed drab in the dim light of underpowered incandescent bulbs and a few candles here and there. A monk was kneeling in a pew at the front of the church, and another appeared to be prostrate in the center aisle, a few steps in front of the altar. One of them was chanting softly.

Loyola stole up the stairs into the balcony, where he took detailed notes on the layout. As he worked, a small group of people entered the church. He fell back into a shadowed corner, hoping they were not here for choir practice.

From his vantage point, he could see the two sentries from the bunkhouse, followed by a slight teenage boy—the alleged visionary Mirsad Mujovic. Behind him came the abbot, Vaso Belosevic, an imposing figure, tall and broad-shouldered, with a bushy black beard.

Before the collapse of Communism, Belosevic had been an officer in the *Uprava državne bezbednosti*, the dreaded secret police of the former Yugoslavia. After Tito fell, Belosevic escaped into religion, taking vows as a monk with the Brotherhood. His skill set proved useful to the military order, and he soon ranked among the Epoch's top leaders. Although Bosnia was his home turf, Loyola assessed from his record that the shabby compound was beneath his station. Whatever they were trying to pull here would be bigger than it looked.

The boy walked up the aisle and genuflected, seemingly oblivious to the monk sprawled in front of him on the floor. He adjourned to a side chapel, where Loyola could see a statue of the Lady of Medjugorje, her head surrounded by a crown of stars, consistent with her reported appearance in the visions from the 1980s. Belosevic hung back, speaking in Italian to a colleague in monastic robes. The acoustics of the chamber were excellent, and Loyola could make out the conversation, despite their low tones.

"Yes, but why here?" Belosevic said. "The Virgin can, presumably, make herself heard anywhere."

"He says it must be here, Father Abbot," the monk said. "He hears her calling, and when he does, he must come here."

Loyola listened intently. He had not been certain that the boy was actually experiencing visions. The entire thing would have been easy enough to stage, and the blackmail dossier didn't require a supernatural explanation.

"I want to minimize his movements around the property," Belosevic said. "They may have access to drones, satellites. Any time he is outdoors, they can see him."

"We could prepare a room in the basement, Father Abbot," the monk said. "But he should get out into the sun and move about. He's already quite frail."

"Prepare the room," Belosevic said. "He can get all the sunshine and exercise he wants when we have accomplished our goals."

"She says someone is here," the boy called out from the side chapel, speaking English. Loyola felt a sudden chill. Who was "she"? His eyes darted nervously around the balcony. He saw no one, and no cameras.

Belosevic looked at the monk, then back at the boy.

"What do you mean?" he asked, also in English.

"A man with blood on his hands," the boy said.

Belosevic shrugged.

"That could be any of us," he said.

"Pledged to an angel," the boy said.

Belosevic frowned.

"Which angel?" he asked.

"Saint Uriel," the boy said, pointing at the balcony.

Loyola's heart leapt, and he ducked down below the balcony railing. He had many questions, but they would have to wait. He was decidedly unprepared for a confrontation; this mission was supposed to be strictly reconnaissance.

A deadly silence had fallen over the nave, and he knew that meant imminent danger. He risked a peek over the railing. No one was visible.

Pulling out his phone, he texted one word to Coll. "DRAMA."

Trading the phone for his Glock, Loyola stilled himself as deeply as possible, quieting his breath and listening for any sound whatsoever. The creak of a floorboard, the rustling of robes, the soft pad of a rubber sole on the stairs. He heard the faint squeak of a door hinge from the far side of the church, near the chapel of the Lady of Medjugorje—most likely Belosevic escorting the boy into a panic room.

While the Brotherhood of the Epoch of Martyrs was formidable, it operated at a lower level than Loyola. But the intelligence provided by Macerata suggested there were twenty-three men on the campus, not counting the abbot and the seer, and each one knew the terrain better than he ever could.

Skill could only get you so far.

The balcony was accessible by two stairwells, and he could hear the rustle of at least one monk coming up each side, perhaps slightly closer on his left. Loyola pressed himself flat against the wall beside the left door. The monk who had been prostrate in front of the altar emerged, wielding a machete. Loyola shot him point blank in the head. The second monk, armed with a club, entered a moment later from the other side of the stairwell, and Loyola shot him center mass. Normally, he would put two in the head to be certain, but he had only brought two magazines with him—eighteen bullets remaining for twenty-one monks.

Loyola descended the stairway. No one was in the vestibule of the church, and no one was in the nave. The electric lights went out. The flickering of candlelight, the only remaining illumination, created too many phantom movements. He had to move outside, where enemies undoubtedly waited.

He kicked open a door, expecting to be greeted by a fusillade. When nothing happened, he decided to risk sticking his head out.

Four monks were standing on the steps, holding ball-and-chain flails in an *en garde* stance, the spiked heads spinning in a wide circle. The weapons were menacing at first glance and ridiculous on the second, as likely to injure their wielders as their targets. The men were cannon fodder, he concluded immediately, meant to distract him while the sentries drew a bead with their Kalashnikovs.

Loyola ducked back into the vestibule, taking a few paces back into a corner then standing ready. In addition to the flailers, he was worried about the two sentries he had seen inside the church. He had to assume they were still there, and could emerge at any time.

As the first two men entered, spinning the flails above their heads, he shot them center mass. One crumpled immediately, the other lurched backward but remained upright. Loyola shot again, this time targeting the head, and the man went down. Their bodies obstructed the door, and their compatriots hesitated to move forward. Loyola could hear noises from the nave—the sentries. The flails were meant to keep him inside, so he decided to leap forward instead, trampling the two downed monks.

The next two flailers were more strategic than the first. The man on his left went high, and the man on his right went low. Loyola dodged the high swing and shot its author in the eye, but the low swing took a small chunk out of his leg.

Loyola lost his balance and fell away from the low-swinger, firing three times. One of the shots connected with the man's shoulder, causing him to drop the flail. Despite the pain, Loyola managed to recover into a crouch and finished him off with one to the head.

One bullet left in the gun, plus one magazine left on his belt. Seventeen monks remaining but only eleven bullets. His leg was bleeding, but the wound wasn't very deep. The flail was a stupid weapon, almost as dumb as the shuriken throwing stars that he was probably going to have to use soon.

Loyola looked back at the church. No one had emerged yet. He swiveled a full 360 degrees to be sure he wasn't missing anything. The cross on top of Mount Krizevac glowed in the distance.

The two sentries finally appeared in the church door and began shooting from cover. Loyola dashed to the left and ran along the side of the building, seeking his own cover but instead finding a third sentry running toward him.

Loyola dropped to a crouch, fired, and hit the man in the chest. Loyola didn't pause to see if the monk went down but immediately sprang into a headlong tackle. He knocked the sentry down and smashed him in the face with the Glock until the man stopped moving.

Loyola swapped the magazine in his Glock, then unhooked the strap and took the dead sentry's Kalashnikov. Spinning around, he saw the two sentries from the church door running up behind him. From a stable kneeling stance, he was able to take them both down with head shots from the long gun.

Fourteen monks remaining, plus the abbot, but at least he had bullets for a while.

Loyola hugged the church wall, awaiting the fourth sentry, who would be coming around the corner any second now. He came, and a short burst from the Kalashnikov finished him off.

Loyola took a moment to mount his night-vision scope on the rifle.

Thirteen monks remained, uncertain location, unknown weaponry. Ten rounds in the Glock, maybe the same in the Kalashnikov. Thanks to the gunfire, they were undoubtedly all on full alert, and probably in motion. There were too many buildings here, and he didn't know the layout well enough. He looked up.

The bell tower. High ground, and only one point of access, through the sacristy. He went in the rear entrance, moving slowly, as the lights were still dead.

He was less than halfway up when he heard someone enter the stairwell below. When a light clicked on, he froze and pointed his rifle downward.

The monk at the bottom of the stairs shouted in Italian. "*Sangue. È qui!*" Blood. Loyola looked down at the stairs. His leg didn't hurt much; the wound was shallow. But it was bleeding freely and marking his passage.

The only question now was whether he should keep climbing or fight here.

He decided to climb. In the belfry, he would have more room to maneuver if and when he ran out of ammo. At least one monk was coming up the stairs, so he squeezed off six rounds of suppressive fire, then dashed up the remaining steps as fast as he could safely manage.

Four-ish bullets left in the rifle, ten in the pistol.

As Loyola emerged into the belfry through a hatch, he realized his mistake. The ringer was electric, controlled from below somewhere. As soon as he entered, the powerful clapper struck the bell, and the resulting sound was deafening, to the point of being painful. It rang again and again. His entire body was vibrating, and his hearing was compromised. He should have stayed in the stairwell, despite the cramped quarters.

Loyola looked over the edge of the belfry railing, estimating the drop at between eighty and a hundred feet. It was highly unlikely he could survive a jump, and even if he did by some miracle, he would be in no condition to fight. He turned his attention to the bell. He was tempted to try to tear it from its mount and use it to block the hatch, but it was securely fastened, and even if he succeeded, he would be trapped. The only realistic escape route led back down the stairs.

Dropping into a crouch, he pointed the rifle at the hatch, and waited. After a long moment, it flipped open violently. Loyola held his fire. No monks surfaced, but a black disc lobbed up and in his general direction—a flashbang grenade.

Loyola was already functionally deaf from the bell, and he definitely couldn't afford any impairment to his vision. Desperately, he flipped the Kalashnikov around, gripping it by its barrel and batting the grenade away with the heel of its stock. The grenade flew over the railing and away, detonating halfway to the ground. A successful gambit, but he lost his grip on the rifle, and it went soaring.

He spun back toward the hatch to find the first monk had already emerged and was practically on top of him. In each hand, the monk held a serrated tactical dagger with a hammer grip. He jabbed at the priest, first with the left, which Loyola dodged, then with the right, which he blocked, twisting the monk's arm around and forcing him to drop the knife. Loyola smashed his forehead into the monk's face, producing a satisfying crunch. The monk staggered, and Loyola executed a shoulder throw, tossing him over the railing. He picked up the dropped blade and stuck it in his belt, then drew the throwing stars, two in each hand.

Two more emerged from the hatch, armed with machetes. Loyola threw the shuriken, nicking one of the monks. Two more stars missed, and a third bounced off one of the monks' robes. Useless weapons. Loyola drew the Glock and shot the first monk point blank in the head. As the man slumped, Loyola used his body to block the second monk's machete swing, but he had to drop the pistol to execute the move. The machete lodged in the dead monk's torso, and the second monk let go of it, adopting a defensive aikido stance.

Loyola jabbed a fist at his opponent's face, which the monk easily dodged, but Loyola's right leg had snaked forward at the same time. Loyola let the momentum of the punch carry him forward into a shoulder block, and the monk went over the railing.

Ten monks remaining.

Loyola scooped up the Glock and snapped it securely into his shoulder holster. He dived into the hatch as the next monk appeared, slamming into him. They tumbled together down the stairs. Loyola kicked the monk away from him and into the next man on the stairs, then staggered to his feet. One of the two monks managed to regain his footing, and Loyola drove an open-hand chop into his larynx. Clutching his throat, the man dropped to the ground. Loyola drew the Glock again and shot him once in the head, then repeated the move for the other one.

Eight monks, seven bullets.

Loyola's hearing was starting to recover, but everything sounded like it was underwater. There was a clamor coming from the stairwell below, but Loyola couldn't tell what it meant. He raised the Glock to eye level, and began advancing slowly. As he reached the final turn, he almost ran into a monk who seemed to be fleeing up the stairs. Loyola shot once, and the man went down.

Loyola advanced around the turn, Glock forward, but too fast. He was caught off guard by another monk framed in the doorway, his rifle pointed directly at the priest's chest. Before Loyola could fire, a shot rang out, and the monk went down.

He stepped through the doorway cautiously and found himself face to face and gun to gun with Calvin Coll, who was wielding an appropriated Kalashnikov. He was wearing gloves and a backpack taken from the trunk of the car, and a pistol was stuck into his belt.

They both lowered their weapons in relief. When Coll spoke, Loyola heard him as if from a distance, as his ears slowly recovered.

"Hell of way to do reconnaissance," Coll said. "I've taken out three."

"Four left then," Loyola said, taking the assault rifle from the most recently fallen opponent. "Plus the abbot and the boy. How did you find me?"

"Guys plummeting from the fuckin' bell tower," Coll said. "It wasn't hard to figure. But listen, this is a real fuckin' mess. Massacre like this is definitely going to get noticed by the authorities."

"Active threats first, worry about later later," Loyola said.

"Easy for you to say, I gotta live here," Coll said. "Any ideas where we'll find the final four? I didn't see anyone on the approach."

"The abbot took the boy into a safe room," Loyola said. "The entrance has to be somewhere around the side chapel. Pretty good odds that the remaining monks are between us and that door."

"I take it you want to breach," Coll said.

"No point in leaving this unfinished," Loyola replied. "They'll just relocate the operation to somewhere more fortified."

The sacristy had two doors that led into the church, in addition to the rear exit leading outside. Loyola moved toward the door closest to the chapel, while Coll took the other one. They edged forward into the church, still dark except for the dim light cast by flickering candles.

Loyola covered Coll as he advanced to take cover behind the pulpit. Then Coll in turn covered Loyola, who ducked behind the altar. As soon as Loyola moved, a barrage of gunfire broke out from the nave. The muzzle flashes revealed the locations of the last four monks, all staggered among the first six rows of pews. They fired continuously in shifts, in a practiced manner that indicated that they had prepared for such a scenario.

Coll looked over at Loyola. The pulpit, made of wood and plaster, was disintegrating quickly under fire. The marble altar was safer, if Coll could get there, but it was hard to see how that would work. Coll made a series of hand signals that Loyola found incomprehensible. He could only shrug and try to provide some covering fire as Coll fished around in his backpack.

Loyola poked his head out on the far side of the altar and unleashed a burst from the Kalashnikov that didn't come close to hitting anything. But the monks stopped shooting for a moment.

He looked back over at Coll, who was in the final stages of sticking a detonator into a brick of C4. Loyola waved at him frantically. The church was a basic wooden structure; that much explosive could bring the roof down. Coll saw him and waved back with a big grin on his face. He pressed a button on the detonator and lobbed it into the pews.

The building shook, but the roof didn't fall. If Loyola hadn't been half-deaf already, the resultant explosion would have done the job.

He didn't allow himself the luxury of reeling, but immediately stalked out from behind the altar, sweeping the barrel of the Kalashnikov over what remained of the nave. The pews on the pulpit-side of the altar had been reduced to char, and presumably two of the monks with it. On the other side, he found one monk dead from a piece of shrapnel, and another with his hands over his head. Loyola shot and killed him. He looked up and saw Coll standing behind him.

"BEEN A WHILE SINCE I USED C4," Coll shouted, his voice barely penetrating the ringing in Loyola's ears. "MAYBE I USED TOO MUCH."

"YOU THINK?" Loyola shouted back.

They raised their rifles into tactical position and moved over toward the chapel. The plaster statue of Our Lady of Medjugorje was somehow intact, although covered with dust from the explosion. Behind it, the blast had shifted the walls slightly, and the outline of a hidden door could be seen. Loyola scanned the area around the statue, but he couldn't find anything that looked like a switch.

He gestured at Coll to turn around. Fishing in the backpack, he found another brick of C4 and matching detonator.

Using the combat knife he had taken from a monk, Loyola cut a thin slice of plastic explosive from the brick and stuck it in the center left of the door frame, where the locking mechanism seemed to be. He set the timer to ninety seconds.

They retreated to a safe distance.

"DOESN'T SEEM LIKE ENOUGH," Coll shouted.

"SHUT THE FUCK UP," Loyola responded.

"NICE LANGUAGE FOR A PRIEST," Coll grinned. "DO YOU KISS THE POPE'S RING WITH THAT MOUTH?

The C4 detonated, leaving a smoldering hole where the door's handle had been. They were far enough away that the blast didn't further aggravate Loyola's hearing. He could make out quieter sounds now, although the ringing continued.

"I'm going in," Loyola said, his voice now only slightly louder than a normal conversational tone. "See if you can find a security office, or the abbot's quarters, and make sure there isn't an alarm going off somewhere that we need to worry about. Scoop up any documents, files or computers you find, and put them all in one location. Once I find the boy, I'll call for extraction and cleanup."

"Roger that," Coll said. "Text me if you need backup." Loyola fished his phone out of his pocket. Miraculously, the screen was intact. Loyola shot Coll a thumbs up then headed through the ruined threshold.

Loyola had expected a modern panic room. Instead he found ancient stone stairs leading down to a catacomb. The modern church above must have been built over the site of a much older one, perhaps a casualty of the war. From its construction, Loyola guessed the catacomb was at least five hundred years old.

The passageway was dark, and Loyola instinctively raised his rifle to look through his night-vision scope, but then realized he had thrown the scope and the rifle it was attached to from the belfry. From the shadows and echoes, he could sense that he was in a fairly wide chamber with a low ceiling. A dim light shone on the far side of the room, and he advanced cautiously, rifle at the ready. He had bombed his way in, so there was not much hope of surprising the abbot.

As he neared the source of the light, he could see it was leaking out from the edges of an ancient doorway. He was tempted to start shooting through the door, but he didn't want to hit the boy.

Loyola kicked the door open instead, then jumped back as the abbot Belosevic, inside, fired off several rounds from a pistol. Loyola ducked inside to return fire, but the Kalashnikov—caked in the dust of multiple explosions—jammed. Belosevic squeezed off another shot and grazed Loyola's shoulder as the priest tackled and disarmed him, kicking the pistol into the shadows.

Loyola's peripheral vision caught the boy cowering in a corner of the room, which was some kind of ossuary, its walls lined with shadowed skulls that seemed to dance in the candlelight. There wasn't time to take it all in, because Belosevic had adopted a karate stance. Loyola opted for Muay Thai.

"Why have you come, servant of Uriel?" Belosevic said.

"You're exploiting this boy, and threatening the Church," Loyola said. "Stand down and come to Rome with me. No more blood needs to be shed this day."

"Exploit?" Belosevic said, indignantly. "You don't know what you're talking about. I serve the Holy Mother, who speaks through this boy. She demands that the Curia reform its wicked ways."

Loyola launched an exploratory punch. The space was tight, constraining their movements, but Belosevic managed to dodge.

"The Church has become irredeemably corrupt," Belosevic said. "The Holy Father lies and threatens and manipulates and bribes to cover up the crimes of his priests. You know this. Everyone knows it. Do you defend it?"

Loyola tried another punch, and Belosevic countered. They repeated the exchange a few times in quick succession, and Loyola started to get a sense of how the abbot approached combat.

"I am sworn to the Holy Father and to God," Loyola said. "Come to Rome, and make your case. If you have right on your side, if the Holy Mother truly speaks through this boy, they will listen. They must."

"Ah, and you can guarantee that, can you?" Belosevic sneered. "You are their pawn. They sent you because you too are corrupt," Belosevic said. "They fear the truths that this boy has received from the Holy Mother. Did they tell you? Did they tell you the sins that she has revealed? You have no idea. What you already know is only the tip of the iceberg."

Loyola feinted a lunge, and Belosevic deftly leaned away.

"If I say to corruption, 'You are my father,' where then is my hope?" Belosevic said. Loyola recognized it as a paraphrase of a line from the Book of Job. "You cannot serve corruption and remain innocent. Look at yourself, assassin. What kind of man are you?"

Belosevic aimed several jabs at Loyola's midriff. Loyola absorbed the blows and boxed the abbot's ears, disrupting his momentum. Belosevic tried to stomp on Loyola's foot, but the priest dodged the attack easily and countered with a raised elbow strike to the abbot's shoulder, aimed at a nerve cluster.

Belosevic's strangled yelp indicated that his aim was true. He staggered back.

"You will regret this day," he rasped. "God will touch your heart, and you will know regret."

Loyola kneed the abbot in the crotch. Belosevic doubled over, and Loyola landed a devastating open-hand chop on the back of his neck. Belosevic crumpled to the ground and lay unmoving.

Loyola turned to the boy, holding out his open hands palm down in what he hoped was a reassuring gesture. The boy stared at him, clearly terrified.

"It's over," Loyola said. "I'm not going to hurt you."

The boy shrank back.

"*Govoriš li engleski*?" Loyola said, hoping he had gotten it right. The boy nodded.

"I'm not here to hurt you," Loyola said, slowly extending his hands in front of him, palms out. "I'm going to take you somewhere safe."

He pulled out his phone. The situation was too FUBAR to rely on the Deacon network for assistance. He would need the Order to intervene directly with transport and clean-up operations, including the construction of a plausible cover story to explain the massacre above.

Opening a powerfully encrypted messaging app, Loyola typed in an alphanumeric identifier, then entered his location as longitude and latitude. "I have the abbot and the boy. Situation stable but serious complications with many casualties. Request immediate extraction and clean-up crew with active measures."

He turned back to the boy while he waited for a response.

"Everything's OK now," he said. "You're Mirsad, right? I'm Frank."

"I know your name, she told me," the boy said, staring at him.

"Who told you?" Loyola asked. "Is it the same person who warned you I was in the church?"

"*Gospa* told me," the boy said.

Loyola recognized the word. It was an old Croatian term for "Lady," and it had been used by the original Medjugorje visionaries.

His phone pinged, and he checked the app.

*Extraction team en route, ETA 30 minutes. Bring in the abbot. Kill the boy.*

He looked up at the boy, who was gazing in his direction, suddenly calm, a slight smile on his lips and the reflection of something distant in his eyes. It was the look of a saint, of a martyr. A sick feeling washed over the priest.

Father Francis Loyola was the *primus sicarius*, the first killer, of the Order of Saint Uriel, the deadly and unstoppable right hand of the Holy Father himself, answerable only to him. In the 862 years of the Order's history, the *primus sicarius* had never refused a direct order. To do so was a canonical crime, punishable by instant excommunication, *latae sententiae*, effective from the moment of insubordination and absolvable only by the pope himself.

For a man with so much unconfessed blood on his hands, it amounted to damnation. An excommunicated man could not make confession. Loyola felt a deep despair twist in his gut. Confession was the ritual, the key sacrament, that allowed him to function as an assassin. He could not afford to lose that divine solace.

The boy stared into the distance and smiled as Loyola drew his gun and took aim.

The ringing was back in his ears, swelling suddenly, louder than even before. Loyola could feel his pulse crashing in his temple, his blood vessels bulging. Another wave of nausea hit him, and his vision went blue around the edges.

He heard a woman's voice.

"What are you doing?" she asked.

He didn't have a good answer.

**Canadian Border, Present Day**

The white, snow-covered expanse of the border was a blank canvas on which to project his memories, which haunted every step he took. They surrounded him as he emerged on the Canadian side, they rattled around in his head as he walked and walked, as he found a car and hot-wired it, as he drove the five hours to Halifax.

Loyola checked into a hotel near the airport. A long shower eased his aching limbs but did little to ease his heart or soul. He thought he had put this life behind him, but it was not done with him. Perhaps it never would be. He fell asleep with a half-completed rosary in his hands.

After a short rest, he boarded the red-eye to Frankfurt without incident, dressed in civilian clothes, stowing a small carry-on with only the basics. He would have to get new weapons in Bosnia, but that would not be a problem.

His first-class window seat had been expensive, but he needed sleep badly, and a long flight was a relatively safe place for that. He was reasonably sure he had thrown off his pursuers, but even if he hadn't, the Bridgewater goons lacked the subtlety required to attempt an assassination in such a controlled environment.

He allowed himself to doze in the plush seat, while the rest of the passengers boarded. After a few minutes, he heard someone taking the spot next to him, dropping a purse in the seat and stowing a carry-on. Loyola opened his eyes and saw an indigo dress with a conservative cut.

Suddenly wide awake, he tensed as the woman took the seat next to him.

Prematurely silver hair peeked out from under a nun's headdress.

She smiled at him.

"Father Loyola," she said. "You can stand down. I'm not here to make trouble. And you should know there's a Sky Marshal six rows back, in case you were thinking of starting something yourself."

"How and why have you found me?" Loyola asked in a carefully measured tone.

"I'm not much inclined to get into 'how,'" she said. "As for 'why,' I am here at the behest of the Holy Father."

"I don't believe you," Loyola said.

"*Ex operibus tuis cognoscent te,*" she said. "*Opus esto, quod quaeris, in mundum inducere.*"

Loyola was normally unflappable, but the Latin code phrase she recited was known to perhaps a dozen people in the world.

*By your works, they shall know you. Be the work you seek to bring into the world.*

"Who *are* you?" he demanded.

"I am Sister Belina Fortis," she said. "I am the *prima sicaria* of the Order of Saint Uriel—the Holy Father's personal assassin."

Even Loyola's practiced poker face could not hide his shock.

"In other words, I'm your replacement," she said, settling into her seat and clicking the safety belt. "I'm sure you have questions. Fortunately, we have six hours to talk."

CHAPTER

7

# Six Hours to Talk

SO MUCH FOR sleep.

The busy work around takeoff provided Loyola with a chance to collect himself and consider his situation, which was less than ideal. He was very unhappy to learn he was still being tracked, but it offered an opportunity as well. He needed information, and Sister Belina Fortis might have it.

"Drinks or snacks?" the flight attendant chirped.

Loyola ordered a Coke. He wanted something stronger, but he needed his wits about him. He watched the drink carefully as the attendant passed it to him. Sister Belina Fortis kept her hands flat on her tray. She ordered a glass of wine.

Once the flight was underway, and the first round of service was complete, they began to talk, leaning in close to each other and speaking in low tones that didn't travel far in the ambient airplane noise. She smelled of expensive soap—Loyola wanted to guess French, but he had little experience with such things.

"Where should we start?" she asked. She spoke with an American accent, but Loyola thought he detected a trace of something else, faint and well-hidden.

"What happened to Arnaud Laroux?" he asked.

Laroux had been *secundus sicarius* when Loyola retired seven years earlier. By the Order's traditions, Laroux should have succeeded to the first position.

"Killed in the line of duty in 2021," she said.

"Where?" Loyola asked. "How?"

"You don't get details," she said. "You could have kept your clearance when you retired, but you opted out."

"Did you take over from Laroux, or was there someone in between?" Loyola asked.

"From Laroux."

"Fine," he said. "You were not part of the Order when I left; I'm quite certain I would remember. What about seniority?"

"Why don't you ask the question that's really on your mind?" she said.

"I'm working my way through a long list of questions," he said.

"Come on," she said, with a smirk. "It's practically written on your forehead."

"Fine," he said, exasperated. "You're a woman."

"Nothing gets past you," she said. "But that's not a question."

"In eight hundred years, the Order of Saint Uriel has never admitted women," Loyola said. "And the *primus sicarius* has always been a priest."

"What does that tell you?" she asked.

"I assume you haven't been ordained," Loyola said.

Her eyes stabbed daggers into him, but her words were carefully mild.

"A girl can apparently only get so far in this world," she said.

"But an exception has been made on other counts, it seems," Loyola said.

"And what does that tell you?" she asked again.

"The Holy Father is even more of a reformer than I thought," he said.

"You're starting to piss me off, Father Loyola," she said. "If you call me a DEI hire, I will kill you where you sit."

"I give up," Loyola said. "What should it tell me?"

"It should tell you that I must be at least twice as good as any man who has ever held the position of *primus sicarius*," she said.

Loyola sat with that for a moment.

"*Any* man, huh," he said.

"Yes," she said, in the most matter of fact tone imaginable.

"Huh," Loyola said.

"Never met a formidable woman in all those years on the job?" she said.

"Met a few," Loyola said.

"But?"

"No but," he said. "Your compatriots in the Order are OK with this?"

"They know me," she said. "And they know my work."

"Even if you're as good as you say, I would expect some resistance."

"Change is hard for some people," she said with a shrug. "That's their problem, not mine."

"Have any other women been admitted to the Order?"

"Not yet," she said. "But the door is open now."

"It must be hard," he said. "Being the first."

"It's not an easy job, no matter who's doing it," she said. "As you well know."

"I would be interested to hear exactly how this came about," he said.

"I'm sure you would," she said.

They sat in silence for a while.

"Sister Belina Fortis," he said. "After Saint Belina?"

"Correct," she said.

"Wasn't she killed while defending her chastity? Around the 1100s?"

"Yes, but that's not the whole story," she said. "The man who tried to defile her was the local lord. His serfs rebelled against him after learning of his crime. They burnt his castle to the ground, and he had to flee. The pope heard about it and excommunicated him. The king heard about it and stripped him of his titles, his land, and all of his possessions. He died penniless in exile."

She flashed him an ice-cold smile.

"Belina is the patron saint of consequences," she said.

"Chicken or vegetarian?" the flight attendant asked brightly.

## Hour Two

Loyola was not a loquacious man, even under the best of circumstances, and this conversation was like no other. Each word was an opening, a gambit that had to be weighed before utterance. Their exchange unfolded in staccato bursts and wary silences, regularly interrupted by food and drink service.

"You were in my church," Loyola said, as he finished his dessert.

Fortis picked at her lasagna.

"I let you see me," she said. "That time."

"You were watching me before the attack?"

"Just Saturday," she said.

Loyola was nettled but remained outwardly impassive.

"You knew about the attack in advance?"

"I knew that a representative of the Epoch of Martyrs had come to Boston for you," she said. "I didn't know why."

"You thought it might be a friendly visit?" Loyola said, quizzically.

"Why not?" she said.

"You must know I killed nearly two dozen of them."

"Enemies become allies, allies become enemies," she said with a shrug. "Situations change. Happens all the time."

"Has the situation changed with respect to the Vatican and the Epoch?" he asked.

She gave him an appraising look.

"You don't know," she said.

"Obviously," Loyola said. He didn't like to betray ignorance, but this was the information that made the entire conversation worth it.

She exhaled sharply.

"Vaso Belosevic has been seen in Rome," she said.

Loyola arched an eyebrow.

"I am surprised that he's at liberty," he said. "I went to a lot of trouble to apprehend him. I assumed he was languishing in the dungeons under the Vatican all this time."

She frowned.

"Are there dungeons under the Vatican?" she asked.

Loyola raised his index finger in front of his lips.

"Are you messing with me?" she asked.

Loyola smirked.

"Someone twice as good as me should already know," he said.

"Be that way," she said, irritated.

"What's Belosevic up to?" Loyola asked.

"Someone half as good as me should have figured it out by now," she said, pulling a magazine out of the seat back pocket and flipping through it.

With a shrug, Loyola closed his eyes and instantly fell asleep.

**Hour Three**

Loyola splashed the tepid airplane bathroom water over his face. He'd managed to grab a few minutes of shut-eye, but his dreams were turbulent.

He looked in the mirror. Was he the kind of man who could not accept a woman as his equal? His better? He didn't think so. If she had been a he, this conversation would be equally antagonistic. Perhaps more so.

Or so he told himself. He was, after all, a Catholic priest, a participant in a system that banned women from equal partnership in the business of salvation. He differed with Church leadership on a wide variety of issues, but he had never considered leaving. The Order, yes, but the Church? Never. Did that make him complicit in all of its worst aspects? The misogyny, the homophobia, the sexual abuse, the lies and cover-ups? Loyola didn't like the first answer that invariably sprang to mind when he went down this path.

He exited the bathroom and walked up and down the aisles for a while. He needed the movement, and he was not in any special hurry to resume the conversation. He took deep breaths and reminded himself of his favorite Proverb: *A fool's mouth lashes out with pride, but the lips of the wise protect them.*

Finally, he returned to his seat. Fortis was sipping a second glass of wine and eating a cinnamon biscotti.

"Peace offering," she said, offering him an unopened package of biscuits.

He placed the packet on his tray table and nodded his thanks.

"Belosevic is in Rome," he said.

"You wiped out about half the Epoch back in 2015," Fortis said. "Belosevic was detained for a time after you brought him in. He was subsequently released under unclear circumstances."

"I see," Loyola said. "Did they tell you why he had been detained?"

"No," she said. "That is one of the reasons we're having this conversation."

"Can you tell me what they did tell you?"

"Belosevic is an apostate, along with his followers in the Epoch of Martyrs," she said. "Signals intelligence revealed he was sending an operative to Boston, specifically to see you. They suspected, or maybe just feared, that you were working with Belosevic. They sent me to find out."

"And?"

"Well, I guess you're not working with Belosevic," she said.

"Why would they even think that?"

"I was about to ask you the same question."

Loyola frowned.

"Let's stipulate for the moment that I'm not going to answer," he said.

"For the moment," she said.

"How do the commandos in the parking lot enter into it?"

"I don't know, and I don't think the Vatican does either," Fortis said. "Do you?"

"No."

"Why would the Vatican think you were working with Belosevic?" she asked.

"That was a short moment."

"I didn't book this flight because of your sparkling personality," she said.

"Who gave you this assignment?" Loyola asked. "The Holy Father himself, or Cardinal Macerata?"

"You're going to have to answer mine before I answer yours."

"Then we're at an impasse," Loyola said.

"Apparently," Fortis said. She tapped on the in-flight video display. "You want to watch a movie? They have *Conclave*."

"Sure," he said.

**Hour Five**

After the movie, Fortis picked up her purse and headed for the bathroom, stopping to stretch for a moment in the aisle. She was tall and lean, and despite the conservative cut of her dress, Loyola found himself noticing her body. He put the thought aside, which was not as easy as he would have preferred.

He considered searching her carry-on while she was away, but it was probably as clean as his. He closed his eyes instead and contemplated the situation.

When Loyola had learned the sniper was with the Epoch, he had hoped the hit was simple revenge. The return of Belosevic hinted at a more complicated and disturbing option—the loose ends of the Medjugorje affair finally coming home to roost. He had to get to Bosnia as quickly as possible, but he would have to lose Sister Belina Fortis first—a task that was apparently easier said than done.

Loyola still didn't know how she had tracked him to Halifax. The Bridgewater people might have tracked him using satellites, but she had known his specific flight. The simplest explanation was that she had access to his Deacon-supplied credit card. The Deacons were legendary for their discretion and independence, but they worked for the Church, and the Holy Father was hard to refuse. Loyola was slightly offended, but there was no reasonable scenario in which they would choose him over the Vatican.

He cursed himself again for failing to retrieve one of his go-bags from the rectory, which he had prepared himself, without help from the Deacons. If he couldn't trust the Deacon network in Frankfurt, larceny would suffice, but it would slow him down considerably. A clean passport and credit card would be even harder to obtain, but he could probably swing that in Bosnia.

Fortis might or might not be twice as good as Loyola, but she had to be at least *as* good, or she wouldn't have lasted five minutes in the job. He was unsure how he was going to get away from her at the airport without causing a scene. If he was lucky, she would be detained at passport control. If not, he supposed he could camp out in the men's room indefinitely.

But that was a two-hours-from-now problem, and the right-now problem was back from the bathroom.

"Are you ready to tell me why they suspected you might be working with Belosevic?" she said, settling into her seat.

"Nope," he said.

"You going to tell me why Belosevic would want to kill you?"

"Revenge," Loyola said.

"Revenge is for amateurs," she said.

"You have a theory," Loyola said.

"I know you killed twenty-three Epoch members in Medjugorje in 2015, and you brought Belosevic in around the same time," she said. "The only explanation I was given was that the Epoch had apostatized. But we don't kill people for apostasy anymore, at least not *just* for apostasy. So I'm not buying that. Medjugorje is, of course, a significant place. But its relevance to this situation is not clear."

"Did you ask Macerata?"

"Did I say Macerata had anything to do with this?"

"I suppose not," Loyola said. "Now that I think about it."

She smiled thinly at him.

"I was told only that the nature of the apostasy was particularly egregious."

"You aren't satisfied with that," Loyola said.

"How do you figure?"

"You're here," he said. "I can't imagine they told you to talk to me."

"In your day, I'm sure you enjoyed wide discretion to get your job done," she said. "It's the same for me. I'm not on a leash."

"Questioning authority is healthy," Loyola said. "It's dangerous to have a fanatic in the role of *primus sicarius*. Look it up in the archives. There's some ugly history."

"Don't assume you know my reasons," she said. "Maybe I just wanted to meet you."

"Why?" Loyola asked, genuinely surprised.

"There is literally no one I can talk to about this job," she said. "No one who really understands. No one I can trust to keep their mouth shut."

"Oh," Loyola said. "I get that. My predecessor died, so I had to rely on confession."

"Sure," she said. "But confession is transactional."

"That's . . . I'm not sure I agree with that," Loyola said. "Anyway, I'm your target, right? You can't afford to have a real connection with me. You might hesitate when the time comes."

Although that was a two-way street.

"Is that where we're headed?" she asked. "Is that how this ends?"

"You've established that I'm not working with the Epoch," Loyola said. "Your orders must have been updated after the attack in the church."

"For the sake of argument, let's say they were," she said.

"I'll assume they didn't tell you to kill me," he said. "Otherwise, you'd have to be some kind of sociopath to seek out this conversation."

"Don't you have to be a sociopath to do this job at all?" she asked. "Wait, do you seriously think *you're* not a sociopath?"

Loyola didn't have a good answer for that.

**Hour Six**

"This is your captain speaking. We will soon begin our descent into Frankfurt Airport with an on-time arrival of 7:10 AM local time. It's a sunny day, forty-two degrees Fahrenheit, six Celsius, winds southwest at five miles per hour. We know you have your choice of airlines, and we thank you for choosing Lufthansa. Flight attendants, please prepare for arrival."

"What happens when we land?" Loyola asked, unplugging his phone from the seat-back jack where it had been charging and stowing it in a pocket.

"We each go about our business," she said.

"Just like that."

"Just like that."

"Why should I believe you?" Loyola asked.

"Believe me, or don't," she replied with a shrug.

Loyola sighed, rubbing his eyes. He looked out the window and saw Frankfurt glittering in the morning sun, drawing ever closer.

"How did you get into this business?" he asked.

She considered before responding.

"I saw injustice up close," she said. "And I couldn't let it go. How about you?"

"I went to war," he said. "And I couldn't put it behind me."

She nodded.

"But you did, eventually?" she said. "Present circumstances excepted."

"I did," Loyola said.

"How?" Fortis asked, in a tone that was a little too casual.

"Do this job long enough, you get caught up in its contradictions," he said. "Not overnight. The seeds of doubt take a few seasons to grow."

"Doubt," she said. "You left the job, but not the Church."

"People fail you," Loyola said. "Institutions fail you. God won't fail you."

She seemed pensive.

"Isn't doubt the enemy of faith?" she asked.

"Doubt makes faith humble," he said. "Faith without doubt is certainty. Certainty begets pride, and pride is the deadliest sin."

He searched his mind for a moment, then spoke.

"Though the pride of the godless man reaches the sky and his head touches the clouds, he is forever dying, standing in his own shit. People will say, 'Where is he?' He flies away like a dream forgotten."

Fortis smiled.

"The book of Job," she said. "Paraphrased a bit."

"Just a bit," he said.

"Why don't you walk away?" she asked. "You don't have to come back to this life. Let me take this cup from you. I'll take out the bad guys. There's no reason you can't go back to your parish once this is over."

He sat quietly for a long time before answering.

"It's not so simple," he said.

"Were you happy there?" she asked.

"Yes," he said, surprising himself with the force of the word.

"Then let it be simple," she said, grasping his arm and looking into his eyes.

Loyola smiled ruefully as he met her gaze.

"I wish I could," he said.

CHAPTER

8

# Friendly Neighborhood Priest

Martina Rocha sat on the edge of the priest's bed and contemplated his room. It was spacious and spare, but not austere. The furnishings were comfortable, and the foot of the bed faced a working fireplace.

A few pieces of religious art broke up the mostly bare expanses of wall. The Sacred Heart of Jesus stared at her from behind glass, an old-fashioned print, somewhat yellowed, perhaps an artifact of the 1950s that Loyola had inherited from a predecessor. Next to White Jesus, a print of a more recent vintage depicted the Virgin Mary with White skin and shockingly blue eyes, her head crowned with a wreath of stars. Rocha was sure she had seen the image before, but she couldn't remember where.

The room showed signs of the cursory search done by her officers after the parking lot massacre. Drawers not quite closed, a closet door ajar, the linens disturbed. A small bookshelf filled with various religious texts in mild disarray.

The room was deeply impersonal; it felt like a preachy Courtyard Marriott.

Pulling on a pair of latex gloves, she repeated the search, slowly and methodically. The closet contained the standard priestly wear, black shirts, suits and cassocks of various weights and cuts. The drawer held white clerical collars, workout clothes, T-shirts, pajamas, and priestly underwear, which was indistinguishable from the secular varieties.

She opened the laptop that sat on the desk. It wanted a password. She tried "JESUSLOVESME," but it didn't work. If she wanted to crack it, she would need IT support, and that would require a warrant. Technically, she should have a warrant just to be in the room, but the housekeeper had assumed the yellow crime scene tape on the door meant that the cops had free rein. The tape should have come down once the diocese announced that Loyola was on retreat, but institutional and bureaucratic lethargy had worked in her favor.

She looked under the bed and found a low flat chest secured by a padlock, which yielded to a few minutes of fiddling with her pocket lockpick kit. Inside, she found mementos of military service. An unloaded Glock 17 pistol sat next to a magazine of ammo and an expert marksmanship badge—a metal cross with a bullseye in its center, and the words "rifle" and "pistol" hanging from tiny chains.

Did chaplains carry guns? She didn't know, and she still hadn't received Loyola's military records. A red, white, and blue ribbon attached to a bronze cross inscribed with the words "For Valor," and a Purple Heart. A few snapshots showed Loyola standing next to heavily bearded soldiers wearing less-than-standard uniforms, suggesting they were some kind of special operations forces.

Did special operations have their own chaplains? Were the chaplains also special? She pulled out her phone and did a quick search. Apparently, some chaplains went through Special Forces training in order to relate more closely to their charges. Another search produced a random website saying the Glock 17 was favored by special operations, for whatever that was worth. While her phone was out, she took pictures of the gun, the snapshots, and the medals. A veteran owning a gun wasn't exactly a news flash, but the context was helpful.

Rocha looked around the room. She was missing something. But what? She went over everything again, even more thoroughly. She felt underneath the drawers for envelopes that might be taped to the undersides, and checked their depth in search of false bottoms.

She went into the bathroom. Nothing interesting in the medicine cabinet, or the linen cabinet, or under the sink. The room smelled of *Irish Spring* and bleach. She sniffed. Too much bleach. Following her nose, she arrived at the toilet tank. Lifting the heavy porcelain lift, she peered inside. At the bottom of the tank was a damaged cell phone. She drained the tank and retrieved it. He had done a good job smashing it up, and it had been stewing in bleach since Sunday. Even if she could get forensics involved, she wasn't sure anything would be recoverable.

But now she knew for certain that Loyola was hiding something.

She put the phone under the sink. If she could contrive a warrant somehow, it would have to be findable.

Pumped up by the small victory, Rocha returned to the bedroom and retraced her entire search, this time even more minutely, again coming up with nothing. But her attention lingered at the closet. Something was off; some detail nagged at her. She parted the cassocks, and felt the slight friction of coat hangers brushing up against the rear wall. Either the rod had been hung off-center or . . .

Grabbing all the cassocks and suits, Rocha threw them on the bed and began a more thorough examination of the back wall, tracing her finger along a barely discernible seam that ran down the center.

Her fingers probed along the wall and under the shelf, coming to rest on a slightly mushy spot. She pushed at it tentatively, and nothing happened, so she pushed again, more forcefully. With a click, the back wall opened at the seam to reveal a hidden compartment. She took a step back, gaping in amazement.

"Goddamn," she said.

A pegboard provided an anchor for hooks of various sizes and shapes. Some of the hooks held what looked to be gun cases of various sizes, and an impressive supply of ammunition was stacked on the floor. She cracked one open and found a sleek-looking semiauto pistol with the serial number filed off.

A duffel bag and two backpacks hung in the center of the pegboard. She dumped them out on the bed, gasping at the rolls of cash that emerged, including US dollars, Canadian dollars, and euros. Multiple passports in various sizes and colors, all with Loyola's photo, and all of them with different names. Several cell phones, a pair of compact laptops, a dozen or so USB sticks, zip ties, bungee cords, various kinds of clamps and fasteners, and an array of tools, some mundane and some exotic—including a lockpick kit that closely resembled her own, and a laminator suitable for creating fake IDs.

"Everything your friendly neighborhood priest might need," Rocha muttered.

What would have been nice to have in this situation was a warrant. But at least she had remembered to bring a fingerprint kit.

* * *

The airport went easier than expected. Fortis had to wait for a checked bag, Loyola did not. They said their good-byes at the carousel.

"Will I be seeing you again?" he asked.

"You might, but you'll never see me coming," she said.

He rolled his eyes.

"Sure of yourself."

"Skill without confidence achieves nothing," she said.

"Hope it works out for you," Loyola said. "Bye."

"*Auf Wiedersehen*," she said, taking out her phone, which seemed to absorb her entire attention as he walked away.

After going through passport control, Loyola found a shop in the terminal that sold prepaid phones. He bought two, then grabbed a coffee and headed for the taxi stand. Fortis—and anyone else still tracking him—already knew he was in Frankfurt, so he booked a room in Sofitel Frankfurt Opera hotel with one of the compromised Deacon credit cards for one last splurge.

The hotel was steps away from the *Alte Oper*, the city's famous opera house, with an elaborate façade that reminded him of Saint Peter's Basilica. As he checked in, he asked the pale young man at the front desk about its statuary.

"Goethe and Mozart, of course," he replied, in a tone that somehow perfectly blended courtesy with condescension. There were several other statues on the façade, most prominently a stiff and angular winged horse, but Loyola thought better of inquiring further.

After checking in, he barricaded himself in the room for some desperately needed sleep. Waking in midafternoon, Loyola unpacked his bags and sifted through the remaining gear. All his weapons were in a storage locker back in Halifax. He had brought three phones, two from Deacon, and those definitely had to go. The third phone had been taken from his go bag at the rectory, and he was cautiously optimistic that it was still secure.

Deacon had provided four passports, which were possibly compromised. He wouldn't need to use them while he remained within the EU's border-free Schengen area, but he would have to risk using one at the Bosnian border. For now, he secreted three in the lining of his suitcase and put one in his jacket pocket. If the event of any entanglements, a compromised ID was probably safer than no ID.

Everything else seemed fairly low-risk. He carefully searched the clothes Deacon had provided. He didn't find any bugs, LoJacks, or AirTags. The plastic case that held his lock-pick tools was also clean.

Loyola had one credit card that he had taken from his rectory go bag on Sunday night, but he had foolishly neglected to grab the matching ID. That meant he could use it for online bookings, but not for a hotel stay or to rent a car. The card was almost definitely safe. The Boston police investigation would have stopped once the diocese had explained his absence and even if it hadn't, he strongly doubted that an overworked local cop would stumble onto his secret compartment.

The credit cards supplied by Deacon would have to go, but not quite yet.

The next question to consider: Who knew he was going to Bosnia, and what could he expect when he got there? Konstantin Stefanidis, back in Massachusetts, was the only person who knew for certain, although he probably assumed Loyola's ultimate destination was Medjugorje, and Loyola had no reason to clarify the matter. Stefanidis was still linked to the Order of Saint Uriel, so Sister Belina Fortis was probably also working under the same assumption.

There was no way to know whether the Bridgewater goons and their sponsors were still tracking him. Loyola was hopeful that he had thrown them off in Bangor, but he couldn't be certain. It depended on whether they had access to Deacon information. He could be sure that Fortis and the Order of Saint Uriel did; there was no other explanation for how she got a seat next to him on the plane.

Careless of her to give that advantage away. Maybe she was hoping to spook him . . . or maybe she was trying to help him for some unfathomable reason.

Best not to go there. With the information on hand, Loyola could only go so far in trying to outthink his adversaries. As one of his mentors had taught him: *When in doubt, assume the worst, and act accordingly.*

* * *

The Spielbank Wiesbaden was a casino located in a palatial art nouveaux complex about a half hour's drive from Frankfurt. Loyola arrived in a stolen car, which he parked in its multistory garage.

In the back seat, he had his carryon and a backpack with the two Deacon phones. He walked up and down the garage, looking at license plates. When he found a car with French plates, he picked the trunk lock and secreted the two fully charged phones in the spare tire well. In a best-case scenario, the car's owners would head home soon, and lead his trackers in the wrong direction. At any rate, he could cross one problem off the list. Now to deal with the credit cards.

Inside the casino, he went to the ATMs and maxed out the cash advance on each card, then he found the restaurant and ordered a massive steak dinner. After he finished, he walked a circuitous surveillance detection route through the casino, looking for pickpockets as he maneuvered. A short, slim man who looked a bit like Peter Lorre was working the room. When he was sure the man had noticed him, Loyola went to the bar and ordered a whiskey. Affecting a drunken wobble, he left the card at the bar, and Peter Lorre wasted no time picking it up. More false signals for any trackers.

Loyola returned to his car and hit the road. The most direct route to Sarajevo would take fifteen hours if he drove nonstop through the night, but he added a few hours to avoid toll plazas that would log his stolen plates. He would also have to steal fresh cars before and after crossing the Bosnian border.

He prayed for an uneventful trip and was pleasantly surprised to get one. A light, cold rain fell for most of the dark drive, but it began to ebb as morning broke and he passed Banja Luka, crossing into the mountainous terrain of Bosnia's central region. The fir trees were laden with recently fallen raindrops that sparkled in the early sun. Outside of Travnik, Loyola was moved by the sight of a ramshackle Christian church along the side of the highway, haphazardly assembled from what seemed like spare parts. A concrete block spire was topped by a rusted metal roof and a simple metal cross. A corrugated metal sheet shielded the entrance from rain and sun, propped up by two rough-cut tree trunks with the bark still on them. Loyola guessed that it would have doubled as a bomb shelter during the war.

As he approached Sarajevo under the Thursday morning sun, he ran another surveillance detection route, taking corners at unsafe speeds and running red lights, behaviors that anyone following him would have to emulate if they wanted to keep up. Coming up clean, he pulled out his sole remaining phone, plugged his destination into the GPS and checked his ETA. Then, typing in digits from memory, he sent an encrypted text message.

*Foxtrot Lima Mike Charlie Bravo Golf. Meet at the white field.* The simple NATO alphabet code should be instantly recognizable to the message's recipient. Frank Loyola, Maximum Caution, Bring Guns.

The phone pinged back at him.

*Foxtrot Lima Mike, more like Foxtrot Mike Lima. C ya.*

*FML.* Loyola had to laugh.

* * *

Not far from Sarajevo's City Hall, Kovači Cemetery sat on a slope, in the shadow of a three hundred-year-old fortress. Here, Bosnia's war dead were memorialized by stark white obelisks, ranging from three to seven feet tall, each inscribed with a mix of Arabic and Bosnian words and names. A bleached bone forest planted squarely in the midst of the city's colorful life.

Loyola didn't know how many people were buried here, but he had been told there were thousands, and he believed it. The terrible signs of war were everywhere in Sarajevo, even thirty years later, from the still unrepaired artillery scars defiantly worn by many of the buildings to the hundreds of red "roses" on the sidewalks, where vividly colored resin had been used to fill in the distinctive craters left by mortar shells.

Little wonder that Loyola felt such affinity for the place. For years, his priestly vestments had covered over the scars of his wars. But he knew they were there, a silent testament to his life's bloody work.

"You must be getting old, man, because I never got this close before without you clocking me," came a voice from behind him. "You always did me the courtesy of pretending, but I knew you knew."

Loyola turned around to find Calvin Coll standing about twelve feet away. It had been almost ten years, but Coll seemed older than could be explained by passing time. His posture favored his right leg, and his eyes suggested something of pain beyond the creakiness of age. The life he had chosen—they had chosen—was brutal to the body. Beyond mere injuries, constant vigilance wrought a vampiric toll.

While Loyola had his share of damage, he'd spent the last seven years rehabilitating his body in peace. But that relative well-being came with tradeoffs. Coll was right; Loyola's head still wasn't in the game.

What was it going to take?

"You got here faster than I expected," Coll said.

"You expected me?" Loyola said, frowning.

"You aren't here because of my message?" Coll said, surprised.

"I haven't checked the digital dead drop since yesterday," Loyola said, "Or the day before. I've been on the run."

"I guess that's probably not a coincidence," Coll said. "Maybe we should go somewhere less out-in-the-open." He waved at the grave markers. "Unless you picked this spot so you'd have a big welcoming committee on the other side."

"Lead the way," Loyola said.

Coll walked him through the grove of white stone markers, trailing his hands affectionately along them as he passed.

"Hey, do Christian martyrs and Muslim martyrs go to the same place?" he asked.

"Beats me," Loyola said.

* * *

They stopped by Loyola's car to retrieve his bags, then sprinted to Coll's Jaguar XJ12 sedan. Loyola guessed it was a 1990s model, although it was in pristine condition. Coll tore out of the parking space erratically and took two corners at a dangerous speed, before initiating a more sedate surveillance detection route.

"I gotta say," Coll began, "being your friend is a hell of a lot. It's a lot."

"Yeah," Loyola said.

"When I told you Zerina and I were talking about starting a family, I meant a cute lil' baby. We were most definitely not planning to adopt a sullen teenage Christian White boy marked-for-death prophet. Don't get me wrong, as a Muslim, I love Maryam. Great lady, virgin, all that. But I gotta tell you, it is not easy trying to run a household where Virgin Mary got *opinions.*"

Loyola stifled a laugh. Over the many years they had known each other, his friend had transitioned from a very strident stance on religion to a more relaxed Bosnian attitude. But despite Coll's no-holds-barred conversational style, Loyola knew he was deeply religious and just as deeply ambivalent about Mirsad's visions.

"OK, I get it," Loyola said. "But you were there. You saw what I was up against. And you could have refused. I would have figured something else out."

"You're a resourceful guy," Coll said. "But I don't figure your Rolodex includes a long list of babysitters with a finely tuned propensity for violence."

"Has someone come after Mirsad?" Loyola asked. "Is that why you contacted me?"

"That kid is his own worst enemy," Coll said. "Doesn't even matter how many papal ninjas are out to get him. His own worst enemy, and a gigantic pain in my ass to boot. The mood swings on this child . . ."

"Calvin," Loyola interrupted. *"What happened?"*

"He ran away," Coll said. "Yesterday. I messaged you as soon as it happened, which I guess you didn't see."

"Are you sure he ran away?" Loyola said. "No one took him?"

"Sure, I'm sure," Coll said. "Told us to our faces he was going. Not sure if you can even call it running away. He's a grown man now and can make his own decisions. And that's exactly what he told me. Zerina was beside herself."

"Did he say why he was leaving?" Loyola asked.

"*She* told him to," Coll said. "Or that's what he says."

"The Lady," Loyola said. "Did she tell him where to go?"

"If she did, he did not share that information with me," Coll said.

"What *did* he tell you?" Loyola asked.

"He thanked us for raising him, and he said we would probably never see him again," Coll said. "He said he had a mission. I tried to stop him. I begged him to wait and talk to you, but you know, his memories of you aren't too rosy."

"Did you put a tracker on him?"

"Through his phone," Coll said. "Don't even need any special gear these days. Downloaded an app I saw on Reddit."

"And?"

"He's in Medjugorje," Coll said. "I didn't want to proceed with retrieval until I talked to you. Didn't expect you to show up like this."

"God *dammit*," Loyola said.

"What? It's natural he'd go back there."

"You know he doesn't have any living family," Loyola said. "If he's there, he's probably with the Epoch of Martyrs. But this is the real problem: The Order of Saint Uriel undoubtedly thinks I'm heading to Medjugorje. I was fine with that because I thought Mirsad was *here*. If he's there, the Vatican might know about it already."

"Oh," Coll said. "Do they know Mirsad is alive?"

"Unclear," Loyola said. He gave a brief account of the last few days.

"All right," Coll said. "I gotta call Zerina, then we better get down there."

"Don't we need to gear up?"

"Your message said to bring guns," Coll said. "You didn't say how many, so I brought 'em all."

* * *

Loyola was no stranger to fast and reckless driving, but he liked it better when he was behind the wheel. Coll was burning up the winding mountain road, which was one lane in each direction. Any time the road straightened out, he pushed to over 120 miles per hour, passing any cars they encountered while darting away from oncoming traffic with hair-raising precision. He distracted himself by relating the events that had led him here.

Loyola guessed they might arrive in Medjugorje in less than two hours. Despite his old friend's complaints, he could plainly see that Coll cared about the boy.

"It wasn't easy, but all things considered, Mirsad seemed like he was doing OK," Coll said. "He seemed happy enough most of the time. Considering what he went through, considering the Lady, I thought he was doing OK."

"He kept seeing her?" Loyola asked. "Consistently?"

"I don't know, man," he said. "He mostly doesn't answer questions. Sometimes he'd go out in the middle of the night, and I'd follow him, and I'd hear him talking to someone, but no one was there. And he always seemed to know shit that he shouldn't, or that he couldn't possibly. Impossible to keep a secret from that kid."

"Phone?" Loyola asked.

"Not until he was eighteen," Coll said. "I didn't want to give it to him even then, but Zerina said, look, he's a man now. He can make his own choices."

"He didn't bolt at the first opportunity," Loyola said, "You must have done something right."

"I think he appreciated us," Coll said. "Or maybe *she* did, and he just went along with it. For fuck's sake, Frank, I'm not a shrink, and I'm not a Catholic, and I wish I'd never gotten caught up in all this Catholic shit. Everybody in the world is down on Muslims, man. Nobody nowhere got a good word for the Muslims. But *you* people are the absolute fucking worst."

"Hey," Loyola said, gently.

"I know, I know," Coll said. "But the *institution* is fucked. You have to know that. I saw *Spotlight*, man. Everybody did. How can you be a part of that?"

A too-sharp retort formed in Loyola's mind, but he said nothing and stared out the window at the long drop off the side of the road they were speeding down.

"All right, all right," Coll said, after a while. "But it wasn't fair putting this on me."

"You're right," Loyola said. "About all of it. And I'm sorry."

Coll leaned the car into a hairpin turn at a stomach-churning velocity.

"All right, all right," he said. "I'm a big boy. I make my own decisions. You didn't make me do shit."

They rode in silence for a while.

"So, what are we getting into?" Coll said eventually.

"That's a damn good question," Loyola replied. "There are a couple of potential scenarios. First is a repeat of last time."

"Not great," Coll said. "We survived, but it was hairy. And we were younger."

"Not great," Loyola agreed. "Second scenario, it's like last time, but with twice as many bad guys. We'll need to find a way to finesse it."

Coll snorted.

"That's one way to put it," he said. "What else you got to ruin my day?"

"Third scenario is a little better," Loyola said.

"Delightful," Coll said.

"It's one of the first two scenarios, except with Sister Belina in the mix. She almost certainly thought I was going to Medjugorje. And we're actually going now, so even if she's still tracking me somehow, it's the same outcome."

"I thought you said this was a better scenario," Coll said. "Isn't she a super-assassin who can easily kick your ass?"

"The jury's out on 'easily,'" Loyola said crossly. "And it might be us and her against the Epoch. It's her against the Epoch, at least. For certain. Almost certain."

"Almost," Coll scoffed.

"Anyway, the enemy of my enemy, et cetera," Loyola said.

"Did that ever work out for anyone, ever?" Coll asked. "What else?"

"One of the first three scenarios except with the Bridgewater guys also involved," Loyola said. "But I don't think that's likely."

"Why not?" asked Coll.

"I'm pretty sure I threw them off the trail in Maine."

"But they're mixed up in this," Coll said. "So they might be here apart from having followed you. They could be aligned with the Epoch. Or the Vatican for that matter."

"The Epoch, not impossible. But doubtful," Loyola said. "And highly unlikely they're working for the Vatican. But anyway, they're based in the U.S."

Coll looked askance at Loyola so hard that he almost drove them off the road.

"Eyes front!" Loyola said, clutching his armrest.

"You really left this life behind, huh," Coll said, casually twirling the wheel as if their lives were not in peril. "Bridgewater is all over this country. Supposedly doing counterterrorism. Even if they're actually here for that and not for your thing, orders can change, know what I'm saying?"

"Yeah," Loyola sighed. "I know all about that."

"Sounds like we're going to need a whole fucking fuckload of finesse," Coll grumbled, pressing the gas pedal to the floor.

CHAPTER

9

# Keep It Together

A HEAVY FOG SHROUDED the woods as they approached the compound. Visibility was limited to perhaps fifteen feet, and the afternoon sun struggled to penetrate the mist. When Loyola looked directly at it, he saw only a hazy and irregular orb that seemed to waver as it labored to break through.

He was reminded of the miracle of Fatima, when the sun danced around the sky with an aura of many colors, offered by God as proof that the Virgin Mary had appeared to three Portuguese children in 1917.

But this was the doing of men. This air was thick and acrid, tainted by fumes from the coal and wood that was still burned as fuel in homes and industries all over the country. No miracle here, only mortal failures wreaking a terrible toll on the degraded planet.

Coll pulled over and parked about a mile and half from the abbey. Their last visit had been ugly and dangerous, and the Brotherhood of the Epoch of Martyrs hadn't even been expecting them. This time, they would be ready. The fog was a mixed blessing. While it would allow them to get close without being detected, the enemy knew the compound well and would be better equipped to maneuver with limited visibility.

Loyola remembered every detail from last time, but he didn't have intelligence on the current situation. It had been nine years since Loyola and Coll massacred twenty-three people on this site. The target would undoubtedly have been hardened since then.

Coll opened the trunk to reveal an astonishing number of weapons. Loyola grabbed an HK416 assault rifle with a suppressor and two magazines, three K-Bar combat knives with quick release sheaths, and a Glock with two magazines. Coll took a suppressed AK-47, two Ruger 1911 pistols, which he stuck in his belt, one K-Bar, and a bandolier that he outfitted with six fragmentation grenades. Loyola arched an eyebrow, but Coll only shrugged.

"I am not in the mood to fuck around," he said.

They donned Kevlar vests, then strapped the weapons over them. Loyola fished around in the trunk for anything else that might come in handy, finding a block of C4 and some detonators, which he put in a pouch. Coll grinned at Loyola, who rolled his eyes.

Perhaps a quarter mile from the abbey, they saw the first defensive emplacements, old-fashioned wooden stockades with a spiked top. Taking cover, they craned their heads to get a better look. Someone was stationed at the stockade, a rifle barrel peeking out from between two pickets. Loyola moved off to the side to reconnoiter, while Coll drew a bead on the defender.

"No one else in the immediate vicinity," Loyola reported back.

"Maybe no one here either," Coll whispered, keeping his rifle steady. "Guy hasn't moved a muscle, not a twitch, since we got here."

"I'm going to approach," Loyola said, drawing a knife in each hand. "No gunfire unless absolutely necessary. They might know we're coming, but we don't need to advertise."

"Copy that," said Coll.

Loyola advanced stealthily, passing the checkpoint, then circling back to approach the sentry from the rear. Coll's assessment had been correct: The man—a monk—was unnaturally still. Loyola put away the knives and got him in a sleeper hold, a precaution that was immediately and obviously unnecessary. The monk was dead, his throat slit, his blood smearing on Loyola's sleeve.

He motioned for Coll to approach.

"Not warm," Loyola said, "but not cold either."

"Recent then," Coll said. Loyola nodded.

"Half an hour?" Loyola said. "Give or take half an hour?"

"What are we walking into?" Coll said.

"No clue," Loyola said.

They advanced another sixty or seventy yards through the fog, and found three more stockades, each manned by a dead monk, one with his throat slit, two with bullet holes between their eyes. Loyola and Coll exchanged a look, but said nothing. They resumed moving, more slowly and cautiously than before.

About twenty yards from the compound, they came upon a full barrier, sandbags stacked in a bunker formation, with eight dead monks inside. The fog was thickening, and it was getting harder to make out the details, but all had been killed by gunfire. Four between the eyes, the others with a collection of wounds that were less precise. Loyola was becoming convinced this was the work of a single attacker, and he could hazard a guess as to who.

Coll looked shaken, but when Loyola met his gaze, he gestured silently: *Proceed.*

The main compound was a charnel house. Several sandbag emplacements were filled with dead monks, some of them still smoldering from the detonation of grenades or explosive rounds. Loyola swept over the scene. Despite the thick fog, he could count at least thirty dead, perhaps more. The compound was eerily silent. They advanced cautiously to one of the emplacements, and Loyola checked the body of a monk who had been killed by a single gunshot.

"Warm," he whispered to Coll.

Coll slumped back against the sandbags, pale, his breath ragged.

"This is what it's like, right?" he said. "For a normal person who comes up against you. This is what it feels like. Sheer terror."

Loyola knew what he meant, but there was no point in saying it. He felt no special mystique regarding death, but killing was ultimately about control, and Loyola preferred to be the one in control.

"Keep it together," he whispered. "Or fall back and let me handle it."

If he could.

In his prime, he might have been able to take on an enemy as well-prepared and entrenched as these monks had been. Maybe.

Coll grabbed his arm and squeezed. Loyola turned.

Through a gap in the swirling mist, a woman's figure loomed.

At first, he thought it must be Sister Belina Fortis, but the woman was too tall. Unnaturally tall, with a hand outstretched as if in a blessing or a warning, and a halo of stars around her head, bathed in a soft glow.

*Gospa*. The Lady of Medjugorje. While it was recognizably the Virgin of the apparitions, her face was twisted with anger.

Loyola had a healthy relationship with fear. Fear kept you alive.

But this . . .

He stood for long seconds, frozen, facing the Lady, who was equally still, her arm extended toward him. His pounding heartbeat marked the passage of time, and his instincts were screaming peril at him. But he couldn't tear his eyes away.

The fog thinned a little.

It was a statue, illuminated by a spotlight.

Loyola could feel Coll's grip slacken as he came to the same realization.

"This shit is doing my head in," Coll muttered.

Instinctively, Loyola swept the surroundings with his gun raised, cursing himself. The distraction had been brief, but it could easily have been fatal, especially if Fortis was still on the scene. Fortunately, there were no signs of movement.

"We gotta find Mirsad and get the fucking fuck out of here," Coll said.

Loyola nodded, as if it would be that easy. He gestured with two fingers toward the church. Raising their guns, they moved quickly to the side door in a tactical formation. The door was ajar, and no sounds could be heard within. Entering, they found more corpses, all monks. A significant number of them had been shot between the eyes.

As they walked up the center aisle, Loyola felt a breeze. The main doors of the church were open. The fog outside obscured his view, but he thought he could hear voices speaking in low tones, muffled by the thick air. Feeling exposed, he motioned to Coll that they should shift their advance to the side aisles. He went left, and Coll went right. At one point, Loyola had to clamber over a cluster of three corpses leaning together, dead hands wrapped around assault rifles that had not saved them, the barrels poking skyward.

They sidled up to the church doors carefully, the voices outside coming into resolution as they neared. One was a woman, the other a man. Loyola recognized both of them—Sister Belina Fortis and Abbot Vaso Belosevic.

He risked a quick peek around the door frame. Fortis was wearing a charcoal gray tactical suit, liberally splattered with blood. She was holding a pistol. An assault rifle hung from a shoulder strap, and she wore a Kevlar vest and a tactical belt with several pouches. The two killers stood just feet from each other, pistols raised in a Mexican standoff. Her gun was pointed at Belosevic, his gun was pointed at Mirsad Mujovic, who stood beside Fortis with a serene expression. Mirsad's face still looked boyish, although he was now twenty-one.

The trio stood out like a tableau against the fog, as if they were the only people in the world. Between Fortis and Mirsad, gaudy lights outlined the distant cross on Mount Krizevac, hazy and indistinct through the thick air.

Any intervention would put Mirsad at risk. Loyola looked over at Coll, who had tipped his phone over the door jamb to survey the scene. Their eyes met, and Coll shook his head. Loyola assumed that meant they were on the same page. But the fact that Belosevic was targeting the boy worried him deeply. He had assumed Fortis would be operating under the same order he had received—*kill the boy*. But in that case, why didn't she simply shoot Belosevic?

The abbot was concluding what Loyola guessed had been a lengthy monologue.

"Our Lady of Medjugorje demands that you renounce the Order of Saint Uriel," he said. "She releases you from your vows. Surely you can see what you have wrought here. Look at yourself. You're a butcher! Your blood-soaked hands are not worthy to touch the hem of Her garment. Turn away from this path! Damnation surely awaits you!"

"The Lady can speak to me directly if there's something I should know," she said. "Until then, the Holy Father is God's representative on earth, and he has commanded me. The boy comes with me."

Loyola looked over at Coll and didn't like the calculating look playing across his friend's face. Coll was trying to find an angle, itching to move. Loyola motioned for him to stay put.

Killing Belosevic would be easy enough; the challenge was to prevent his death spasm from killing Mirsad. The only way around it, from this angle, would be to shoot the barrel of Belosevic's pistol and knock it off target. Loyola was an extraordinary marksman, but he wasn't confident he could make the shot. And there was a chance he would deflect the bullet toward Fortis.

He looked at Fortis. She was almost perfectly impassive, but he detected the slightest narrowing of her eyes. She had seen him.

It was now or never. He couldn't predict what she would do next, and he couldn't hold Coll back much longer. Loyola stepped fully into the doorway, his gun at eye level, sighted on the barrel of Belosevic's weapon.

*Audentes Fortuna juvat.* Fortune favors the bold.

It was not a prayer, but it would have to do.

Time seemed to stop as he pulled the trigger.

Metal struck metal with a loud crack as Loyola's bullet found its mark.

Reflexively, Belosevic squeezed the trigger, but the impact had deformed his gun's barrel and it blew up in his face.

Shrapnel scored his hand and face, and he collapsed to the ground screaming.

Loyola swiveled his aim to Fortis and found her gun pointed at him, so perfectly sighted between his eyes that the barrel looked like a dot. Mirsad had not flinched and was still standing next to her as if nothing had happened.

Coll stepped into the doorway and took aim at Fortis. She glanced at him, but her aim did not waver.

"If you think I can't take both of you out and walk away, you're wrong," she said.

"We're just here to take Mirsad home," Loyola said.

"The Holy Father has blessed this young man with an audience," Fortis said, "and I'm escorting him to Rome. You can come, if you like, but you're not stopping me."

"Calvin is the boy's father," Loyola said. "It's up to him."

"Tell the pope to email me, and we'll do a Zoom," Coll said.

Fortis laughed.

"It doesn't work that way," she said. "But I appreciate the brass balls."

"I'm not Catholic. 'Pope' don't mean shit to me," Coll said. "I follow the Prophet Muhammed, and the mountain can damn well come to me."

"I think you have that backwards," Fortis said. "Anyway, I *am* a Catholic, and I have orders, and I intend to follow them."

"It doesn't have to go down like this," Loyola said.

"Should have thought of that earlier," she said. "Should have brought Mirsad in the first time. Why didn't you? Did they pay you? Threaten a family member?"

Loyola arched an eyebrow.

"Is that what Macerata told you?" he asked.

"I don't know why you keep bringing him up," Fortis said. "I received my orders directly from the hand of the Holy Father."

Loyola frowned. He relaxed his stance slightly, and lowered his gun until it was pointing at the ground. Neither Fortis nor Coll budged.

"What were you told about that first mission?" Loyola asked.

"You were ordered to bring the boy to the Vatican," she said. "The mission went sideways, and the boy was killed, or so you reported. I was told that new intelligence suggested the boy was alive, and here he is. So why did you do it?"

"I was ordered to kill the boy," Loyola said, glancing at Mirsad. He seemed unfazed by anything happening around him, eyes shining and distant, a faint smile tugging at the corners of his mouth. "I disobeyed."

For the first time, Fortis seemed to be taken by surprise.

"Who gave the order?"

"It came through the secured app," Loyola said. "But Cardinal Macerata gave me the assignment originally. The Holy Father had instructed me long ago to obey Macerata's orders as if they were his own. Before this, I never had any reason to question them."

Fortis frowned.

"Macerata is still in play," she said. "But in this case, I received my orders directly from the Holy Father."

Loyola glanced over at Coll. Although he kept his demeanor professional, Loyola could see the muscles of his jaw bunching up. In his peripheral vision, he could see Belosevic on the ground, moaning softly. Fortis was ice cold and motionless, her gun resolutely pointed at Loyola's head.

It was in everyone's interest to deescalate the situation. If it went on much longer, someone was going to get shot. Maybe multiple someones.

"Why don't you ask Mirsad what he wants?" Fortis said.

Loyola and Coll looked at the boy—not a boy, but a man, and capable of making his own decisions. Mirsad seemed to hear them from a great distance. His focus slowly returned to the scene, and his expression of serene detachment gave way to a more troubled mien. He looked at Fortis, then at Loyola, and finally at Coll.

"I want to go home with my dad," he said. "But *Gospa* wants me to go to Rome."

As if on cue, dazzling lights pierced the mist in the sky over the cross of Mount Krizevac. A beating sound rose in the air, mysterious for a moment, but then familiar—the rotation of helicopter blades, growing nearer by the moment. Fortis frowned and cast a glance over her shoulder while keeping her gun perfectly centered on Loyola.

"Your ride?" Loyola asked.

"Unfortunately, no," she said.

"Fuuuuuuck," said Coll.

"What are we dealing with?" Fortis said.

"Most likely our friends from the parking lot," Loyola said. "They're with a mercenary outfit called Bridgewater."

Fortis gave him a sharp look. She knew something, but there was no time.

"What are we doing with this asshole?" Coll said, gesturing at Belosevic, who was rocking back and forth, cradling his head.

Fortis put a bullet in Belosevic's head before anyone could react.

"God damn," Coll said. "Was that necessary?"

"He might have had information," Loyola said crossly.

"We'll never know," Fortis said, holstering her pistol and hoisting the assault rifle, a NATO-style CZ Bren 2 configured with a long barrel. "Fight or run?"

"They have gear, they may have numbers," Loyola said.

"I'd suggest putting a sniper in the bell tower, but if these guys are gear heads, they might just knock it down," Fortis said. "And we've got to get the kid out of harm's way."

"There used to be a panic room in the church, but I imagine it's been decommissioned since my last visit," Loyola said.

"Where's your vehicle?" she asked.

"Mile and a half to the south," Loyola said.

"We're all pals now, is that it?" Coll muttered.

"All right," Fortis said, ignoring the aside. "Mine is about a mile southeast, but it's a two-seater. I can take the boy to Rome, and you two can meet me there."

"Fuck that," Coll growled.

"He's safer with me than with you," she said, matter-of-factly. "Much safer."

"Ours is a four-seater," Loyola said. "We all go together, and we can figure out what happens after, after."

Fortis looked at Loyola, then at Coll, taking their measure. She radiated supreme confidence, and Loyola could clearly see that the question was not whether she could defeat them but how long it might take, given the rapidly approaching helicopter. And the boy might not take kindly to seeing his father executed.

"How much time do we have before the chopper gets here?" Loyola asked.

"Less than five minutes, but you know that," she said. "You just want me to know that you know that I'm thinking about it."

He shrugged.

"If you two are going to be measuring your dicks for a while, can you do it inside?" Coll said. "We're too exposed for all this conversation. If they've got rocket launchers, we're sitting ducks."

Fortis nodded. Loyola took Mirsad's arm as gently as he could and steered him through the doors. Coll closed them and immediately began placing slices of C4 in strategic positions around the vestibule.

"Setting the timer for eight minutes when I say go," he said. "We exit out the back, take advantage of the smog. Maybe we get lucky."

Loyola turned to Mirsad, worried about the distant look in his eyes.

"Mirsad, can you run?" he asked.

"*Gospa* says to run," he replied.

"Swell," Coll said. "Then let's the five of us get going."

* * *

They were a quarter mile into the woods when they heard the explosion. Loyola and Coll stepped into the clear for a moment to risk a look. They had gotten lucky; the helicopter was low over the church when the C4 detonated. It lurched wildly as the pilot attempted to right his craft, but the turbulence was too much, and the copter tipped over and crashed into the building. Loyola watched the bell tower come down with some satisfaction.

"Get back under cover, you idiots," Fortis hissed. "Reinforcements *en route*."

They ducked back into the woods. Loyola could hear a truck or trucks closing fast, clattering over the bumpy road that provided the only vehicular access to the promontory. Visualizing the approach, he concluded that they had probably seen the explosion. Loyola motioned for everyone to lie flat and said a silent prayer that *Gospa* wouldn't give them any trouble.

An armored personnel carrier rumbled past them, then another.

"We're too close to the compound," Fortis whispered. "We have to move."

Loyola nodded. They covered another three-quarters of a mile. As they neared Coll's Jaguar, a glow could be seen in the haze. Fortis motioned them to stay put, then disappeared into the mist. She returned within moments, carefully emerging from the exact spot where she had vanished in order to minimize any misunderstandings.

"I count at least twenty-five guys, heavy gear," she whispered. "They found your car, and they're searching in an expanding perimeter. We have maybe four minutes."

"You took out more than that back at the base," Coll said.

"I had a lot of strategic cover to work with," she said. "The monks weren't armored, and I didn't have any civilians to worry about, at least not until the end."

Coll looked at Mirsad, then at Loyola, then finally at Fortis.

"Where's your vehicle?" he asked her.

She gestured back and to the left.

"Armored?" he asked.

"Sturdy," she said. "It'll take some punishment, but it can't compete with the vehicles we just saw."

Coll turned to Loyola.

"What's the safest play for Mirsad?" Coll asked.

Loyola thought for a moment.

"You and I start a fight," he said. "When we've got their full attention, Sister Belina blasts through and doesn't stop until she reaches the border."

Coll looked at Mirsad.

"You want to go to Rome, son?"

Mirsad suddenly looked less like a saint and more like a boy.

"*Gospa* wants to go," he said. "I guess I do too. Can I, Dad?"

"You're a grown man," Coll said, thickly. "You can make your own damn decisions."

"Then I guess I want to go," Mirsad said. "For now anyway."

Coll nodded.

"I guess it's settled then," he said.

Mirsad suddenly threw his arms around Coll.

"Be careful, Dad," he said.

"You too," Coll said.

Loyola looked at Fortis.

"You OK with this plan?" he asked.

"It's the best bet," she said. "I imagine we'll see you in Rome."

"You better fucking believe it," Coll growled. "Don't try to stop us."

"My orders are to bring the boy to the Holy Father," she said. "No one said anything about stopping you."

She paused.

"Yet," she added.

"Enough," Loyola said. "They're here any second."

Fortis turned to Mirsad.

"Let's go," she said, pointing. "That direction. Run as fast as you can. I'll be right behind you."

He took off. Fortis turned to Loyola.

"Good luck," she said. "I look forward to continuing our conversation."

She disappeared into the fog.

"She flirting with you?" Coll said. "Is that allowed?"

"We have a task," Loyola said. "Let's focus on it."

* * *

The first squad of four Bridgewater mercenaries didn't stand a chance. Using their knives and the cover provided by the deepening mist, Loyola and Coll managed to take three down silently. The fourth squeezed off a loud burst from his assault rifle before Loyola shot him in the head with the Glock.

Voices erupted from the woods around them—too many. Coll threw a grenade at the loudest cluster. After the screams died down, the remaining mercs took the hint and stopped their chatter. Loyola and Coll raised their rifles and took cover behind the trunk of a large downed tree. Leaden footsteps crushed through the brush, enveloping them in white noise that seemed to come from every direction.

Loyola became very still, listening, watching, then suddenly firing into the mist. A man groaned, and his body fell heavily. The sound sparked more movement, and Loyola fired again, twice, followed by Coll, twice. More bodies fell, and the remaining commandos unleashed a barrage of automatic weapons fire that made up in volume what it lacked in precision. Several shots thudded into the tree they were crouched behind, and they ducked even lower.

A brilliant light suddenly cut through the mist—the high beams of an Aston-Martin coupe, which roared into life and swiftly peeled away. As the Bridgewater soldiers started firing at the vehicle, its lights clicked off, and Loyola and Coll sprang into action, targeting every muzzle flash that appeared in the mist. At least eight more commandos went down, as the car vanished into the fog.

"How many you do think are left?" Coll said, breathing heavily.

"Too many," Loyola said, "and they've almost certainly called reinforcements. We have to get to the car and get out of here."

"Agreed," Coll said.

They fought their way through the brume, encountering and dispatching eight more Bridgewater fighters before reaching the Jaguar.

"Twenty-five guys, my ass," Coll said.

"She said 'at least' twenty-five,'" Loyola replied.

"Man, taking her side already," Coll said, shaking his head. "You got it bad."

"Not funny," Loyola said curtly.

"I mean, it's a little funny," Coll said. "It would be funnier if it wasn't my son's life on the line. I hope she's really taking him to Rome, and I hope she's not getting the same order you got. She might be the type who follows orders."

"If she wasn't trying to keep him alive, she would have just shot Belosevic back at the church," Loyola whispered. "It wouldn't have mattered if he got off a shot at Mirsad on his way down. We'll see them in Rome."

Four men had been left behind to guard the car. Working in close synchronization, Loyola and Coll silently took out the two with knives, but the second pair required gunshots, triggering a large commotion from nearby. They took cover behind the car, moments before a fusillade exploded toward them.

"Get off my fucking car!" Coll screamed, rolling around to the back bumper and then advancing with his rifle blazing. Loyola came around the front, moving more judiciously, in a series of head shots chosen carefully to conserve ammo. The commandos kept emerging from the mist, seemingly endless. Loyola counted nineteen before the shooting stopped, and he had no idea how many Coll had taken out.

The woods fell silent. Loyola felt an icy grip on his heart.

"Cal," he said, first in a low tone, then repeated it more loudly. He ran in the direction where he had last seen Coll and found his friend sprawled on the ground, surrounded by Bridgewater goons. Blood was pouring from the hole where his left eye should have been.

"Cal," Loyola shouted, not caring if anyone heard. "Cal! Can you hear me? Hang on brother!" He knelt down. Coll's face was a mess but he was breathing. Loyola quickly checked for other wounds, and finding none, hoisted Coll over his shoulder and carried him to the Jaguar. Like its owner, the car was wounded but still alive, roaring in affirmation when he turned the key.

Loyola secured Coll in the back seat and took off down the highway, the car shaking violently from the rough road and the damage it had sustained.

Prayer had become a ritual of repetition for Father Francis Loyola, but when he turned to God now, his words were raw and intimate, shouted over the din of the vibrating automobile. He pleaded for his friend's life with the sincerity of a child, offering all manner of bargains that he could not keep.

# CHAPTER 10

# Sixty-Forty

IT HAD BEEN many years since Loyola had seen a comrade fall. Among all his protective instincts, detachment was the one that had atrophied the most in retirement. His heart didn't stop pounding until he pulled up to the clinic.

Medjugorje had no hospital, but the Sovereign Military Order of Malta ran a small facility for Catholic pilgrims who had come to pay their respects to the Lady. Loyola was acquainted with the administrator, a German priest and doctor named Josef Armbrüster. They had crossed paths when Loyola was working in Ukraine many years earlier. The doctor had not been formally briefed on the precise nature of Loyola's work, but he had seen enough not to ask questions.

The gloomy, unabated fog made it feel late, but the sun had only just gone down, and Loyola found Armbrüster in his office. He examined Coll and bandaged the wound.

"He was lucky only to lose an eye," Armbrüster said, as he finished the dressing. "It looks like whatever did this barely missed his brain. I can't do any more for him here. He'll have to go to the hospital in Mostar for tests and further care. I assume you will want me to arrange that?"

"I would be grateful," Loyola said.

"What should I tell them about the cause of his injury?"

"Is the cause evident?" Loyola asked.

"Not necessarily," Armbrüster said. "What's your friend going to say when he wakes up?"

"He'll probably pretend to be disoriented until he hears from me or someone else he trusts," Loyola said.

"I'll tell them I found him in my parking lot, and I don't know what happened," Armbrüster said. "Which is technically true."

"Thank you," Loyola said, sincerely, clasping the man's arm.

"Is there anyone who should be informed?" Armbrüster asked.

"I'll take care of that," Loyola said.

* * *

Loyola straightened his clerical collar and stared at his reflection in the mirror. It had only been five days since Boston, but he could swear he had lost twenty pounds. A heavy shadow itched on his face, but he didn't shave the stubble. It was less than a full beard, but it helped obscure his identity. He considered shaving his head, but he decided to save that step in case he needed it later.

He looked and felt gaunt, despite sleep and a shower. His night had been plagued by nightmares, driving for hours and hours on dark featureless stretches of winding mountain roads, capturing and prolonging the urgency and frustration of the previous day's events.

Even in his dreams, he knew he had to face Coll's wife at the end of his journey.

Zerina was not naive. She knew the man she had married, she knew what he did for a living, and she knew the kind of people who were his friends. But she was fiery and fiercely protective of her husband. When Loyola entered the hospital room, he found her sitting next to his bed. She leapt from the chair and threw her arms around his neck then pulled back and slapped him, hard.

"Look what you did to him," she cried. "Look at his face."

The hospital staff had re-dressed Coll's wound. Loyola knew the eye was gone, and he could see now that Coll would wear a significant scar along his temple, which the bullet had miraculously only grazed.

"I'm sorry," he said. "It's my fault."

"I know," Zerina said bitterly, then after a moment, "I know it's not. Those terrible men took Mirsad. Where is he now? Where is my boy?"

"He's in Rome," Loyola said, "or nearly there. *Gospa* wanted him to go."

"*Gospa, gospa, gospa,*" she said. "That bitch has brought us nothing but pain."

Loyola felt a pang, but he didn't respond.

"You are the Catholic," she said. "Do you believe this shit?"

Loyola shrugged carefully.

"I don't know what to believe," he said.

"Rome," she spat the name as if it were a curse. "And who is watching over him there? Didn't they want him dead before? Isn't that why he came to us?"

"A . . . friend of mine is watching over him," Loyola said. "I trust her to keep him safe."

"You trust her, but who trusts you?" Zerina shot back. "Cal trusted you. Look where that got him."

"I'm sorry," Loyola said.

"I know," she said, the anger suddenly dying down again. "He trusted you because you saved him once. And you saved Mirsad once. And maybe this time, he would have died going after Mirsad alone instead of . . . this."

Loyola didn't know what to say, so he said nothing.

"Are you going to bring Mirsad back to me? To us?"

"Yes," Loyola said.

"You swear?" she said. "You swear on God? As a priest?"

"I swear by all that is holy," he said.

"Then go," she said. "I will tell him you were here."

Loyola nodded sharply and left.

* * *

Rocha was sound asleep when her phone pinged—the Google News alert she had set up for Monsignor Gasparo Biancardi. Rubbing the sand from her eyes, she sat up in bed and opened the story. Reuters was reporting that the Vatican had issued a formal statement expressing its deep sorrow over the second brutal al Qaeda attack on the Brotherhood of the Epoch of Martyrs in Medjugorje, Bosnia. She almost put the phone down and went back to sleep, thinking it was the story she had already seen, when her sleep-fuzzed brain locked onto the word *second.*

Waking all the way up, Rocha stumbled to the coffee maker, barely lifting her eyes from the phone as she clumsily got the pot started.

"The slaughter comes nine years after al Qaeda-linked militants attacked the abbey in 2015, killing twenty-three," she read aloud. "Last night's attack was even deadlier than the first, with fifty-one confirmed dead and six more missing. Among the dead were a significant number of elite operatives working for Bridgewater Global, a military contractor tasked with a counterterrorism mission in several countries around the world. An unknown number of terrorists were also killed in the clash. Since the death of Ayman al Zawahiri in 2022, al Qaeda has largely . . ."

She put down the phone and took some coffee from the still-percolating machine, sloshing it into a mug as the basket dripped onto the heating plate with a hiss and a scorched smell.

She googled "Bridgewater AND Catholic." A number of news results appeared. The company's CEO, Lloyd Bridgewater, was in Rome to celebrate Christmas. One of the more recent stories included a grip-and-grin between Bridgewater and a cardinal named Niccolò Macerata. She could find little information in English about Macerata, except a lone story that mentioned he was a confidant of the pope.

Rocha googled "Bridgewater AND Biancardi," but found nothing except today's news stories. A search for "Biancardi AND Macerata" brought up a group photo of people who worked for the Vatican's Secretariat of State. Another bell rang as the caffeine started to do its work—Loyola had supposedly worked as a diplomatic liaison for the Vatican. That meant the State Department, surely.

She repeated all of the previous search terms in combination with "Loyola" but found not a single hit. "Did you mean LOYALTY?" Google asked unhelpfully.

Medjugorje . . . Loose puzzle pieces suddenly clicked together. She did an image search for "Lady of Medjugorje" and confirmed her half-formed thought. Scrolling down the Wikipedia page, she found multiple images based on descriptions of the apparitions—the Virgin with her head surrounded by a halo of stars. It was the same image she had seen on the wall of the hero priest's room.

She had many connections now, but where did they lead? More than enough to convince her that something needed to be investigated, but much less than enough to justify continuing to work the case in the face of a direct order to stop. The mere existence of links did not constitute evidence, especially when all the entities were naturally linked by their strong involvement in the same religion.

The guns in Loyola's closet were another matter however, illegal by virtue of the serial numbers being filed off. She would need a warrant to go back and get that evidence, but she would need *some* kind of evidence to get the warrant.

Something more than "these Catholics know each other" and "the priest had a suspicious picture of the Virgin Mary."

She glanced at the clock. It was 6:30 AM, and she already had the kind of headache she usually got at quitting time. Some days she hated her job.

* * *

The Jaguar was a disaster, barely fit for the road, and the bullet holes peppered all over its body would attract police attention. Loyola dumped it a secluded spot just outside of Medjugorje and sent the coordinates to a digital dead drop so that Coll could retrieve it later. Loyola hiked back into Medjugorje with all the supplies he could fit into a rucksack and returned to the clinic, where he found Armbrüster in his office.

"How is he?" Armbrüster asked.

"He'll live," Loyola said. "The doctors said the damage was superficial except for the eye. The *policija* will probably come around with questions."

"Don't worry about that," Armbrüster said. "They might not even bother, and if they do, I'll handle it. There are a lot of guns in this country, not as many as yours perhaps, but enough. These things happen."

Loyola nodded.

"Plus, there was a terrorist attack last night, it seems, and I am sure they will be busy with that," Armbrüster said. "The abbey of the Brotherhood of the Epoch of Martyrs. Second time that the terrorists hit the place. Just terrible."

Loyola got up and closed the office door.

"Father, you've done so much for me already," he said.

"All for the church," Armbrüster said.

"I have one more favor to ask," Loyola said.

"Certainly," Armbrüster said.

"Hear my confession."

Armbrüster nodded and drew the Venetian blinds. The office was small, and the light leaking through the slats gave the room a suitably confessional feel. He swiveled his chair slightly, so that they were looking past each other.

"Bless me Father, for I have sinned," Loyola said. "It's been five days since my last confession. These are my sins."

He took a deep breath.

"I killed at least fourteen people . . ."

"At *least*?" Armbrüster said, with a sharp intake of breath. "In *five days*?"

"It was a combat situation," Loyola said apologetically. "Well, parts of it were. It's hard to keep track in that setting."

"Combat initiated by whom?" Armbrüster asked.

"Not by me," Loyola said. "I think all of these could be considered self-defense, but maybe I could have found nonlethal ways to deal with some of them. Uh, maybe."

"I—all right," Armbrüster said. "Go on."

"I stole five cars," Loyola continued. "I lied to a variety of people who work for airlines and passport control. I took the Lord's name in vain and used vulgar language several times."

Armbrüster sat silently for some time, waiting.

"I, uh, had some impure thoughts," Loyola added, finally.

"*That's* what you held back?" Armbrüster asked.

"I'm usually better about that," Loyola said sheepishly.

"But not about killing?" Armbrüster said, incredulously.

Loyola paused. The seal of confession sat over their conversation, but he still instinctively hesitated to disclose details.

"I used to do certain work at the direction of the Holy Father," he said. "That work often involved violence and deception."

"I am not entirely ignorant of such things," Armbrüster said. "*Used to*, you say."

"I retired seven years ago, Father," Loyola said. "A few days back, I was attacked, apparently as a consequence of work I had done before for the Vatican."

"So these murders to which you are confessing, they were not carried out at the direction of the Holy Father," Armbrüster said.

"Not murders," Loyola said, defensively. "Killings. In self-defense. But you're correct that the Holy Father did not direct me in this matter."

"You 'think' they were self-defense,'" Armbrüster said. "That's what you said."

"Yes," Loyola said. "I didn't seek any of these people out. They were trying to capture or kill me, or one of my friends."

"And the lies as well. And the cars. These were to preserve your life?"

"Less directly, but yes," Loyola said. "I was being tracked by the enemies of the Church, and I lied and stole to evade them."

"Enemies of the Church, or *your* enemies?" Armbrüster asked.

"Both," Loyola said. "I think."

"Again, you 'think'," Armbrüster said. "Are you certain, or are you not?"

"Uh, sixty–forty?" Loyola said uncomfortably. "I take your point, Father. Regardless of the reason, the people in question were definitely trying to kill me. One hundred percent. And they kidnapped my friend's son."

"I see."

A long silence ensued.

"Let me ask you this, Father Francis Loyola, and do not dare to lie in the presence of God," Armbrüster said finally. "Why have you come to take confession? Do you truly believe you have sinned?"

Loyola paused to collect his thoughts before responding.

"My actions were sinful by their nature, but perhaps not sinful due to their context and intent," Loyola said. "To be honest, I have always struggled with that question. My practice has always been to confess everything, and let my confessor decide. It's not the first time I've had a conversation like this, and different confessors have given me different answers. I guess I would say it is important to me to confess, to seek forgiveness, regardless of the outcome."

"I see," Armbrüster said. "Do you feel contrition? Do you repent of your actions?"

"I do," Loyola said.

"You are a priest," Armbrüster said. "Tell me what repentance means."

"That I sincerely intend not to sin again," Loyola said.

"But you think that perhaps you have not sinned," Armbrüster said. "In which case your repentance means nothing. Let me ask this another way. Do you intend to kill again?"

It was a reasonable question, one that Loyola might have asked if he was sitting on the other side of the confessional, if he had lived a different sort of life.

"I do not *intend* to kill anyone," Loyola said. "But it is very possible, maybe even probable, that I will have to defend myself or someone else again before this matter is finished."

"Your act of contrition includes a promise to avoid the 'near occasion of sin.' Do you intend to *seek out* situations in which you would feel killing is justified?"

Another silence.

"There's a boy's life at stake," Loyola said, eventually. "In addition to my own. I intend to take steps to make the boy safe and to ensure the safety of the Church, which may be a related issue. My own life is secondary to those concerns, but I'd prefer to keep it, all other things being equal."

Armbrüster sighed.

"I do not profess to know your burdens," he said. "But I am profoundly skeptical that this life you have chosen can be endured without lasting moral stain. Here is your penance. After the present matter is concluded, you must find a calling in which you save lives and do not take lives, and you must stay in that calling for the rest of your days. If you fail to carry out this penance in full, you must disclose that failure to your future confessors, so that they may ponder whether you deserve absolution."

The penance was just, perhaps even transformative, rekindling a spark of hope, a glimmer of light in the oppressive darkness of Loyola's soul.

"If you sincerely accept this penance, I will give you absolution," Armbrüster said. "If you do not accept it, I cannot."

"I accept," Loyola said. The words hung in the air like a vow. For any Catholic, the sacrament of confession offered moral solace and the opportunity to start anew. For a man like Loyola, who walked so fine a line between virtue and vice, it carried even more weight.

"I will hear your act of contrition," Armbrüster said.

As they each recited the words that led to absolution, Loyola felt a weight lifting from his shoulders, a hint of the possibility of a better life.

All he had to do was survive long enough to see it.

CHAPTER

11

# A Short Stint in Purgatory

LOYOLA WANTED NOTHING more than to speed. But he was driving a stolen car, and carrying a compromised passport. The consequences of getting pulled over were far out of proportion to the hour or two he might gain by speeding.

He didn't have to like it.

The trip was long, and Loyola stopped to indulge in a hot meal outside of Venice—pasta carbonara and a single glass of chianti in honor of the fact that no one had tried to kill him today. After dinner, he found an unmanned parking garage, drove all the way up to the roof, where few other vehicles had parked, put his seat back and tried to sleep.

Loyola had known true exhaustion in his life, but he had hoped those days were behind him. After seven years of relative peace, his body had quieted, and it protested the return of adrenaline, and its persistence. The uplift of his confession had faded, and the grimness had returned. He worried that a switch had been thrown, and that it could not be turned off so easily. What if he was meant only for violence? Perhaps it was hubris to think he could throw it off so easily, whether as a result of God's plan or his own human failings.

He was freshly confessed; perhaps it would be better if he simply did not wake in the morning but went freshly scrubbed into the Kingdom.

Except for the cars he'd stolen after confession. Well, a short stint in purgatory was probably still better than he deserved.

Mired in such thoughts, he finally gave into weariness and fell asleep. When he opened his eyes, the sun was higher in the sky than he had anticipated. But he felt more prepared for the trials to come.

Rome had always been a sanctuary for Loyola—a place to which he returned when the mission was over, for physical rest and spiritual healing. This time was different. The crisis was ahead of him, not behind.

* * *

Rocha decided to make a murder board in her living room, rather than the office, since the investigation was officially over. The department had trained her extensively in the use of link-mapping software, but the exercise had only kindled her visceral love for colored yarn connecting photos secured to an oversized bulletin board by thumbtacks.

In the center, Father Francis Loyola, with a string connecting him to a photo of the massacre at the car lot. Above him, the Vatican cleanup artist, Gasparo Biancardi, author of many press releases and dossiers. To the left, she pinned up a picture of the Lady of Medjugorje, connecting her to both Loyola and Biancardi.

Cardinal Macerata and Monsignor Biancardi, colleagues at the Secretariat of State, linked by a length of yarn. Lloyd

Bridgewater, connected to both Macerata and the Lady of Medjugorje, the latter by virtue of this week's attack.

She was interrupted by the ping of an email. Emil Moussa was an Interpol officer she had met at a conference some years back. At her request, he had forwarded crime-scene photos from the newest Medjugorje massacre. "Something stinks," he wrote, "but the Bosnians aren't asking for help."

She was floored at the number of bodies in the photos. Several pictures showed dead monks scattered all over the abbey grounds, which were covered with sandbags, as if they'd been expecting trouble. The church was completely bombed out, with the husk of a downed helicopter visible in the ruins.

A second batch of pictures showed the Bridgewater casualties, which were also extensive. A number of burned bodies had been recovered from the wreckage of the helicopters, and many other operatives had been killed in assorted ways, including several by gunshot wounds to the head.

She peered closely at the photos. Shot in the head while wearing body armor. She flipped back to the photos of the monks and found even more headshots, many of them remarkably precise.

Just like in the movies.

Rocha had seen this movie before.

She printed the pictures and walked back to the murder board. She put a photo of the headshot kills at the abbey between the Lady of Medjugorje and the parking lot massacre, and connected them with yarn. On her laptop, she called up the photos she had taken at the rectory, sending one to the printer—the expert marksmanship medal, which she pinned underneath Loyola's photo.

Was the marksman priest somehow behind all of this?

"This is fucking nuts," she said aloud. "Absolutely fucking bananas."

Returning to her computer, she switched to Signal, the encrypted messaging app, which she used to reply to Moussa with thanks and a new request. Could he run a set of fingerprints for her, strictly on the downlow? Please and thank you.

"Sure," he messaged back immediately. "But you've piqued my interest now, Martina. What are you getting yourself into?"

"Fuck if I know," she replied. "But I'll probably regret it."

* * *

Using his one clean credit card, Loyola booked a rental on the *Viale Vaticano*, near the Vatican Museums, with a rooftop terrace view over the walls that enclosed Vatican City. A Christmas tree in the living room reminded him of the date—December 22, the last Sunday of Advent, and the first time in nearly seven years that he had missed Sunday mass.

Loyola had been planning to again discuss the coming Jubilee year, this time with a sermon about hope. He wondered how his parishioners were doing and what they must think of him. His life in Boston seemed impossibly distant now. Armbrüster's penance rose again in his mind, but it was too soon to give it any serious thought. But he could not go back to his parish. His old life had come roaring back with a vengeance, violently crowding out all other possibilities.

Loyola could not continue like this. He would get out or die trying. His eternal soul was at stake.

Inevitable, perhaps, that he should worry about damnation. The nature of Loyola's work involved constant compromises. He sped through gray areas as if they were red lights on an empty road at night. To presume that he always made the right call would be hubris, and so Loyola frequented the confessional, as his predecessor had before him, as Sister Belina Fortis would for years to come. For the *primus sicarius,* death could come at any moment. The stain of mortal sin was a burden best cast aside, and frequently. And the confessional, with its sacred seal, was the only place he could speak candidly about his feelings and experiences.

Loyola went to the terrace with a pair of binoculars. The evening was seasonably warm for Rome, in the upper forties. He wore a black cassock, the armor of God. The uniform comforted him, and it was perfect camouflage here, just steps from Saint Peter's Basilica. No one would notice one more priest. He was just part of the scenery.

The lights of the Vatican and the hum of its constant activity also gave him comfort. As he swept the scene with the binoculars, he could see priests and monsignors and cardinals walking to and fro, engaged in animated conversations about the business of the church. The occasional small group of nuns could also be seen gliding along the flagstones, not exactly segregated, but not exactly included.

Loyola wondered how Sister Belina Fortis felt when she visited this place, and he felt a sudden pang of shame. She would likely never know the glow of welcome and inclusion that he had experienced. The church had progressed in some ways, but the Vatican was still unmistakably patriarchal. It was a sort of masculinity, he thought, but bent and pent, perhaps even warped, by the opposing strictures of power and self-denial. He didn't know how to fix the problem. Loyola was a simple man, or so he liked to tell himself.

The violent part of his life had always been situated outside these walls, never following him past the threshold. But now the Vatican was the source of his current danger and the threat to Mirsad. He would never be able to face Coll if he failed to bring the boy back safely.

Loyola would do whatever it took to protect Mirsad, but he flinched at the idea of perpetrating violence on these sacred grounds. There must be some other way.

If Fortis was telling the truth and the Holy Father had summoned Mirsad, the boy was likely being kept in the *Domus Sanctae Marthae*, Saint Martha's House, a hotel-like building on the other side of the wall that faced Loyola's terrace. The *Domus* was built in part to house the College of Cardinals when they assembled in a conclave to elect a new pope. Because of the extreme secrecy around that process, the building was designed with security firmly in mind. It would be hard to get to Mirsad without being detected, and at any rate, Loyola was not going to shoot his way into the Vatican.

He considered walking in the front door. It was an appealing notion. He was not, technically, in any sort of trouble, and he was certainly permitted to enter, as a tourist if nothing else. He could probably demand an audience with Macerata or the Holy Father himself, and given the bodies he had buried for them, he would get it.

On the other hand, he had enemies everywhere, some almost certainly within Vatican City's walls. Fortis knew he was coming, and she would probably have warned the Holy Father. Would she have told Macerata? And whose side was she on, really? She had declined to fight him in Medjugorje, but she also got what she wanted—Mirsad. The mission was the priority, and picking a fight with a potentially dangerous foe would have put the mission at risk. Now, she and Mirsad were ensconced in the Vatican, perhaps the only place in the world where Loyola would feel inhibited about unleashing violence.

Although Rome was considerably warmer than Boston, Loyola started to feel a chill in the night air, and he returned to the apartment. As soon as he crossed the threshold, he sensed that something had changed since he left, an instinct acting at a subconscious level to put him on alert. He drew the knife he had strapped to his calf and silently inched his way through the suite.

In the brightly lit living room, an old man was sitting on the sofa. He was wearing a red flannel shirt, blue jeans, and sneakers. Loyola was so taken aback by the very un-Italian outfit that he didn't recognize the man until he spoke.

"I'm glad to see you made it here in one piece," said His Holiness Pope Nicholas VI, Bishop of Rome, Patriarch of the West, Vicar of Jesus Christ, Successor of the Prince of the Apostles, Supreme Pontiff of the Universal Church, Primate of Italy, Archbishop of the Roman Province, Sovereign of Vatican City, Servant of the Servants of God—and apparently, Awkward Wearer of Skinny Jeans.

"It's been a long time, Francis," the pope said. "I wish we could just talk about your ministry in Boston, but we have a great deal to discuss, and very little time."

He motioned to the coffee table as Loyola stood there gaping.

"I brought wine," the Holy Father said with a smile. "You look like you could use a glass."

CHAPTER

12

# A Killer With a Conscience

LOYOLA KNELT TO kiss the ring, but the Holy Father wasn't wearing it.

"It wouldn't be a very good disguise, would it?" he laughed. "Please sit."

Loyola settled into an overstuffed chair. He would have preferred a corner seat with his back to a wall, out of habit and for practical reasons. It was very unlikely they were alone here. But he couldn't exactly squeeze onto the couch next to His Holiness, as if they were two pals settling down to watch a football game.

The pope poured two glasses of what looked to be an expensive Chianti, then raised his in a toast.

"To the Blessed Virgin," he said. "May she watch over us always."

Loyola took the other glass and returned the gesture. He sniffed it inexpertly and took a sip. It was very good, and on some other occasion, he would have enjoyed the indulgence. But he needed his wits about him, so he put it back down on the coffee table. They sat silently for a moment as the pope took a long draught. According to protocol, Loyola should wait to be addressed, but this encounter was nothing if not unusual.

"Holy Father," he began, in a humble tone. "I have many urgent questions."

The pontiff nodded.

"To address the most obvious one," Nicholas said, "your successor chose these clothes."

Loyola stifled a laugh. He had met the pope many times in the course of his work for the Order of Saint Uriel. The pontiff was known for being genial and good-humored, but Loyola didn't remember any moments as surreal as this.

"I presume she is here, Holy Father," he said.

"She is, but she insisted on remaining out of sight," the pope said.

"I understand, Your Holiness," Loyola said.

"I'm out of uniform, so we can dispense with the honorifics," the pope said. "Call me Nick."

After a pregnant pause, the pontiff laughed heartily at the horrified look on Loyola's face.

"That was a joke," he said. "But seriously, you can drop the major formalities for now."

Loyola nodded sheepishly.

"Allow me to anticipate your more important questions," the pope said. "I will start nine years ago. Acting as my deputy, Cardinal Macerata assigned you to handle a situation in Medjugorje. This you know."

Loyola nodded.

"The initial mission was sanctioned by ourselves . . . by me," the pontiff continued. "The Brotherhood of the Epoch of Martyrs had sent communiqués to the Vatican that sparked great concern. The first was intended to demonstrate the legitimacy of the visions. It contained sensitive information of a theological nature that only an archbishop of Rome would know. As such, it strongly suggested that the visions were authentic.

"The second communiqué contained sensitive information of a secular nature that could create significant legal problems for the Church if widely disseminated. This information could have been uncovered through more mundane means, albeit not easily. This communiqué had the tenor of a threat. If the visions were not formally acknowledged, it was implied, the information would become public. It was at this point that Cardinal Macerata and I determined that you should investigate."

The pontiff took a sip of wine.

"A third communiqué was sent, unbeknownst to me," he said. "It was intercepted by Cardinal Macerata, to whom I had delegated this matter. The third communiqué described a prophecy that the Holy Father would be threatened with assassination by a hidden hand. The murder was to take place at the start of a jubilee year."

Since the Year of Our Lord 1400, the sitting pontiff had declared a jubilee every twenty-five years, except when an extraordinary jubilee was announced to meet some especially pressing need. Ordinary jubilee years were focused on various religious remembrances, grappling with sins great and small, and the pursuit of justice.

On a practical level, a jubilee involved a number of public ceremonies and observances, starting with the ceremonial opening of the sealed *Porta Sancta*—the Holy Door—in Saint Peter's Basilica during Midnight Mass on Christmas Eve.

The door was set to open in just two days.

Loyola took a moment to process all of this.

"Cardinal Macerata withheld this information from you, Holy Father?" he asked, finally.

Nicholas VI nodded.

"How did you discover this omission?" Loyola asked.

"Sister Belina brought Mirsad to me," the pope said. "I spoke with him for a long time, and he explained many things to me. The prophecy, of course, but he told me something that caused me even greater distress and pain."

Loyola could hear real emotion in the Holy Father's voice, and he leaned forward to listen.

"Mirsad told me that you had been ordered to kill him," the pope said, "and that you refused."

Loyola bowed his head.

"It is true, Holy Father," he said.

"For the *primus sicarius* to refuse a papal order is grounds for instant excommunication, without the need for an investigation or formal finding," the pope said in a gentle tone. "Even more grievous, almost unforgivable, you have continued to act as a priest and perform the sacraments, knowing this."

"Yes, Holy Father," Loyola said, his heart filling with dismay, unable to meet Nicholas's gaze. It was all he could do not to drop to his knees. "I confessed the sin to one who gave me absolution. But I have been haunted all these years by the fear that he did not have the authority. That God had not forgiven me."

"Fortunate for you, then, that I did not give this order," the pope said.

Loyola had known that this was a possibility, even at the time. But to hear it said out loud was transfigurational. He had been holding something cold and ugly in his heart of hearts for nearly a decade, and it abruptly unclenched and released. For all this time, he had labored under the nagging fear that his ministry had been tainted by this unpardonable sin. Loyola sagged with relief, as if a flood of bile had suddenly exited his body. His hands shook, and his eyes threatened to betray the extremity of his emotion.

He wondered where Sister Belina Fortis had stationed herself. He hoped that she couldn't see him like this, see his open uncontrolled emotion, which could only be perceived as weakness in a man like him. But she was surely watching.

"Francis," the pope said, his voice now inflected with sadness.

"Holy Father?"

*"Why didn't you ask me?"* Nicholas said.

"Holy Father," Loyola said, his voice breaking. "How could I?"

Loyola had wanted to ask, of course. He had wanted to confront them, Macerata and the Holy Father both. But his vows were sacred and unambiguous. He was not in the habit of questioning orders. He couldn't afford to be. His job was to kill, and his obvious talent was only redeemed by the grace of his service to the church. If the purity of that service were opened for debate . . .

The psychology that allowed him to contain all of these contradictions was fragile, built on an edifice of faith. Loyola's refusal to kill Mirsad had cracked the foundation of that resolve, slowly eating away at him. To confront this cancer directly was unimaginable. If he pulled at loose strings, the entire enterprise might unravel, revealing that he was not, after all was said and done, a warrior for God's justice, but just another man who relied on deeply held beliefs to justify mass murder, no better than any other terrorist or war criminal.

The magnitude was too great. Loyola could not face the dilemma. He could only silently bear it, until he could not bear it any longer, and then he retired.

He buried his face in his hands.

"You should have trusted me, Francis," the Holy Father said, placing a hand of consolation on Loyola's head.

"I'm sorry," Loyola said.

They remained in silence for a long while.

* * *

The pope excused himself to use the washroom, and Loyola went into the kitchen to run cold water over his face. He sensed Fortis before he saw her. She was wearing a full nun's habit, in indigo hues naturally, an unruly lock of her prematurely silver hair peeking out from her headdress.

He didn't bother to ask if she had been listening.

"What would you have done?" he said.

"Honestly, I don't know," she said. "If I'm really being honest, I think a lot about how the Holy Father sees me. He calls me his 'little experiment.' If I refused, I would worry it would be seen as proof that a woman can't do the job."

"So you would have done it?" Loyola asked.

"I might have done what you did," she said. "But honestly, I can say whatever I want if it's hypothetical, but when it's real . . . I just don't know."

"Now that you know the full context, does it change how you think about me?" he asked.

"I have a rich inner life," she said, in a retort as quick as it was bone dry. "It doesn't leave me with a lot of time to think about you."

Loyola stepped forward, very close to her. She raised an eyebrow at his proximity but didn't step back. She smelled as good as he remembered.

"Does he make jokes now?" Loyola asked in a conspiratorial *sotto voce* whisper. "I don't remember jokes."

She put a finger to her lips.

"I am the bearer of a sacred trust," she said. "I'm sure you understand."

* * *

"Here is where we find ourselves," Pope Nicholas VI said, as Loyola settled back into his chair. Fortis joined them now, standing in a corner of the room that allowed her to see both the front door of the apartment and the passage that led to the terrace.

"Our investigation has revealed that Cardinal Macerata arranged for the release of Vaso Belosevic, with whom he made an agreement," he continued. "We believe that Macerata is implicated in a plot to assassinate me, and that all of his actions are fully explained by a desire to prevent Mirsad from delivering the Lady's warning to me."

"You and Mirsad were the only free agents who could potentially expose Macerata's duplicity," Fortis said to Loyola. "They might have let sleeping dogs lie with respect to you, except that Mirsad sent a message to the Epoch compound out of the blue. We only caught it because we had Belosevic under surveillance."

"Mirsad initiated that contact with the Epoch, by the way," Nicholas said. "He told us he was following his Lady's instructions."

Loyola frowned.

"Why would the Lady place him in harm's way?" he said.

"The question presumes the Lady is not a delusion," Fortis said, dispassionately.

"We need not debate the visions now," the pope interjected. "But for what it's worth, when Mirsad showed up at the compound, he triggered a series of events that ultimately led to our discovery of the plot and Father Loyola's reactivation."

Fortis looked like she was biting off a comment.

"At any rate, we have ample evidence that the warning must be taken seriously," Nicholas continued. "Macerata seems to believe in it, or he would not have hidden it from me. Even it's simply self-fulfilling, our situation remains the same."

Loyola and Fortis nodded their assent.

"The Brotherhood of the Epoch of Martyrs tried to blackmail the Church back in 2015," the pope said. "That effort failed, due to Father Loyola's actions. Cardinal Macerata tried to suppress the contents of the boy's visions in order to advance his own ambitions. Should I die, he will likely become the next pope."

He took a deep breath.

"Cardinal Macerata gave the order to kill Mirsad and spare Belosevic nine years ago. He is directing the plot, or at minimum, allowing it to proceed."

"Holy Father, if I may," Fortis interjected.

"Yes, my child," he said.

"Cardinal Macerata has been seen with Lloyd Bridgewater, whose mercenaries have been tracking Father Loyola and who attacked us at the Epoch of Martyrs compound on Thursday. Surely we can presume Macerata is directing the plot and not just letting it happen."

Loyola raised an eyebrow at her willingness to challenge the Holy Father, but said nothing. Maybe if he had been less deferential to authority ten years earlier, they wouldn't be in this mess.

"Perhaps we *could* presume," the pope replied. "But I will not. The picture is not yet complete, and there are still many moving parts."

Fortis nodded.

"The Bridgewater mercenaries are adequate muscle, but they're bulls in a china shop," Loyola said. "I don't think you could trust them with an assassination of this magnitude. You need someone willing to die for the cause."

"You suspect one of the military orders," the pope said.

"Current or former, yes," Loyola said. "Especially if it's going to happen at Midnight Mass. Saint Peter's Basilica will be packed with thousands of people for Christmas Eve. Anyone hoping to operate in that environment would have to know it intimately."

"There are four active military orders under the Vatican's supervision, and a handful that are not, such as the Epoch of Martyrs," Nicholas said. "Of these, only the Order of Saint Uriel has regular access to the Vatican and its secrets. There are twelve active-duty members of the Order, as per tradition, and perhaps twenty or thirty who are retired or who have transitioned to support roles."

"The active members are loyal," Fortis said, emphatically.

"There are other ways to learn the landscape," Loyola said.

"Be that as it may," Nicholas said. "I am loath to take chances. The jubilee door opens on Tuesday. We must be prepared to defend the ceremony."

"If Sister Belina is right and the active members are trustworthy, we should bring them in," Loyola said. "We can't do this alone."

"Sister Belina may or may not be right," the pope said, "but none of the twelve are in Rome at the moment except for her. Macerata may have arranged that. He has been running the Order as my deputy for decades, and I have only now been given reason to question his loyalty. If we summon the rest of the twelve, he will know."

"The Swiss Guard?" Loyola asked.

The Swiss Guard was the Vatican's security force. The Guard's members were elite military personnel, highly trained and very lethal. They dressed in suits and ties most of the time, akin to the American Secret Service, but on ceremonial occasions such as Christmas Eve, many of them would be decked out in absurdly colorful renaissance-style costumes, broad blue and gold stripes with red trim, including scarlet-plumed helmets.

"Cardinal Macerata plays an important role advising the Guard," Nicholas said. "At best, we should expect them to be leaky. At worst, some may be traitors. Either way, alerting the Guard almost certainly means warning our enemies."

He paused and locked his gaze with each of them in turn.

"There's a reason we're meeting here and not in the Vatican," he said. "The only people I trust are in this room."

Loyola wanted to urge the pontiff to step back from the public event, but he knew it would be pointless. Nicholas VI had served time in a Communist prison for his beliefs. He was not known for backing down in the face of threats.

Still.

"It's nearly impossible to defend Saint Peter's Basilica with just two people," Loyola said. "Especially with thousands of civilians in harm's way."

"Fifteen to twenty thousand in the church," Fortis said. "Tens of thousands more in the square. It's a nightmare scenario."

"We will have the usual security, and I can enhance it somewhat without attracting undue attention," Nicholas said. "And we have a full day to prepare. Use it. Scout the locations. I grant you free run of the city, but you must not be seen, or at least you must not be noticed. Macerata must not know you're here."

"A nun in the Vatican might as well be invisible," Fortis said in a perfectly uninflected tone, as if she was describing the weather.

"Perhaps," the pope said. "But Macerata will not fail to notice *you.*"

She acknowledged the point with a nod.

"Can we narrow down the possibilities?" the pope asked.

"We can probably rule out a bombing or a hit squad," Fortis said. "They will want to avoid anything that suggests a plot or conspiracy, anything that would prompt a lengthy investigation, anything with massive geopolitical ramifications, and anything that might complicate a conclave. They will want to make it look like mental illness or a grudge against the Church. That means a lone assassin."

"But it only needs to *look* lone," Loyola said. "We should assume they have access to discreet support personnel, and we should assume there's a backup plan if the first assassin can't get to the target. But they have to hide the size of the operation, so that will limit the support team's options."

"Meaning?" the pope asked.

"We can't just stop the first assassin," Loyola said. "We have to expose him. If we stop him without exposing him, if he aborts or escapes without taking his shot, they can switch to Plan B. We'll try to anticipate every possibility, but killing or apprehending the first assassin puts an end to the Christmas Eve threat, and hopefully gives us the evidence we need to get to Macerata. And once the shooter is down, we can call in the Swiss Guard. Even if some of them are compromised, they won't be able to wish away a general emergency call."

"We also need to expose them without exposing *you*," Fortis said to Loyola. "There are going to be cameras everywhere. There are a lot of Catholics in Boston, and a lot of them will be watching over the Internet. Some might even be here in person. You're already a local hero. It is imperative that you are not seen saving the pope on live TV."

"Haven't they moved on yet?" Loyola grumbled.

"You *will* keep a low profile," the pontiff said in a commanding tone. "The Order of Saint Uriel is one of the Vatican's most sensitive secrets, and any public scrutiny of the Order would have unimaginable consequences. Even my death would be preferable. You must stay out of sight. No further discussion is required."

"Yes, Holy Father," Loyola said, bowing his head.

"Back to strategy," Fortis said. "A sniper seems like the most obvious approach."

"Saint Peter's is huge," Loyola said, thinking aloud. "There are an almost endless number of places to situate a shooter. But they're limited by their need to avoid scrutiny. It can't be a miracle shot from a mile away, or hanging upside down from a zipline. A short-range snipe, or even better, a run-up. Someone with a knife or a handgun at close range, an attack that looks more lucky than smart."

"Almost anyone entering the square on Christmas Eve will have to go through scanners and metal detectors," Fortis said. "The best way to smuggle in a weapon would be to do it in advance."

"You have a lot of ground to cover," Nicholas said, standing up on stiff joints that belied his youthful personality. "Get an early start."

Loyola and Fortis stood as well.

"I'll secure the perimeter," she said, stepping into the hallway outside the apartment. "Give me five minutes."

"Of course," Nicholas said, straightening his red flannel as Fortis vanished. "This shirt is quite comfortable. I might need some of these for around the palace."

Loyola wasn't sure if this was another joke. He tried to look ambiguously amused.

"What do you think of your successor?" the pontiff asked.

"She's extremely formidable," Loyola said.

"She would have to be, wouldn't she?" Nicholas said. "How do you feel about a woman in the role? A modern-day Thecla to your Paul."

Loyola smiled at the reference. Of course, Paul and Thecla hadn't been killers. Or at least Thecla wasn't, and Paul had given it up.

"I've seen enough to believe she earned her place," he said. "And more importantly, I trust your judgment."

"Is she better than you?" the pontiff asked, with a smile.

"I couldn't say, Your Holiness," Loyola replied.

"Would she have refused the order to kill Mirsad?" the pope asked.

"I don't know," Loyola said. "Maybe."

"Anyone can pull a trigger," the pope said. "I need a killer with a conscience. That is one of many reasons that you have been sorely missed. I regret that I did not cultivate a closer relationship with you when you served as *primus sicarius*. If you were to come back, I can promise it would be different."

"Thank you, Holy Father," Loyola said. "But I'm done with this life. After this matter is concluded, I need to know God can find some other use for me."

"I will bless whatever you choose to do after this mission," Nicholas said.

"One last job," Fortis said, returning from the hallway. "Just like in the movies."

Loyola tried not to think about how those movies typically ended.

* * *

Rocha slept fitfully, too close to the surface, waking to grope for her phone every twenty minutes or so. The Signal message from Moussa finally arrived at three AM, jolting her into a fully alert, if highly enervated, state.

"A partial print found at the scene of a mass casualty cold case," Moussa wrote. "I would very much like to speak with the owner of that print."

The attached PDF, labeled "Garde-le-château, 2010," was a collection of police files written in French, which she couldn't read. Swearing, she Googled the title, and found a Wikipedia page, "The Garde-le-château massacre." It rang a bell.

She gasped as she read the overview, then tabbed back to the PDF, scrolling down until she found the pictures. They were horrific. No wonder she had remembered.

At least ninety people dead, although some bodies were in a state that made it hard to be sure. In one place, in one day.

Who the fuck was Father Francis Loyola?

Beloved parish priest. Former military chaplain.

Mass murderer?

Rocha returned to Signal and messaged Moussa. He responded immediately.

"You have my full attention now, Martina," he typed. "This guy must be a witness at least. Maybe something more? I can justify questioning him. Do you have a name?"

"I have several," she replied, typing a list of the aliases she had found on passports in Loyola's secret room. On an impulse, she withheld his real name. There was still the problem of her illegal search, and the fact she was under direct orders to drop the investigation. This was not the first time she had played fast and loose with procedures. If she was caught, it could be a career-ender.

"I can't tell you where I got these names," she wrote, "but they might be linked to the prints. Run them and see what you come up with. And please, Emil, keep this between us for now."

Emil sent a frowning emoji.

"I'll need some provenance to take action on this evidence," he said.

"I can't," she replied. "It's all off-book. If you can't do it, I'll understand."

"You will be the death of me," he replied, with a winking emoji. "Stay tuned."

CHAPTER
13

# Some Fucking Spaghetti

Saint Peter's Basilica was fractal, packed with exquisite and extraordinarily dense detail. Every floor, wall, ceiling, and column was adorned, inscribed, frescoed, or sculpted, and each element had layers of meaning and symbolism. The lives of hundreds of saints were depicted, each with their own unique elements and events, often witnessed by celestial beings. Ancient names and Latin words sat on faceplates, wrapping along borders, climbing pillars like ivy. Gold and silver could be found everywhere, from the delicate leaf filigree on a painting to heavy reliquaries the size of a large dog. Mortal remains were embedded and interred in the twenty-five altars and more than one hundred documented tombs within the church itself and in its two subterranean levels, the oldest dating all the way back to Saint Peter, the apostle and first pope.

You could spend an entire life exploring and never reach its limits.

Father Francis Loyola often felt he had barely scratched the surface, despite how much time he had spent there. It was impossible to miss the building's aura of infinite complexity, but a deeper understanding eluded him.

The statue of Saint Longinus was one of the church's many edifices. According to tradition, Longinus was the Roman centurion who stuck a lance into the side of Christ as he hung on the cross, then repented of the act, crying out "Truly this was the son of God." The statue depicted the moment Longinus came to his famous realization, the blasphemous spear still brandished in his hand, a look of sanctified wonder dawning on his face.

Loyola wondered what it must have been like, that epiphany, the sudden realization that he had witnessed the most important moment in human history.

Longinus was a soldier, and Loyola felt a certain affinity.

Behind the statue, a short flight of stairs led to the Vatican Grottoes, the first and most public underground chamber beneath the famous church, below the basilica proper and above a much older maze of catacombs.

Loyola followed Sister Belina Fortis down the stairs into a wide, well-lit hallway populated by tourists and lined with alcoves and chambers. A few steps beyond the entrance, they passed a small, simple chapel in honor of the Lady of Guadalupe with a reproduction of the miraculously created image associated with the sixteenth-century apparition—the Virgin's self-portrait, in a sense. The image depicted her with olive-tinted skin, in contrast to the blue-eyed Lady who had appeared in Medjugorje. Did the Lady continually remake herself in solidarity with those who witnessed her? Or did the people who saw her simply imagine her to be like them?

Loyola had no answers, but the icon was a sharp reminder of why they were here. He crossed himself, wondering if Fortis had chosen to use the public entrance precisely so they would pass by this chapel. He had little sense of what she thought about Mirsad and his visions, aside from skepticism. He had to admit he had very little insight into what she thought about anything.

Fortis led, but Loyola knew where they were going. As they progressed, the flamboyantly ornate architecture became simpler, giving way to cream-colored walls and a series of themed chapels, some behind wrought-iron gates, others cordoned off with velvet ropes. The tombs of popes were everywhere, many of them relatively humble markers.

They proceeded down the corridors, behind one of the velvet ropes, past a statue of Pope Pius VI kneeling in prayer, and through an unobtrusive service door that opened onto a rough, unfinished corridor, cool and damp. They picked up the pace, taking several turns that led to a heavy steel door secured by a keypad—distinctly unlike the antique locks found everywhere else in the basilica.

Fortis typed nine digits faster than he could track, and the door swung open to reveal the rarely used Papal Situation Room.

The chamber was much as he remembered it, although the equipment had been updated in the years since he visited. The square footage was similar to that of a high school gymnasium, but the space felt crypt-like and claustrophobic thanks to its low and vaulted ceiling, supported by pillars every twenty to thirty feet. Latin inscriptions covered nearly every surface, including prayers for God's guidance and admonitions against any force of evil that might interfere with the work of the Church.

An open space in the center of the room featured a circular table with workstations, surrounded by oversized freestanding computer monitors.

Fortis sat down at one of the workstations and activated several screens showing St. Peter's Square and Basilica from a dizzying array of angles. Loyola had always liked the view from here, because so much of the Vatican's art was invisible from normal vantage points. But this was not the time for sightseeing.

She deftly controlled the views, paging through shots of the highest elevations that a sniper might seek out, finding nothing but pigeons and seagulls.

"You're confident they won't try a long-distance shot?" Fortis said.

"I have absolute faith in God," Loyola said. "Everything else is open to discussion."

Fortis called up cameras that showed the topside of the massive colonnades that bordered Saint Peter's Square, where 140 larger-than-life statues of saints stood sentry on the roof. Most of them were completely inaccessible except from behind. Loyola wondered what it must have been like to sculpt these giants, knowing that the public would never get a good look at their faces, a miracle of craftsmanship visible only to God—at least until the invention of zoom photography.

Below, the square teemed with thousands of people, some tourists and others the stewards of the Church, preparing for Christmas Day.

"The Holy Father won't be outside during the Mass," Loyola said. "Whatever they're planning, it'll have to take place inside."

"He'll be on the balcony Christmas Day," Fortis said.

"The prophecy said that the assassination would take place at the start of the jubilee year," Loyola said. "That means during the Mass, probably very close to the unsealing of the Holy Door. We should focus our efforts there."

"You believe this prophecy?" Fortis asked, and he again detected skepticism.

"Macerata does," Loyola said, "or he would have acted before now. He withheld the prophecy from the Holy Father for nearly a decade, and he's repeatedly tried to take Mirsad out of the equation. No reason to do any of that unless he believes. And if he believes, he'll follow the script."

"The Holy Father didn't say whether the prophecy described a *successful* assassination," Fortis said. "Not when talking to me earlier, and not when telling you about it."

"Yeah," Loyola said. He had noticed that as well, but he saw no point in dwelling on it. Prophecy or not, predestination or not, the job was unchanged—spare no effort within the reach of human striving to save the Holy Father.

Fortis returned to the keyboard, and the monitors reconfigured to show the interior of the basilica from dozens of different angles. A few clicks of the mouse, and the monitor directly in front of them revealed several views of the Holy Door. After the pope opened the door, he would lead a procession past Michelangelo's marble masterpiece of pain and sorrow, the *Pietà*, depicting the Virgin Mary cradling her son's lifeless body after it was taken down from the cross.

"The best defense is to stay close," Loyola said. "I should be part of the procession. I can wait for him to make his move, then head it off."

"We're keeping you off TV, remember?" Fortis said, exasperated.

"I could wear a disguise," Loyola said.

"Uh huh," Fortis said. "Or I'll dress like a man and do it. Let's try to stay focused."

She switched the view on the monitor to show the nave.

"Picture him walking up the aisle with five thousand people on each side," she said.

"Once he's past the jubilee door, the next best time to strike will be during the Mass, when the Holy Father will be mostly stationary," Loyola said. "Seated, or at the lectern, or at the altar."

Fortis called up the cameras that covered the main altar.

"The high-ground options are limited," she said. "You can go up the many, many stairs to the top of the cupola dome, but I don't see how you can get a shot from that angle. A bomb could bring the dome down, but that would result in a lot of collateral damage and a major international investigation."

"If the idea is to pass this off as the work of a lone nut, the assassin needs to be captured or killed, quickly and cleanly identified with a backstory of mental illness," Loyola said. "A bomb in the dome doesn't get us there."

"There are the reliquary balconies," Fortis said, pointing at the screen.

The main altar was surrounded by four massive pillars, known as piers, with statues at their bases and hollow interiors. The statue of Saint Longinus was one. The others commemorated Saints Veronica, Helen, and Andrew. Interior stairways led down to the grottoes and up to balconies that housed some of the church's most sacred and important relics—the spear of Longinus, pieces of the True Cross, and more. All four balconies faced the altar.

"Great vantage point for a sniper," Loyola said, running his hand over his face as he thought through scenarios. "Pretty exposed, but thanks to the layout, no one would be able to rush you before you take the shot."

"The relics are protected by motion detectors," Fortis said. "Doesn't leave much time to get into position and make the shot before someone comes to check."

"We should check for any signs of tampering," Loyola said. "But my gut says it's too tricky."

"All these options are too tricky," Fortis said. "It's not an easy mission."

She toggled various views of the main altar, and they stared in silence for a while.

"If not high ground, what about low ground," Loyola said, pointing at one of the cameras displayed on the screen.

Directly in front of the main altar was the *Confessio* of Saint Peter, an open, sunken chamber at the level of the grottos, above where Saint Peter's bones were interred in the necropolis below. The *Confessio* was ornate and resplendent, filled with art and valuables, and surrounded by ninety-five brass lamps affixed to a heavy marble railing. The space was accessible to the church via a short flight of steps in front, but locked gates connected it to the grottoes on the left and the right sides. A glass-paneled viewing area in the center, beneath the stairs and accessible through the grotto, offered a view but no access.

"Someone could slip through one of those gates during the Mass without being seen," Loyola said. "Maybe."

He pointed at the main lectern, which was directly in front of the *Confessio.*

"Clear close range shot right there," he said. "During the homily."

Fortis nodded.

"But look at this, too," she said, pointing. "During the readings, the Holy Father will be seated here, right in front of the statue of Saint Longinus, with another entrance to the grotto right behind him."

"Good place to stage a run-up," Loyola said. "Very John Wilkes Booth."

"The grottos will be locked up and closed to the public during the Mass," Fortis said, "but there are plenty of places to hide down here, and plenty of places to hide weapons."

"The locks are ancient," Loyola said. "A ten-year-old with a multitool could beat them."

"There are two doors to the *Confessio*, plus the door to the grotto behind Saint Longinus, and grotto doors behind the other three pillars for good measure," Fortis said. "That's a lot of territory for two people to cover."

"Does Macerata have access to these cameras?" Loyola asked.

"Quite possibly," Fortis said.

"Can you replace the live feed with a looped recording while we investigate? We don't want him to see us poking around."

"Give me a couple minutes," she replied, launching into a flurry of keystrokes.

* * *

"He's in Rome," Moussa said on Rocha's Zoom screen. "I matched a credit card to one of the aliases you sent me."

"Son of a bitch," Rocha said. "Who the fuck is this guy?"

"Who indeed?" Moussa said. "Why won't you tell me where this information came from? I looked up your recent cases on Google, and I think I have a guess."

Rocha was alone in her apartment, but she leaned in close to the monitor as if someone might hear.

"Illegal search," she whispered. "I could get fired. I could go to jail."

Moussa massaged the bridge of his nose.

"Garde-le-château is the most important unsolved cold case in our files," Moussa said. "If this guy knows something about it, I want to interview him. But he must be dangerous. You've met him, yes?"

"For the sake of argument, let's say I have," Rocha said.

"Would he speak with you?" Moussa asked. "He's an American, so I'm worried he'll *shoot first and ask questions later*," he said, making a finger gun and drawling in what he must have hoped was an approximation of an American accent.

"Maybe," she said, with a thin smile. "I don't know. We talked for like ten minutes on one occasion, and he was probably lying for most of it."

"I can second you to Interpol for a few days," Moussa said. "I don't need to have the whole case locked down. But he's in Rome now, and I don't want to wait. I can put the request in today. *Immédiatement*."

"I don't know," she said. "My boss is itching to stick it to me."

"*Merde*, then call in sick," Moussa said. "I'll pay for your flight myself if I have to. Just get here, and we'll figure how to justify it later. As your people say, better to beg for forgiveness, *oui*?"

"I have always lived by that principle," Rocha laughed.

"Christmas in Rome, what could be finer?" Moussa said. "And perhaps we will unwrap a mass murderer. Get on the next plane. I will pick you up at the airport."

* * *

Loyola and Fortis checked the reliquary balconies first, finding no signs of tampering, then proceeded to investigate the grottoes, starting with the lavishly decorated brass gates that led to the *Confessio* of Saint Peter. The north gate was locked but with some give. It clanked and squealed loudly when Loyola tested it. The south gate also clanked but didn't squeal.

Loyola ran a finger along one of the hinges, and it came away slick.

"WD-40," he said, sniffing.

"We have a winner," Fortis replied.

They spent most of the rest of the day searching the grottoes for concealed weapons. The process was painstakingly slow, due to their need for discretion, and the fact that many prospective hiding places were off-limits. There was no discreet way to pop open the lid of a papal sarcophagus.

As they worked, they quietly exchanged ideas about other avenues of attack, trying to make sure they hadn't missed anything.

"Poison?" Loyola asked. "Something that would look natural?"

"The only thing ingested during the Mass would be the communion bread and wine, and it would be ingested by multiple people," Fortis said. "We're assuming they don't want a body count."

"Fire?" he said. "Make it look like an accident?"

"Fire isn't a very surgical weapon," she said. "Even if they're extremely clever, there's no way to be sure it reaches the target."

"Pressure-triggered microexplosive?"

"A landmine? In Saint Peter's? Are you serious?" Fortis said. "I can't imagine how you could install one in his path without being detected, and then you also have to worry about someone walking over it first."

In the end, they found nothing and came up with nothing.

"Does it matter if we find the weapon?" she asked. "We know where they're going to strike. We just need to be there to stop it from happening."

"Sounds simple," Loyola said. "That's why I don't like it. I still think I should be near the Holy Father. I can be ready for anything that way."

"We've been over this," Fortis said, rolling her eyes. "Be less famous next time."

With no comeback readily available, he moved on to practical matters.

"Can we get the cameras on a portable device?" he asked. "Phone or tablet?"

"I can probably arrange that," she said.

"We'll need to be concealed," he said. "If we stop him too soon, they'll go to Plan B, and then we're cooked, because we don't know what Plan B is."

"How do you see this playing out?" she asked.

"Before Mass starts, we hide in the grotto near the gates to the *Confessio*," he said. "Lights off or down, which shouldn't raise eyebrows, since it's supposed to be closed."

"Booby-trap on the *Confessio* door?" she asked.

"Good idea," he said. "Let's do it. Beyond that, we need to cover our asses in case we've read this wrong."

"I can put discreet motion detectors in the nearby hallways, and we can track them on our phones," she said.

"Good," he said. "What other gear should we have?"

"Nothing exotic or too 'professional,' just in case we're detected by bystanders, killed in the line of duty, or arrested by the Swiss Guard," she said. "Sidearm of choice. Knives. Pepper spray. Taser, if you like, or a baton."

"So, no grenades," Loyola deadpanned.

"No grenades, no assault rifles, no night vision, no body armor, no acid, no napalm, no trained crocodiles," she said. "And try not to damage any of the literally priceless relics and artworks stuffed into every inch of our surroundings."

"The cameras will record everything," Loyola said.

"Monsignor Biancardi can take care of cleanup and info ops," Fortis said. "As always. Let's stay focused on the task at hand."

Loyola had never really liked Biancardi, but he appreciated the monsignor's work, especially in the wake of missions that went sideways. The Vatican's active measures operation always found a reasonable explanation—even for Loyola's latest entanglements.

"Fine," Loyola said. "The killer shows up, we stop him. Once he's subdued, we call in the Swiss Guard on an open radio channel. The conspirators will have someone monitoring the main frequencies. They hear that he's busted, they shut it down. Biancardi cleans up. We remain on alert just in case."

"If the assassin spots us and flees?"

"It's imperative that we put him down before he gets away," Loyola said. "If he escapes in any kind of shape to signal his withdrawal, they can go to Plan B."

"Agreed," Fortis said. "It ends here. By any means necessary."

"Anything else we can do now?" Loyola asked.

"I think we've got this," Fortis said, in an uneasy tone. "Right?" Loyola was caught off guard. It was the first time she had allowed him to see anything but overwhelming self-confidence.

"My luck hasn't been running great lately," Loyola said, meeting her frankness with his own.

"We don't need luck," Fortis said, shaking it off. "We have faith. But say your prayers just in case. I'd feel better if we knew what Plan B was."

"We've been at this all day," Loyola said. "We've covered as much physical territory as we can. If we were going to figure out the other line of attack, we would have by now. Maybe there isn't one."

"I hope *this* isn't Plan B," she said gesturing toward the *Confessio*.

Loyola shrugged away the icy finger of doubt that her comment prompted.

"Me too," he said.

* * *

When he got back to the apartment, after dark, Loyola checked his digital dead drop and found a new message waiting.

*What's a man have to do to get some fucking spaghetti in this town?*

A phone number was attached.

A rush of feelings came over him. Frustration at his friend for not taking time to recuperate. Annoyance at the distraction. Then, finally, relief. The number of people Loyola could trust in Rome had just increased to three.

He texted *Piazza de Popolo* to the phone number, splashed some cold water on his face and went out. The *piazza* was a ten-minute cab ride away, but Loyola walked, attempting to center himself in the cool night air. The streets were busy but less buzzy than usual. The *taverne* were relatively empty, their customary patrons instead flitting from shop to shop, searching for last-minute Christmas provisions.

Loyola found Calvin Coll lost in thought, staring at the seventy-foot obelisk that stood lonely in the center of the square. He didn't seem to notice Loyola's approach, but he spoke without turning his head.

"Why is it covered with hieroglyphics?" Coll asked.

"Emperor Augustus had it shipped here from Egypt around 1 BC," Loyola said. "Spoils of the war with Cleopatra, if I remember correctly."

"Cultural appropriation," Coll said, shaking his head solemnly.

"Would it help if I told you Cleopatra was Greek?"

"Fuck no," Coll said. "That's worse!"

He turned toward Loyola. The entire left side of his face was raw, and his eye was covered by a heavy bandage. Loyola winced but did not look away. The wound was his responsibility.

"What are you doing here, Cal?" he asked. "I'm sure the doctors didn't clear you to travel looking like that."

"I'm here for my boy," Coll said. "Simple as that. And spaghetti."

They left the square, walking a short distance to a homey restaurant called Rollo Pollo, a favorite of Loyola's from years gone by. The owner recognized him—Loyola was still wearing his cassock and collar—and escorted them to a semiprivate corner table in the rear of the establishment. His show of hospitality was darkened only by his clear disapproval that neither man was interested in ordering wine to accompany their dinner. As they waited for the food, Loyola filled Coll in on what had happened since they last met.

"The main thing is Mirsad is as safe as he can be for now," Loyola said. "After tomorrow, I don't see why the conspirators would need him anymore."

Coll frowned, then winced as the movement pulled at his bandages.

"These guys think the visions are real," Coll said. "They're never going to stop coming for him."

"Hopefully we're going to take out the whole operation," Loyola said. "We stop the assassination, get the clearest possible picture of the conspiracy, then go after the masterminds. Mirsad can be protected here, or if you want to take him home, I'll do everything I can to arrange for security."

"Catholic security," Coll scoffed.

"I can work outside the Order on this if you prefer," Loyola said. "Up to a point."

"Uh-huh," Coll said. "And if he decides he wants to stay here?"

"The Order can protect him," Loyola said. "That is by far the safest option."

"Motherfucker, the Order can't protect the pope, how are they going to protect Mirsad?" Coll asked.

"We haven't failed the pope," Loyola said.

"Yet," Coll said.

Loyola shrugged. He wasn't above lying in the line of duty, but he wouldn't lie to Coll. Anything could happen tomorrow, and they both knew it.

"Moving Mirsad tonight is too risky," Loyola said. "As of now, it's possible they don't even know he's here. After tomorrow, you can talk to him and decide how to handle things going forward. But I don't think we should move him before then."

"What happens if you get killed when this thing goes down?" Coll asked.

"Sister Belina will help you," Loyola said.

"Is that so?" Coll asked.

"I'll make sure she knows," Loyola said. "And the Holy Father. If they want my help tomorrow, and my silence thereafter, that's the price. Mirsad gets to talk to you, and he gets to decide his own future. No games. No conditions."

Coll stared at him for a long while, his one eye somehow more intense than ever, perhaps making up for its lost twin.

"All right," he said finally. "Don't let me down, Frank."

"I won't," Loyola said. "I swear it."

"The safest thing for Mirsad is taking these assholes down," Coll said. "So how can I help?"

"You're in no condition to work the field," Loyola said. "But I could really use you in the chair, on cameras and comms."

"Done," Coll said.

After dinner, they parted ways. Coll's hotel was a short distance from the restaurant, and he looked exhausted.

"Sleep as late as you need to," Loyola said. "Text me when you're ready."

Loyola walked along the Tiber River on his way back to the apartment. As he turned to cross the bridge, he paused to admire the cupola of Saint Peter's where it loomed over the surrounding structures in the middle distance. Whatever strange road had brought him back to Rome, he hoped that tomorrow would be the end of it. But a nagging instinct refused to let him draw consolation from the thought.

"Penny for your thoughts," came a voice from behind him.

He turned with a highly disciplined calm to meet the gaze of Sister Belina Fortis, unwilling to give her the satisfaction of seeing him jump.

"Thinking I need a long vacation," he said. "You?"

"I was just wondering why you would risk operational security by briefing a civilian about our incredibly sensitive plans," she said.

"The question implies I trust you more than him," Loyola said.

"You don't trust me?" she said. "Still?"

"You're spying on me," Loyola said. "I wasn't spying on you."

"I wasn't spying on you," she said. "I was spying on *him.* I set up an alert on his bank cards, and I saw he was in town. I wanted to make sure he wasn't going to do anything stupid. Good thinking on my part, as it turns out."

"If you were listening, then you know I want him in the chair tomorrow," Loyola said. "You and I can only cover so much ground. We need someone to monitor the cameras and manage communications."

"The Vatican's security and surveillance systems are a tightly guarded secret," Fortis said. "He's not even Catholic."

Loyola rolled his eyes, and Fortis laughed.

"Fair enough," she said. "Our worst enemies are Catholic at the moment. But still, it's a big ask."

"It's a big job," Loyola said. "But there's no one else in Rome we can trust."

She sighed.

"If it goes south, I'm blaming you," she said.

"If it goes south, it won't matter," Loyola said. "The new pope will come after us first. And he can't kill us any deader than dead."

"He could excommunicate us," she said. "One-way ticket to hell."

"There are rules," Loyola said. "It would be invalid in the eyes of God. Probably."

"Oh, well, *probably*," she replied. "That's OK then."

"A little faith, Sister," Loyola said.

"And a whole lot of luck, Father," Fortis replied, disappearing into the night.

CHAPTER

14

# Oh, How They Pound

ROCHA TORE OUT of her apartment and drove to the airport with a flashing siren magnetically clamped to the top of her car. She got the last available seat on the last flight of the evening, packed with holiday travelers seeking to welcome Christmas Eve in Rome. It was a middle seat in the rear of the plane, impossibly small, wedged between two people who were not especially small. The flight was too warm, the food was terrible, her seat wouldn't recline. She was jacked up with adrenalin and couldn't sleep, although she managed a sort of prolonged doze.

At the crack of dawn, Rome time, Moussa picked her up at the airport in a rented Volkswagen Golf, and they drove straight to Loyola's short-term apartment, just outside the walls of Vatican City, which had been rented with a credit card under the name Jonas Wojtek, an alias that appeared on one of his passports. The curtains were drawn, but not opaque. She could see that a light was on inside.

They parked in front of an espresso bar a few yards away so Rocha could caffeinate and try to clear her pounding head. She wished she had insisted on going to a hotel first, as she had a growing sense that her travel clothes were not just rumpled but ripe. At least they could sit outside while she drank her Americano. A small handful of early-morning patrons loitered in low-key conversation, old men smoking cigarettes, with newspapers tucked under their arms. The light was tentative and cloudy gray, the air cool and damp. Her hoodie had been too warm on the plane but was now too thin to keep the chill out.

"What's our jurisdiction here?" Rocha asked.

"I got us added to the Interpol Major Event Support Team, which is assisting with security for Midnight Mass," Moussa said, sliding her a badge that said IMEST in big block letters. "They provide mostly data-related support, running IDs and fingerprints through our database, checking vehicles, and so forth. The two of us are, as they say, 'surplus to requirements,' although if a security incident breaks out, we might be called on to help. If we have to go into the Vatican, we should be able to move freely through the checkpoints."

"Can we arrest 'Wojtek'?" she asked. Moussa had signaled that he understood the situation, but Loyola's true name had not yet been spoken between them.

"We do not have that authority," Moussa said. "We would have to ask the *Carabinieri* to make the arrest, or the Vatican police, if he's inside the walls."

Rocha frowned.

"The Vatican might be caught up in . . . whatever this is," she said.

"'Whatever this is' brings us to the other problem," Moussa said. "Unless you're holding out, we do not yet have a crime to accuse him of. The illegality of your search means we can't prosecute him for forging identity papers. With respect to Garde-le-château, he can at best be described as a person of interest. We are a long way from arresting anyone."

The partial print matched to Loyola had been found on an unidentifiable fragment of metal outside a devastating blast site at Garde-le-château. A full set of prints had been found on a discarded stiletto that had been used to kill at least a dozen victims, but those did not match Loyola. If they had, things would be simpler.

Rocha conceded the point, grumpily.

"Other than the document forgeries, are you even confident that he has committed a crime?" Moussa asked.

There was little point in continuing to hold out. Rocha gave him a short summary of her investigation so far, including the parking lot shootout, the Medjugorje connection, and the apparent public relations clean-up measures of one Monsignor Gasparo Biancardi.

"Everywhere Loyola goes, a body count follows," she said. "He has a connection to Medjugorje. He has a secret panel in his bedroom closet hiding cash, illegal guns, and fake passports. Normal people don't keep a stash like that. Criminals do."

"So 'person of interest,'" Moussa said, gently.

"Fine, yes," she replied sharply. "You flew me out here. You must think there's something more going on here."

"What I think and what I can prove are two different things," Moussa said. "Thus we investigate. Unless you want to inform the Vatican that we suspect an imminent threat to the Holy Father. That's the only way I can see to escalate this without more proof. But the Vatican has been cleaning up after this guy, or so you believe. Alerting them to our interest may be the same thing as alerting him."

"Can we search the apartment?" she asked.

"No," he said. "We have two lawful options. We can go knock on his door and ask him what he's up to, or we can wait to see where he goes."

"I say we knock," Rocha said.

"But if he sees you, he will put together that you've searched his place in Boston," Moussa said. "He'll burn the alias he's currently using and get a clean one, and there goes our best chance of tracking his activities."

She wanted to argue, but . . .

"Also, this body count you mentioned, I prefer not to be added to it," he added.

"Why do you have to be so fucking reasonable?" Rocha grumbled.

"There are limits to my reasonableness," Moussa said. "Or you would not be sitting here. If we can get something on him, you can take it home and use it to get a search warrant. But for now, we can't let him see you. So keep your hood up. Do you have sunglasses? Good. Put them on. There's no sun, but hopefully he'll just think you're hungover. No offense, but you kind of look the part."

Flipping him off, Rocha took out her phone and scrolled with as much gravitas as she could muster, as if she were reviewing case files, but it was just TikTok.

* * *

Rocha was on her third coffee when she saw Loyola emerge from the rental, and her nerves were so jangled with caffeine that she worried she would levitate out of her seat. He had added a few days' worth of beard since she saw him last, but he was dressed as a priest, and his craggy features were unmistakable. Fortunately, he crossed the street immediately, walking along the city wall to the arched entrance of the Vatican Museums. Once inside, they were bound to lose him. She started to rise from her seat, but Moussa put a hand on her arm.

"Whatever he may be, an amateur he is not," Moussa said. "We must tread carefully."

When Loyola was completely past the threshold, they made their move. The museum was closed for the holiday, but Moussa flashed his ID, and they got in without challenge, skipping the metal detectors and X-ray machines.

As they passed through the gate, she was hit with a blast of sensory overload, not just the art and ornamentation, but people everywhere—not just people, but priests, dozens of men dressed exactly like Loyola, all striding purposefully in one direction or another.

But Loyola's gait was slightly different from the rest, like a boxer or a dancer. He was always pitched slightly forward, his balance skewed toward the balls of his feet rather than his heels, ready to change direction or velocity at a moment's notice. It was a subtle tell, but unmistakable once you noticed it.

Rocha grabbed Moussa's arm and silently directed his gaze. They followed at a great distance, as the priest weaved confidently through the corridors, like he had been there a thousand times before.

* * *

Emerging from the Museum, Loyola walked a long ambit through the city to approach the basilica through Saint Peter's Square, so he could scan the preparations and security perimeters. It was packed with busy people, at least a thousand, a tiny fraction of the crowds yet to come. The people were distributed in clumps and clusters. Electricians on ladders checked the twenty thousand lights on the eighty-foot tree that towered over the scene, matching the height of the obelisk in the center of the square. Beneath the tree was a massive nativity scene, serving as backdrop to a choir of twenty-some boys rehearsing the "Carol of the Bells."

*Hark! How the bells, sweet silver bells*
*All seem to say, "Throw cares away"*
*Christmas is here, bringing good cheer*
*To young and old, meek and the bold*
*Ding, dong, ding, dong, that is their song*
*With joyful ring, all caroling*
*One seems to hear, words of good cheer*

The song's accelerating tempo and escalating scale pounded into Loyola's brain, a metronomic earworm of steadily increasing tension, as he crossed the square and headed toward the basilica entrance.

*From everywhere, filling the air*
*Oh, how they pound, raising the sound*

It reminded Loyola of a frenetic old poem that had lodged itself in his head for unhappy weeks when he was in high school.

*Keeping time, time, time,*
*In a sort of Runic rhyme,*
*To the tintinabulation that so musically wells*
*From the bells, bells, bells, bells,*
*Bells, bells, bells—*

On the whole, he would have preferred "Silent Night."

He scanned the square again. In the distance, back the way he came, too far to make out faces, almost too far to bother with at all, two figures caught his eye. He'd glimpsed them in the museum, he realized, and they had been on the far edge of his perception then as well. And perhaps he had passed them on the street before that?

The Vatican was his home turf, and its crowded and elaborate halls were dizzying even for frequent visitors. Losing them would not be a problem, even if they were professionals. But their mere presence was worrisome. No one was supposed to know he was here. And they had apparently been following him for a while.

Despite the frenzy of the past week, his instincts were still rusty, and his limitations presented a danger—not only to himself but to the Holy Father.

He had to do better.

*Oh, how they pound, raising the sound*
*Oh, how they pound, raising the sound*
*Oh, how they pound, raising the sound*

* * *

In the Papal Situation Room, he found Coll and Fortis embedded. Coll was seated at a workstation, already up to speed with the controls, flicking windows and camera views around the array of monitors faster than Loyola could take in their contents. Despite his adept handling, Loyola could see small movements of his head and neck, signs that Coll had not adjusted to the loss of an eye. Loyola worried that his friend was not up for this, but it was too late to change course.

"Everything cool here?" Loyola asked, cautiously.

"All's well," Coll said. "We reached an understanding. She'll kill me if I fuck up the Vatican, and I'll kill her if anything happens to Mirsad."

"Seems fair," Loyola said. "Sister Belina, have you checked on Mirsad today?"

"Of course," she said. "He said the Lady had a message for you. 'Beware the guardian of the castle.'"

"What's that mean?" Loyola said. "A reference to Macerata? Do we have to worry about the Swiss Guard?"

Fortis shrugged. Loyola looked at Coll.

"No idea," Coll said. "Lady doesn't say shit to me, never has. But Mirsad did ask Sister Belina to tell me he was sorry for all the trouble he caused. If you ask me, the Lady oughta told him it's not his fault. If she was real, she would. Tell me I'm wrong."

"Did you tell Mirsad that Cal was here?" Loyola asked.

"Nope," Fortis said.

The music swelled on repeat in Loyola's brain.

*Gaily they ring, while people sing*
*Songs of good cheer, Christmas is here*
*Merry, merry, merry, merry Christmas*
*Merry, merry, merry, merry Christmas*

He shook his head in an effort to dislodge it.

"Where are we at?" he asked.

"We got gear," Coll said, gesturing at an encrypted portable radio rig on the desk in front of him. Fortis gave each of them a tiny earbud so discreet that most observers would never spot it. Loyola was familiar with the technology. The microphone pointed into the ear canal, able to detect even the quietest of whispers by capturing the vibrations they created in the bones of the skull. It slipped securely into place.

Coll handed Loyola and Fortis clean encrypted phones from a cabinet in the back of the situation room.

"Vocal comms will be on radio only," he said. "These are only for video—if I need you to see something, or if you need me to see it."

Loyola nodded.

"What's the situation upstairs?" he asked.

"Lots of activity," Coll said, waving at the monitors, all filled with motion. "Too much to keep track of it all, but no glaring red flags so far. Did you know there's a fucking coffee shop on the roof of the church? Who comes up with this shit?"

"Can you play back these streams?" he asked Coll.

"Sure," Coll said. "What do you want to see?"

"About fourteen minutes ago, the square. Northeast corner. Two people, one male, one female. The woman is wearing a peach-colored hoodie and sunglasses. The man's in a beige trench coat."

"Hang on," Coll said, as the images zipped into fast-forward. "These two?"

"That's them," Loyola said. "They were following me." Glancing over Coll's shoulder as he zoomed in on the image, Fortis sat down at a nearby workstation and unleashed a furious flurry of keystrokes. Loyola was surprised the keyboard didn't catch fire. He looked at the image Coll had isolated.

"I don't know the man," Loyola said. "The woman looks vaguely familiar. Do we have other angles?"

Fortis flicked a series of images onto one of the monitors, following the two back through the surveillance grid. In one of them, the woman had taken her sunglasses off so that she could rub at her eyes.

*"Shit,"* Loyola said.

"I don't like the sound of that," Coll said.

"She's the Boston cop who investigated the sniper attack at my home parish," Loyola said. "Martina Rocha."

"I like that even less," Coll said. "Is the guy from Boston too?"

Fortis called up an image of the two entering the Vatican Museum. The man was waving a badge at the security guards manning the main gates.

"Interpol," Fortis said, unleashing another burst of typing. "Moussa. French. He's assigned to IMEST for Midnight Mass. Looks like Rocha has been seconded to IMEST, too, both as of last night."

"Can you get them unassigned?" Loyola asked.

"Not without raising a lot of questions," Fortis said. "Questions that would look even worse if the attack on the pope goes forward. What does she have on you?"

"She shouldn't have anything," Loyola said. "Monsignor Biancardi cleaned up after the attack. She should have just dropped it."

"Did you leave any evidence?" she asked.

"I had a stash in a hidden panel in my bedroom closet," Loyola said, shifting uncomfortably. "But she would have had no reason to go looking. I was the victim, not the perp. And the case should have been kicked out of her jurisdiction."

"Does anything in the stash lead here?" Fortis asked.

"My one clean credit card," Loyola said, even more unhappily. "I didn't have time to go back and retrieve the matching passport."

"Well, she's here now," Coll said. "And they were clearly tailing you. Whatever the reason, that's one more piece of shit in our sandwich. Is it possible they have backup?"

"Anyone else from Boston on the IMEST Team?"

Click click click.

"I don't see anyone," Fortis said. "No other late additions either."

"Do we currently have eyes on Rocha and Moussa?" Loyola asked.

"They're in the square," Coll said. "They look like they're still looking for you."

"Where's Macerata?" Loyola asked.

"He's been staying at the hotel," Fortis said, the *Domus Sanctae Marthae*. Mirsad was housed there as well, hopefully as far from Macerata as possible.

"Has anyone come or gone?" Loyola asked.

"We only got set up a little before you arrived," Coll said.

Fortis called up a hallway view, centered on a closed door.

"This is his room," she said.

"How far back does the tape go?" Loyola asked.

"Twenty-four hours," she said, rewinding. Except for a room service breakfast, no one had been to the room this morning. She continued reversing into the evening. At around 8:15 PM, a heavyset older man in a cassock emerged from the room. She paused the video so they could get a better look at him, then Loyola and Fortis spoke simultaneously.

"Biancardi!"

"Oh yeah, Biancardi," said Coll. "That explains everything. I have just one question. Who the f—"

"He does information operations for the Vatican," Loyola interjected. "You will recall the cover story for our first visit to Medjugorje. He's the guy who comes up with it, and if necessary, manufactures evidence to support it. He's a disinformation artist who cleaned up a lot of my messes back in the day."

"He would normally work with Macerata then," Coll said. "Right? It's not necessarily suspicious that he paid a call."

"Not necessarily," Loyola said. "Except for the timing."

"We just made a second big mess in Medjugorje," Coll said.

"True," Loyola said. Fortis had resumed rewinding. At 7:37 PM, another man exited the room—a layman in a business suit.

"Lloyd Bridgewater," Fortis said. "Macerata and Biancardi might have legitimate business together, but if Biancardi is also covering up for Bridgewater, that makes him part of the conspiracy."

"Has to be," Loyola said, itching at his beard. "That's bad news for us. We've been operating from a presumption that the conspirators will be operating in high stealth mode. If they have Biancardi on board, they still won't have *carte blanche*, but it definitely expands the range of possibilities. He wouldn't be able to paper over the pope being killed, but he could smooth over a lot of inconvenient details. So we might be looking at a bigger team, or a more aggressive team. We need to rethink our preparations."

Fortis continued rewinding.

"I want to see if they entered together," she said.

When the time-stamp wound back to 7:15 PM, another man emerged from the room—a monk dressed in the robes of the Benedictine order. He was raising his monastic cowl over his balding head, but his gray-bearded face was clearly visible.

"Who is that?" Coll asked.

"I don't know him," Fortis said.

"I do," Loyola said, nausea sweeping over him. "It's Konstantin Stefanidis. A former member of the Order of Saint Uriel."

*Beware the guardian of the castle . . .*

In French, *garde-le-château.*

Loyola had not given the abbot a second thought since leaving his monastery in Plainfield, Massachusetts. If he were here . . . with Bridgewater and Macerata and Biancardi . . .

Bridgewater's goons had picked Loyola up soon after he left Plainfield. Deacon hadn't betrayed him after all—Stefanidis must have put a tracker in his car.

"Stefanidis had the skills to become *primus sicarius*," Loyola said. "The Holy Father declined to elevate him because he believed Stefanidis was motivated by a love for violence more than love for God."

"That's bad, right?" Coll said. "That sounds bad."

"He's one of the most dangerous men I've ever met," Loyola said.

Fortis silently backed the video up. All three men entered the room together at six PM sharp, welcomed by Macerata.

"That's it," Fortis said. "That's the conspiracy."

"We've run right out of luck," Loyola said grimly. "It's down to prayer now."

He took a deep breath and began to tell the story.

CHAPTER

15

# The Garde-le-château Affair, 2010

"YOU ARE FAMILIAR with the Cathar heresy," Cardinal Macerata said.

Loyola nodded. Catharism was a gnostic heresy of the Middle Ages. Based in France, the Cathars had challenged Catholic doctrine with respect to the Trinity and the Sacraments. While Church historians did not entirely agree about the details, the Cathars were said to have favored a sort of sacramental euthanasia for the aged and infirm, known as the *Consolamentum*. The sect also accused Rome of immorality and corruption, which made them popular with the local aristocracy.

Cutting to the chase, they made a lot of powerful enemies.

In 1209, Pope Innocent III declared a bloody crusade to suppress the heresy and later dispatched the Inquisition to finish the job. By the fifteenth century, the original sect had been almost completely eradicated. Historians outside the Church, and even a few inside it, described the campaign as one of the most successful genocides in human history.

The story was not Loyola's favorite, and he was grateful that the Church had repudiated such practices under Pope John Paul II. While Loyola's assignments often pertained to heresy in one way or another, he had never been assigned to kill on the basis of simple belief. There had always been a complicating factor.

In this case, the complicating factor was extreme.

A sect claiming to be modern-day Cathars had been quietly recruiting on college campuses for several years, attracting adherents with impressive technical skills to support a demented program to create the Four Horsemen of the Apocalypse and thus bring about the End Times. About one hundred neo-Cathar adherents had taken up residence at Garde-le-château, an abandoned medieval fortress at the top of an improbably steep mountain in France's Languedoc region, where a small team of biochemists were close to summoning the First Horseman, Plague, in the form of a weaponized virus, deadly and highly contagious.

"Our intelligence is limited," Macerata said. "We don't know whether all these neo-Cathars are directly committed to the millenarian goals of the leadership. The plague research is compartmentalized. Only a handful of people know about it, even at the site. You will have to assess the situation on the ground prior to taking any action."

"Is the compound protected by a military order?" Loyola asked. He wasn't a historian, but he recalled that the Cathars had been blamed for the assassination of church figures back in the day.

"They have security, but we don't have good visibility," Macerata said. "It might be quite pedestrian, or it might be formidable. This is one of several reasons we have assigned this task to you rather than working with the French authorities. The laboratory, all materials therein, and everyone working directly on the program must be sanitized. Nothing and no one can be permitted to escape. There is no room for error."

"I understand, Your Eminence," Loyola said, bowing his head.

"Another question, less pressing but of interest, is whether this group has any real connection to the historical Cathar heresy," Macerata said. "To make this determination, I have assigned a member of the Dicastery for the Doctrine of the Faith to accompany you on this mission in order to collect intelligence."

Loyola frowned. The Dicastery for the Doctrine of the Faith was the modern name for an office associated with infamy—the Inquisition, an institution originally founded to crush the Cathars, as it happened. While it seemed unlikely that such an ancient enmity could be relevant today, Loyola didn't like the resonances, and he didn't like working with partners he hadn't personally vetted.

"Your Eminence, I must respectfully object," he said. "A civilian will only hamper my ability to operate. Surely this question is of secondary importance. It can be investigated over time, without incurring so much risk."

"The Holy Father believes this question is very important indeed," Macerata said. "Fortunately, your companion is not a civilian. In fact, he is a former member of the Order of Saint Uriel—Monsignor Konstantin Stefanidis. Although he is no longer with the Order, we cooperate on sensitive matters from time to time."

Loyola knew the name but not the man. Stefanidis had once been a rising star within the Order, the youngest priest ever to earn the position of *secundus sicarius.* But he disappeared from the scene a few years before Loyola joined the Order. No one would speak of the reason for his departure, but the Dicastery was a prestigious assignment—not exactly an ignominious exile.

Perhaps Stefanidis had simply been moved to the injured reserve list. The job was extraordinarily hard on the body, and no one operating at that level could afford to go into the field with even the slightest weakness or disability.

"You will investigate the biolab," Macerata said. "Monsignor Stefanidis will investigate the theological issue. The lab and everything connected to it must be comprehensively sanitized. Use your judgment, but err on the side of ending the sect's capacity to create this weapon or any like it in the future. That includes eliminating their sources of expertise, *in aeternum terminale.*"

Loyola sometimes disliked Macerata's carefully parsed language, which he interpreted as a way to distance the cardinal from the visceral realities of the job. They both knew what he meant—kill the scientists. Why not be direct? Loyola did not have the luxury of distance. Why should the people who gave the orders?

But "Yes, Your Eminence," was all he said.

* * *

Stefanidis was in Paris for reasons that he did not volunteer and Loyola did not probe. After an exchange of emails, they agreed to meet in Perpignan, on the Languedoc's eastern coast. They would obtain a car from the Deacon network, then drive together through the mountains and forests for two hours to reach Garde-le-château.

The monsignor appeared to be a couple of years older than Loyola. He had an engaging smile, a genial baritone, and a receding hairline over a salt-and-pepper beard. Loyola's first instinct was to like the man, and his second instinct was to question his first instinct. The gregarious façade masked an intensity that might be religious fervor or something else entirely. He had a lot to say about heresy in general and the Cathars in particular, much of which went over Loyola's head.

"There are only eight major heresies," Stefanidis explained as Loyola drove. "Denial of God the Father, denial of Christ's godhood, denial of Christ's death and resurrection, denial of the Trinity, denial of the Virgin Mother, denial or distortion of the seven sacraments, denial of the resurrection of the flesh, and denial of the apostolic succession. All heresies contain, directly or indirectly, at least one of these components. But when you mix and match, suddenly there are thousands of variations."

This sounded credible enough to Loyola, but he couldn't really judge. Stefanidis struck him as someone who wanted to be sure you knew he was a genius. Loyola had met many such people, some of whom were in fact geniuses, many of whom were not. Stefanidis was intelligent, Loyola was sure of that, but in his experience, intelligence did not always travel with truth and accuracy.

"The Cathars were implicated in many sins," Stefanidis said, animatedly. "The Church kept remarkably complete annals. Some of their practices were relatively innocuous, fasting and celibacy, appropriate when done for the right reasons. But they believed the material world was the source of all evil, and the spiritual the only source of goodness. This led them to deny the incarnation of Christ and the resurrection of the flesh, among other things. Some denied the undivided divinity of God the Father as well, following the gnostic tradition that there existed a good God and an evil God."

Stefanidis continued for some time. Hopefully, there wouldn't be a quiz.

It was a long drive, and for a while Loyola appreciated the conversation. He encouraged the other man to continue with occasional questions in his characteristically laconic style.

He was genuinely interested in Church history, and he could not discuss his own work, even with a former member of the Order. Being a good talker might get you far in the world, but being a good listener could keep you safe. Macerata had vouched for Stefanidis, even suggesting he still served the Order in some manner, but something about the confluence of events and personalities didn't sit right. Loyola had learned to trust his inner voice on such matters.

Stefanidis launched into a lecture about the Cathar sacraments, some parts of which were new to Loyola, others were vaguely familiar. The sect's most significant and controversial innovation was the *Consolamentum*, a form of baptism that, like its Catholic equivalent, wiped away sins.

Unlike orthodox Catholics, many Cathars were baptized twice—once on being confirmed into the faith, and again when they were approaching death. After receiving the second *Consolamentum*, sick or aged Cathars undertook the *endura*—a near-total fast in which they refused life-giving sustenance. In the eyes of the Church, the *endura* was tantamount to suicide, a grave sin dressed up in sacramental robes.

"The *endura* was intended to preserve the state of grace created by the *Consolamentum*," Stefanidis explained. "Its purpose was to hasten the death of the believer, so that they would not be able to sin again. But there was also an element of purification to the *endura*, through suffering and refusal to partake in the material world. This is key to understanding the community at Garde-le-château. Their misguided goal might be to inflict a sort of global *endura*, an apocalyptic purification of a sinful material world."

"Doesn't seem like an idea that the original Cathars would come up with," Loyola said. "Unless I'm missing something."

"Ah, but they could not have foreseen modern science and its potential," Stefanidis said. "Who knows what obscenities they might have carried out if the Church had not suppressed them during the Albigensian Crusade and subsequent missions."

"'Suppressed' is one word for it," Loyola said.

"The Church has done terrible things to control this sect," Stefanidis agreed, his tone mild. "Terrible things indeed. It got so bad that Pope Alexander IV had to give inquisitors permission to absolve each other's sins after torture sessions. The papal bull was called *ut negotium*, strictly 'a matter of business.'"

Loyola grunted disapprovingly.

"Such practical language for something so transcendent," Stefanidis said, as if that was what Loyola meant. "What more intimate bond could exist between men? Each cradling the other's immortal soul, washing it clean, lifting it up?"

"Are you serious?" Loyola said incredulously. "This was done to sanctify torture."

"Are you and I so different from those men, Francis?" Stefanidis asked.

"Yes, we really are," Loyola said.

"Do you not seek confession after a mission?" Stefanidis asked. "I did, when I was in your Order. Every time."

"Well," Loyola said, uncomfortably. "Yes. But . . ."

"You do what the Holy Father calls on you to do," Stefanidis said. "No matter what. Would you torture if he asked you? You don't have to answer that. But consider how civilians would talk about the things you *have* done, if they found out about them? Are you really so different? This is a different age, to be sure, but are we not the terrible means in the service of God's indescribable ends?"

"I don't punish people for what they think or what they believe," Loyola said, letting an edge creep into his voice so that his feelings would not be mistaken. "I protect the Church, and I protect innocents. Nothing more and nothing less."

"As does the Dicastery," Stefanidis said. "As it has always done. We maintain the sacred traditions of the church. We protect the souls of the innocent from dangerous knowledge."

"The Dicastery has repudiated the tactics we're discussing," Loyola said. "As did the Holy Father. John Paul II called the Inquisition sinful, and he prayed for the Church to be forgiven."

"You could say he acknowledged that times have changed," Stefanidis said. "The challenges of today are different, and they call for different solutions. Perhaps the challenges of tomorrow will require yet another approach."

"That is . . . definitely not what the Holy Father said," Loyola said.

"Ah, Francis, consider yourself blessed that you have not spent a career parsing the words of holy men," Stefanidis said. "The Church does not exist only in the here and now. It is eternal, coexistent in every time and after the end of time. If we do not carry the golden thread of tradition forward, if we do not protect it with our lives, and even at the expense of others, we might as well be Presbyterians. We are Catholics. We are the Church, and we embody its history. Some things do not change. Some things must not change."

Loyola had never been one to beat a dead horse. They drove on in silence.

* * *

The fortress of Garde-le-château sat atop one of the Languedoc's many steep mountaintops, accessible only by a winding, one-lane dirt road. According to Stefanidis, the original Cathars had also lived on the site. The Crusaders climbed a sheer cliff wall to mount a surprise attack from the rear, leaving no survivors.

Loyola found an elevated spot from which to do reconnaissance on the castle, a mile or two away.

"The Crusader assault was led by Arnaud Amalric, who later went on to carry out the massacre at Beziers in 1225," Stefanidis said. "He is best remembered for the order he gave on that occasion: 'Kill them all. God will know his own.'"

"Sounds like a swell guy," Loyola said, peering at the castle through powerful binoculars. He was tempted to try the cliff himself. The fortress had seen better days, but the access road was dotted with utility poles, and he was worried about video surveillance. The angle made it difficult to see what was happening inside the compound, but he didn't spy any sentries manning the walls. The element of surprise would make things simpler and keep collateral damage to a minimum.

The neo-Cathars did not appear to be especially militarized. As far as Loyola could tell, most of the castle's inhabitants were young men and women, hardly an elite fighting force. Macerata's dossier indicated that many had been recruited from French universities, mostly humanities majors.

The biolab was both physically and organizationally compartmentalized, located in a heavily fortified central building that had served as an armory hundreds of years earlier. The scientists had dormitory rooms inside the central complex. According to Macerata's dossier, the rank-and-file believers knew something important was happening inside, but they didn't know what. There would surely be some kind of security, but Loyola saw no indication that the location was a hard target.

"We're going to be here for a while," Loyola said to Stefanidis, setting up a camera with a long lens focused on the castle gates and connecting it to a laptop. "Smoke 'em if you got 'em."

The monsignor did not got 'em. He pulled out a rosary and sat on the hood of their rental car, watching as Loyola methodically examined every visible detail of the compound through his binoculars, taking notes and drawing diagrams in a spiral-bound book of graph paper.

"You're more thorough than your predecessor," Stefanidis said after a while.

"I prefer to see trouble coming," Loyola said.

"Perfectionism has its downsides," Stefanidis said. "There's nothing more dangerous than believing you've covered all the angles."

"I'm not a perfectionist," Loyola said. "And professionalism isn't arrogance."

"Ah, but arrogance is a necessary sin," Stefanidis said. "For someone like you or someone like me. You believe you are qualified to decide who lives or dies. I believe I am qualified to decide who goes to heaven and who goes to hell. You can't get the job done without a measure of arrogance."

"I don't decide," Loyola said. "I do as the Holy Father commands. As for who goes to heaven or hell, I'm pretty sure that God alone decides that. If you're doing your job right, you're the guy who explains His reasons. Nothing more."

"A humble killer," Stefanidis scoffed. "Do you wash the feet of your victims?"

"I refuse to be baited," Loyola said. "Another professional practice."

Stefanidis shrugged off the riposte.

"There's a truck going up the mountain," he said.

Loyola turned his attention to the binoculars. A bright yellow cargo van was carefully threading its way up the treacherous mountain road. Big blue letters on the side of the box read LA POSTE. Loyola opened his satellite-connected laptop and did a quick search. Mail was delivered to the village daily. Searching further, he found the depot from which the vehicle originated.

"A lot easier than the Crusader route," Loyola said.

"But not nearly as much fun," Stefanidis grumbled.

* * *

After considering several scenarios, Loyola decided on a two-pronged approach. Shortly after midnight, he made his way to the nearest postal depot and stole a van from what appeared to be a reserve lot. Ideally, he could return it the next day, and no one would be the wiser.

He pulled it around to the warehouse. Once he figured out the storage system, he was able to retrieve a pair of uniforms, a small bag of items addressed to Garde-le-château, and a dolly full of random packages for camouflage purposes. He sifted through the pile as he loaded the van and returned a parcel that seemed to contain medical equipment and another wrapped as if for a child's birthday. Satisfied with his haul, he concealed the truck near the bottom of the mountain.

The next morning, he and Stefanidis followed the regular postal worker from the depot and on to his route. Stefanidis drove the rental car, while Loyola monitored their location on his phone. When they reached a sufficiently isolated spot,

Stefanidis closed the gap, and Loyola rolled down the window to discreetly shoot out two of the truck's rear tires using a modified nail gun supplied by Deacon.

The vehicle rolled roughly off the side of the road. Loyola guessed it would take at least two hours for a repair truck to arrive and do its work. Longer, if they were lucky, but he wasn't going to count on that. The nails would make it look like an accident.

Stefanidis had argued for a predawn assault, frontal and swift, but Loyola wanted to minimize collateral damage and maximize his opportunity. His assignment was to destroy the lab and kill the scientists working on the Horseman project. The most efficient and foolproof strategy was to strike during working hours, when they would all be together in one place.

Speeding forward to where the van lay hidden, the two men quickly changed into the blue-and-yellow postal uniforms. Encrypted radio earpieces completed the ensemble. Stefanidis looked distinctly awkward, his magisterial beard and aristocratic mien sitting uncomfortably in a working man's clothes. Loyola was more at home in the uniform, but he would be riding in back. If all went to plan, no one at the castle would lay eyes on him.

Stefanidis pulled into the courtyard and backed into a spot next to the central building. Pulling his cap down as far as possible and tilting his head downward, he hoisted a satchel full of mail and headed for the village's administrative building. The monsignor's mission was to find the castle town's library as discreetly as possible and make a quick survey of its contents, bringing anything of religious interest back to the van in his satchel.

Meanwhile, Loyola slipped out the back of the van, carrying a satchel of his own, filled with thermite-composite bombs—specially designed incendiary devices that burned hot enough to melt steel and reduce any biological materials into an ultrafine, sterile ash.

The biolab was a compact, windowless suite of modern rooms that had been built into the castle's stone-walled armory. There was only one entrance, guarded by a man dressed in jeans and a T-shirt, awkwardly cradling an unsuppressed M-16 rifle. The sentry didn't look very professional, but Loyola couldn't afford to try a nonlethal approach. The M-16 was deafeningly loud and even a single discharge would raise an alarm throughout the complex. Loyola took the man down with a single, suppressed shot to the head.

The door was locked with a keypad that was silently defeated by a Deacon-supplied magnetic device whose workings Loyola barely understood. Cracking the door open, he searched for any signs of cameras in the dimly lit hallway beyond.

One pointed directly at the door. He holstered his Glock and retrieved a paintball gun with a long narrow barrel from the satchel. He pushed the door forward incrementally, until he could get the barrel through the aperture. The air-powered gun was almost completely silent, and the paintball was filled with a viscous glittery substance. If someone was monitoring the camera feed, they would see something that looked like a visual glitch rather than a total failure. By the time someone thought to check it out, he would hopefully be long gone.

He dragged the dead sentry inside and shut the door behind him. Macerata's intel was good but it had not included a floorplan, so Loyola was on his own from here. The hallway ran along the east wall of the building, with three doors on his right, evenly spaced. He placed a timed thermite charge with a radio detonator under the body of the sentry, then advanced to the first door.

No light could be seen leaking from the frame, and Loyola heard no sounds when he pressed his ear against the door. He opened it slowly, revealing a small and shabby computer server room. The machines were outdated and dusty. He placed a thermite charge on top of the server rack, then continued down the hall.

The second door opened onto a locker room, also dark. After confirming it was empty, he looked around. The room held eight lockers—six for scientists and two for lab assistants, if Macerata's dossier was correct. The lockers were unsecured, and all had clothes and phones inside, indicating his targets were all on site.

He placed two thermite charges at strategic locations and continued on.

Light bled from the gaps around the third door, near the end of the hallway. From the spacing, he could tell it was the biggest area, and he could hear sounds from within. It had to be the lab. Pressing his ear to the door, Loyola judged that no one was very close. He dropped to the floor and snaked a tiny endoscopic camera underneath. The closest person was seven or eight feet away. He pulled the camera back and readied himself. He had nine bullets left in the magazine and a second mag on his belt, but he wouldn't need it.

The secretive nature of the project meant he probably didn't have to worry about cameras inside, but there would be a panic button somewhere. He would have to move faster than anyone could react, which should be doable. These scientists were killers, but they worked in sterile conditions far from their victims. He doubted any of them shared his intimate experience with violence.

Loyola turned the knob slowly and silently, opening the door just enough to get clear of the latch. He took a deep breath, then surged forward.

The two men nearest him were engaged in an animated conversation in French. His entrance was so unexpected that they didn't have time to be startled. Two suppressed head shots and they hit the ground. He wheeled around the corner and found three men working at computers. Three shots, same result. At the far end of the room, two men were in a corner in front of a lightbox wall covered with abstract images that Loyola assumed to be microbes. He shot them.

The remaining figure was a woman in a white coat, wearing goggles, latex gloves, and a respirator mask. She was loading a bottle filled with liquid into an autoclave. On one side of the autoclave was a large freezer, and on the other was a rack filled with petri dishes and test tubes.

Most of the objects in his field of vision were fragile, and some of them were bound to be lethal. She could drop the bottle, or stagger into the rack.

He couldn't afford to take the shot.

Loyola advanced on her swiftly, angling his approach so that she would back into the freezer. He took the bottle away from her, carefully placing it inside the autoclave. She didn't resist. Her eyes were resigned, perhaps even jaded, as if she had been living with the specter of death so long that it held no terror at the last.

He put his hands around her throat and applied gentle pressure. She didn't fight.

Loyola made a swift survey of the room. In addition to the standing freezer, a door at the far end led to a walk-in freezer with a biohazard icon on the door. When he opened the freezer, his stomach turned violently. Most of the freezer was stuffed with plastic bags marked as biohazards, but against the back wall, on a set of lighted shelves, were rows of jars containing human fetuses.

His hands shook as he placed thermite charges in the freezer.

Emerging, he placed incendiary devices in every corner of the room and in the center, with extra charges around the equipment and computers. He moved back through the hallway, placing charges there as well. He set a timer for ten minutes just in case anything went wrong, then synchronized it with his rugged Casio G-Shock wristwatch. He had used much more than was necessary, so that there could be no doubts. When the devices detonated, the entire lab would be reduced to white-hot slag. Nothing would be recoverable.

All evidence of the contagion, every trace of their horrific work, would be immolated, destroyed beyond recognition in an eruption of hell on earth.

Loyola checked the time. The entire operation had taken less than twelve minutes. He reached for his earpiece and activated the radio.

"T minus ten," he said in a low voice. "Acknowledge."

He waited a couple of precious minutes but got no response. It was possible that Stefanidis was simply unable to talk because someone was nearby, but Loyola was uneasy. The monsignor was an unknown quantity. He could not have risen to the second rank in the Order of Saint Uriel without formidable skills, but his personality was a problem, perhaps the problem that had ultimately disqualified him—his admitted arrogance, an unshakeable certainty in his own judgment combined with a short fuse. Such qualities were a poor fit for the *primus sicarius*, who operated with unparalleled discretion in matters of lethal harm. When on a mission, Loyola had been blessed with more latitude for unilateral action than even the Inquisition. He had to be very careful never to abuse it.

His values were what separated him from the monsters of yore, no matter what Stefanidis said.

Loyola waited three precious minutes for a response, with the timer ticking down. Finally, he growled "T minus seven" into the earpiece and set himself in motion. As he reached the door, he heard a deafening noise and for a terrifying moment, he thought the incendiaries had gone off early. But the sound was ahead of him, not behind. Grabbing the M-16 from the dead sentry, he broke into a run.

The bright sunlight stung his eyes as he emerged. The van was where he had left it, unattended, but a clamor of voices was coming from the direction of the courtyard that lay between the vehicle and the administrative building. A burst of M-16 fire rang out, and then another. Loyola followed the sound.

The sight that met him in the cobblestone courtyard was chilling.

An incredible number of bodies, he couldn't tell how many, were splayed in a radial pattern around the center of the square, where a statue of Saint Michael the Archangel loomed over a dried-out fountain. In front of the fountain, Konstantin Stefanidis stood, drenched in blood, a stiletto in one hand and in the other, a 1900 Model Luger pistol, which had been modified with an unusually long barrel, likely to improve aiming precision. Neo-Cathars, some armed with clubs and others with guns, clambered over the bodies of their comrades in an attempt to reach him.

Stefanidis made no effort to withdraw and took no offensive actions. He simply stood, almost perfectly still, as they rushed him. When some unfortunate attacker came within range of his blade, he dispatched them with swift and ruthless efficiency. Anyone who tried to take a shot from a safe distance got the gun.

The neo-Cathars had not been highly trained, but their sheer numbers would have overwhelmed any ordinary man. Even Loyola could not imagine fighting off so many by himself.

Every one of Stefanidis' strikes, near or far, was pinpoint accurate.

The attackers seemed to ebb back and flow forward with a metronomic rhythm, staccato bursts of violence unfolding at an almost hypnotic pace, falling lifeless to the ground.

The spectacle was strangely, brutally beautiful.

Stefanidis was playing defense, and ordinarily, Loyola would not have hesitated to join the fray. But these were amateurs, cult members, and all the intelligence suggested they were oblivious to the nefarious schemes unfolding behind the lab's locked doors. And Stefanidis was making no attempt to retreat. He stood there, almost placid, daring them to approach him. And they approached. And they died. They were fanatics, they could do no less.

Loyola was paralyzed for a long moment, long enough for three more to die.

Then reinforcements began to arrive, a large contingent of young men with M-16s. While they showed more signs of training than their predecessors, they were still obviously novices, rushing forward with sloppy posture and no formation. But novices with machine guns were dangerous enough. Loyola took cover behind a stone wall on the edge of the courtyard and began picking them off, one by one.

Stefanidis moved, finally, snatching a rifle from one of the fallen that surrounded him and taking cover behind the fountain. A deafening exchange of gunfire ensued, and the ranks of the attackers slowly thinned. In the rear, someone was trying to herd a group of unarmed people—noncombatants who were perhaps less experienced with violence or less fanatically committed to the cause—steering them away from the action, toward the stone warehouse that housed the lab, a reinforced area that they thought would be safe.

Loyola's gut twisted.

He ducked behind the wall and looked at his watch.

Thirty-one seconds.

Perhaps thirty noncombatants, maybe more, all retreating in the direction of certain death.

Heedless of the danger, Loyola leapt to his feet and sprinted after them. The armed men unleashed a volley of bullets in his direction. The shots went wild, but some of them hit a stone column as he passed it, spraying stone shrapnel at his face. He could feel the blood begin to run, but at least it had missed his eyes.

"STOP!" he screamed. *"Arrêt! Danger!"*

The group of bystanders saw him coming, face bloodied, rifle still in his hands. They panicked, running away screaming, continuing toward the old stone warehouse they hoped would provide refuge.

A blinding light, then an unbearable heat, breaking over him like a storm, like a wave. He felt the skin of his face dry and begin to crack.

Loyola dropped flat to the ground and rolled down a short flight of stone stairs.

The blast was almost silent.

But the screams . . .

Loyola lay numb.

The voices stopped, mercifully.

Behind him, the gunfire continued a while longer, then, finally, it too stopped.

He heard footsteps. When they got close, he sprang to his feet.

Stefanidis was standing there, blade in his right hand, gun in his left. Loyola slapped the knife out of his hand. It went clattering across the courtyard.

"What happened?" he snarled.

"They discovered me as I was finishing in the library," Stefanidis said evenly, seemingly unbothered by Loyola's aggression. "I couldn't leave you behind, obviously, so I waited. I was forced to defend myself, so I did."

His face was impassive, but his eyes were smirking.

At least that was how it seemed to Loyola.

Behind him, the armory building collapsed, thunderously.

"Let's go," Loyola said, without looking back.

The postal van had been reduced to slag, parked too close to the blast site. They broke into another vehicle and sped away.

"Funny thing," Stefanidis said in a conversational tone, as he drove down the mountain path. "They weren't Cathars after all. Just a fairly pedestrian millenarian cult that appropriated the name. I have to admit, I was disappointed. Garden-variety heresy, hardly any doctrinal points of interest."

Loyola rolled down the window, letting the wind blow painfully over his blistered face. The sound of moving air was not loud enough to drown out the screams that echoed in his ears, but at least he wouldn't have to listen to Stefanidis talk.

CHAPTER

16

# Not a Creature Was Stirring

EVEN COLL WAS rendered speechless by Loyola's account.

"I asked the Holy Father afterward," Loyola said. "It wasn't the first time Stefanidis had created such a problem. That was why he was dismissed from the Order. After Garde-le-château, he was dismissed from the Dicastery as well, then assigned to run a monastery in western Massachusetts."

"To a cushy retirement post," Coll said incredulously. "What's a motherfucker gotta do to get defrocked from this operation."

"I wasn't consulted," Loyola said. "Believe me."

"How does this change things?" Fortis asked. "The job remains the same."

"Stefanidis is capable of anything," Loyola said. "We'd assumed the goal of the conspiracy was to elevate Macerata, and we planned accordingly. Stefanidis might have a different goal. He might be out for revenge, or just trying to amuse himself. He's a madman. And with Biancardi as part of the cabal, they have a much wider range of motion than we anticipated. They can paper over a lot of irregularities."

"Protecting the Holy Father remains our top priority," Fortis said.

"The Holy Father might not even be the target," Loyola said. "Stefanidis might be planning another massacre. There will be fifteen thousand civilians in the basilica."

"The Lady didn't say anything about a massacre," Coll said. "And even as I hear the words coming out of my mouth, I see the problem with them."

"I need to get up to the main floor of the basilica," Loyola said, pacing back and forth like a caged animal. He glanced at his watch. It was not yet noon, but the basilica would be filling up with hundreds of people tasked with preparing for the evening Mass. "We missed something. We must have. I need to be out there."

Fortis sighed.

"Even before this development, I figured you might be like this," she said, gesturing toward a table a few feet away. Loyola saw a monk's hooded robe, a pair of Buddy Holly-style glasses, a hair clipper, and a lighted makeup mirror.

"If you go up, your hair stays down here," Fortis said. "Non-negotiable."

"Deal," Loyola said, quickly.

"Keep the beard," she said.

"That's a generous description," Coll scoffed.

"But clean it up. Make it look like it's on purpose, rather than . . . this," Fortis said, ignoring Coll and gesturing at Loyola's face.

"All right," Loyola said, striding over to the table.

"We absolutely cannot afford for you to be seen and recognized," Fortis said. "The Holy Father was very clear."

"I heard him," Loyola said, irritated.

"He asked me to remind you," she said. "In no uncertain terms."

"All *right*," he replied, with mounting exasperation.

* * *

It took all of Loyola's self-discipline to walk with the slow, deliberate grace that befitted his brown Franciscan robes. His body wanted to pace and pound, to incarnate his state of mind—taut, predatory, paranoid.

*Oh, how they pound, raising the sound.*

He forced himself to breathe deeply.

*Hark! How the bells, sweet silver bells*
*All seem to say, "Throw cares away"*

"Are you *singing,* motherfucker?" came Coll's voice in his ear.

"Sorry," Loyola whispered. "Subvocalizations. The earbud is extremely sensitive."

"You can mute it by tapping your palm once over your ear," Fortis said helpfully.

Loyola's eyes swept over the basilica, searching for anyone or anything out of place. He had been at it for hours now, with no new insights. The church was closed to tourists ahead of Midnight Mass, simplifying the landscape somewhat, but the number of clergy, monastics, and support staff nearly made up for the ordinary crowds. Loyola began to pick up on clusters—groups of nuns working on flower arrangements, men in overalls setting up chairs for the evening's congregation. When he spotted anyone who wasn't part of a cluster, anyone who seemed idle or alone, he flagged them to Coll, who used the cameras to capture their faces.

"Can you run facial recognition?" Loyola asked.

"Fuck no," Coll said. "You think is this *Mission: Impossible*?"

Loyola made his way to the massive Holy Door, which the pope would open to mark the beginning of the Jubilee Year. The door featured sixteen bronze panels that depicted the history of humanity, from the Garden of Eden through the life of Jesus and ending with a metadepiction of Pope Pius XII opening the door itself after it was extensively renovated in 1950.

If the plan was meant to conform to the prophecy, the assassins would not be likely to strike before the door was opened. After finding out about Stefanidis, Loyola was less certain than ever that the prophecy mattered, but he didn't have an alternative scenario—at least not yet. And too much of the plotters' activity had revolved around Mirsad.

After opening the door, the pope and his attendants would process past the *Pietà*. Loyola scrutinized the chamber that housed the statue. Unlike the Holy Father, the *Pietà* was protected by a thick pane of bulletproof glass, installed in the 1970s after a deranged man vandalized the statue. The barrier was probably indestructible enough to render the space useless for an attacker.

He walked the processional route. The crowd at large might be fairly safe; they would be screened with metal detectors, and it would be challenging to aim and fire a weapon without the crowd fouling the shot, intentionally or otherwise. He scanned the hall. Very high windows on all sides offered vantage points for a sniper, but getting to them without being detected from the inside would be impossible, and the outside would be difficult.

"Cal, do you have visuals of the exterior?" Loyola asked.

"Sure do," Coll said.

"Keep an eye out for someone doing a Spider-Man," Loyola said. "Climbing to get to one of the upper tier windows for a snipe."

"I only have two eyes," Coll said. "Actually, I only have one. But I'll do what I can."

As he completed the dry run of the procession, Loyola arrived at the altar and the *Confessio* of St. Peter, surrounded by the four statues standing guard, each at the base of a massive pillars. The Holy Father's throne was located just in front of St. Longinus, along with chairs for his retinue. Loyola's gut still told him that this was the place, bounded within the four piers.

He looked up. A walkway around the interior of the dome was accessible from the rooftop near the coffee shop. It was fenced due to a spate of suicide jumps dating back to before Loyola was born. The fence was a tight grid that would make it virtually impossible to point a long gun down toward the church. Still . . .

"Cupola walkway?" Loyola said.

"Sister Christian is putting motion detectors at the entrance," Coll said.

Loyola scanned the area around the *Confessio* again and again, taking in as many details as possible. If he couldn't anticipate every line of attack, he could at least imprint the topography in his mind. If and when the time came to act, swift navigation would be crucial.

When his eyes returned to the basilica entrance, he spotted Rocha and her Interpol colleague walking down the center aisle. Cursing, he walked toward the statue of Saint Longinus wielding his spear, pacing himself so as not to draw attention. He took the stairs behind the statue and, once out of sight, descended hastily into the grotto.

"Cal, you gotta keep eyes on the cops," he snapped. "Warn me if they're nearby."

"I'm doing my best, partner," Coll said, and his voice was strained. "But I'm watching fifty monitors with 50 percent of my normal eyes."

Loyola regretted his tone.

"Copy that," he said.

"They're heading toward the spear guy," Coll said.

Loyola had walked the labyrinthine grottoes multiple times in the past twenty-four hours. Losing two newcomers would not be that difficult, but Rocha's arrival added a new and volatile element to his job. He was accustomed to being the hunter; now he would have to stalk his prey while someone else was stalking him.

*Oh, how they pound, raising the sound*

* * *

The boys' choir launched into yet another rendition of "The Carol of the Bells," at least the third, maybe the fifth. Rocha couldn't keep track because the song was now unshakingly implanted in her brain.

She looked at Moussa, who was scanning the square yet again, seemingly unbothered by the music. They had circled the square twice without spotting Loyola. Moussa gestured at the basilica, and Rocha nodded.

As they started up the stairs, Rocha felt an unfamiliar sensation of awe. She had been raised Catholic and had long since left the religion behind, but the building was incredible, and it was impossible to separate it from its origins in faith. She was not tempted to believe. She had seen too much for that. But she almost wanted to.

It was easy enough to switch it off. The protective instinct that blunted her emotions at the scene of a homicide kicked in. She was surrounded by grandeur, but also great danger. She could not afford distractions.

The interior of the church was the opposite of what Rocha had expected. Not hushed but buzzing, as priests, nuns, and lay people flitted from spot to spot in what she assumed were preparations for Midnight Mass. As they entered the nave, a man in overalls to her right was squeegeeing a large glass barrier. It took her a minute to focus past him and see Michelangelo's *Pietà* on the other side of the glass. She gasped.

*Focus, Maria,* she told herself sternly. *You're not a tourist.*

They walked slowly down the center of the church, where workers were setting up rows of chairs for the evening service. In unspoken synchronization, Moussa took the right side, and she took the left, scanning the crowd with eyes practiced at picking out details.

They were so focused on the sides that she almost missed what was right in front of her—a man standing beside a pit in front of the main altar. It was too far to make out his face, but he was bald and wearing glasses. Rocha was about to move on when she saw him walk to the right. The superficial details were wrong, but he had Loyola's fighter's gait. The man ducked behind a statue of a Roman centurion and disappeared.

Rocha grabbed Moussa's arm and directed him toward the statue, forcing herself to keep a casual pace. There was no telling what Loyola would do if he perceived a threat, but she needed to confirm whether it was him, or some other martial arts priestly murder machine who just happened to be nearby.

Her nerves jangled as they approached the statue. There had been no sign of the man since he ducked behind, and she was afraid he was lurking, ready to strike. With a combination of relief and disappointment, she discovered there was a stairway behind the statue.

"The grottoes," Moussa said. "Many popes are entombed below."

His words prompted a vivid image, which was fortunately quickly dispelled. The good news was that the grottoes were modern and well-lit. They wouldn't be brushing away cobwebs and crunching bones under their feet. The bad news quickly became apparent. The sublevel was a maze of rooms, and their prey was nowhere in sight.

"Should we notify the Swiss Guard?" Moussa asked.

"Are we still worried he's working for the pope?" she replied.

Moussa shrugged.

"Well, let's take a look around at least," he said.

Rocha nodded miserably. Everything about this adventure felt like a wild goose chase, and pacing through labyrinthine catacombs wasn't helping things. The fatigue was also starting to catch up with her, and her head was pounding.

*Oh, how they pound, raising the sound*

CHAPTER

17

# The Holy Door

"I NEED TO BE up there," Loyola said, for at least the fourth time.

"I agree we need to cover upstairs," Fortis said. "Which is why I am going to do it. My presence won't raise alarms with the cabal, and more importantly, I'm not being stalked by Interpol."

"I don't—"

"Like it, yes, I know," she said, exasperated. "Too bad. We need someone covering the grottoes, and it's got to be you."

"You guys are badasses, but two is not enough," Coll said, breaking to the argument before Loyola could respond. "Call in the cavalry. You've got me, but I can barely sit up in this chair. We're cooked without more people."

"We can't call anyone," Loyola said, for what seemed like the fifth time. "Stefanidis was part of the Order. He's working with the deputy chief of the Order. We don't know who we can trust."

"I know who we can trust," Fortis said with a sharp tone. "The Twelve have not been compromised. But the Holy Father has spoken. Anyway, it's too late. The rest of the Twelve are scattered across the globe. I can't get anyone here in time."

"Fuck those guys," Coll said. "Let me make some calls."

"Out of the question," Loyola and Fortis said simultaneously.

"Only Catholics got a dog in this fight," Coll said, ignoring them. "Bring in some unaffiliated muscle. Someone from outside the circle of shit."

"Even if I thought that was a good idea, we don't have time to get anyone up to speed," Loyola said. "The only thing that could make this situation worse is a bunch of trigger-happy mercs who don't know the lay of the land."

"And even if *he* thought it was a good idea, *he's* not in charge here," Fortis said. "*I* am. And I say it's not happening."

Loyola instinctively bristled, but he bit off a retort, because he knew she was right. She was the *prima sicaria*, and he was retired. He was still rusty as hell, and he was honestly unsure if he had been better than her when he was in his prime.

Something something age and guile. Anyway.

Coll snickered.

"Never did I ever think I'd see Father Frank Loyola whi—" Faced with baleful gazes from both Loyola and Fortis, he thought better of completing the sentence.

"Fine," he said. "We'll do it *Die Hard*. But don't say I didn't warn you."

* * *

Since 2009, for various reasons, Midnight Mass had not been held at midnight, but this year it would start at ten PM and run until midnight. People began lining up for admission to the service around seven PM, a slow process thanks to the many security checks.

In the basement, Loyola and Fortis geared up, while Coll made his way to the chair after a brief nap. He was in evident pain and blood seeped from the edges of his bandage.

"You all right?" Loyola asked.

"Fuck no," Coll said, "but I got this."

"No doubt," Loyola said. "But let me change that dressing before you get sepsis."

Coll wanted to protest, but he knew Loyola was right. Loyola found a first aid kit in one of the desk drawers and began the messy job. He felt a stab of guilt as he exposed the wound, raw and ugly, inflamed and roughly stitched. The doctors in Mostar had removed the ruined remains of the eyeball and implanted a piece of silicon to hold the socket's shape, sewing the lid shut over it. Eventually, after some healing had taken place, they would be able to reopen the lid and replace the silicon placeholder with a cosmetic prosthesis. Loyola had no idea how Coll was functioning at all, let alone how he had managed to drive from Mostar to Rome in this condition. But his son was in danger, and perhaps that was explanation enough.

Loyola's decisions had led to this.

He cleaned the wound carefully, dabbing it gingerly with antiseptic and an antibiotic ointment, then gently applying fresh, clean gauze. He finished by putting an eyepatch over the dressing. Coll was uncharacteristically silent throughout.

"Thanks, partner," he said, when Loyola finished.

"Least I could do," Loyola said gruffly.

Fortis was checking her weapons and holstering them. On the table in front of her lay a slightly old-fashioned habit, black-and-white, floor-length and baggy enough to conceal her tactical pants and black body suit. Her fighting style was oriented toward freedom of movement, so she eschewed armor.

"No indigo?" Loyola asked.

"The whole point of having a very recognizable style is that it confuses people when you switch it up," she replied. "Macerata would spot me instantly and at a distance in indigo. Hopefully he'll look right past the penguin style."

A collapsible baton disappeared into one of the pouches on the pants, and she slung a bandolier with at least a dozen knives over her shoulder. She had two ankle holsters, and she filled them with snub-nosed pistols modified with bobbed hammers that would not catch on her clothes when drawn. As she strapped the upper part of the holster to one calf, Loyola could see it was unshaven, covered with a fine silky down as silvery as the hair on her head.

Loyola pushed the thought out of his head. His life was dedicated to God, and at any rate, he had his own gear to prepare.

Under his black shirt and Roman collar, he donned a lightweight Kevlar vest. Over the shirt, a Glock in a shoulder holster, and a bandolier with a row of throwing knives. A second Glock went in an ankle holster. then he strapped on a tactical belt that held four magazines, two suppressors, a multitool, a pouch full of zip-ties, and a flashlight. In his pants pockets, left- and right-handed brass knuckles with a serrated surface reminiscent of a meat tenderizer.

Over everything, he pulled on robes, white and gold vestments as suitable for concealing weapons as they were for celebrating Christmas. It was the uniform of the evening and would draw no undue attention.

Fully outfitted, he tried a couple of quick moves. The gear felt heavy, especially with the vestments on top, and he worried that his loadout would slow him down. But he was loath to give anything up when he didn't know what to expect.

Fortis had three ID badges on lanyards. She gave one to each of the men and put the third around her neck, hiding it beneath her robes.

"These will get you past the Swiss Guards," she said. "Coll, it won't probably be enough to get you out of hot water if someone finds you. When we reach the point of alerting the Swiss Guard, you need to grab the radio and get out of here ASAP, just in case this room is activated."

"Anything else?" Loyola asked.

"Negative," Fortis said.

"I got nothing," said Coll.

"Time to break out the grapes of wrath," Loyola said, making the sign of the cross.

"Amen," Fortis said, crossing herself.

"You had to make it weird," Coll sighed, shaking his head and taking his seat.

* * *

The boys' choir from that afternoon was now installed toward the front of the church, backed by an organ and some brass players. The boys, whose ages ranged from nine to fourteen, were dressed in white robes and singing something chantlike, their words smearing into the muted instrumental sounds like an undulating phonetic soup.

Rocha was annoyed. "The Carol of the Bells" had been stuck in her head all day, thanks to those jerks. It was only fair that they sing a rousing rendition of "Holly Jolly Christmas" or some such to dislodge it.

*Hark! How the bells, sweet silver bells*
*All seem to say, "Throw cares away"*

She tried to make the earworm more tolerable by imagining the song as a heavy metal anthem, electric guitars in a winding arpeggio backed by a heavy bass line. But the new version just accentuated her attenuated nerves.

Rocha was walking down the aisle that ran along the north wall, paced by Moussa on the south. The service was still an hour from beginning, but the place was packed. At intervals, she passed members of the Swiss Guard. Despite their ridiculous stripey RenFaire uniforms and ceremonial halberds, Moussa had assured her they were quite formidable.

She caught one of them sweeping the crowd with his eyes, even as he remained at rigid attention. He clocked her, noting her Interpol ID and giving a slight nod of professional respect. Rocha returned the favor.

Various other religious types were attending to various last-minute tasks around the basilica. A monk was lighting candles up toward the front. A nun in old-timey robes was walking up the aisle toward Rocha. She was tall and youthful in appearance, despite an unruly lock of silver hair that peeked out from under her veil. The sister passed the detective with eyes reverently downcast.

For some reason, she reminded Rocha of Loyola, even though the two couldn't be more different. It took her a minute to figure out what it was—gait. Like the priest, the nun was poised on the balls of her feet, adjusted only slightly to account for a different center of gravity.

Rocha turned. The nun was disappearing out the back of the church.

Had to be her imagination.

* * *

In the grottoes, Loyola walked a circuit around the two entrances to the *Confessio* and the four stairwells that led up to the altar space, with special attention to Saint Longinus, who would be standing directly behind the Holy Father when the Mass began.

He kept his pace brisk but relatively normal. He couldn't cover all the entrances at once, no matter how fast he walked, and it could be a very long evening. Coll was watching motion detectors all over the grounds, which would hopefully give them an edge when the time came.

The grottoes were normally closed for the holiday, and only the emergency lights were on, giving the space an appropriately funereal vibe.

"I think your cop made me," Fortis said over the encrypted radio channel.

"She couldn't possibly know who you are," Loyola replied, puzzled.

"Game recognizes game," Coll said. "She turned around to take a gander at you, but she hasn't moved in your direction. Maybe she was just checking out your ass. I'll try to keep an eye on her, but mad monks take first priority."

"Do the best you can," Loyola said. "Maybe we can figure out how to use them to our advantage, but I don't kill cops."

"If you can help it," Coll said.

"If I can help it," Loyola admitted.

* * *

Fortis passed the *Pietà* on the way to the foyer. The stark marble portrait of the Virgin had a definite presence that had always stirred something in her heart.

But recent events had altered her regard.

The drive from Medjugorje to Rome was twelve hours. Mirsad had slept for the first several hours, exhausted by the traumatic events at the Epoch compound. They stopped for a fast-food breakfast when he woke, and after that, they talked for a while. She asked him about the Lady, and the answers she received were troubling. When all this was over, she would need to think about whether she believed the visions were real.

But for now, she had to keep her mind on the job.

Fortis took up position in a relatively shadowed corner of the foyer, which was dimly lit for dramatic effect. Staffers were setting up cameras to livestream the pope's opening of the Holy Door, now less than half an hour away. Two Swiss Guards stood sentry at the door, and a number of cardinals had gathered nearby, easily identifiable by their gold and white vestments and scarlet skullcaps. Macerata would join them soon, and Fortis would have to balance her priorities—keeping a close eye on the pope while avoiding being noticed by their enemies.

Loyola's plan to expose the plot in order to stop the plot was shaky from the beginning, in her opinion, and even more so now that they knew Biancardi the fixer was involved. Simply deterring an attack tonight might derail the conspiracy entirely, simply by desynchronizing the plot from the prophecy. Were the conspirators true believers, as Loyola had argued? Or were they cynics using the prophecy for camouflage and misdirection?

The number of unknowns had ballooned in a few short hours, particularly with the identification of Konstantin Stefanidis. Fortis had never met the former *secundus sicarius*, but she had read the Order's files on him. He was an apex killer with a towering intellect and arrogance to match, standing in sharp contrast to Macerata's quiet and calculating strategist.

Macerata might be the most-obvious beneficiary of the plot, but Stefanidis was not the kind of man to play second fiddle to someone else's ambitions. Fortis was certain he must have reasons of his own, and she was far from certain that his reasons pertained to the prophecy. Stefanidis was a former Inquisitor; he would require extraordinary proofs in such matters of faith.

Speaking of the devil . . .

A group of Benedictine monks in traditional robes entered the foyer from the square. Most of them were chatting amongst themselves amiably, but one was scanning the area, silently and intently. She eased back further into the shadows.

"Sister Christian, you have Stefanidis at ten o'clock," Coll said in her ear.

"I see him," she replied. "It looks like he's going to be in the procession."

After the Holy Father opened the jubilee door, hundreds of people would follow, a ritual act associated with special blessings. The foyer was already filling up with participants—priests, monks, nuns, and lay people from all over the world invited as guests of honor, all dressed in religious robes or secular finery. The cardinals and the pope would take a left at the *Pietà* then process down the center aisle. The procession would split in front of the *Confessio,* with half going left and the other half going right, toward the statue of Saint Longinus.

The pope and several cardinals would take seats in front of the statue as hundreds of people passed by. The entire procession would take about ten minutes, a high-risk window with many moving parts. If Stefanidis was part of the procession, if he had smuggled in a gun, if he took the right-hand turn at the

*Confessio*, he would have an easy shot at the Holy Father. Even an amateur could hit the target at that distance.

But there would be no escape—multiple cameras would be pointed at the spot, and the lights were very bright.

"Loyola, would you say Stefanidis craves martyrdom?" Fortis asked.

"Not necessarily," Loyola said. "But he might not fear it."

"I think I need to stay close to the Holy Father," she said, outlining her thinking in quick, terse sentences. "Too many opportunities to take the shot, regardless of whether it's Stefanidis or someone else."

"Is there any chance he could recognize you?" Loyola asked.

"We've never met," she replied. "And my picture isn't exactly in the Vatican's directory of employees. But I can't rule it out, given Macerata's role in the conspiracy."

"If he did recognize you, it might work to our benefit," Loyola mused. "If Plan A is above ground, seeing you on point could push them back to the grottoes, where we have more flexibility to take action without creating an international incident."

"Do it," Coll said.

"Agreed," Loyola said, and she could hear the strain in his voice. He might be retired, but he desperately wanted to be near the action. And she suspected that he still didn't entirely trust her skills. Patriarchy was a hell of a drug.

* * *

The darkness of the vestibule of Saint Peter's Basilica was dispelled by a spotlight that revealed the Holy Door. Twelve feet tall and more than seven wide, the portal's brass panels gleamed in the sudden flare.

A second spot switched on to reveal Pope Nicholas VI. Surrounded by dozens of cardinals in splendid vestments, he was dressed in simple white robes, a plain gold stole, and a white skullcap.

"In the name of the Father, and of the Son, and of the Holy Spirit," said Nicholas VI. "God is joy, and God is love, and may God's joy and love be with you all. We are gathered here to celebrate the birth of Jesus Christ, and to celebrate the start of this jubilee year, during which we are reminded of God's infinite forgiveness and his gift of transcendent hope . . ."

"Macerata just joined the cardinals," Coll said. "Very late."

Fortis had fallen back to a position with the religious orders, mingling with a group of Carmelite nuns whose habits resembled her own. The bishops and cardinals were between her and the Holy Father, but she would attract too much attention if she shouldered to the front. She planned to pass through the jubilee doors with the Carmelites, then break away once inside the nave of the church, fast-walking the north aisle to take up a discreet position near the Holy Father, just behind the pier that housed Saint Longinus.

"Movement on your six, sister," Coll said in her ear.

Fortis sensed the approach, through an indescribable combination of sensory inputs that had always served her well—sounds, shadows, the indirect movements of bystanders, perhaps something else as well. She didn't turn but shifted slightly into a more ready stance. It seemed unlikely he could try anything with so many people packed together, but she wasn't entirely sure of his rationality.

As Stefanidis edged into her peripheral vision, she saw his hands in front of his chest, palms together and fingers upright, a prayerful pose that also served to indicate that he wasn't brandishing a weapon.

His eyes were forward, on the Holy Father.

"Blessed Christmas, Sister," he said, without turning his head.

"Blessed Christmas," she replied.

"An auspicious year, to be sure," he said. "The jubilee is a fine tradition, one of our finest. Tradition is so important, wouldn't you say? The very heart of our church."

"Our tradition is very important," she said mildly. If he was trying to bait her, he would have to try harder.

"And all these men," he said, with a very subtle emphasis on the last word. "The direct successors of the apostles, consecrated and ordained to lead us."

Fortis suddenly felt the presence of peril in this conversation, twisting like a knife.

"May God bless and guide them, Brother," she said with as much saccharine as she could muster. "And may he guide you too."

"'He guides me in paths of righteousness' for his name's sake," Stefanidis said. "Though I walk through the valley of the shadow of death, I will fear no evil."

"My second favorite psalm," Fortis said, biting back an urge to comment on how pedestrian the passage was.

He looked at her now, side-eye, mouth curled in a smile that seemed genial, a smile that seemed to hide no vipers.

"What's your favorite?" he asked.

"The fear of the Lord is instruction in wisdom, and humility comes before honor," she recited.

"Fascinating," he said, sounding almost delighted. "I'll see you again."

He faded back into the crowd, disappearing into a cloud of Benedictine monks.

"Do we have a problem?" Coll asked in her ear. "Sounds like we have a problem."

"Sure, but we already knew that," she whispered, far too quietly for anyone in the room to hear, but just loud enough for the ultrasensitive microphone in her earbuds to relay.

Her attention returned to the pope, who was coming to the conclusion of his jubilee speech, after which he would open the Holy Door and pass through. It was rare for Fortis to entertain any distractions from the pontiff's words. She loved him like a father, valued his wisdom, and most of all his compassion. He was a kind man who took pleasure in helping others.

Fortis also did not crave martyrdom, neither did she fear it. But she would gladly give her life to protect this man.

Nicholas paused to regard the men who surrounded him, wordlessly looking one after another in the eye. The cardinals of the Church, the servants of God, and one who would betray him for personal gain. She detected no anger in his gaze.

"Most of all, the jubilee is about forgiveness," Nicholas said. "In 1750, to inaugurate the jubilee celebration, Pope Benedict XIV urged believers to take up God's infinitely generous offer of eternal forgiveness. He asked 'What is the will of God but your salvation? To fulfill this will, the Church calls you. To all who ask sincerely, the Church promises forgiveness.' Benedict urged believers to undertake a war by means of peace, to fight for the salvation of God's children by abandoning all thoughts of hatred and harm."

Nicholas looked down at his open hands, then clasped them.

"Who among us can aspire to such dignity?" he said. "Jesus told us to turn the other cheek, truly the most difficult thing He asks of us. A commandment that tests us all, even those He has chosen to speak for Him, even those He has chosen to lead the faithful. We struggle, we fight, we fail. We can only strive to match God's limitless kindness and know, that when we fail, as we so often do, that the Church promises forgiveness. All of us rely on that promise. And so must I."

He looked up again, and his face was serene.

"Amen," he said. Walking up to the Holy Door, he rapped on it three times with his knuckles. It slowly swung open. Nicholas VI stepped over the threshold.

The jubilee year had begun.

CHAPTER
18

# Midnight Mass

"I've got motion at the northeast entrance to the grottoes," Coll said. "Frank, you're on. Looks like four . . . no six. Dressed like monks, carrying duffel bags full of who knows what but probably guns. Sending photos to your phone."

Danger was marching toward him, but Loyola felt relief more than anything. Maybe the *Confessio* was Plan A after all. They were in with a shot to finish this. A definitive takedown, followed by a very visible deployment of the Swiss Guard, and maybe the whole thing was over.

Nothing in his recent experience suggested it would be so easy.

"OK, the guns are out of the bags now," Coll said. "Assault rifles. They're pros, approaching in a *very* cautious tactical formation. Probably take, six, seven, eight minutes to reach your position. They'll be coming up the long north corridor, likely heading for your spear guy."

The Holy Father was just now reaching his chair, in front of the statue. The attack team could afford to take its time; the Mass would continue for nearly two hours.

"Copy that," Loyola said. His phone vibrated, and he pulled it out. Coll had sent photos of several monks. One was a tall and powerfully built man with a pug nose that had clearly been broken multiple times.

Loyola recognized him—one of the monks from Stefanidis' abbey back in Massachusetts. He felt a certain amount of relief. If these operatives were the abbot's men, it suggested Fortis was right, and the Order of Saint Uriel may not have been compromised. One less problem to worry about.

"Whoops," Coll said. "Two of them have broken off and are headed toward me."

"Shit," Loyola said. "Get out of there."

"I can handle this," Coll said. "But you're going to be on your own without surveillance support for a few minutes. Don't assume these guys are the only thing you have to worry about."

"Your eye . . ."

"Seeing twenty-twenty times one," Coll said. "That's why I always carry a spare."

Loyola cursed, but he couldn't leave his post, not even to save his friend.

"I feel guilty enough as it is," Loyola said. "Try not to lose anything else."

"Amen the fuck to that," Coll said. "It's a coin flip whether the four assholes will get to your position before the two assholes get to mine, so be ready. Sister Christian, you hearing this?"

"Copy," Fortis said, sounding stressed. "I don't like leaving you boys alone down there, but I have to keep eyes on Stefanidis. I'm sorry."

"Absolutely," Loyola said. "And you need to be in position if any of these guys get past me."

"I'm near Saint Longinus," she said. "If anyone comes up those stairs, I'll know it."

"No chance of that," Coll said. "We got this. Right, Frank?"

"We got this," Loyola said.

"We hope," Coll muttered under his breath.

"You know we can hear you, right?" Loyola said.

"Just don't start singing again," Coll said. "I'm down an eye already. I can't afford to gouge my ears out too."

Loyola heard Fortis snickering over the earbuds. No one had lost their sense of humor yet, so things must not be too bad.

*Oh, how they pound, raising the sound*

* * *

Rocha and Moussa walked together down the aisle on the south wall of the basilica, keeping pace with the leading edge of the procession. A priest holding a large cross led the way, followed by a squad of people dressed like geriatric altar boys, then another priest holding up an ornate, gold-colored bible. A gap, and then the pope was next, flanked by two Swiss Guards, and followed by a small army of mostly old, mostly White men in scarlet skullcaps.

The trailing end of the procession seemed to go on forever. Behind the red hats were white bishop hats, then monks in robes and nuns in habits, then what looked like priests, then more monks, then what looked like ordinary people. Rocha scanned the nuns for the tall, silver-haired one from before, but she didn't seem to be part of the procession.

When the pope reached the altar, he turned to the right, along with his retinue. A chair had been set up in front of the statue of the spear guy who guarded the staircase to the grottoes. The Swiss Guards took up a position close to the seat.

Rocha spotted the tall nun standing next to the massive pillar that housed the statue, a sole individual out of place in a carefully orchestrated scene, situated so her line of sight included both the pope and the staircase. None of the three other statues surrounding the altar came with a similar watcher, Rocha noted.

Rocha elbowed Moussa, using her eyes to direct his gaze toward the scene.

"What do you make of that?" Moussa asked.

"She's worried about something coming out of the grottoes," Rocha said. "We saw Loyola go down there earlier. No way it's a coincidence."

Moussa frowned.

"Do you think Loyola is going to try to kill the pope?" he asked. "Should we call it in?"

Rocha thought about it.

"Is there another entrance to the grotto?" she asked.

"There are several," Moussa said. "Each of the four piers, the pillars around the altar, hides a staircase. But she would surely notice us accessing one."

"What's the next closest?" Rocha asked.

Moussa pulled out his phone.

"Outside of the basilica, and then quite some distance. If we walked to the exit, then ran to the grotto entrance, it would still take ten, fifteen minutes."

Rocha surveyed the scene. The procession coming up the center aisle split in front of a lantern-festooned pit that was somehow part of the altar. Half the people went left toward them, and half went right, toward the pope and the nun and the statue with the spear. The nun was watching the procession. Her bearing seemed casual, at least to anyone who wasn't paying attention.

Rocha looked over at the pillar on the opposite side of the altar from spear guy. It featured a statue of a woman with a distressed look on her face, holding up a cloth in a manner that Rocha assumed to be significant.

"Let's use the staircase over there," Rocha said. "There are a lot of distractions and obstructions between her and us. We might get away with it." Moussa nodded.

They began to make their way toward the pier, trying to look casual, at least to anyone who wasn't paying attention.

* * *

With the luxury of a few minutes warning, Loyola was making preparations. He removed his white and gold vestments. His standard black suit would not raise alarms if he was spotted, and it offered better camouflage in the dimly lit grottoes.

He ducked into a chapel memorializing Pope John Paul II, from where he could see the attackers before they reached any of the exits that led to the altar above. The only way he could miss anyone was if they came down from the altar space, and Fortis was monitoring the four piers upstairs.

Working quickly, Loyola drew both his guns and screwed on the suppressors. Even suppressed, the sound of gunshots would reverberate up and down the hallways, but the echoes would make it hard to get a fix on his location. He moved the brass knuckles from the pockets of his robes to his tactical belt. He peeked around the edge of the chapel with his night vision scope. The assault team was getting close.

He took a slow, deep breath and centered himself. Even if they were formidable fighters, there were only four. This was a best-case scenario. He could handle them easily, stay out of sight, then call in the Guard when it was over.

Fortis' voice crackled in his ear.

"Loyola, you have Interpol incoming," she said. "They're going down the stairs that lead to the Chapel of Saint Veronica. Just two, but it's your cop and the other one. Nothing I can do."

Loyola gave a heavy sigh. A verse from the book of Psalms came into his mind.

*Pride is as a chain about the neck of the wicked;*
*Violence covers them as a garment.*

His first thought was to call in the Swiss Guard, now rather than later. Even if the Guard was compromised, it would be difficult for a traitor to hinder a response to armed men in the building. But these monks were not ordinary killers. They were professional assassins, trained under Konstantin Stefanidis. The Swiss Guard would eventually prevail by virtue of superior numbers, but many of them would die, and the fighting could spill into the basilica in any number of ways. Stray gunshots could penetrate weak spots in the grotto ceiling. Gunfire or explosions could cause structural damage, collapsing sections of the basilica floor, or worse.

Safely taking down the assault team was tricky enough, but eluding Interpol was another thing entirely, unless he was willing to kill them. With them blundering about, he couldn't protect all points of egress to the basilica above. In such chaos, a shooter could get through, endangering the pope and everyone around him.

Coll's voice came through the radio, his whisper amplified by the earbuds.

"I have motion at the Chapel of Saint Veronica, but I also have motion at the southern entrance by the Piazza Braschi. Looks like six more monks."

"I thought you were taking cover," Loyola said.

"I pulled a monitor and keyboard under the table with me," he said. "Might as well make myself useful while I wait. Lucky for you I did."

"We're fucked," Loyola said. "I can't act freely with Interpol down here, and they'll call it in as soon as they see what's going on. Then I'll have the Swiss Guard down here too. It'll be a massacre."

Loyola took a deep breath.

"I'm going to try to handle this," he said. "But if I can't, be prepared to evacuate the basilica."

"I can get an evacuation request to the Guard, but they will have a lot of questions," Fortis said. "And I can't leave the Holy Father."

"If things go south down here, tell the Holy Father what we need," Loyola said. "They'll obey him without question, and he trusts you without question."

She took an agonizing second to think about it.

"Copy that," she said. "Good luck, and the Lord be with you."

"And also with you," Loyola said.

"Allah be with you both," said Coll, "but tie your camel."

* * *

The door closed behind them, abruptly muting the sound of organs and choirs. Rocha drew her weapon halfway down the stairs, and Moussa followed suit.

They emerged into a darkened room, dim emergency lights casting barely enough illumination to avoid obstacles. She activated the flashlight on her phone and stuck it in her blazer's breast pocket, facing forward. It barely penetrated the gloom, casting shadows everywhere, on the walls, on the ceiling. A short and elaborately decorated passage led to a juncture with a curved corridor.

"Left or right?" she whispered.

"Right," replied Moussa. "I think."

They moved forward carefully, passing a chapel with a portrait of the Virgin Mary that Rocha knew well as a Mexican-American and a former Catholic—the Lady of Guadalupe. The image was said to be miraculous. She wondered if it was the original and hoped she wouldn't leave a bullet in it.

Beyond the chapel, she saw a bright glow. A thick glass wall on their left, flanked by stone saints and small stone lions, opened onto a fabulous space crammed with detail. She could see lanterns on the left and right, which she recognized from the pit upstairs. The glow must have been coming from the main church. As they passed, she imagined she could hear the muffled sound of the choir above.

*Oh, how they pound, raising the sound*

If this was the pit, then the spear guy's stairs should be directly ahead.

Rocha tensed. She felt certain Loyola was here.

As they passed through the illuminated zone, her eyes struggled to adjust, as she heard a rustling sound behind her. She wheeled to see Moussa slumping to the ground. Behind him was Father Francis Loyola, the white square of his priestly collar like a beacon or a target in the darkness. She raised her weapon and pointed it at the square, but her view was blocked by something rushing at her.

It was his fist. It landed cleanly and precisely on her chin, ringing the bell.

As she lost consciousness, she heard a gun go off. She was pretty sure it was her own.

* * *

"Goddammit," Loyola growled.

The good news was that her shot missed him, probably just damaging a priceless and irreplaceable work of art. The bad news was that her gun was not suppressed. It was a Boston P.D. standard-issue Glock 27, 40mm, deafeningly loud in the silent grotto. The approaching assault team could not have missed it.

So much for the element of surprise.

"What happened?" Coll and Fortis said in his ear simultaneously.

"Interpol is down, nonlethal, but one got a shot off," Loyola said. "It's about to get hot down here."

"Should we evacuate?" Fortis asked.

"If you don't hear from me every two minutes or so, evacuate," he said. "I'm going to try to keep this under control."

The gunshot would bring the assault team to a halt while they assessed the risk and waited for backup, the six additional men that Coll had monitored at the southern entrance. Loyola used the time to drag Moussa and Rocha to the Chapel of the Patron Saints of Europe, a small room dominated by a big, black, stylized crucifix. They would be out of the line of fire, but he wasn't sure how long they would remain unconscious. After a moment's hesitation, he zip-tied their hands and feet together. In the event that he didn't make it, they were more likely to get killed by wading into the fray than by being discovered here.

He searched them, confiscating their phones and radio earpieces and smashing them with the heel of his gun. Rocha was carrying keys and a multitool. He placed all of it, along with their guns, on top of the altar, several yards away from where they lay. He would be long gone, or dead, by the time anyone found them.

*Any public scrutiny of the Order would have unimaginable consequences,* the Holy Father had said. *Even my death would be preferable.*

"Checking in," said Fortis.

"Check," said Loyola.

*You should kill them*, said a cold, practical voice in his head. *They will expose you.*

"I won't," Loyola said.

"Won't what?" Coll said in his ear.

"Never mind," Loyola said. "How you doing?"

"The wolf is at the door," Coll said. "Going radio silent while I deal."

"Don't die on me," Loyola said.

"No promises," Coll said, and his microphone clicked to mute.

Loyola dropped to his belly, crawled forward and pulled out his night scope. He could see two men advancing, closing in on the corridor that led to the Chapel of Saint Longinus, but very slowly. They were holding long guns, probably AR-15s, undoubtedly with night-vision scopes. They hadn't spotted him yet.

It was imperative to prevent anyone from accessing the church above.

He was more likely to lose control of the situation in a firefight.

Loyola rolled into the corridor silently, arms folded over his chest to keep his weapons from clattering on the marble floors.

No gunshots came, and he allowed himself a moment of relief. Then he dashed down the corridor to the chapel, taking a position just inside the threshold, his back flattened against the wall, quietly transferring a knife from his bandolier into his hand.

One monk would enter while the other one covered. If he moved fast enough, he could take them both out before a shot was fired. He waited.

"Check," Fortis said.

The barrel of an AR-15 peeked into the chapel. Loyola grabbed it and yanked, jerking the man just enough into the room to expose his neck. Loyola jabbed it with the knife, then put his whole weight into wrenching the rifle from his hands. Executing the move put him in the entrance, in full view of the second man, who was already raising his rifle to shoot. Loyola threw the knife with pinpoint accuracy, into the second man's eye socket, with enough force to reach his brain. He went down like a sack of rocks.

"Check," Loyola said.

Eight to go.

* * *

It was the first time at the Vatican for Brother James and Brother Paul. They had memorized the floorplan, but they weren't prepared for the visceral sensation of awe and antiquity that its collection of art, relics, and tombs inspired.

"We gotta come back here as tourists," Brother James said, as they passed the statue of Pope Pius VI kneeling in reverent ecstasy and entered the much less awe-inspiring service corridor.

"For sure," said Brother Paul.

The unfinished tunnels extended like a maze before them, but their training had been thorough, and they quickly located the Papal Situation Room. The code they had been given for the keypad worked, and they entered.

The large chamber was dark, except for one brightly lit computer terminal directly in front them. It was a little disappointing, given what they had been told to expect, but it would probably be more impressive when all its systems were activated.

Brother Stephen put down his gun and sat at the keyboard. It took only a moment to log in. As he searched for the app that controlled the monitors, with Brother Paul looking over his shoulder, a pop-up window opened, then another, and another, followed by the "blue screen of death" that accompanied a system failure.

"Dammit, what?" Brother James said, squinting at the error message.

"What does it say?" Brother Paul asked.

"It says . . . 'you're fucked'?" Brother James said. "Uh-oh."

The first shot took Brother Paul in the head. Brother James groped for his gun, but the second shot hit him square in the chest. His vest absorbed much of the impact, but it felt like a donkey had kicked him in the sternum, and he fell backward.

Calvin Coll emerged from the shadows, towering over the monk with a double-barreled shotgun extended in front of him.

"Who the devil are you?" Brother James asked, his tone almost plaintive.

"I'm the motherfucker you lost the Crusades to," Coll said, then he pulled the trigger.

* * *

Sister Belina Fortis was too disciplined to fidget, but events were testing her heroic composure to its limits. She was a warrior, not a bodyguard, and every inch of her body strained to run down the stairs and join Loyola in the fray.

The one thing she absolutely couldn't do.

Her most pressing problem at the moment was Konstantin Stefanidis and the fact that she couldn't see him. The last fix she had on his location was during the procession. She was certain he had passed through the jubilee door, but he must have peeled off before reaching the altar. He could be anywhere.

"Check," she said.

"Check," said Loyola.

"Check and mate," Coll said. "Your eyes and ears are back online."

"Perfect timing," Fortis said. "I've lost Stefanidis. I know he went through the jubilee door. I need to know what happened after that."

"Stand by for rewind," Coll said. "Frank, how you doing?"

"Two down," Loyola said. "Eight to go."

"Bravo Zulu," Coll said. "Keep in touch. Sister Christian, your guy ducked out of line immediately after going through the jubilee door. Headed toward you and Saint Centurion then . . . kind of disappeared?"

"Can you expand on that?" Fortis asked.

"There's a space directly behind you," Coll said. "On the far wall, there are three altars with some kind of paintings.

Camera coverage in the middle has a couple of dead spots. He disappeared into one of them."

Fortis craned her head back.

"It's the confessionals," she said. "There's less coverage in the transept there, in order to protect people's privacy. If he ducked into a booth, he could still be there, or he could have used it to change clothes."

"I'll look for someone matching his description in different clothing," Coll said, "but middle-aged White guy is the style of the season."

"Do what you can," Fortis said. She adjusted her position slightly to improve her view of the transept.

Unfortunately, the move put her in line of sight for one of the Midnight Mass livestream cameras. The surveillance cameras could be wiped or altered after the dust settled, but the livestream was being archived in real time by news services. She couldn't find a spot where she could see what she needed to see and stay off the feed. But there was nothing she could do about it, so she put it out of her mind.

* * *

*Oh, how they pound, raising the sound*
*Oh, how they pound, raising the sound*
*Oh, how they pound, raising the sound*

Oh, how it pounds.

Her head. Pounding.

Rocha came to consciousness with a start. She was in a darkened room, but her eyes had been closed for a while, and she could make out the outlines of things—wooden pews, some kind of decorations on the wall, an oversized crucifix hanging ominously over it all. Her hands and feet were restrained, zip ties by the feel of it. Moussa was lying next to her, and she felt a brief stab of panic, but she was able to get her bound hands to his neck, and she found a pulse, going strong.

She sat up. As consciousness returned more fully, she found herself with questions. First, and foremost, why was she still alive? The evidence might still be inconclusive from a legal standpoint, but she was convinced Loyola was a deadly killer with a body count beyond the dreams of most serial killers. Why would he hesitate to use lethal force on them?

Some part of her wanted to believe he was a good guy. Perhaps it was a remnant of her Catholic upbringing, a lingering belief in the priesthood that somehow persisted despite everything she had seen as a Boston cop. Or maybe it was the testimony of his parishioners, who had described a man of few words but open heart. Or maybe it was just something in his demeanor. He had almost certainly lied to her during their short face-to-face encounter, but he possessed some aura of decency that she found hard to discount.

Moussa had asked her if Loyola was here to kill the pope. She wasn't sure she bought that, but she didn't have a lot of alternative explanations either.

Rocha began groping around the room for some sort of implement that she could use to cut or grind down the zip ties. She had heard of perps who dislocated their thumbs to get out of them, but she had no idea how that worked, or if it worked. And at any rate, it wouldn't get her feet free. There were some candlesticks on the altar. If they were metal, if they had sharp edges . . . If there were matches to light the candles . . .

When she reached the altar, the flaw in her plan became apparent. She lacked a good way to hoist herself up. She could get to her knees, but the marble was smooth, and she kept falling back. She tried to hook her zip-tied hands around the corner, unsuccessfully, but something hard and metal fell with her as she slid back—her multitool.

Rocha opened it with her teeth and began sawing away at the zip-ties. Whatever the fuck was going on here, she wasn't out of it yet.

* * *

When the two scouts failed to report back, Brother Ignatius began to worry that the plan was going off the rails. He tried to radio Brother James and Brother Paul, hoping they had successfully taken control of the surveillance system, but he got no response from them either.

Whoever was interfering with their plans, it wasn't the Swiss Guard and it wasn't Interpol. Either force would already have armed platoons rushing down the stairs amid a storm of radio traffic, which Brother Dominic was monitoring closely.

It could only be the Order of Saint Uriel. According to their intelligence, just one of the Twelve was in Rome—the accursed woman. Ignatius was eager to take her down, but cautious. By every account, she was a formidable killer, despite the impurity and fallibilities of her gender.

But that was why Brother Samson had come on this mission. The pug-nosed giant had been trained by the abbot himself.

The eight monks huddled together as Ignatius whispered orders. Four would undertake a frontal assault, while Brother Samson flanked their opponent. Two chosen martyrs would take advantage of the distraction to rush the south door into the *Confessio* and finish the job, carrying only handguns. Ignatius would stay back. If the first wave failed, it would be up to him to complete the mission.

An elaborate backstory had been fabricated for them, a mishmash of Internet forum posts and tragic childhoods that would sate the media's need for explanations. As soon the deed was done, Macerata's handful of plants in the Swiss Guard would storm down here to clean up as best they could, and any lingering irregularities would be explained away by Monsignor Biancardi.

They broke the huddle. Each one knew his work, and they were all prepared to die if necessary, in order to save the Church.

If God was for them, who could stand against?

* * *

"Team of four making a frontal approach," Coll said in Loyola's ear. "One more trying to flank you. Two more shifting to the southern corridor. I think they're heading for the south *Confessio* door. One is staying back."

Loyola frowned.

"I'm not sure our precautions will be sufficient to take down two of them," he said. "It might hold, but . . ."

"Copy that," Fortis said. "I can see the *Confessio*, but I can't turn my back on Stefanidis, assuming he is where we think he is. Do we have eyes on him yet?"

She sounded extremely tense.

"Working on it," Coll said. "But there's a lot going on right now."

"Focus on Stefanidis," Loyola said. "I can handle things here."

It was big talk, but probably true, if he could avoid being distracted by the situation above. He turned his attention to the oncoming assault. Two heading down the south corridor. They were almost certainly heading for the iron *Confessio* gate that had been lubricated with WD-40, where Fortis had prepared a surprise for them earlier.

Four advancing toward his position. One trying to flank him, according to Coll. Loyola wasn't sure how that was supposed to work, unless his opponent had access to the service corridors, but he didn't want to distract Coll from finding Stefanidis.

One thing at a time.

Loyola was perched at the top of the long hallway that connected the grottoes to the Chapel of Saint Longinus. He would have to risk leaving the post in order to secure the *Confessio.* He backed up as far as he could, then ran as fast as he could, hurling himself across the north corridor.

Loyola heard the crack of gunshots splintering the walls behind him as he dove and slid into the southern corridor, where he found the two attackers were much closer than he had expected. Rolling into a kneeling stance, he put a bullet in the first one's head. The second dashed past him toward the *Confessio* gate. Loyola ignored him and took cover behind the pillar demarcating the northern corridor.

With stealth now out of the question, the four frontal assailants were approaching fast, no doubt hoping to distract him from the *Confessio.* Loyola risked sticking his head out from behind the pillar to put down some suppressive fire. He shot one man dead. Two of the remaining monks started firing at him, while a third took cover. Loyola glanced nervously up the curved hallway toward where he had stashed Rocha and her partner. Loyola berated himself for not securing them more thoroughly. If someone came at him from that direction, he might hesitate, which could prove fatal.

No time to overthink. The pillar that sheltered him was vibrating against his back as it absorbed automatic weapons fire.

Could anyone hear this upstairs? Probably not, hopefully not. The floors were thick, and the service was pretty loud.

When the fusillade paused, he emerged from cover and took down another member of the four-man team. One of the remaining two put down covering fire while the other tried to advance.

The dim emergency lights flickered and echoes of an undulating scream wound through the hallway. The man Loyola had let pass had discovered Fortis's lethal electrified booby trap at the *Confessio* gate. He took advantage of the distraction to pop out from behind the pillar and take down another member of the squad in the northern corridor. Only one remained in the corridor. Loyola was about to take another shot when he was hit by a ton of bricks from behind.

He twisted as he tumbled painfully to the ground and found himself staring into the face of the gigantic pug-nosed monk from the abbey in Massachusetts.

Brother Samson loomed performatively, then hoisted Loyola to his feet and threw him thunderously against a wall. For a long terrifying moment, Loyola wasn't sure if the loud crack that followed was the fracture of his spine or a priceless fresco.

The wave of pain that washed over him suggested his spine was intact.

"Check," Fortis said in his earpiece.

"Talk to me, Frank," Coll said. "Who the fuck is that guy?"

Loyola wheezed some kind of sound into the transmitter but couldn't manage to form a word. He rolled, as Samson came at him again, barely evading a nightstick the monk had produced from somewhere. Its impact left a crater in the fresco that Loyola's back had softened up.

Loyola had dropped his firearm when he hit the wall and reaching for the ankle holster would leave him open to the nightstick, so instead he slipped his fingers into the serrated knucks on his tactical belt. His limbs were sluggish, but they obeyed his commands, and he struck Samson in the face several times, drawing blood. The monster roared and hit him with a mighty backhand, throwing Loyola to the ground again.

This would be a stupid way to die, he thought.

A gunshot rang out. Samson flinched, but did not fall, slowly turning, with an expression of rage painted on his bloodied face.

How? It couldn't be Coll. The Papal Situation Room was too far away.

Another shot. Samson flinched again, his shoulder kicking back. The third bullet hit him in the head and emerged from the back of his skull. For an impossible moment, Loyola feared that the giant might somehow survive, but then his body finally went slack and he sank to the ground.

As the monk's bulk slumped to one side, Loyola was able to see his rescuer.

Martina Rocha stood frozen in place, her service pistol still smoking and now pointed at Loyola's chest.

"Don't move, motherfucker," she said.

"Check," said Fortis in his ear, urgently. "Do I need to evacuate up here?"

"I'm going to need a minute," Loyola said to both of them, raising himself onto one knee with great pain and a lot of difficulty.

A shadowy figure emerged from the darkness behind Rocha, holding an assault rifle—the last of the forward attackers. Loyola had already been inching his hand toward the ankle holster; he drew and fired faster than Rocha could react. The police officer heard the man collapse behind her and lurched to one side, angling to get a look. He was impressed with her discipline—she didn't take her gun sight off of him for a moment, nor did she reflexively pull the trigger.

"What the fuck is going on here?" Rocha demanded, swiveling her gaze back to Loyola.

The priest considered trying to disarm her, but he could see her muscles twitching with adrenaline, and he didn't like his odds. He pointed his gun toward the ceiling, conspicuously removing his finger from the trigger.

"I just saved your life," Loyola said. "And I could have killed you before, but I didn't."

Her aim didn't waver.

"I swear on my eternal soul that I will not resist arrest after this is over," he said. "If you want to arrest me in the morning, I'll come peacefully. But tonight, I have a job to do. They've come to kill the pope. I intend to stop them."

She stared daggers at him.

"I don't know how or why you're here," Loyola said. "But you must have been following your instincts. What are your instincts telling you now?"

She lowered her gun.

"Goddammit," she said. "I better not regret this."

Loyola nodded firmly. He moved toward the last man he had downed, removing his Benedictine robe. The hood might suffice to keep Loyola's face off camera if he went upstairs.

"Checking in," he said, putting his hand to his ear as a signal to Rocha that he was talking into a microphone. Fortis did not respond. Loyola looked up at the ceiling. A rumbling vibration that he sensed more than heard, a foreboding of something gone terribly wrong.

"Frank, get the fuck upstairs," Coll said. "It's Stefanidis."

Loyola turned to Rocha.

"There's one more monk down this corridor," he said, pulling the brown robe over his head. "He's the leader of this squad. There's another assassin upstairs, but he's above your pay grade. I need you to take out the guy down here, then call it in to the Swiss Guard."

She gave him one last penetrating look, but she nodded and turned her attention to the corridor.

"How will I—?" Rocha said.

"There's no one else down here," Loyola said. "Shoot anything that moves. I mean it. This is not your average Boston perp. If you try to arrest him, he *will* kill you."

Loyola allowed himself a precious moment to take a deep, centering breath, for which he was rewarded with a stab of pain that he attributed to one or more cracked ribs. Raising the monk's hood over his head, he dashed down the hallway toward the stairs, with all the speed his battered body could muster.

CHAPTER

19

# To Save Us All From Satan's Power

"Do I need to evacuate up here?," said Sister Belina Fortis, urgently.

"I'm going to need a minute," Loyola said.

The music was loud, a six-piece horn ensemble accompanied by the organ and a choir, sufficient to drown out the muffled action downstairs. But the readings were about to start, and she wasn't sure the mayhem would stay below much longer. Fortis had nerves of steel, but even she had her limits.

Her impulse—always—was to run toward the fight, but she couldn't leave her post while Stefanidis was still at large. Loyola could handle things below. The real battle was up here.

"Sister Christian, Stefanidis is coming out of the confessional," Coll said in her ear. "Dressed in Swiss Guard stripes, looking absolutely fucking ridiculous, and coming up on your six."

"Check," she said.

"I have Frank muted, he's talking to Interpol right now."

"Is he calling it in?" she asked. If the threat below was concluded, it was time to blow the whistle. That was supposed to be the end of it. But Stefanidis was already in motion, and it was hard to imagine that he would abort. The assault below felt like a feint, designed to keep them busy while the real attack played out above.

"Closing in," Coll said, interrupting her analysis. "No visible firearm, but he's got a poleaxe thing."

"A halberd," she said.

"Whatever," Coll said. "On you in thirty, twenty-nine, twenty-eight, twenty-seven . . ."

What was the play here? A highly visible insider assassination, televised in front of the whole world, would torpedo Macerata's hope of ascension.

*We'd assumed the goal of the conspiracy was to elevate Macerata, and we planned accordingly. Stefanidis might have a different goal.*

"Fifteen, fourteen, thirteen . . ."

Would he be willing to strike here, in front of all these cameras? In front of the Church and the entire world?

*Any public scrutiny of the Order would have unimaginable consequences. Even my death would be preferable.*

She had her orders, but she knew her heart. She would not let harm come to the Holy Father, not if she could stop it, even if it meant exposure. Nicholas had done too much for her, placed too much trust in her. She would not let him die.

The only serious question was whether Stefanidis was the final boss, or if another player remained hidden. She didn't think so. Her crash course on Stefanidis indicated he was a narcissist and an egomaniac. In his mind, if he couldn't get the job done, no one could. There would be no Plan C.

She turned to face him, taking a few steps forward and getting out of the line of sight for the closest livestream camera.

Stefanidis beamed at her, as if he had been waiting all his life for this moment. His right hand held the halberd. His left hung at his side, then flicked, causing a throwing knife to drop from his sleeve. In a flash faster than she could see, he launched it underhand.

Fortis made an instant calculation. She could easily dodge or deflect, but the blade might hit someone else. Instead, she clapped her hands together sharply, closing in front of her chest like a prayer and capturing the blade just before it hit her chest.

It was razor sharp, slicing her hand.

The wound was shallow, but it burned.

Poison!

Fortis wasn't sure how much time she had before it took effect. She wanted to shoot Stefanidis, but he was surrounded by hundreds of priests who had been seated in the north transept and were now on their feet, not yet fleeing, but on the edge of panic. She dashed toward Stefanidis instead. Close combat would be riskier for her, but less likely to result in collateral damage.

Stefanidis brought the halberd's point forward with both hands, but she whipped out the collapsible baton and cracked it against the wooden handle in a mighty blow, snapping the medieval weapon in two. She heard a collective gasp from the onlookers, which sounded almost like an appreciative "whoa" to her ears.

She tackled him, and they both hit the ground. Another wave of shocked exclamations rose up around them, quickly scaling into alarmed shouts.

Fortis landed on top of Stefanidis, clawing at his eyes, but he grabbed her wrists in a steely grip and held them at bay. She headbutted him, eliciting a satisfying crunch from the cartilage in his nose. He got a knee up somehow, and shoved her off to one side, attempting to rise. She locked an arm around his neck, putting her full weight into keeping him on the ground while squeezing his windpipe. He was bulkier than her, but she pressed her knees into the back of his knees, preventing him from standing.

A few of the younger priests now moved forward, and Fortis realized how much trouble she was in. Stefanidis was dressed like one of the Swiss Guard, and it was unlikely anyone had seen him throw the knife. Her hand was bleeding heavily, and she was sweating in reaction to the poison. She looked like a lunatic, and now the real Swiss Guards were starting to arrive on the scene. She didn't want to hurt them, but to protect the Holy Father, she would.

If she could.

Her head was swimming. Both her arms were now locked around Stefanidis' throat, and the new arrivals were clawing at her, trying to pull her off target. She tried to get enough leverage to snap his neck, but there were too many on top of her now, and the poison was sapping her strength. Stefanidis managed to loosen her grip enough to rasp out a few words over his shoulder, low enough that no one else would hear.

"When you get to hell, remember: *It was all your fault*," he said.

Then the Swiss Guards were pinning her arms. As she was dragged back, her habit rode up, and one of the Guards saw the pistol strapped to her shin.

*"Pistola!"* he shouted. "She has a gun!"

People in the immediate vicinity took up the cry, which spread through the church like wildfire. Up to now, the action had not been visible to worshippers in the main part of the church. But the word reverberated around corners, gathering volume as it was repeated and repeated.

"Gun! Gun! *Pistola!*"

Stefanidis stood and straightened himself while the Guardsmen piled onto her. As the poison overcame her, and she passed into darkness, the last thing she saw was his fiendish grin, perhaps foreshadowing the hell that surely awaited her.

* * *

Martina Rocha was pretty sure her days as a cop were numbered.

There had been good days and bad days, to be sure. But she was throwing it all away, if she even survived the night, which was less than certain.

Why had she trusted Loyola?

It wasn't the collar. She was thoroughly estranged from the faith of her youth, with no hidden regrets.

He had saved her life, true, but only after assaulting her minutes earlier.

He possessed a certain force of personality.

But when the decision point arrived, her memory of his parishioners tipped the balance. Every one of them had vouched for his integrity and his generosity, often emotionally, often emphatically.

As a cop, she knew all too well that deadly sins could be buried beneath a mountain of goodwill. Her gut told her this was not one of those cases.

In Boston, Rocha's instincts had warned her Loyola was hiding something. In Rome, here and now, those same instincts said he was telling the truth.

Her eyes had adjusted to the low light, but she couldn't see the monk Loyola had warned her about. She remembered there were two corridors, north and south, and a sort of church space in the wide center aisle, complete with an altar and pews. She advanced in that direction, stepping as softly as she knew how.

A small sound echoed from the north corridor as she crept up to the stone altar and crouched to take cover behind it.

Another small sound. The rustling of a robe. Close by.

She reached into her pocket and found her multitool.

Time for a little misdirection.

When she was fairly sure the monk had passed her position, she lobbed the tool into the north corridor, in the direction from which he had just come.

In the dark, with so many unknowns, it was a risky move. If he spotted her, if she had misjudged his position, if . . .

The tool hit the floor, the impact echoing loudly.

A short burst from an automatic weapon ensued, thankfully pointed in the direction of the noise. Rocha emerged from behind the altar and fired repeatedly. The muzzle flash generated enough light to dilate her pupils, effectively blinding her, but she kept firing until the magazine was empty. One way or another, one of them was going down.

The cacophony of gunfire was deafening to her in the stillness of the grotto, and she wondered if anyone above could hear it. She couldn't tell if the monk's body had hit the ground, but she could smell gunpowder, and she was still standing.

Moving forward cautiously, she tripped over his body. As her eyes readjusted, she laid hands on the monk's AK-47. Slinging it over her shoulder, she headed upstairs.

* * *

Loyola burst out from the stairwell behind Saint Longinus and almost ran into a cluster of uniformed Swiss Guardsmen, arms locked and encircling the Holy Father. A half dozen more plainclothes Guards were closing on his location, raising their pistols toward Loyola and shouting "HANDS ON YOUR HEAD" in four different languages. The pope's voice, impossibly strong, rose above the din of panicking civilians, who were swarming toward the exits.

"*HIC VIR SERVUS DEI EST*," he cried. The armed Guardsmen responded instantly, pointing their pistols skyward and adopting a deferential pose.

"Instructions, sir?" one of the plainclothes officers asked.

Loyola recognized him as Armand Morello, a Guard commander who had met Loyola on several occasions and who knew him as an authority figure.

"Downstairs isn't safe," Loyola said. "If a monk comes up those stairs take him down, but there are two plainclothes Interpol officers down there, who are working with me."

Loyola looked around. The closest exit from the basilica led into the Treasury Museum, a serene statue of Jesus Christ flanked by three popes looming over the threshold. Unlike the main exits, the museum gate was locked, so it wasn't clogged with fleeing worshipers.

"Cal, do you have eyes on the Treasury?" he asked.

"It's clear except for security personnel," Coll said.

The Treasury held some of the Vatican's most precious artifacts under constant guard and close surveillance. It was the closest thing to safe in this situation. The next nearest exit would be some way down through the nave, on the north wall near the roof access, but the panicked congregation had choked off that route.

"Frank," Coll said. "Fortis is down, and I've lost sight of Stefanidis."

A cold chill ran down Loyola's spine. He had barely met Sister Belina Fortis, but he suddenly couldn't imagine a world without her.

Loyola peered around the pillar housing Saint Longinus and saw a cluster of guards around someone on the ground. The Holy Father suddenly appeared at his side, having imperiously swept past his bodyguards.

"Go to her, Francis," he said. "No harm must come to her."

Loyola nodded.

"All right," he said, "but you have to get out of here now. Morello, take the Holy Father out through the Treasury Museum. Don't let him go back to the residence until they've swept it for explosives and toxins."

"Yes, Father," Morello said.

"When you activate the Papal Situation Room, you'll find a couple of dead bodies and a civilian working the chair," Loyola said. "The live one is with me, and he's to remain at his post."

Morello barked orders in Italian, and the phalanx of Guardsmen swept Nicholas toward the museum, struggling to get past a cluster of hysterical people who had not yet moved toward a viable exit.

One of Morello's men remained behind to escort Loyola to Fortis. They found her lying on the ground, her face ghastly pale and sheened with sweat. Her habit was covered in blood, but he could see only one small wound on her hand.

Loyola turned to his escort.

"It's poison," he said. "Call this number." He recited the digits of an emergency line connected to Rome's Deacon network. "Tell them 'contingency delta, priority one, *extrema unctio statim*.' Don't move her until they come. If she regains consciousness, do what she says. On the authority of the Holy Father."

The Guard pulled out a phone.

"Stefanidis heading for *il papa*," Coll said in his ear. "At your two o'clock. You gotta move *now*."

He wheeled about. Through the chaos, he saw one Swiss Guardsman calmly striding toward the Treasury door. Unlike the other Guards, he was bearded.

Loyola broke into a run, slowed by the need to weave through the remaining congregants and priests, who were running in every direction, some confused by fear and others simply unsure where to find an exit.

"STEFANIDIS!" he shouted.

The bearded man cocked his head, recognizing the voice. Time seemed to slow as Loyola watched the calculations play out in the other man's body language, his weight shifting subtly away from his forward momentum, readying a new move. He cast a regretful look at the Treasury gate, as the last of the pope's protectors passed through and secured the door against intruders.

Stefanidis shrugged and tossed a resigned smile over his shoulder at Loyola, then turned and dashed into the nave of the church, where fleeing worshippers clogged the aisles.

"*Oremus, ludamus*," he called out.

The first word meant "let us pray." Loyola didn't recognize the second word; his Latin was limited to a collection of memorized prayers and code phrases. But he assumed it was some kind of demented serial killer shit. He set off in pursuit.

* * *

Despite Loyola's adrenalin-stoked perception of time, only moments had passed since violence first broke out in the basilica.

He picked his way through the chaos of the mob as quickly as he could manage. Stefanidis seemed to be making better progress toward the exit, and Loyola discovered why when he stumbled onto the first body, an elderly priest, half trampled by the crowd, but with the same deathly pallor and sheen of sweat that Fortis had worn. After pushing several more steps into the crowd, Loyola came upon another body, a young woman in a wheelchair, bedecked in her Christmas finery, then another, a middle-aged man in some sort of ethnic costume, clutching an orthopedic cane in a death grip.

Stefanidis was killing anyone who slowed him down.

"Cal, call the Swiss Guards and tell them there are more poison victims in the nave," Loyola said.

"Don't need to call, they're right here," Coll said. "They apparently have orders to leave me be, but they don't seem real happy about it."

"I'll smooth it over later," Loyola said.

"Focus on living that long," Coll said.

The first couple of bodies had shown no signs of blood; Stefanidis had nicked them strategically, or perhaps he had used a syringe. But as Loyola waded forward, the bodies began to get messier, bloodier.

For a moment, Loyola thought Stefanidis was trying to spook him, but then he realized the broader purpose. The crowd was pulling away from him in horror, parting like Moses at the Red Sea and closing in his wake, making it harder and harder for Loyola to keep pace. For a moment, Loyola considered trying to take a shot from a distance, but too many things could go wrong.

The screams of the crowd were deafening.

Stefanidis cut toward the north wall of the Cathedral and entered the Chapel of the Blessed Sacrament. Inside, past a spectacular sixteenth century pipe organ and to the left of its stunning gold tabernacle, Loyola knew he would find an exit that led to the Patio of Saint Gregory, and from there into Saint Peter's Square. If Stefanidis made it into the Square, with panicked people running in one direction and an army of emergency responders running in the other, Loyola would never be able to catch up with him.

"Be careful, Frank," Coll said. "He threw something. Can't see what."

Loyola pushed forward, no longer able to afford the luxury of being gentle.

"Make way!" he cried out. "*Polizia! Carabinieri!*"

A few people complied, despite his monastic garb, and Loyola reached the chapel not long after Stefanidis exited. As soon he stepped inside, something detonated in the alcove behind the organ. Its massive pipes came crashing down in front of him, rolling and colliding with each other, reverberating as if they were massive tuning forks, a clamor that was deafening yet strangely sacred.

Loyola managed to avoid being crushed, but he fell backward, his ears ringing. His broken ribs stabbed into his lungs when he hit the ground, rendering every breath an agony, but he hauled himself to his feet.

Coll was saying something, but Loyola couldn't make it out. He clambered over the fallen pipes toward the exit, which was miraculously unobstructed. He burst out onto the Patio of Saint Gregory and, to his dismay, found more bodies. As his ears started to recover from the explosion, he could hear people screaming. He looked around wildly, but he couldn't find his target.

Loyola would be damned if he let this monster get away.

Coll was shouting in his ear, the sound muffled at first, then clarifying.

"LEFT!" Coll said. "LOOK LEFT!"

Loyola spun. He saw a flash of blue and gold stripes at the end of a long walkway as Stefanidis disappeared through a threshold that led toward the stairs to the basilica's rooftop terrace.

Loyola's stomach knotted. The roof offered no opportunity for escape. It could mean only one thing. The attack had not yet ended.

* * *

Lieutenant Gilberto Tancredi of the Swiss Guard had no idea what the fuck was going on, although he would never use language like that in such a holy place.

First, a nun had attacked one of the Guard, then the victim had slipped away somehow, and then someone had pointed out that the victim had been wearing a beard, which was strictly forbidden for a Guardsman. So maybe the nun had her reasons, but they couldn't know, because she had fallen ill, and then the Holy Father had ordered him and his commander to obey a deranged-looking monk, who had instructed him to call a phone number and recite a Latin phrase.

To make matters worse, a woman emerged from the grottoes and strode up to him purposefully. She had an AK-47 slung over her shoulder, and the plainclothes Guards drew their weapons, but tentatively lowered them when they saw the Interpol badge hanging around her neck, which she was brandishing assertively.

"There are several armed monks in the grottoes below," she said to Tancredi in an American accent, having somehow intuited that he was in charge of the scene. "Most are dead or disabled, but proceed with extreme caution. One of my colleagues is also down there. He's unconscious. Where's Loyola?"

"Who's Loyola?" Tancredi asked.

"Monk's robes, shaved head, heavy stubble, looks slightly insane," she said.

"Did you say Loyola?"

A man in an expensive suit walked up to them. He was carrying a leather satchel.

"You know him?" the woman asked.

The man looked at her suspiciously, then at Tancredi.

"You called for assistance," he said. "*Extrema unctio*."

Tancredi pointed at the nun. The man raised an eyebrow but wasted no time. In a flash he was by the nun's side, fishing in the satchel and emerging with a large syringe. Tancredi flinched as the man jammed the syringe into the nun's chest and emptied its contents. He removed it, grabbed her wrist and took her pulse.

A long moment passed in silence, and then the nun sat up abruptly, her eyes feverish but clearing rapidly. She looked around, then said to no one in particular, "Where's the Holy Father? Where's Loyola? Where's Stefanidis?"

"You really need to rest," the man in the suit said. "Your system . . ."

The nun put her hand to her ear, signaling that she was listening to someone else. She turned to Tancredi.

"You need to put guards at every access point that leads to the roof," she said. "Wait an hour, and if no one emerges, storm the roof with as many people as you can muster. If anyone except me or Loyola tries to exit the roof, kill them."

"Who are you?" Tancredi said plaintively.

She pulled herself to her feet and looked at the woman with the AK-47.

"I need your gun," the nun said.

"Hell no," the woman replied. "I'm coming to the roof."

The nun grabbed a halberd from a nearby Swiss Guard who was too taken aback to stop her. The man looked at Tancredi, who just shrugged helplessly.

"Fine," she said. "No time to argue. Let's go."

They took off. Tancredi considered following them, but then another man emerged from the grotto staircase, prompting another round of drawn weapons and shouting. The man raised his hands over his head. Tancredi saw that he had an Interpol badge around his neck.

"What the hell's going on?" Emil Moussa asked.

"I am sure I do not know," Tancredi sighed.

* * *

Halfway up the stairs, Loyola paused to nurse his aching chest. He was caught by a coughing spasm, and when he took his hand away from his mouth, it was spattered with blood.

"Not a lot, at least," he said.

"Not a lot of what?" Coll asked.

"Never mind," Loyola said. "Do you have eyes on the roof?"

"Yes," Coll said. "But they've disabled some of the cameras."

"They," Loyola said, his heart sinking.

"At least six, maybe more," Coll said. "Cavalry is on its way. You don't have to do this alone. Just wait."

"They aren't up there for a coffee social," Loyola said. "The attack is still ongoing. Could be bombs, could be worse. I can't afford to wait."

"The pope is e-vacked, and Stefanidis is on or heading for the roof," Coll said. "Loyola is in pursuit."

"I know?"

"Sorry, I wasn't talking to you. Patching you in."

"No time to argue," Fortis said in his ear. "Let's go."

"Sister Belina," Loyola said, his relief palpable.

"Check," Fortis said. "En route to you. Rocha is backing me up."

"It's not safe for her," Loyola said.

"It's not safe for you either," Fortis said dismissively. "We're coming your way, and the Swiss Guard are sealing off the roof. I didn't stick around for a briefing, but the *Carabinieri* have got to be mobilized by now, and they're probably coming with choppers."

"Roger that," Loyola said, as he resumed climbing. "We need to end this before they get here. Otherwise it's going to be a massacre."

* * *

"Are you OK?" Rocha asked, as they climbed over the fallen organ pipes, following in Loyola's wake. "You were kind of on the verge of death a few minutes ago, yeah?"

"Feeling much better," Fortis said, in a less-than-reassuring manner. "Wide-spectrum antitoxin."

"Is that a real thing?" Rocha asked.

"Lucky for me," Fortis said. "I'm Belina, by the way."

"And you somehow know my name," Rocha said.

"Father Loyola recognized you," Fortis said.

"Right," Rocha said. "But who are you, and who is he, for that matter, and what the flying fuck is going on here anyway?"

"There's a man on the roof who came here to kill the pope," Fortis said. "And an unknown number of highly trained killers accompanying him. You should think about sitting this out, but if you don't, I strongly recommend that you hang back and try to pick some of them off from a safe distance."

"I'm a cop, not a soldier," Rocha said. "What are you?"

Fortis shrugged.

"I'm one royally pissed-off Bride of Christ," she replied.

"This is insane," Rocha said.

"Divine madness," Fortis said with a grin, as she got clear of the pipes and threw open the door.

* * *

At the top of the stairs, Loyola paused to catch his breath, then stripped off the monk's robes. If death was waiting for him out there, he would face it as a priest, proudly wearing his Roman collar, the armor of God.

The door to the roof opened onto a spacious terrace. To his left, in the center of the roof, was a café and gift shop. Directly in front of him, a broad walkway led to the basilica's massive cupola dome. In the other direction, a tall safety fence kept visitors away from the famous stone statues of Jesus and his apostles that gazed out upon Saint Peter's Square from the top of the basilica's façade. The scene was washed in sepia tones by dim electric lights.

Loyola wanted to stick his head out for a better look, but he was certain there would be sentries, and he wasn't ready to fight yet.

"What have we got?" he whispered.

"The Guard is still here, and they are still none too pleased with me, but apparently have their orders," Coll said. "I'm putting you on speaker so they can hear for themselves that the Black infidel is on the level."

"Fine," Loyola said. "What can you see?"

"We're up to at least ten monks on the roof," Coll said. "Stefanidis is in the café, for fuck's sake. Hell of a time for a coffee break."

"He must have something stashed," Loyola said. "Weapons, maybe a bomb."

"Maybe not, he just came out with a cup of espresso," Coll said. "But wait, there are two guys behind him, and they're wheeling a cart with large crates that look like they might hold Stingers or some other kind of rockets. Also, the mad monk has traded his poofy striped costume—no offense, fellas—for a brown monk's robe like the others are wearing."

Loyola cursed himself silently. They hadn't searched the café. It had been crowded with people during the day, and they never circled back.

"Tell the Guards to tell the *Carabinieri* to keep their choppers back until I can take out the artillery," Loyola said. "Are the monks heading for the dome?"

"The Guards can hear you," Coll reminded him. "And yes, the mad monks are heading toward the dome."

The assassination attempt had failed. Loyola couldn't think of any reason for the plotters to convene on the roof except to go out in a blaze of glory, collapsing the dome of the basilica, beneath which so much history had played out.

But something didn't sit right. If the goal of this exercise was to elevate Macerata, what was the point of a shabby and conventional terrorist attack? It would cheapen their sacrifices, and in its wake, the Church would rally around Nicholas, empowering him to easily sideline the scheming cardinal.

The dome might be the obvious target for someone else, but not for Stefanidis.

"The ladies are maybe four minutes behind you," Coll said. "Maybe six. I strongly recommend you wait for them. I can hear how ragged your breathing is."

"What is Stefanidis doing now?" Loyola asked.

"They . . . are no longer moving toward the dome," Coll said. "They've stopped by the bell tower on the south side of the roof and appear to be unloading."

Loyola's mental map flashed red, even as he heard a sharp intake of breath over the line from Coll.

"Where's the Holy Father?" he asked.

"I see it," Coll said. Loyola could hear Coll's fingers hammering rapidly on a keyboard. "He's in a safe room in the Treasury Museum."

The dome wasn't the target—the museum was. If their ordinance was powerful enough, or aimed carefully enough, they could collapse the whole building on top of the Holy Father.

"Get word to . . ."

A burst of electronic noise suddenly erupted in his ear. The monks were jamming the signal—probably not theirs specifically, but all over the Square.

Loyola popped the earbud out. Hopefully Coll could get a word of warning to the Holy Father, but he couldn't count on that happening fast enough.

No more time to think. He had to go in.

* * *

"How many stairs?" Rocha asked skeptically.

"Two hundred and something," Fortis said.

"There's an elevator," Rocha said, pointing.

"If you like getting shot when the bell rings."

Rocha thought for a minute.

"Let's send it up without us in it," she said. "Might buy Loyola a distraction."

"Or it might screw up his stealth play," Fortis said.

"Which do you think is more likely?" Rocha asked.

Fortis pressed the call button. The elevator car was already there, and the doors slid open. She stuck her head inside, then looked up at its ceiling.

"I have a better idea," Fortis said, pulling off most of her habit, except for the headdress, to reveal a black body suit, tactical pants, and an astonishing number of knives on a bandolier.

"I hate it already," Rocha said.

* * *

The Swiss Guards in the Papal Situation Room were not having a merry Christmas, and things were getting less merry by the minute, as they watched dozens of screens with camera feeds go blank, one at a time.

"You heard the man!" Coll said. "Get the pope the fuck out of that building. Anywhere but there. Radios are down, you have to go on foot. GO NOW!"

The Guards dashed out of the room.

Coll grabbed his double-barreled shotgun, a pocket full of shells, and a belt full of grenades. He still hadn't adjusted to his missing eye, and he couldn't handle anything more precise. He pulled a set of gold-and-white vestments with a cross motif over his head to cover it all.

As he turned to leave, he caught a view of himself in a mirror and cursed—a Muslim wearing the symbol of the Crusaders, fighting to save the pope.

"The things I do for this man," he muttered and headed out.

* * *

Loyola was certain that at least two monks were waiting on the other side of the door to the roof. Only two, if he was very lucky. Stefanidis and the rocket men were on the other side of the long building that housed the cafe and gift shop. If he could take out the sentries quietly, he might be able to surprise the others—depending on how many there were.

Loyola drew his Glock and was about to launch into motion when he heard the ding of an elevator bell behind him.

*Shit.* He flattened himself against the wall just as the sentries responded, storming into the covered stairwell with assault rifles raised.

The door opened, but the elevator was empty. The monks exhaled, lowering their weapons and beginning to turn. Loyola would have only a moment to act before they spotted him. But then a lithe figure swung down from the elevator's ceiling and barreled into them.

Sister Belina Fortis yanked the first monk's rifle forward and smashed her forehead into his nose. When his hands went limp, she wordlessly passed the weapon to Loyola, while spinning to plant a sharp elbow in the second man's throat. His larynx cracked with a sickening sound, and he sank to the ground.

It was over in the blink of an eye.

Maria Rocha dropped down through the elevator's ceiling hatch, gamely but with somewhat less grace.

"You have the right to remain silent," she said to Loyola.

He stared at her blankly, unsure of how to respond.

"It's a joke for Christ's sake," she said.

"Very funny," Loyola said, without inflection. He turned to Fortis.

"At least eight more, maybe others," he said. "Probably others, maybe a lot. All trained by Stefanidis."

"You look like shit," she said.

"You too," he said.

Footsteps were approaching.

"Brother Marco," someone called. "Report!"

"Stefanidis is on the south side of the terrace," Loyola said, speaking low and fast. "He's still trying to kill the Holy Father. Whoever gets free, goes over there. Whoever gets a shot, takes it. No egos."

Fortis nodded. She retrieved a halberd from the elevator and bounded through the door, planting the polearm's shaft on the ground and using it to vault into the fray. Rocha's eyes widened, as Loyola checked his weapon.

"Stay here," he said. "Pick off anyone you can. Try not to kill one of us."

"If I kill you, I won't get to arrest you," Rocha said, dropping into a kneeling stance and raising her weapon.

Loyola waded into the melee.

Fortis was a whirlwind, and three monks were already on the ground. Four more were rushing toward her from different directions, unable to draw a bead and worried about shooting each other. The halberd flashed across one's throat, and he fell backward in a spray of blood. Loyola had trained himself to count every enemy and every shot fired, but the chaos here surpassed him. Bodies were flying everywhere. Rocha popped out of the stairwell and picked off one, then another. No matter how many they killed, more seemed to arrive.

Loyola dashed past the madness to cut a mostly straight line between the cupola on his right and the central bell tower on his left. One of the monks noticed his charge and pivoted to intercept. Loyola put a bullet between his eyes without missing a step.

A six-foot white metal fence separated him from the south side of the terrace. He vaulted over it and found himself facing the rear of the central structure.

He kicked open the back door of the gift shop, startling the four monks who were stationed in a long room lined with a variety of papally blessed tchotchkes—posters, rosaries, medals, scapulars, and more.

Loyola rushed forward, slamming the first monk into a wall covered with crucifixes of all shapes and sizes, which clattered to the floor from the thunderous impact. The second monk pointed a weapon at him, but Loyola was moving too fast. He grabbed the barrel and yanked the weapon out of the monk's hands, then kicked the monk in the testicles, dropping an elbow on his neck when he doubled over.

While this was happening, the next two monks managed to aim their weapons, and Loyola jumped to take cover behind the counter as a fusillade hit the wall above him, which displayed an array of blessed waters and oils. The torrent of bullets showered him with broken glass and holy water for what seemed like an impossibly long time. When the shooters finally paused their barrage, Loyola surged upward with his weapon raised, taking them down with two ruthlessly precise shots.

Time was running out. Stefanidis must be nearly ready to fire his rockets.

Loyola ran faster than he had ever run before, his muscles screaming with exhaustion and his chest heaving despite the pain in his ribs.

* * *

Rocha picked off yet another monk. Yet her tally was a fraction of the casualties racked up by the nun, who seemed to tap into some primal force of violence. Rocha was beginning to understand some of the past body counts her investigation had uncovered.

Well, "understand" might be overstating it.

She almost jumped out of her skin when the elevator bell dinged behind her. She hadn't even noticed it leaving. As the doors slid open, she saw an older priest in white-and-gold vestments, wearing an eye patch and carrying a shotgun. She fired in his direction, but it went wild. He jumped backward with a yelp, pressing himself flat against the elevator wall and out of the line of fire.

"Rocha!" he said. "I'm with Frank!"

"Why should I believe that?" she demanded.

"Fair point," he said. "I got nothing."

Something about his tone was reassuring.

"Fuck," she said. "You better not kill me."

Calvin Coll exited the elevator and took cover on the other side of the door.

"How's it going out there?"

"The nun is terrifying," she said.

"That's for damn sure," Coll said. "Where's Frank?"

"He's trying to get to the Big Bad, I think."

"OK," Coll said. "I'm going after him. Cover me?"

"Why the fuck not?" Rocha said.

"You're OK, lady," Coll said. "See you on the flip side."

He ran in the direction Loyola had gone, threading a path among an impossibly large and still growing pile of dead and disabled monks.

* * *

Loyola had no time for subtlety. He came crashing out of the central building, guns blazing, making a beeline toward the southern bell tower, a dome smaller than the cupola, but still sixty feet wide and over a hundred tall, with massive stone arches that opened onto a cavernous belfry.

Stefanidis and his two accomplices were almost ready to unleash a barrage that would destroy the Treasury Museum and kill the Holy Father. The monks were bolting the rocket launcher to the terrace floor, but when they heard Loyola approach, they dropped their equipment and turned to meet him, opening fire while Stefanidis took cover.

Loyola dived and rolled, ignoring the agonizing pain in his ribs. As he rose from the floor, he put the closest monk in his sights, but an unstoppable cough wracked his body as he pulled the trigger, and his bullets missed the mark, flying into the belfry and ricocheting inside. The basilica's massive bells were too large to be moved by such a small impact, but they set off a soft and haunting vibrato tone.

*Oh how they pound*

The monk Loyola had been aiming at landed a shot on him, center mass. Loyola's Kevlar vest absorbed most of the impact, but his cracked ribs went off like fireworks. Loyola rarely resorted to full auto, but he raised his rifle, squeezed the trigger and held it down, spraying the scene indiscriminately. When the smoke cleared, both monks were down, and the bell continued its eerie keen.

Loyola took cover behind the massive tower, his back pressed against its base. The abandoned rocket launcher was in front of him. Coll had been wrong; it was considerably larger than a Stinger. Loyola didn't recognize the model, but he could see Chinese characters on the crate. The monks hadn't finished mounting its stand to the floor, and the tube was lying on its side, the front of the barrel pointed toward the gift shop.

Stefanidis was somewhere on the other side of the bell tower, probably with a pretty good idea of Loyola's position. The arches that opened on to the belfry were above his head, and he wouldn't be able see to the other side unless he hoisted himself up.

"Give it up, Stefanidis," Loyola called out. "There's no escape."

"There is no escape," Stefanidis agreed, his voice ethereal and distorted. "There is only the mission." The voice seemed to be right behind him, but when Loyola whipped around, he found no one there. The acoustics of the bell tower were playing tricks on him.

Loyola looked up. Stefanidis might have climbed up to the level of the arches in order to claim the high ground and take advantage of the confusing acoustics.

Loyola advanced a few feet to where a short flight of stairs hugged the tower wall. Cautiously poking his head up into the archway, he tried to turn the trick back on Stefanidis, directing his voice into the resonant space.

"The mission makes no sense," Loyola said. "How did Macerata talk you into this?"

The ploy apparently worked; he heard a scrambling sound, as Stefanidis tried to get a fix on his location. Silently enduring the pain in his chest, Loyola hoisted himself the rest of the way up on to the ledge of the belfry.

His adversary was not visible in dim lighting, so Loyola slowly inched his way along the ledge, his back against its pillars that separated the arches, moving clockwise around the tower.

"Macerata," Stefanidis spat, dripping with scorn. His voice seemed to be moving now as well, but with the acoustics and his own movement, Loyola couldn't be sure. "His ambitions mean nothing, except as a means to compel his support."

"Then why this sacrilege?" Loyola asked, inching further around the bend.

"Sacrilege?" Stefanidis said, incredulously. "Have you forgotten who I am? I have served the Order of Saint Uriel, and I have served the Dicastery for the Doctrine of the Faith. Sacrilege? Far from it, my actions are consecrated to God! God has chosen me to stop the apostasy of Nicholas!"

The voice seemed to emanate from in front of Loyola now, and he slowed his advance to a crawl, using every sense to prevent a surprise encounter. Loyola lowered his voice slightly, in the hopes of confusing Stefanidis, who was undoubtedly engaged in the same exercise of echolocation.

"Apostasy?" Loyola said. "He's the pope!"

"Ah, Francis, you are out of your depth," Stefanidis asked, sounding amused. "There is precedent. Pope Marcellinus, for instance, the first and last to take the name, became an apostate in the fourth century by offering worship to a false god to save himself from persecution. The church tried to cover it up, but it is known."

Loyola risked peering around the next column. He found no sign of Stefanidis.

"Nicholas doesn't worship a false god," Loyola said. "And the pope is infallible. By definition, he cannot be apostate."

"Only when he speaks *ex cathedra*," Stefanidis said, as if he were talking to a child. "He must invoke the power of his office to claim infallibility, and he must do so publicly. It's not a license to do whatever one wants."

"I still don't get it," Loyola said. He paused and listened, focusing his senses and praying for inspiration. "What's your beef?"

"My beef?" Stefanidis said mockingly. "You are such an American, Francis. My *beef* pertains to the accursed woman."

"A specific woman?" Loyola said. "Or women in general?"

"Your successor, obviously," Stefanidis said.

"Sister Belina?" Loyola asked, puzzled. "You object to her position in the Order? Is that what this is about?"

"You really don't know," Stefanidis said.

"I know she's at least as formidable as I am, probably more so."

"Fool!" Stefanidis hissed. "She's a peerless killer. *That* is not the issue."

"Then what?"

"The *primus sicarius* has always been a priest!"

"So what?" Loyola said.

"You still don't understand?" Stefanidis asked, incredulously. *"He ordained her."*

"What?"

A wave of shock washed over Loyola. He had spent previous little time pondering the reason for the conspiracy. Men sought power, the same now as it had ever been. And his work rarely concerned itself with motive. But this . . .

*He calls me his "little experiment."*

*No harm must come to her.*

Belina Fortis was a priest. The first and only female Catholic priest.

The ramifications sent his mind spinning. He instinctively rebelled against the idea. He had been a priest too long, he was steeped in the Church's parochial traditions and unchanging nature. But equally strong currents arose in response—his love and respect for Pope Nicholas, and his still-formative relationship with Fortis, rapidly forged through combat and the urgency of crisis, a state of exception that allowed something to take root in him with unexpected strength. It was something new in his life, but already deep.

Almost no one in the world could understand what it meant to head up the Order of Saint Uriel and deliver the wrath of God on behalf of the Church itself. In a very real way, Loyola and Fortis had no one except each other. Whatever creed and duty demanded, his first and most authentic instinct was to take her side.

He heard the scramble of footsteps, as if from a distance, driving all of these thoughts from his mind. Stefanidis was making his move—and the sound was coming from the direction of the rocket launcher.

Loyola jumped down from the ledge and raced back in the direction he had come. Stefanidis was closing in on the launcher. When he saw Loyola, he drew two stilettos and adopted a fighting stance.

*Fuck that*, Loyola thought, raising his rifle. But something slammed into him from one side—another monk, someone he had missed. The monk ripped the rifle from Loyola's hands. Before his opponent could use it, Loyola slipped his fingers into the brass knucks and unleashed a series of blows on the man's face.

The monk dropped, but Stefanidis now had his hands on the rocket launcher, and he was hoisting its barrel in Loyola's direction. Loyola ran toward him at a speed that would break Olympic records, his feet barely touching the ground, as if he was nearing escape velocity. He crashed into Stefanidis, and the rocket launcher fell heavily on the ground.

Something broke loose inside of him.

Loyola had survived this long because of a glacial cold at the center of his being. He was the man who never lost his cool, never acted impetuously, always stuck to the plan. It was the only way to survive the horrors he experienced and the horrors he inflicted as the *primus sicarius*, the pope's assassin.

But it had been years since he inhabited that role. Since then, he had discovered the joys of community and connection, the satisfaction of playing a role in lives of ordinary people, overseeing their weddings, births, and funerals. He had taken the cold as far as he could and found something warm beyond it. Stefanidis and his thugs had thrust him back into that old life, sent him back to the killing fields. He had returned to violence without the old safeguards, and all of it erupted now as rage.

*Rage.* Loyola swung his fists again and again, relishing the way the brass knuckles tore into his enemy's flesh.

*Rage.* A part of himself that he had refused to face, that he had entombed in ice, bound it up in heavy chains of cold steel for so many years.

His indiscriminate attack was devastating, but it also left him open. Loyola felt one of Stefanidis' stilettos slide into his hip, just below the Kevlar vest. His left leg buckled, and he fell to the ground. Stefanidis lurched backward, his face a bloody mess, but he was possessed with an ecstasy and somehow remained on his feet. He dropped the knives and groped for the rocket launcher.

Stefanidis put his hands on the weapon and lifted it with some difficulty.

Then came a blast, and another.

Stefanidis jerked backward as if a puppeteer had yanked his strings, but he did not fall. His robes and the skin of his arms shredded in sync with the blasts. Loyola could see the bones of his fingers through a mess of ruined tissue and blood.

But Stefanidis did not release his grip.

When Loyola hoisted himself to his feet, he saw Calvin Coll standing next to the bell tower with a smoking double-barreled shotgun in his hands.

"Fuck the Inquisition!" he shouted triumphantly.

"RUN!" Loyola shouted to Coll, as he stumbled toward Stefanidis. Coll looked at Stefanidis, grasped what was about to happen, then dove to the floor and rolled.

Loyola fell on top of Stefanidis and they toppled together, as the mad monk triggered the weapon. The rocket launched, skidding across the terrace floor crazily, like a skipping stone, then it seemed to bounce at an acute angle, striking the top of the bell tower dome and exploding.

Loyola felt a scorching heat, and then the ground turned to rubble beneath his feet, the crest of a wave of collapsing stone that carried him along like a surfer riding the curl. Stefanidis was torn away from him by the force of the collapse.

Loyola felt terror at the scale of a tremendous and impossible fall.

His last thought was of Satan being cast down from Heaven.

* * *

Loyola opened his eyes on a scene of devastation.

Marble and stone surrounded him, beams and pillars, pieces of art.

He had prevented Stefanidis from killing the pope, or so he hoped, but Saint Peter's Basilica had not gone unscathed. As his vision cleared, he realized that the roof had collapsed and they had fallen into the church. He found himself staring at the granite head of Pope Pius VIII, which he recognized as the statue that once loomed over the gate to the Treasury Museum. He felt a stab of fear for the Holy Father, but as he craned his head around a bit, he could see the damage was mostly confined to the basilica.

Loyola tried to move but his leg was pinned. He was near the top of a precarious-looking pile of rubble. The basilica had been evacuated, at least as far as he could tell. If there were bodies, he couldn't see them.

He heard a cough, and he coughed reflexively in response, his mouth filling with something salty that was almost certainly blood. He turned his head toward the source of the sound.

Konstantin Stefanidis lay a few feet away from him. A stone arch had crushed the lower half of his body, and he looked pale—almost certainly due to internal bleeding. When Stefanidis saw that Loyola was awake, he managed a weak smile.

"Francis," he said. "Do you remember our talks back in France?"

"I remember," Loyola said. His throat felt raw.

"Do you remember the papal bull I told you about?" Stefanidis continued. "*Ut negotium*, allowing the Inquisitors to absolve each other's sins?"

"I remember," Loyola said.

"Will you hear my confession?" Stefanidis asked.

Loyola paused and thought about it before speaking.

"All right."

"Bless me Father, for I have sinned. It has been a week since my last confession."

He coughed wetly for a moment, then continued.

"I lied and conspired against the Holy Father," Stefanidis said. "I acted with intent to kill. In my defense, I had reasons. An apostate pope is unimaginable, intolerable, to one such as I. And I was perhaps the only person with knowledge of the apostasy and the will to do what had to be done."

"I still don't really understand," Loyola said. "Nicholas is God's representative on earth. If he did it, it must be God's will."

"Francis, it is not that simple," Stefanidis said, coughing again. "If he had announced it *ex cathedra*, with a formal declaration of doctrine, we would not be here, regardless of what I might personally think. But this . . . this was underhanded. The act of a coward. A reward for his pet, done outside the *depositum fidei*, the traditions of the Church. Infallibility takes place in the light of day. No, Francis, this was apostasy. I am certain of it."

"You killed innocent people," Loyola said. "And put others in harm's way."

"I killed innocent people," Stefanidis admitted. "To this I confess. But harm's way? Do you want to lay your own sins at my feet as well? I did not force you to kill anyone. I did not force *that woman* to kill anyone. Or is this your confession to me?"

"Arrogance," Loyola said "You were convinced you knew better than the Holy Father, so convinced that you chose mortal sin rather than admitting that you could be wrong."

"I accept this accusation," Stefanidis said. "I have been arrogant, and I am sorry."

He coughed again.

"Give me my penance," he said. "I do not have much time. I must make my act of contrition."

"No," Loyola said.

"No?"

"You have not repented of your sins," Loyola said. "I don't think you even regret them. You have no remorse. You would do it all again."

"Francis . . ."

"No," Loyola said. "You don't deserve absolution, and I cannot, will not, give it."

Stefanidis laughed weakly, then coughed up a large amount of blood. Then his ruined face took on a sorrowful mien.

"Think well on this, Francis," he said, and Loyola heard something like real fear in the man's voice. "I will not live to reach another confessor. You are deliberately choosing to send me to hell for all eternity."

Loyola felt the decision twist inside of him. He had undoubtedly sent many men to hell during his career, but it had always been incidental to killing them. This was different, somehow, crueler. He wasn't sure if his resolve was ugly or righteous, but it was unshakeable.

"Yes," Loyola said. "That's exactly what I'm doing."

Stefanidis made a strangled sound, which could have been laughter or tears.

"Then neither will I absolve you. We will go down into hell together, you and I. Has there ever been a pair of priests more deserving?"

"Probably," Loyola said.

Stefanidis laughed a little at that, then his head lolled back, and the light went out of his eyes.

Loyola heard voices approaching, rescuers perhaps, but they seemed to be shouting him from a great distance, or underwater. His mouth was full of blood, and he felt a mounting pressure in his chest. His vision went blue around the edges, and he thought he felt a soothing hand on his brow.

He was hot, then cold, then nothing at all.

CHAPTER

20

# The Weary World Rejoices

LOYOLA WOKE UP in the back of an ambulance, to the sound of the dashboard radio playing "O Holy Night." He sat up too fast and was rewarded with a blast of pain in his ribs and some fuzziness in his vision.

It was better than waking up in hell, which he had more than half-expected.

"Easy there," came a voice from the fuzzy zone. "Even a tough motherfucker like you needs to slow down for a concussion and a set of cracked ribs."

"Calvin," Loyola said, weakly. His voice was hoarse, but he no longer seemed to be coughing up blood.

"That's right, brother," Coll said. "You got the job done, but you made a hell of a mess. There are a lot of people wanting to talk to you, but I have instructions to take you to the big guy first."

"Nicholas," Loyola rasped. "He's alive?"

"Alive and well thanks to you," Coll said. "Can you walk?"

"He really shouldn't be up and around," a medic said.

"Take it up with the pope," Coll said.

With Coll's help, Loyola managed to get to his feet. He was steadier than he had expected to be, but every inch of his body ached, and his hip felt fragile where he had been stabbed.

"You want a wheelchair?" Coll asked.

"No, I got this," Loyola said.

"Figured," Coll said. "Badass like you can't be trusted to do the sensible thing. Lean on me then."

"You drove ten hours to Rome one day after your eye was shot out," Loyola said.

"Yeah, but that was an emergency," Coll said. "Everything's cool now."

As his vision started to clear, Loyola could see they were in Saint Peter's Square, surrounded by dozens of ambulances and police cars. The statue of Jesus on top of the basilica's façade, and the saints of the Colonnade looked down on them serenely, apparently unharmed. But behind the façade, Loyola could see clouds of black smoke.

"How many?" Loyola asked.

"Too many," Coll said. "But most of them were killed by Stefanidis inside the church. A few trampled in the panic, more than a few heart attacks. But most everyone was out by the time you brought the house down."

"The damage . . ."

"The pope said, and I quote, 'tell that asshole not to worry about it,'" Coll said. "Most of it can be repaired or restored. It could have been a lot worse."

"Did he really say 'asshole'?"

"I swear to Allah," Coll said. "Well, look who we got here."

Martina Rocha was standing in front of Loyola. Her Interpol partner, Emil Moussa, was right behind her.

"Am I being arrested?" Loyola asked.

"Funny thing that," Rocha said. "The only thing I really had on you was as a person of interest in the Garde-le-château massacre. But it turns out the dead guy we pulled out of the rubble next to you was a perfect match for the fingerprints found on a bloody stiletto left at the scene."

"Fast work," Loyola said.

"Your buddy here suggested we check," Rocha said.

Loyola nodded. He didn't want to volunteer any additional information, since he was not without liability in the incident. And of course the Order of Saint Uriel was a closely guarded secret, or at least he hoped it still was.

"We're supposed to meet with the Vatican's Secretariat of State after things calm down a bit," Moussa said, "but we're inclined to call it a closed case."

Loyola smiled weakly.

"Your boss won't mind if you come back empty-handed?" he asked Rocha.

"Ah well, that," she said sheepishly. "I may have been fired."

"On Christmas?" Coll exclaimed. "That's cold."

"I think we'll be able to find something for her at Interpol," Moussa said. "Solving Garde-le-château is a feather in her cap. Of course, there are many loose ends. I don't suppose . . ."

"My man has a concussion," Coll interjected, "and he's late for an audience with the pope."

"Just so," Moussa said with a smirk. "Maybe we'll clear it up someday."

"Maybe," Loyola said.

"Come on now," Coll said. "That's enough."

* * *

They found the Holy Father in a secure basement room, down a long hallway lined with Swiss Guards, a mix of plainclothes and uniformed men. As Loyola passed, each Guard snapped to attention and saluted.

Loyola was deeply uncomfortable. He was a creature of the shadows, and even such semi-public recognition made him feel profoundly exposed. The Holy Father had instructed him to protect the anonymity of the Order of Saint Uriel at all costs. He had surely failed spectacularly.

They entered a sleek, modern space, a cross between a briefing room and a comfy hotel lobby. A number of people were working phones and computers in a low buzz of activity. At the far end of the room, sitting in a chair that was not exactly a throne, but not not a throne, was Pope Nicholas VI. Standing at his side was Sister Belina Fortis. Her face was dirty, but she had changed into a clean indigo pantsuit and matching headdress.

Sister . . . Loyola's muddled brain remembered. Father? Mother?

Nicholas smiled at his approach. In the Holy Father's presence, Loyola became acutely self-conscious. His priestly suit was caked with dust and blood, and he was suddenly aware that he could smell himself.

"I am truly glad to see you up and moving, my son," the pontiff said.

"He needs rest," Coll said.

"Of course," Nicholas said. "But may we have a few private moments first?"

Coll looked at Loyola, who nodded.

"This Catholic shit, man," Coll muttered, as he went to find a seat. "Never ends."

Nicholas led Loyola to a private room with a few comfortable chairs and a table with water bottles and snacks. Fortis followed along, ready to offer support if needed, but Loyola managed on his own.

He tried to stand at attention, but the pope waved at him imperiously.

"For God's sake, sit," he said. Loyola complied, and Fortis quietly left, closing the door behind her.

"Holy Father," Loyola rasped. "I beg your forgiveness."

"Are you fucking kidding me?" Nicholas asked.

Loyola gaped.

"Father Francis Loyola," the pope said, more formally, "you saved my life and countless more by preventing Konstantin Stefanidis from destroying the Treasury Museum while it was filled with security personnel. *Forgive you*? I am here to *thank* you."

"But the basilica . . ."

"Francis, stop," Nicholas said, impatiently. "I believe this is what they call 'Catholic guilt.' I will have none of it. You have served God admirably."

"But the Order, the need for secrecy . . ."

"Ah that," he said. "Here is the situation in which we find ourselves. First, and most important, Stefanidis is dead. Unfortunately, Cardinal Macerata fled before we could arrest him, as did Lloyd Bridgewater. I have some leverage over the cardinal, but his deep involvement with the Order of Saint Uriel makes him a powerful foe. He knows where the bodies are buried, literally."

Loyola nodded.

"This is a serious problem, but one that can be resolved another day," he said. *"In aeternum terminale."*

Loyola nodded.

"Monsignor Biancardi was not as well-prepared as his coconspirators," Nicholas continued, "to his great misfortune but to our advantage. He was still packing his bags when Sister Belina detained him. I have persuaded the monsignor to repent of his treason and turn his considerable skills toward the remediation of our current public relations crisis."

"You must have been quite persuasive," Loyola said.

"Sister Belina went to his quarters directly from the roof, and I think it's fair to say she was not overflowing with Christian charity," Nicholas said. "The monsignor was anxious to make amends."

Loyola laughed.

"With the help of the Deacons, we have cleaned up the dead monks in the grotto," Nicholas continued. "The ones on the roof shall be deemed tragic victims of the terrorist attack, which was a 'lone wolf' operation conducted by one Aris Stavros, a cult leader and a once-in-a-generation villain, whom we have learned was also the author of a notorious mass murder in Garde-le-château in 2010."

"Will that work?" Loyola asked, incredulously.

"Fortunately, Monsignor Biancardi's original plan to protect Macerata required only slight adjustments," Nicholas said. "He has already unleashed a horde of Internet conspiracy theories to muddy the water with outlandish claims about what 'really' happened. Few of them are as outlandish as the reality, but if someone someday somehow stumbles onto the truth, it will be dismissed as online nonsense."

"But the footage?" Loyola asked. "Surely much of this was captured on camera."

"Less than you might think," the pope said. "The livestream stopped when the fighting began, and we've taken care of the surveillance. Unfortunately, many people saw your successor's fight with Stefanidis. Biancardi has put out the story that one of the Guardsmen was working undercover as a nun for some reason."

Nicholas laughed, and Loyola smiled, but the anecdote brought him back to earth.

"Did Monsignor Biancardi reveal anything to you about the motives of the conspirators?" Loyola asked, cautiously. "The real ones, I mean."

Nicholas VI met Loyola's gaze.

"What did Stefanidis tell you?" he asked.

"He said you had apostatized."

"Specifically."

"I think you know," Loyola said.

"Many would agree with him," Nicholas sighed. "Do you?"

Loyola shrugged.

"It's above my pay grade," he said. "But I trust you. I believe in you."

"What do I always tell you, Francis?" Nicholas said with a rueful smile.

Loyola smiled back at him.

"'People fail you,'" he recited. "'Institutions fail you. God won't fail you.'"

"I am a man," Nicholas said. "I declined to invoke infallibility when I did this thing because I was feeling fallible when I did it. And of course, I am at odds with our institution."

"You are God's representative on earth," Loyola said. "And you're also a good man. Where you lead, I will follow. But you are . . ." He paused, then lifted his open hands and gestured at Nicholas. "-the pope."

"Once infallibility is invoked, it is forever," Nicholas said. "When God grants me certainty, I will be certain. Until then, I try to do my best."

Loyola shifted uncomfortably in his chair. His ribs hurt most, but the rest of him wasn't in very good shape either.

"I've kept you too long, my son," Nicholas said. "You need to rest. But tell me, is there anything I can do for you? Name it, and it's yours. You don't have to decide now. When you're ready, I'll be here."

"Will you hear my confession?" Loyola asked.

"Of course," Nicholas said.

Loyola crossed himself.

"Bless me Holy Father, for I have sinned . . ."

* * *

When Loyola emerged, he felt lighter. He was weary and injured, but he was right with God, and he hoped to stay that way going forward.

The outer chamber was buzzing with activity as the Church's professionals dealt with a multitude of problems and tasks resulting from the evening's events. Loyola passed a cluster of people talking about the Christmas Day Mass and its customary papal address from the balcony of the basilica overlooking Saint Peter's Square. The Holy Father insisted he would appear, but his aides were deeply concerned over security and the building's structural integrity. Loyola smiled. Nicholas would prevail, and his address would be spectacular. He hoped he would be awake to see it, but he had some doubts.

Loyola looked around for Belina Fortis, but his eyes landed instead on Calvin Coll, who was standing in a corner chatting with Mirsad. The boy smiled and waved without turning his head. Loyola walked over to them stiffly.

"Did the pope fire you?" Coll asked. "You really fucked this place up."

"Ninety days probation," Loyola said.

"A White man can get away with anything," Coll said, shaking his head.

"Mirsad, I hope they have been treating you well," Loyola said.

The boy nodded vigorously.

"After all this," Coll said, waving his arms, "he says wants to go sightseeing. I told him we're going to have to see what his mother thinks."

"Has the Lady spoken to you since the big explosion?" Loyola asked.

"Gospa says you did well," Mirsad said. "She says Belina did too."

Not Sister Belina, Loyola noted.

"What about you?" Coll asked. "Which life are you returning to?"

"Neither," Loyola said. "Time for something new."

"The Lady says your work is not yet finished," Mirsad said.

"It's done for today," Loyola said.

Loyola clapped Coll on the shoulder, and Coll hugged him in response, heedless of the priest's ribs. It hurt less than Loyola expected.

* * *

A room had been reserved for him at Saint Martha's House, but Loyola wasn't ready to sleep. Too many thoughts were rattling around in his head. He emerged back onto Saint Peter's Square and approached the basilica. Someone tried to wave him off, but one of the Swiss Guards recognized him and let him pass with a grin and a razor-sharp salute.

The front of the basilica was not too much worse for wear, although everything was covered with a thin gray layer of stone dust, which also swirled through shafts cast by the electric spotlights erected for emergency workers.

One minute, everyone had been celebrating a joyous Christmas, then everything was frozen in place by unthinkable tragedy. Loyola had been to Pompeii once, and the scene reminded him of that.

But Saint Peter's would rise again, of that he had no doubt.

He passed through the jubilee door, running his hand over its panels, as so many pilgrims had before him. The *Pietà* lay beyond, safe behind its glass wall, one of the few surfaces not touched by dust. The Holy Mother, captured by Michelangelo in her moment of unspeakable grief. He wondered if she liked the statue, or if it was too painful for her to look upon.

He moved on through the basilica. The damage was terrible, but also less than he had feared, mostly contained in the left transept where daily Masses were usually celebrated. The floor was covered in debris, but he couldn't see any sign that it had caved in, which meant the grottoes might have been spared the worst of it. Except for a few bullet holes here and there, but who was counting?

He walked over to Saint Longinus, who stood sentry as if nothing had happened, his spear upright, his face ecstatic, his robes billowing around him.

Belina Fortis was kneeling nearby, her face turned toward the altar, her fingers counting on an olive-wood rosary. Her eyes were closed, and her lips were moving. If she was anyone else, he would think she had not noticed his approach.

But she wasn't anyone else.

Fortis concluded her prayers, crossed herself, and turned toward him with a smile.

"I almost died here," she said, gesturing back toward the confessionals.

"Me too," Loyola said, gesturing toward the giant pile of debris.

They both laughed, and then she grew serious.

"The last thing Stefanidis said to me, what I thought might be the last thing I ever heard, was that this was all my fault."

"He was insane," Loyola said. "And also wrong."

She shrugged.

"I chose a hazardous path," she said. "I don't fear death, but I fear failure. I fear what I am capable of, and what my choices yield. You understand this."

"Some of it," Loyola said gently. "But I think the cross you carry is heavier than mine."

Fortis stepped closer and looked him straight in the eyes, seeking to read something within. But Loyola's eyes were practiced liars, and whatever she was seeking, she didn't find. She smiled and shook her head.

"What will you do now?" he asked.

"I remain the *prima sicaria*," she said. "I imagine my next mission will involve Cardinal Macerata. He's too dangerous to let be."

Loyola nodded.

"They say he's descended from Machiavelli," he said.

"That's what I heard too," she said. "I could use your help."

He held her gaze for as long as he could bear it. For a moment, he allowed himself to imagine a different sort of life than the one God had chosen for him.

"I have a penance to complete," he said, finally.

Loyola turned and limped off into the night.

# ACKNOWLEDGMENTS

I WANT TO START by thanking my beta readers circle, whose feedback and support are absolutely irreplaceable, telling me what I got right and what I got wrong, including vetoing some of my wilder/dumber ideas: Roberta Bortolini, Megan McBride, Sam Jackson, John Horgan, Caitlin Fitz Gerald, Brett Friedman, and Larry Berger. I write for them before I write for anyone else.

Effusive thanks are due next to the people who ushered this book into the world, including my agent, Wayne Arthurson of The Rights Factory. At Crooked Lane Books, thanks to my editor Marcia Markland for believing in this project, Julia Abbott, Thaisheemarie Fantauzzi Perez, and many others on the production and marketing teams.

A lot of research went into this book, and I would be remiss if I did not give a special shoutout to everyone who has spent their time and labor documenting every inch of Saint Peter's Basilica and then posting that information online. I visited the Vatican in 2014, but I had no inkling of this book in mind at that point, so I did not run around looking to see which stairwells went where or searching for secret passages in the basement. A crucial resource was the website stpetersbasilica.info, which includes annotated and illustrated floor plans of the Basilica, and the countless contributors, tourists and otherwise, whose photography and 360-degree views make it possible to view almost every inch of the structure in Google Maps. Any errors in the description of Saint Peter's are mine, some no doubt accidental and others done intentionally to smooth over fight choreography and other such hifalutin literary concerns. Similarly, the history of the Catholic Church presented here is heavily embellished and in some places entirely invented, a literary construct loosely inspired by reality but not in any meaningful way beholden to it.

Finally, and most importantly, my wife Janet has enabled everything I have accomplished in publishing, as first reader, editor, and constant inspiration. While this is true about all my books, this book owes her a special debt, since it was directly inspired by something she said and numerous subsequent conversations that shaped both broad and specific decisions about the story. She gets all my thanks and all my love and an equal share in any success that I manage to eke out in this crazy world.